GUARDIAN
of
THIEVES

USA Today Bestselling Author
LICHELLE SLATER

Cover by Angel Leya
Editing by The Writer's Assistant
Formatting by Lichelle Slater of Dragon Scales Publishing

Sands of Wonder

The Sultan and The Storyteller
(Prequel & part of *The Villain's Ever After* series)

Daughter of Thieves

Guardian of Thieves

Sheblom
Dorus
Zunbar
Balim
Ailorn Mountains
Halmu
Narshiz
Crehat

Spells

Akshifak – I reveal you

Amsikik – I catch you

Anadi al-ma' – I call the water

Aouasif – windstorms

Ashriq – brighten/shine/light up

Barq – lightning

Ibtaqi – slow down

Iftah 'aqlak elai saouf ara zikratak – Open your mind to me so I can see your memory

Iftah el samawat – open the skies

Iftah ya bowaba – open portal

Iftah ya simsim – open sesame

Inhar – collapse

Inhal – dissolve (remove spell)

Inshat – become active (such as energy/force)

Iqrab – come forth

Ishfa el-jerouh – close these wounds

Itrabati – be wrapped up

Itshad – be pulled

Jalid – ice

Qowetik melki – Your power now belongs to me

Salalem – stairs/staircase

To: You

Yes, you.

You beautiful, amazing, gorgeous person.

My amazing reader and fan.

Thank YOU for your continued support,
for reading an indie author,
for choosing today to live.

One

"My name is Irilibus. I am here to request custody of the criminal Mihrage."

The forty thieves had only just escaped from our village, which had been burned to the ground by the royal guard. We had been preparing to journey to the caves in the Ailorn Mountains when Babkak had appeared with Irilibus, a man I'd met while trying to escape the desert with Prince Abudar, Princess Mithra, and my recently discovered brother, Arash, only ten days ago. Irilibus was a practical stranger who had turned us over to The Veil. And there he stood, demanding possession of Mihrage.

I turned to my second best friend—the young man a few years older than me with orange skin and dragon horns, one of which had a golden band clasped around it. I'd only recently learned that band symbolized Mihrage's exile.

Not trusting the man who had already betrayed me once, I stepped between Irilibus and Mihrage. "He isn't going with you," I said firmly. "You exiled Mihrage, which means you cannot come back six years later and collect him to make him pay for a crime for which he's already been punished for. You exiled him."

I felt Mihrage close to my back, but he didn't try to move me out of the way.

Irilibus's gaze shifted from over my shoulder to lock with my eyes. "You have no say in this matter."

I folded my arms. "Mihrage is an adult and therefore no longer your responsibility or concern. You can't control him anymore. Besides, you were willing to betray the prince and princess. If anyone should be arrested, it's you," I said stubbornly.

The weight of Mihrage's hand settled heavy on my shoulder.

I didn't break eye contact with Irilibus.

"Why do you expect me to return to Narshiz?" Mihrage asked.

Irilibus's gaze hardened. "To undo what you started."

"Started?" he asked.

"Your curse spread from Narial to all of our people. Not only is she turning to stone, but somehow all of my people have become birds or fish. We have had every faith healer and wizard try to break your curse, but none can. They say only the source of the magic can unravel it."

Mihrage's shoulders lifted and fell as he sighed. "How many times must I tell you it wasn't me who cursed her?"

Irilibus didn't respond.

Mihrage shook his head and pulled on my shoulder, turning me to look at him. "She was a dear childhood friend of mine. I should try—"

"You don't have to," I interrupted. "He kicked you out for something you didn't do. And even now he is trying to control you! You don't owe them anything!" I sucked in a breath to calm myself. "Has he even tried to contact you once in the last six years?"

His eyes shifted away from mine to look at a distant spot over my shoulder. When his brows softened, I followed his gaze to see what he was really looking at—Taraji.

She stood with concern written all over her face. Her normally bright smile was gone, and her stunning dark brown eyes had lost their sparkle. The two, likely bonded through the love they shared, exchanged some silent conversation I wasn't privy to.

If lovers could do such things, I wouldn't know.

The boy I thought I was falling for had a fiancée and had made it clear he was choosing her. Even if Abudar had been taken by The Veil, he wasn't my responsibility anymore. Roseline could save him.

But if I lost Mihrage . . . the thought made my stomach churn.

"If you're going with him, so am I," I said, interrupting Mihrage's and Taraji's gag-worthy looks. I dusted a speck of sand off of my shoulder and looked down at Igborg, my turquoise dragonling. "Hop on in. We're going with Mihrage." I opened my colorful hand-sewn bag that had once belonged to my father. It was one of the few things I had left of him.

Mihrage finally came out of his stupor. "What? You can't come with me."

"And why not?" I raised a brow.

"If Caspara is coming with you, so am I," Taraji said. She stepped up to my side and pulled her scarf over her freshly braided hair. Her mother must have done it, because it was in neat little braids from the front of her head to about her ears and then fluffed in an impressive afro.

I shrugged. "I guess we're both coming."

"Me too!" Igborg announced as he crawled up my leg and into his normal spot in the pouch.

Mihrage looked over at our leader as though Farhad

would side with him and object to our joining them.

Instead, Farhad nodded to us. "We can send more thieves with you, if you'd like. We protect our family." He lowered his chin a bit, giving Mihrage a look to remind him that he was, indeed, part of our band of thieves.

I wrapped my arm around Mihrage's shoulders. "Why on earth would we allow you to go on your own? You're stuck with us forever."

The corner of his lip tugged in a bit of a grin he struggled to hold back. "If you get me in trouble, I'm leaving you to be arrested." He pulled away from my arm to retrieve his backpack.

I laughed. "No you wouldn't."

He playfully rolled his eyes, knowing full well that he wouldn't ever leave me.

Taraji's mother, Leila, made her way to the front of the band of thieves, grabbed Mihrage by the front of his shirt, and pulled him down so he was eye-level with her. "You will come home to us."

He looked to Taraji for help. She offered none, so he cleared his throat softly and nodded. "You have my word."

"And you will bring Taraji home."

"Are you certain Taraji should go?" Babkak asked.

Taraji hugged her father. "I will be safe. Mihrage has magic, and Caspara is arguably the best thief we have left."

"But you'll be going to the academy soon, and we need to spend time together."

"Baba, I'm growing up." She kissed his forehead. "This is just a little adventure beforehand."

"We will return," Mihrage reassured them.

"Good." Leila threw her arms around Mihrage. She was practically his adopted mother anyhow. She'd always looked out for Mihrage. She then pulled me into a hug. "The same rules apply to you. You must return as well."

I squeezed her tightly. "I will."

I looked back in the direction of our home. I could no longer see the smoke from the fires that had destroyed them. My father was buried there. And now that the thieves were headed south to the Ailorn Mountains to make those our home, I wouldn't be able to visit as frequently as I would like. Perhaps we could move the graves closer, or better, return and rebuild that town, once we knew we would be safe there.

I shook my head and refocused my attention on the moment, on what was happening now. Taraji and I would be traveling with Mihrage to his previous home in Narshiz, likely passing through Balim on the way, which meant if Prince Abudar had been taken by The Veil, I might be able to stop by and rescue him.

Even if he wasn't my responsibility . . . he was still the prince.

My gaze darted to my tattoos, the marks that I was some sort of important sentinel to protect the land. Even if I only protected the thieves, at least I was fulfilling part of my supposed destiny. Unfortunately, Prince Abudar had the same tattoos, making him my special "other half." But I had no desire to partner up with Abudar, especially since he had a future wife to deal with.

"The fastest way to get back to Narshiz is to take a ship," Dablin said.

He was one of the trusted leaders of our little band of thieves, along with Babkak and Farhad. My father had been the fourth leader, before he'd been murdered. That reminder sent a pang through my chest like someone had driven a dagger through my heart and I had to suck in a breath.

"There is a harbor near the Ailorn Mountains," Farhad said. "You can all travel with us until we arrive there. Then we shall give you some supplies and you can be on your way." He looked at Irilibus. "And it will give me time to see if I trust you with three of our children."

"That's not fair," said Isline, Taraji's younger sister. "I want to go on an adventure!"

Taraji laughed. "You're too little."

"Why should *you* get to go? You're not old enough either," she countered.

Taraji bent over to meet her sister's eyes. "Baba and Mama need you to help get the new house ready. And I expect you to be grown up and help with that."

Isline finally pouted and relented with an "Okay," then leaned to Mihrage and peered up at him. "Why does he look exactly like you?" She pointed rather obviously at Irilibus.

"Because he is Dalarian, just like I am," Mihrage answered.

"Why would he want to arrest you, though?" Isline asked.

He sighed. "It's . . . complicated. He is the leader of my people and feels I did something wrong."

"What could you have done wrong?" Taraji asked.

"Did you try and steal something?" Isline whispered.

He chuckled. "No, I didn't."

"Although he did try and steal from my father when he first arrived in our village," I said.

All eyes shifted to me before going back to Mihrage.

"It's true," he confirmed.

"He's never been good at stealing things," I said in a loud whisper to Taraji's sister, making her giggle.

"But then what happened?" Isline asked.

"My father brought him home and fed him, then took him to speak with the leaders. I don't know what happened that night, but he stayed." I shrugged.

Mihrage smiled a little. "He took me to them to see who was willing to help raise me. They all said they would help, but it was Babkak who gave me a little home and helped the most."

Isline grinned, proud of her father.

"Let's move!" Farhad called, coaxing our people to get going after the disruption.

Once everyone began to walk, Farhad and Dablin flanked Irilibus. Mihrage stayed in front of the other Dalarian, near his adopted family and didn't once look over his shoulder at his previous leader. I was in front of him, walking alone. Because I no longer had a family.

"Tell us a bit about this curse," Farhad said to Irilibus once Isline rushed on ahead.

"I don't mean to be rude, but it's none of your business."

"She's slowly turning into stone," Mihrage answered, still not looking over his shoulder.

"Who?" Taraji asked.

Finally, Mihrage glanced back. "An old childhood friend."

"And she's becoming stone?" Farhad asked.

Mihrage nodded. "And like I said, I don't have that kind of magic."

Taraji took him by the hand. "Remember a few days ago when Prince Abudar and Caspara warned you that he was coming?" She spoke softly, and I hoped Irilibus couldn't hear.

"I had hoped he wouldn't find us, especially after the village was destroyed. How did he find us? Who would have known?"

Taraji shook her head. "I don't know."

"See? You should have run," I teased.

Mihrage wasn't amused.

I bit my lip. "I'm sorry, I shouldn't tease. You seem nervous. Are you sure you want to go?"

He nodded uncertainly. "I should."

Two
Mithra

The afternoon sunlight filtered through the sheer white curtains, shielding the dining room from the blazing heat of the sun. I lazily stirred my spoon in my coffee, watching the branches of the tree in the courtyard sway in the wind. It was peaceful.

Quiet.

Abnormally quiet.

Likely because Abudar had been abducted by The Veil the night before and a letter had been sent to our parents announcing it.

It was my first step in getting recognized.

It *had* been a peaceful and quiet morning, but my peace and quiet were interrupted when my mother and father entered, carrying their conversation with them.

"I simply don't understand why they're holding him for ransom in the first place!" Father was saying in frustration. "And what was Abudar even doing in the desert last night?"

"If you noticed, Caspara is gone too. She must have had something to do with it," I offered.

Father looked at me as if barely noticing I was present

in the room. It wasn't the first time I'd seen that look, and annoyance stirred my stomach.

Growing up in Abudar's shadow, I had come to expect barely being noticed. But all of that was beginning to change. With Abudar gone, my parents would finally see me.

Mother shook her head. "Caspara had a lot going on, discovering her family, losing her father, trying to accept being a sentinel. What could she possibly gain from giving Abudar to The Veil?"

I stopped stirring my coffee and rested my hands in my lap. "Mother, Caspara could have been offered money. Sands, even the chance to be rid of the responsibility of being a sentinel at all might have been enough for her to turn him over! You heard how she complained about it."

Mother sighed.

Caspara wasn't a terrible person, but she was the only one I could pin this on. And I was going to seize that opportunity.

I cleared my throat. "Have either of you spoken with Roseline? I haven't seen her all morning."

Mother nodded. "I informed her of Abudar's disappearance. She wants to help, but what could she possibly do?" Mother wearily put her face in her hands.

For a moment, I felt a pang of guilt burn in my chest.

I didn't *want* my mother to hurt, but this was the only way they would see *my* strength and power.

I found myself reaching out and grasping her hand. "Mama, he's going to be all right."

"But what if he isn't?" Her voice cracked. "Do you think Caspara really betrayed our trust in such a way?" She lowered her hands, giving me such a desperate look, I hesitated to answer. "We opened our home to her, and I spoke with her about her father. She was upset, but I didn't think she was upset enough to ever do this. I thought she was fond of Abudar."

The ruby in my pocket heated and I placed my hand on it. A tingle moved up my arm and shoulder, into my throat, and across my tongue.

"She would do this. Her father was killed while he was a prisoner in the palace," I said without a single thought. "This could be her revenge for you not finding his killer. Or because Abudar broke her heart."

Mother looked over at Father in a silent exchange.

He shook his head and shrugged one of his shoulders. "I suppose Mithra could be right. We did nothing to help her while we expected her to just fill her responsibility as a sentinel. We wanted her to step up when she didn't even know what it meant. We gave her nothing in return."

Mother dried her cheeks and stood. "I need a few hours to come up with a story that will help her."

"Be careful," I warned.

Mother shifted her look to me.

"It's that . . . well, you've only just received your power back. You could accidentally create a new problem instead of helping. Be careful."

She nodded and left the dining room.

It was rare for Father and I to be alone. He usually left with Abudar to teach him something sultanly. Without Abudar there, it was just the two of us and an awkward silence that grew increasingly uncomfortable.

Father heaved a sigh and his eyes fell on Abudar's place at the table. "I know you two haven't always gotten along, but perhaps you could help us bring him home. Perhaps you and Roshanak can open a portal to sneak in and bring him home? I am going to draft a letter to The Veil right away and see what they want in exchange for his return, but just in case . . . perhaps we should be ready for something else." He looked at me. "Can you find a way in?"

I swallowed hard. He never asked me for anything. I nodded slowly. "I'll see what I can do, Father." I rose from my seat and walked to the doorway, but paused. When I looked over my shoulder, he was once again staring at Abudar's empty place. "He's going to be fine, you know. The Veil have no reason to harm him."

Father nodded and gave me a smile that didn't reach his eyes.

I walked to my room and sat in front of my mirror, running my tongue over my teeth.

The whole world was stopping for Abudar. My father had pleaded with me for help because at least he noticed I even had magic.

After the Desert Trials, I was convinced the royal guard had only been sent out to recover Abudar, because he was next in line for the throne. Had I been out there on my own, would anyone have fought so hard to find me?

"You appear to be angry."

I spotted Arash in the mirror. He lounged in the chair beside my bed, one leg slung over the arm rest. He had his chin on his fist.

I turned in my seat and raised a brow. "How did you sneak into my room?"

He snorted and rolled his eyes. "Mithra, you only ward your bedroom door." A sly smile appeared on his handsome dark face. His green eyes were particularly playful today.

"Then I shall have to start placing wards on my secret

entrance too." I stood and walked to the painting beside my bed that led to a secret tunnel.

Arash rolled his head to follow my movement without moving the position of his body. "Who said I used the secret tunnel?"

"What other way could you have slipped into my room?" I placed my hands on my hips.

He grinned and rose to his feet. The sunlight glinted off the sword earring dangling from his right ear. "If I told you, you'd find a way to ward that one too. How am I supposed to act as your bodyguard if you lock me out?" Arash stopped in front of me and looked down, his nose inches from mine. "How can I keep you safe?" He stroked my cheek with his knuckles.

I rolled my eyes.

He chuckled and gently took my chin and pressed his lips to mine.

I melted into his touch and wrapped my arms around his neck.

Arash had a way of reaching the parts inside of me no one could. He was the only one who could tease me without losing their head, and he knew it. His lips caressed mine and his hand on my spine pulled me against his body.

"You know you'd lose your life if anyone caught you in here," I whispered against his lips.

"I know." He kissed me again.

"I wouldn't ever forgive myself if that happened."

He pulled back to search my gaze. "Then we'd better not allow it to happen." He kissed my forehead. "Because I could never leave you with such heartache. What is the plan now that your parents know about Abudar? Are you going to bring him home?" Arash let go of me.

I felt my lips tighten and rolled my eyes. "Why is everyone so worried about him? If he's such a powerful sorcerer, why can't he find his own way out?"

Arash caught my wrist. "After everything you went through with him going through the Dragon's Lair and across the desert, you're still cold toward him?"

"And what has he done to make me want to like him?" I demanded. "Caspara was the one who got us out, not Abudar."

"He *did* help us get away from The Veil, though," Arash countered.

I snorted. "Right. He was *so* helpful. I would have gotten us out anyway." I pulled away from him. "I should visit Shorix before my father or the military have to get involved. I had hoped they would take a day before they worried, but apparently someone in The Veil sent a letter."

Arash wrapped his arms around me from behind and I looked forward into the mirror. His eyes locked on mine. "Mithra, you don't need to be in competition with him."

I raised a brow. "We've always been in competition. You know that."

He heaved a sigh. "I'm only saying, you don't have to take it out on him."

"I've punished my parents by having him taken, and my father didn't even know how to talk to me this morning." I pulled away from Arash's arms. "I know Abudar being gone won't change things immediately, but I had at least hoped they would change a little."

"You know they're going to figure out a way to bring him home. And then what happens to your plans?"

I glared at him, fury burning in my chest. I didn't know the answer to his question, but how dare he try and tell me my plan wasn't going to work! "If you don't get out of my room now, I'll scream."

He frowned and lowered his arms. "You wouldn't."

I sucked in a breath.

He held up both hands. "Fine! I'll go." He walked to my bedroom door and opened it. "Mithra, you know I'm always here for you. I'm the one always at your side." His eyes were once again soft. "Don't shut me out."

I didn't reply.

Arash heaved a sigh and shut the door behind him.

I rubbed my hands over my face and considered bringing Abudar back. I could be a hero, then.

But you don't really want to save your brother. If he returns, you'll once again be invisible. It's time for your family and the kingdom to see how much power you truly have.

The words came into my mind as though someone were beside me. I turned in a circle, my heart thumping against my ribs.

"Arash!" I called and ran for the door.

Silly girl. Reach into your pocket. What is there?

Keeping my back against the door and my eyes on my empty room, I reached into my pocket and felt the smooth ruby I'd found inside of the cave nearly two weeks ago. I had searched for this ruby because, if my grandfather's journals held any truth, this ruby was enchanted. According to those journals, he had once had it on top of his staff.

I looked down at the ruby in the palm of my hand, my heart still thumping.

I am here to help you.

Was the ruby the speaking to me?

I lifted it closer to my face. "That voice is you? You're

speaking to me?"

My door burst open, slammed into my back, and sent me stumbling. The ruby flung into the air and clattered against the stone floor.

I spun around. "*Itrabati.*"

Arash stood just inside of my room with his sword in hand, though the spell I'd instinctively cast bound his arms to his sides and held him still.

"You scared me!" I scolded.

"You yelled for me! What else was I supposed to do?"

"I often call your name." I walked over to him and leaned into his face, but the fear of him bursting in was gone.

He frowned in a near pout. "You were scared when you called for me. I heard it in your voice. Let me go now."

I kissed him, enjoying his moment of frustration, before I lowered back down onto my feet and said, "*Inhal,*" which removed the spell I'd cast.

"Why *did* you call me?" Arash asked, sheathing his sword. He wrapped his arm around me and pulled me close.

I looked in the direction I'd seen the ruby fall and visually searched the floor for it. "I thought I heard someone in here with me." My heart had been racing since the voice spoke, but with Arash's comforting presence, my heart had calmed. "Remember that stone I retrieved in the caves?"

He nodded. "The one that belonged to Khorshid?"

"Yes." I paused a moment, a bit unsure how I should tell him that the stone had just spoken to me.

Arash tilted my chin to look back at him. "What is it?"

"I can't find it." I was being honest while simultaneously avoiding answering that the stone was definitely enchanted. I wanted to talk to it more before sharing anything with him.

Arash released me and got on his hands and knees to search the ground for the ruby. I was grateful for him sparing me the humiliation of crawling around myself. Plus, I rather preferred looking at him.

"Ah, I found it." Arash reached under the table displaying various kinds of potted plants. I noticed his hand flinch, and then he leaned back on his ankles and turned to me with concern lining his brow. "Mithra . . . this stone has a lot of energy. It burns."

I walked over and took it from his hand. "Yes, it does."

He blinked, pulled out of his trancelike state, and looked up at me. "What is it about that ruby that makes me wonder what you're hiding?"

I placed the stone in my pocket. "Who says I'm hiding anything?"

He frowned and got to his feet. "I came in here because you yelled my name. You said you thought you heard a voice, and then you talked about the ruby. Is it the ruby that spoke to you? Is that normal for enchanted artifacts?"

I shrugged. "I don't know, to be honest. I haven't been exposed to many enchanted items, in spite of being the princess and being trained by the grand sorceress. Mother and Father don't have any they use for them. Roshanak does have a book that writes down the spells she creates, but I've never heard it actually have a voice."

"Do you think you should ask her about this? Obviously, you can't tell her you found your grandfather's stone from his staff, but perhaps you could ask her if it's possible for enchanted artifacts to have a voice. If they're sentient." Arash shrugged.

"That's not a bad idea . . . or I could ask Shorix." I

tapped my bottom lip in thought. "I do need to visit her anyway."

He smiled. "It is pretty amazing that you've encountered this. I can't wait to see what new spells you might be able to cast."

I couldn't help but feel my heart relax in happiness. Arash was right, he'd always been at my side. He'd always supported me, and to hear him excited about this ruby made me realize just how perfect he was for me. Marriage might be a few years away, but at least I had someone by my side, someone who always saw me even when my family didn't.

I gave Arash a kiss. "I'll be back in a few hours."

He kissed me again. "I'll be here when you return."

"*Iftah ya bowaba,*" I said, swirling my right hand in a circle with my left hand palm out toward the wall.

A glowing purple ring of magic formed with sparks of red. When the ends touched, the space on the inside of the ring went wavy, like the desert sands on a hot day.

With one step through the portal, I exited my bedroom and stepped out onto an overgrown path in a humid forest and stood before an incredible moss-covered building. The Veil's new sorceress tower was positively charming.

The main level of the tower was a building with three floors and a deeply sloped roof from the middle to the corners. The corners had carved wood that curled upward like tree roots, and a carved animal stood on the precipice of the roof at the front of the building. At one time it may have been a phoenix or griffin, but the details had worn away.

Attached to the building and standing on the edge of a shallow cliff stood a tower with six floors and an opening between the top of the tower and the roof, almost like the lighthouses I'd seen near the Zunbar harbor.

It obviously still needed repairs. From where I stood I could see a crack in the roof, and the stones at the back corner of the main building had slumped into a decaying pile. The Veil had only just relocated there, and I'm sure they were busy at work keeping the sorceresses calm and making them feel at home.

However, I was positive that with their combined efforts and repairs, The Veil's tower would rival that of the Zauberin Academy in beauty and size.

I entered through the front doors and found an entrance with a beautiful mirror, a well-worn (but recently dusted) rug, and two armchairs by two empty pots I assumed would soon be filled with plants. To my right was a room with a fireplace and staircase. The room on my left was smaller but with more seating and lots of windows. A good handful of young women were in there chatting with one another, likely gossiping about their current state and making assumptions as to what Shorix had planned for them. Some might have been missing their families. But I knew they would see that learning from Shorix would be better for them.

I entered the room on the right, which had rows of tables and chairs, so I assumed the room behind the entrance would be the kitchen.

A young woman trotted down the stairs with a bucket and rags and paused before her foot hit the bottom. "Princess Mithra? How did you know where we'd fled?"

It was a good question. One I didn't know how to answer. When I summoned my portal, I had thought only of Shorix. I had been taught that in order to create a portal, sorceresses had to have been at that location or have seen a picture of it. However, I felt one hundred percent confident I would arrive where Shorix had moved the sorceresses. And I had.

Perhaps the gemstone had played a hand in my arrival.

I clutched my pocket. "I am here to meet with Shorix. Direct me to her."

She seemed to be fumbling for a way to re-ask the question I'd avoided, or perhaps to come up with a reason why she shouldn't take me, until I raised my brow.

She snapped her teeth shut, set her bucket on the floor, and said, "Follow me."

I followed her back up the stairs, where there were a few doors, all of which were closed. I imagined those rooms would be bathrooms or bedrooms, and the third floor was the same. However, there was an additional hallway on the third floor that led to the main level of the sorceress tower.

The first floor of the tower was a wide-open space with bookshelves circling the outer wall and then organized in rows in the center with plenty of tables and couches to sit on to study.

We began the arduous trip up the stairs and through the levels of the tower. The next floor was split in half with two different rooms, the third was a large, open practice space, and the next two floors mirrored the second. The sixth floor of the sorceress tower had individual rooms I assumed were for the teachers.

I guessed correctly, because the girl stopped by one of the doors. "This is Madam Shorix's room. Please forgive me for not being more—"

"It's fine." Why in the sands of time would Shorix *choose* to live on the sixth floor of the sorceress tower? It was agonizing! I knocked on the door.

"You may enter."

The door swung inward, revealing a beautiful bedroom with ancient-style carved furniture, but a window that let light pour in. There was a bed up on a risen part of the floor behind the desk at which Shorix sat.

"Ah, Princess Mithra!" Shorix rose to her feet, clearly surprised, but she smiled easily. Her veil hung from one ear and she didn't bother pulling it up as she approached me. "It has been some time since we've visited."

I closed the door behind me. "I wanted to have a word with you. I was also curious to see where you'd managed to settle. I finally managed to sneak away from the palace for a few moments." Not waiting for an invitation, I sat in one of the plump armchairs.

Shorix sat in the opposite chair. "The sorceresses we brought with us are . . . apprehensive. Many we've spoken with are upset we brought them here, which is to be expected when it wasn't their choice."

I found myself smiling, which made Shorix grin as well. "Once they realize we are doing this *for* them, they will change their thoughts."

Shorix nodded. "It may take some time. I must confess, your idea to set up on a small island was perceptive. We have been able to speak with the girls and have managed to begin *some* lessons without interruption. With time, I have a feeling many will finally understand what we want and join our cause."

"Our goal in all of this is to share all types of magic with the women, correct?" I asked.

Shorix nodded.

"And once they trust us, I can have them on my side to make a bid for the role of grand sorceress." It was a new goal, one I hadn't even quite settled on myself, but I blurted it out like a fool, catching the head sorceress off guard.

Shorix raised her brows and her lips parted. "You wish to become the grand sorceress of the palace?"

"Yes, I do," I confirmed with a nod. A giddy rush shot through my body.

"After Roshanak retires?"

"No. I mean as soon as possible. I know I still have things to learn, but I feel as though Roshanak isn't even sharing spells with me she is sharing with Abudar."

She gripped her skirt. "Speaking of Prince Abudar, I am afraid the idea to bring him here was not a wise one. I trust you and know your aspirations, but I still do not understand why we need to have him held captive here."

I scowled. "Everything would have been fine in that regard if *you* hadn't written to Roshanak or my mother to tell them where he is. You're hiding on an island because of him. He revealed your location in Balim to our parents. Had I not warned you of his betrayal, you and your sorceresses would have been arrested."

It wasn't a complete lie. I had spoken with Shorix in Balim and told her I would support her movement to share magic equally with all women who possessed the gift of magic. In fact, it was under my direction that The Veil took the girls who had participated in the desert trials, including those who hadn't finished. Because those who hadn't finished the trials had fought for the right to learn magic beyond their one gifted element, and since they wouldn't get to attend the Zauberin Acadamy, they were more likely to join Shorix's cause.

She looked over at the papers on her desk. "Yes, you're right. But Roshanak sent me a letter, and your mother . . . I fear we need to release him so they don't discover our private academy. Let me take you in as a student. That will begin—"

I felt like she'd sucked the air from my lungs. "No," I interrupted, finally finding my voice. "Not yet. There is still so much I can do while he is here."

"Like what?" she asked. "All we wanted was to be treated equally. If we return the prince to the palace, we can achieve that. What more could we need?"

I shook my head. I wasn't ready for this yet! This wasn't what I had hoped for. "Abudar shouldn't have magic, based on our laws," I spat. "How is it even possible he has magic?"

Shorix's head tilted slightly. "Years ago, men *were* allowed to have magic. But they abused the power and wars constantly destroyed the land. Sheblom used to be one giant island, but when their wars broke out, the land itself broke apart from their chaos. Gods or leaders, whichever story you believe, decided to control the greed of men by putting women in charge. Men with magic were banished from Sheblom until no more existed. However, perhaps Abudar has magic because of your grandfather?"

I shrugged. "He was born with magic. With Mother being a magic user herself, who is to say his powers didn't come from her? Mother and Father tell us stories constantly about how he would make things happen even before he could speak, but that doesn't mean his powers came from Khorshid."

Shorix shrugged. "Perhaps it could be as simple as us needing him to be the sentinel for our world right now."

"And he's growing stronger and stronger. Shorix, if you let him go, he will undermine everything! He will take the throne as sultan *and* sorcerer. Imagine what would happen to the women of our land! We've already been suppressed by my grandfather's laws, and if Abudar keeps his magic . . ." My thoughts raced and I raised my hand to massage my forehead.

What place would I have in a world such as that?

"You have many worries, Mithra."

I lowered my hand. "I don't want to become expendable. Please keep him here, just for a few more days. I'll . . . put together a plan where I can save him and you don't look like awful people." I stood.

Shorix got to her feet as well. "I think you should visit your brother first." Shorix guided me over to her door. "We're taking good care of him. Don't worry."

I rolled my eyes. "I wouldn't care if you weren't. But I have things to do. I'll return and visit him then."

"Mithra, he would like to see you."

She had no idea how much I despised my brother. "If he sees me before he's freed, he will know I had a hand in it. He will report that to my family when he returns home. I cannot visit him until it is time."

"As you wish, Your Highness," Shorix replied and curtseyed.

I allowed her to open the door for me, then paused and looked at her. "I did have a question for you, one I forgot to ask. Are enchanted artifacts sentient? Do they speak?"

She blinked. "What a peculiar question."

I didn't answer that with anything, not wanting to hint to her that I was in possession of such an artifact.

Shorix pursed her lips in thought. "I do not know the answer to that question. In all of my studies, artifacts are enchanted through magic only, and magic itself may be alive, but not sentient to the degree you could have a conversation with it. I don't know if that answers your question."

I smiled politely. "Thank you. As I said, I shall return another day." I opened the portal again and returned to my bedroom.

If magically enchanted artifacts couldn't speak, how was it possible I had a ruby in my pocket that did? What part of magic didn't even a head sorceress understand?

Three

Masts grew out of the horizon like dead trees reaching out of the desert sands in search of a foothold in the sky. My throat tightened with nerves. It was so soon. I thought it would have taken us longer to reach the harbor and standing there with the ships visible, I suddenly felt anxiety like I'd never felt before grip me.

I was leaving behind the only family I had left. If I got lost, would I ever see them again?

"We should only be gone a few weeks," Mihrage said to Babkak and Leila. "Although I can't promise I'll bring Taraji back with me," he added with a teasing grin, eyes locked on Taraji.

She rolled her eyes.

I chuckled. "I'll bring her back, Leila."

Leila hugged her daughter and quickly dried a tear she didn't want us to see. "You had better get going. Be safe."

Babkak hugged Taraji next, and then the adoptive parents hugged Mihrage again, followed by me.

"You really can't let me go?" Isline complained after Taraji had given her a hug.

"No. You need to help get our new home set up. *That* will be an adventure."

"That will be boring."

Taraji laughed.

Mihrage picked up his pack and shouldered it. I adjusted the straps of my own while I turned to follow Irilibus. Taraji vowed yet again to be safe and repeated that she would be coming back and not to worry.

We left the thieves behind.

Our family.

Hopefully, the palace guard believed they'd killed everyone and wouldn't search for them beyond the town we left behind. I wanted to come home to everyone I knew, even if the location wasn't the same.

Taraji slipped her hand into Mihrage's and the three of us followed Irilibus to the docks.

The tiny harbor hosted mainly small fishing boats, with a handful of merchant ships double the length of one of the boats but still smaller than the majority of the ships I'd grown up seeing docked in Zunbar's harbor.

"Are you part dragon?" Taraji asked, looking at Irilibus. "I've asked Mihrage that question since we met, and he's never given me a straight answer."

Irilibus glanced at the younger Dalarian.

Mihrage rolled his eyes and shook his head. Taraji was sneaky asking another one of his race for answers he wouldn't give.

Irilibus shrugged. "I like to think we are. There are stories passed down that say a dragon fell in love with a human and he learned to shape-shift into a human form for her. When they had children, they were half-human, half-dragon and were branded as Dalarian. But in all of my searching, I cannot find proof that ever happened."

"And yet you stand before us with orange skin, dragon horns, and dragon eyes," I threw in.

Mihrage laughed. "Does that mean you are from the sands because your skin is brown?" He shook his head. "None of us know where we truly come from."

"I know where I came from. From my father and mother," I answered.

"With some magic involved," Taraji threw in. She pointed to her arm, hinting to me of the tattoo on my own— my mark of the sentinel.

I rolled my eyes. "Yes, well, I'm still not convinced Telama wasn't wrong when she gave me this tattoo. And our conversation got moved away from Mihrage." I looked back up at him.

He shrugged and grinned. "I'm fine with that."

I folded my arms.

"Wait here," Irilibus commanded.

Once he was out of earshot, I turned to Mihrage. "Do you need to prepare us for anything before we leave all safety behind?"

He didn't look at me. "I do not know the state of the city I grew up in. I know as much as you do right now, and if Irilibus is being honest, then perhaps my people have changed. I don't know what that means." Finally, his blue eyes turned to me. "But I'll keep both of you close to me. The Dalarian are not particularly fond of strangers, which is why we inhabit one of the islands away from the mainland."

"How long are we going to be on the boat?" Taraji asked.

Mihrage shook his head. "Maybe a day at most. We aren't very far, though it seems like it."

"I have to confess, I'm a little worried about finding everyone when we get back," Taraji said.

"You're not going to be lost." Mihrage took her hand.

"Caspara and I will keep you safe."

I nodded. "I already promised your mother and father. It's too late to leave you behind now."

She rolled her eyes but grinned.

Irilibus approached and pointed his thumb over his shoulder. "I managed to charter one of the trading ships. Unfortunately, they are stopping at Halmu this evening to restock on their shipments, but they can take us to Narshiz in the morning."

"I've never been to Halmu," I said. "It will be a fun adventure." I tried my best to smile. I could tell Mihrage wasn't pleased about the delay, because I wasn't pleased either, but the expression on his face didn't change. I nudged him. "Have you ever been to Halmu?"

"Once." He nudged his head toward the docks. "Let us be on our way."

Irilibus turned and led the way through the palm-tree forest to the boat we would be taking.

There was nothing impressive about it. In fact, the aged wood on the hull had been patched more than once, and I cast Taraji a wary glance.

She widened her eyes at me in response, but neither of us voiced our concern.

The docks reeked of fish and seagulls, sharks, and other larger fish that circled the end of the dock for the scraps the fishermen tossed over.

"Have you ever been on a boat?" Taraji suddenly whispered in my ear. "Because I haven't."

"I've only ever snuck on them when they were in port," I answered back.

"Don't worry," Mihrage cut in. "You'll both be fine."

"Is your magic brain telling you we will be, or are you

just being kind?" Taraji pressed her index finger against the middle of Mihrage's forehead.

"I'm being kind. But I've been on a lot of boats, and you really are going to be fine. We're only sailing a couple of hours." He took her chin and kissed her.

I tried my hardest not to roll my eyes. In secret, I was envious.

"Do you need a kiss too?" Mihrage asked.

"No!"

He threw his arm around my shoulders and kissed the top of my head. "*Mwah!*"

"Mihrage!" I laughed and pushed him away.

He grinned playfully.

Taraji giggled, and I was very grateful for her not being jealous.

"Kids, we need to get on," Irilibus said.

We all gave him the same silent look—did he really just call us "kids"?

The piece of wood leading from the dock to the ship seemed just about as sturdy as the boat, which is to say not at all. The end resting on the railing of the boat rose and fell with the ship and the waves.

I sucked in a breath. I was used to scrambling up and down buildings, yes, but the boat rocked and with it, the plank of wood I was supposed to cross. Walking on the unsteady wood wasn't what made me nervous. Falling from it and into the ocean's unknown depths did.

Like a little rat, I scurried across the weak piece of wood and onto the rocking deck of the ship, but didn't find relief until I had crossed the deck to a crate and sat down. My stomach rose and fell uncomfortably.

Taraji followed, arms straight out to the side for

balance, but she made it. Mihrage had no issues walking on, nor did Irilibus, who took up the rear.

Taraji sat on the crate beside me while Mihrage leaned his back against the mast.

"I am not used to the earth rocking," I said aloud. I looked out over the rise and fall of the waves, which bade the ship to rock with them. I settled my attention on Irilibus. "Do you even remember me?"

He studied my expression.

"I was a little beat up, but I was there that day. In Balim. When you handed us over to The Veil?"

Irilibus's lips tightened. He remembered me.

"Us?" Mihrage asked.

I gripped the edge of the crate under my bum and tried to steady myself. "He betrayed Mithra and Abudar—and in turn, me and Arash—so The Veil would tell him where you lived, Mihrage. He was willing to turn in the prince and princess, for what? So you could get revenge for what he allegedly did to that girl?" I snorted, refocusing my attention on the leader. "That's pretty pathetic."

"Hoist anchor. Lower sails!" the captain bellowed.

Irilibus's strange eyes watched me. When Mihrage stared at me like that, I always felt he was reading my mind. With Irilibus, it felt more like he was trying to figure out what to say.

Finally, he spoke. "It was an opportunity that landed in my lap. I needed to lift the curse before it becomes permanent, and when you all showed up, it was too much of a blessing from the gods to turn it away. To have members of The Veil finally tell me where to find my son, I would have done almost anything."

My jaw dropped. *Mihrage is his son?*

Mihrage visibly flinched.

"You never told them about your family?" Irilibus asked, his brows furrowed.

Mihrage flexed his jaw and folded his arms over his chest before glancing over his shoulder. "What family? The one from which I was disowned?"

In spite of unsteady footing, Taraji leaped to her feet and crossed the deck to Mihrage. She wrapped her arms around him and held on, even if he was stiff.

He slowly relaxed his arms and wrapped them around Taraji. "I never lied to you," he said to her. "I only . . . I didn't want to tell you the whole truth. Being exiled was difficult enough. If I'd told you all I had also been disowned . . . I was afraid no one would want me."

Taraji straightened and held his face. "You know better now. And I will never judge you for holding back. I don't know what you went through or what that felt like."

I looked back at Irilibus, whose expression was mute. "You hate your son enough to betray the royal family to find him?"

He shook his head. "It's not like that. I've—"

Mihrage interrupted him with a scoff.

Irilibus glanced at him, then looked back at me. "In spite of what he may feel, I've never hated him."

"He seems to believe that," I said sarcastically. "What sort of father banishes their own child for a curse he didn't cast?"

Mihrage gave me a look that was somewhere between warning and gratitude for standing up for him.

"I had to keep my people safe," Irilibus countered. "Not only that, but he cursed his own sister."

I glanced at Mihrage, whose expression hadn't

changed. When I turned back to Irilibus, I asked, "Then why were you living in a hut in the desert with your wife?"

He ran his hand over his face. "You don't know what it's like to have an entire race of people leaning on you for answers and support. Looking at you when everything begins to fall apart. Demanding answers and justice."

"And I was easy to pin everything on because I was so young," Mihrage threw in.

I understood Mihrage's feelings. I felt the same way toward Roshanak when it was revealed she was my mother. I was still processing this information.

"Mihrage . . ." Irilibus started.

He held up his hand, cutting him off. "I agreed to come back and help, but after I visit her and use my magic to see if there's anything that can even be done to resolve the problem, I'm leaving and I will return *home* with Taraji and Caspara."

Irilibus's jaw tightened, but he nodded. Although the ship was small, he moved to the furthest place at the back of the ship, giving us—or rather, Mihrage—space.

Taraji gave his hand a squeeze. "You can always talk to me."

"I know," he said softly. "And I should have when Caspara warned me, but . . . I didn't know how. I'm sorry for keeping this from you."

She shook her head. "No more secrets from now on, okay?"

Mihrage kissed her lips softly. "Okay."

Igborg nudged his head out of the gap at the corner of my pouch and peered up at me with large eyes. "The earth is moving."

"That's because we're on a boat. I don't think it's going

to get any better until we get back to land."

He flicked his tongue. "I no like boats."

Four

Halmu was far more beautiful than I could have ever imagined. Unlike Zunbar, which was a bustling city on the northern coast of the main island with shade provided only by fabric and buildings, Halmu was a city on the southern coast shaded by trees and bushes as tall as me. Some were palm trees, others had thick trunks or long spiny branches. Not to mention the thousands of flowers splashing color in contrast to the red sand.

"Your mouth is hanging open," Taraji said.

"How could yours *not* be? Look at this place!" I leaned my hands on the ship's railing. "Now, I could live in a city like this."

"Every city has an underbelly," Mihrage reminded me. "You should know that."

The buildings were built similarly to those in Zunbar, but with a dark gray stone instead of mud and clay or orange rocks hewn from the earth. One large building in the distance caught my eye. It was stark white and had a gold-and-turquoise dome.

The sailors pulled the ship to the dock and one of them slammed down the gangplank we'd used to board.

"We'll see you in the morning," Irilibus said, placing a handful of coins into the hand of the man I assumed was the captain.

Taraji, Mihrage, and I picked up our packs and disembarked the ship, entering a small crowd of traders and sailors traveling from the docks to the city and back again. The ground beneath my feet swayed as though I was still on the boat, and I flung my hands out to steady myself, accidentally striking Irilibus in the chest.

"You'll get your land legs back," he said and stepped around me.

"I'm sorry. I didn't mean to hit you."

He turned his head, nodded, and said, "Follow me. I know of a tavern we can stay in. Stick together, though. Sometimes unsavory folk tend to stay here. It's the biggest port on the island, other than that in Zunbar."

"We should probably visit the market too so we can get some more food," I suggested.

"And because I want to see what it looks like compared to Zunbar," Taraji added with a beaming smile that made her eyes light up.

Mihrage glanced at his father. "Is Halmu safe enough to explore?"

I rolled my eyes. "Mihrage, you haven't been my personal bodyguard for the past sixteen years. Don't start now." I looped my arm through Taraji's and began leading her down a road I assumed led to the city due to the arched entrance in the distance and foot traffic headed that way.

Mihrage mumbled under his breath and hurried after us. But he called back over his shoulder, "I think we should find an inn that doesn't double as a tavern. Where the women will be safe." He stepped around a woman carrying a bundle of fabric on her head in order to catch up to us.

I laughed. "Don't worry, Mihrage. I've got a dagger and

Igborg. I can protect myself. Taraji has magic, and she can help too. We're not incapable of keeping ourselves out of trouble."

"*You* are never able to keep yourself out of trouble," he chided back, but at least offered a smile. His eyes were tight, though, and I knew he was uneasy.

I couldn't tell if he was uneasy from being around his father, being in an unfamiliar city, or if Halmu was truly so dangerous.

Taraji stopped him and whispered, "Mihrage, we don't have to do this. We don't have to go with your father or do anything for him. You don't owe him a thing after what he did to you."

"I know. But I suppose it's in me to help because they're my people. And I suppose I *am* a bit curious to see what's happened with this curse." He lifted her chin. "But you can stay here with Caspara and return home to the thieves tomorrow. I'll be back in a couple of days."

She snorted. "You're a fool if you think I'm leaving you alone with him. Who knows what he might try if he's already exiled you *and* gave the royal kids to The Veil to find you?" She leaned up and kissed him. "We already promised to stick together. I'm not leaving you."

I was relieved when Igborg poked his head out of the pouch, nose twitching as he sniffed the air. "Where is here?"

"This is a city called Halmu." I reached down and scratched under his chin.

"It smells."

I laughed. "Good smell or bad? Maybe you smell the flowers." I walked to the side of the road, checked to make sure no strangers were close enough to see him, and stopped to hold him out to a bush covered in flowers with vibrant orange-and-yellow petals.

His nose twitched again and he tilted his chin to peer up at me. "I like."

I bent over and smelled them too. "Mm, I like it too. Maybe when we get to our new home, we might have a place to grow some flowers. We might be close to a river."

He grinned a sharp-toothed grin. "Taylin help!"

"The jinni? Hm. That's a good idea. I'll have to ask him." I laughed, then set Igborg back into my pack beside the lamp, much to his disappointment. "I'll take you out when we get some food. I don't know if people here see lizards."

"No lizard. Dragon." All I could see was his nose.

"I know, and that may be frightening to people. Stay hidden until I let you out." I patted his head.

Igborg protested by letting out a grumbling whine as I caught up with the others.

Mihrage chuckled. "Not happy about being kept away?"

"Not at all. He's getting so big and heavy." I readjusted my pack.

"I did notice that," Mihrage said. "He may not be able to stay hidden in your bag for very much longer."

I hadn't ever thought about Igborg growing up, at least not in size. I thought he would remain a cute, small dragon forever.

"Maybe your jinni can tell you about dragons," Taraji said. "He seems familiar with Igborg and has lived a long time."

I nodded. "That's actually a great idea. I wonder why I never thought about talking to him. He might be able to tell me how big Igborg will get and what type of dragon he is."

"Speaking of dragons," Mihrage mumbled and stopped to point to the Ailorn Mountains to the north. "Didn't you say something about waking a dragon while you were trying to escape from the Dragon's Lair during the Desert Trials?"

Barely visible, high above the mountains, floated the silhouette of a dragon. No one around us seemed to notice, even though dragons hadn't been seen in our land for decades, maybe even centuries. Even Igborg didn't belong here. He had been imported as a gift for Abudar's birthday last year, if Mithra was correct.

"It must be staying away from the cities?" I wondered out loud.

"I hope there's a big treasure in that mountain to keep it occupied," Taraji whispered.

I shook my head. "It would have to be bigger than what was hoarded in the caves, and I can't imagine anything more than that. He's got to be looking for food."

"Let's hope it doesn't want to eat us," Mihrage said. He placed his hands on our backs and urged us to keep walking through the people.

Although the streets of Halmu weren't nearly as crowded as Zunbar's, they were far more colorful. With vibrantly dyed fabric hanging across the streets for shade, the varying races in their native clothing, and spices and food, I couldn't help but feel we'd traveled to an entirely different world!

We purchased a little bit more food—I bought Igborg some fresh meat and nuts, and then a bundle of dried fruit for myself.

However, my ears perked as I handed the man my coin. A merchant at a nearby table was speaking to a client. "Yes, I heard there was a new castle too. Though, I don't know how anyone could see a castle through the storm around Daryabar."

"Daryabar?" The stranger burst into laughter. "An island that exists in fairytales?"

The merchant scowled. "It is real. We hear about it all the time from the sailors that pass through. The only new tale is that of the castle now appearing out of nowhere."

A castle? On an island that supposedly didn't exist? Or did in tales?

"Caspara, we need to get to the inn before the sun sets and I don't remember how to get back," Mihrage said with a little smile.

I understood what he meant. The world looked entirely different at night. Casting one more look at the merchant and his client to see if I would hear anything else, and realizing I wouldn't, I followed my friends back in the direction from which we'd come.

I had never stayed in an inn. The only time I'd entered an inn was to break into a room or two or three to steal. In spite of my adventurous nature, the only time I'd traveled beyond Zunbar was when I entered the Desert Trials to find the magic lamp for my mother, Roshanak. Of course, I hadn't given it to her, and I didn't doubt she was still looking for it.

The oddly shaped inn stood out from the buildings surrounding it. A tall central building with four floors stood between two shorter buildings that reached out from it like welcoming arms. The architect had built little rooms in these "arms" and undoubtedly in the main building as well, and there was also a walkway of stone in front of the doors leading to the main building and a statue in the central space surrounded by plants.

"I've never seen a place with so many plants," Taraji said, her lips spread into an enormous grin.

"Wait until we get to Narshiz," Mihrage said. "This place pales in comparison."

She shook her head with a giddy laugh. "I find that highly unlikely."

Mihrage chuckled.

A man a good two heads taller than me exited just as we reached the doors of the main building. He nodded his head in a polite but silent greeting, and the sun glinted off of the golden tattoos on his face.

"Thank you," I said, since he held the door for me.

"You'll see all kinds of people here. It's probably best not to talk with them," Irilibus stated.

"I'm a pretty good judge of character," I said without looking at him.

The room was packed with paint-chipped tables, mismatched chairs, and people of every shape, color, and size. Beautiful bronze lanterns hung overhead, lighting the room. Women and men bustled through the organized chaos inside, taking orders and carrying trays of food or drinks.

"I'll get us a room," Irilibus said and began pushing his way through the crowd to get to the front.

"We might as well find somewhere to sit. I'm ready for some dinner," Mihrage said. He glanced my way. "You're being unnaturally quiet."

"To be honest, I feel overwhelmed. My thoughts are in a million places," I answered. It was true. My thoughts bounced from dinner and the wonders of this place to my people, my father, speaking with Taylin, and worrying about Igborg as he grew up. My mind even briefly wondered if Abudar had made it home yet.

In fact, I was so distracted, I had even forgotten my promise to let Igborg out to eat until he climbed out of my bag as soon as we sat down.

"You're supposed to stay hidden," I scolded softly and tried to push him by the head back into my pack.

He dug his claws into the wooden table and let out a shriek.

"Igborg!"

"A dragonling?" a man to my right said, leaning over for a better look. He appeared to be in his late twenties and had long black hair, which was tied at the back of his head. He wore a sun-faded purple band around his head, and his neck, shoulders, and arms were covered in tattoos.

"Now he's seen you," I said to Igborg and pushed on his chest. "Get back inside!"

"No! I been in all day!" he protested. "Hungry!"

The stranger quirked a grin and held out his hand, which had meat in it.

Igborg snatched it without hesitation.

I rolled my eyes. "Traitor."

Igborg looked up at me with a sheepish glint but still flicked the meat into the air and caught it, practically swallowing it whole.

"How long have you had him?" the man asked.

"You seem familiar," Mihrage interrupted.

The man's dark eyes drifted to Mihrage. "Do I?" But he grinned in a way that confirmed Mihrage's statement, or at least looking like he knew what Mihrage meant.

Mihrage studied him in return, unable to place his face.

"The name is Sinbad." The stranger extended his hand to me.

"Caspara," I replied and took his hand.

To my surprise, he pulled my hand to his lips and kissed the back. "Where are you from? He leaned a little further to take me in completely. "Clearly not from Halmu. Women here don't dress the way you two do, in pants and men's tunics."

I pulled my hand away, the hair on my neck prickling. "Who said tunics were only made for men?"

He grinned. "I stand corrected."

"We're from Zunbar," I answered as Mihrage said my name in warning. I looked at my best friend. "What's he going to do? Follow us back to the city and be disappointed when he realizes I have nothing to my name but a tunic?"

"You said you were a good judge of character," Mihrage replied, his voice low, barely audible over the ruckus of the inn. "He is not a good man."

I turned back to Sinbad. "And what do you do? Try and use your charm to attract girls a decade younger than you and hope they fall for your off-handed complements?"

He grinned and laughed. It was only when he tilted his chin back I spotted the tattoo on his throat and the golden hoop earrings in his ears. "I am not that old. Twenty-one to be exact, but I get your hint." He held out his arms and stood. "I'll give you a silver coin if you guess my career." His cocky grin reminded me of Abudar.

I folded my arms. "A piece of silver? That's a boring wager. Give me five silvers."

He lowered his arms. "Now, I like you. Five pieces of silver it is."

I looked the man up and down. "You'd better twirl in a circle."

He obeyed, not realizing I was mocking him.

I looked over the man's garb—salt-worn vest, earrings,

tattoo, bandana, not to mention the men who sat at his table. "Your garb reminds me of pirates," I finally stated.

"That's because I am one, beautiful." He bowed at the waist.

"It's Caspara." I frowned. I'd already been swept off my feet by Abudar's flattery, I wasn't about to fall for Sinbad's.

"Point taken." He set five silver coins on the table and patted Igborg on the head before taking his seat.

"Sinbad!" a man hollered over the crowd.

Those nearest us stopped conversation to see what was going on as the man made his way to Sinbad's table.

Sinbad jumped back to his feet. "Petra!" He wrapped his arms around the wide man.

"You've returned from one of your grand adventures!" Petra held Sinbad at arm's length. "And in one piece! I'll pull up a chair so you can share the story." He dragged a chair over from the nearest table and plopped down.

A few more people leaned in to hear.

Sinbad turned his chair around and sat with his arms on the back. "Where to begin? The last time I left here." He rubbed his hands together. "I had obtained a crew I'd never sailed with before." He moved his hands dramatically as his voice took on a mysterious, story-teller tone. "As you know, we were seeking the Treasure of Turue, but before we could even make it to the island of Daryabar, the men I hired staged a mutiny. These low-life rats tied me up, stole my map, and locked me in the brig for three days!"

Daryabar? I'd heard that name somewhere.

An audience gathered, and each man and woman leaned forward in anticipation of his story. I hated to admit I was one of them and wanted to know what happened, whether or not it was true.

"Did they feed you?" someone in the sea of faces asked.

"Nay, nor did they provide water." Sinbad held his hand to his throat and gave a dramatic gulp.

"Can you believe this story?" Mihrage mumbled under his breath.

Irilibus returned and took his seat, telling Mihrage there was only one room available, so we would have to share, while Sinbad continued his story.

"On the third day, they lowered anchor in a bay somewhere. They dragged me to the beach of this island I'd never before seen in all my days upon the sea. Piles of gray rocks stood up from the ground like skeleton fingers of a giant, and the only plants I could see were dying trees or sagebrush. I knew they were about to maroon me there and shamelessly pleaded for my life." He climbed onto the table and knelt, acting out clasping his hands in front of him to plead.

"I thought he was tied up," Mihrage pointed out as he sipped from his glass.

I chuckled. Mihrage's sarcasm was almost as amusing as the story.

Sinbad flung his arms out. "Before the crew could get away with their sordid plan, a cyclops appeared from the forest!"

The crowd gasped.

"A cyclops?"

"No such thing!"

Sinbad pointed to the crowd. "No such thing you say? And yet an enormous man with one eye in the center of his forehead showed himself to us!" He placed his hands together in a circle shape on his forehead. He jumped on top of the chair and crouched. "I thought we were done for! Me, bound to a tree, left to die by my own crew! But the cyclops didn't notice me at first. His gaze settled on the crew running away and thought that they would be fun to consume for his dinner. He chased them down, scooped them up in his hands, and ground their bones to make his bread!"

I was with Mihrage. Sinbad was a bold-faced liar. Still, his story was at least fun.

Someone stopped by the table so we could order food, and I used Sinbad's silver pieces to get a pile of raw meat for Igborg.

"How did you escape, then?" someone asked.

Sinbad pulled the dagger from the back of his pants. "I said I was tied to a tree, I never said I wasn't without an escape plan. I cut my bonds, but before I snuck back to the ship, I had to retrieve my map. The cyclops hadn't eaten the men's clothing."

Mihrage raised his brow and sarcastically said, "What, the cyclops took the time to strip your men of their clothing before eating them?"

Sinbad's eyes darted to Mihrage and he hesitated just long enough for me to identify he hadn't considered how preposterous that sounded. But he quickly retorted, "Would you want fabric stuck in your teeth? I had to sneak past his snoring form and bulging stomach to comb through every pocket until I recovered what was mine. I wasn't a fool, and couldn't carry on to the secret island steering a ship on my own, so I did the only thing I could. All by myself, I sailed back here to Halmu. Now, I seek a new crew, one that will not betray me and leave me for dead."

"You sailed a ship all by yourself?" someone said in

disbelief.

Sinbad extended his arms. "Ask everyone who saw me dock. Did any crew disembark?"

"No," someone muttered.

"It's true. I saw him too."

"Aye, all alone."

Sinbad nodded.

"You seek a new crew?" Petra asked.

"Well, I still haven't uncovered the Treasure of Turue." He shrugged and sat back down in his chair. "I will not stop until I discover what it is."

"What is it supposed to be?" I asked, then felt a tad embarrassed when all eyes shifted to me. I'd been so enthralled, I hadn't noticed I'd eaten everything on my plate.

Sinbad smiled at me. "I believe it may be a griffin egg."

Mihrage snorted his drink out of his nose and wiped his arm across his face. "Griffin egg? Griffins haven't existed in our land for ages."

"But they may exist in other lands, could they not? Think about it! An entire world and not one griffin still alive? That is what we believed about dragons until the desert dragon rose from its slumber less than two weeks ago. And this young woman has a pet dragonling!" Sinbad gestured his hand to me.

If the room wasn't already captivated enough, it suddenly fell so quiet, all I heard was the *chink* of a spoon or fork clattering against a plate.

I put on a stiff smile. "He's just a lizard." I held up my blue-green Igborg for the room to see and silently prayed he would keep his young mouth shut. "A uromastyx lizard from Zunbar. That is all."

"I've had enough stories to put me to sleep," Mihrage said, rising to his feet and yawning loudly. His father stood as well. "Good luck on your treasure-seeking journey, Sinbad."

The pirate clicked his tongue. "Hopefully we shall meet again. I'm curious to know about you. We haven't seen Dalarian around for some years."

"That is a story I will not tell to a room full of strangers," Irilibus said firmly.

"Perhaps you're ashamed to admit they all left your land?" Sinbad raised his glass to his lips.

Irilibus arched a brow. "I am not falling into your trap to correct you and tell my story. Good night."

I kissed Igborg on top of the head and whispered, "Thank you" before setting him in my bag. I snuck him a final piece of meat before I too stood and joined Taraji and Mihrage in following the Dalarian leader through the dining room.

"I'm done with stories too," someone said. "Where is the music?"

From the corner of the room, the musicians began to play a joyful song to replace the awkward silence we left behind. I exhaled in relief.

Mihrage cleared his throat. "Remember when you said you were a good judge of—"

"Shut your lips. I never said I trusted the pirate," I interrupted.

"You gave him your name *and* showed him Igborg. He's a notorious troublemaker and steals from men who rightfully earned their rewards. Sinbad has a reputation I'm shocked you haven't heard. I wouldn't be surprised if he's got someone watching where we will sleep so he can try and slip in to steal Igborg for himself," Mihrage said sharply.

I blanched. "Why would you say something like that?"

He sighed. "Because it's true. There are all sorts of rumors about Sinbad."

"Like there are rumors about you?" I countered.

He frowned. "That's not the same thing. Rumors come from some truth."

"Or none at all."

"Knock it off, you two," Taraji said. "We're all safe and fine. I'll lay a spell on the sand outside of the door to suck in anyone who tries to enter our room after we've all gone in."

"You can do that?" I asked.

Mihrage raised his brows. "That would be impressive."

"I've been practicing for when I get to go to the academy," she said proudly.

I'd somehow forgotten about that. She'd completed the Desert Trials and now had the opportunity to attend the Zauberin Academy with the other sorceresses who had also completed the trials. I wouldn't be one of them. When we returned home, Taraji and Mihrage would leave me to pursue their futures—Taraji to become one of the most amazing sorceresses in all the world, with Mihrage at her side as her husband, likely raising the beautiful little children they would someday have while using his own magic to help the people in their little town.

And me? I would go back to being Almas, the thief. Because I couldn't face the thought of leaving everything I knew to be a sentinel alongside a greedy prince.

The room was small, with one bed. I didn't fight or even ask for it. Instead, I laid out my bedroll, slipped the magic lamp under my rolled-up robe which acted as my pillow, and set my bag beside me.

Igborg climbed out and snuggled against my leg.

Mihrage was unsuccessfully trying to talk Taraji into sleeping on the bed until Irilibus finally said, "I'll sleep in it and you two can stop arguing." He kicked his pack under the bed and removed his shoes.

Taraji smiled a bit at Mihrage. "See? You should have taken it."

He rolled his eyes.

With only one bed in the room, we were provided extra bedding. I laid out my own and settled down and closed my eyes. Someone blew out the candle, and I stroked Igborg's spiny back until I drifted off to sleep.

Five

I bolted upright, my heart clinging to my throat like a blob beetle that stuck itself to the livestock and sucked their blood.

Something was wrong.

Something was very wrong.

All of my senses fired—my ears zeroed in on the distant sound of the ocean, the slight breeze in the leaves outside the window, and I could have sworn the sound of footsteps. My nose picked up the scent of rum, and my eyes focused on a shadow that slipped out the window. Or maybe it was the curtain in the breeze, but . . . I didn't remember any of us opening the window to allow a breeze in.

I tossed the blanket aside and sprinted the three steps to the window, then leaned out to see if I could spot the shadow, but even my trained eyes couldn't spot anyone or anything.

I overreacted. It was just a trick of the light. Sinbad's stories got to me.

But when I turned to my bed, I realized what was wrong.

Igborg wasn't there.

"Igborg?" I whispered, trying to call for him without waking the others. I had to remind myself to breathe.

Igborg would sometimes get too hot and lie directly on the floor or decide he was hungry and wander around and find some bugs to eat, but he always stayed in the house. After Sinbad had announced to everyone in the inn that Igborg was a dragon, I had it fixed in my mind that the shadow that had entered the room had taken him, and I couldn't shake that thought.

"Igborg, where are you?" I whispered a little louder and knelt down to dig through our bags to see if he was sneaking some extra food.

"What are you doing?" Taraji asked sleepily.

"I can't find Igborg."

"Did he go outside to get something to eat?" She propped herself up on her elbow.

I shook my head. "I don't think so. He ate a big dinner. And I don't know if he would go out in a strange place like this." I bit my lip and rested my hands in my lap. "I think . . . I think someone took him," I confessed.

Taraji sat up and crawled over to me. "Do you really think so?"

"I didn't leave the window open, and I don't remember any of you leaving it open, but it is." I gestured with both hands. "And I swear I saw a shadow, but it could have been my mind playing tricks."

"Why are you two awake?" Mihrage grumbled. "It's not even dawn yet."

"Igborg is missing," Taraji answered for me.

"And I think I saw someone leave the room through the window," I added. "But it may be my imagination."

He sat up and rested his arms on his knees, giving his sleepy mind a moment to comprehend what we'd just said. His attention focused on the open window and he stood.

"Do you think you can tell what happened?" I asked.

He shook his head. "Like I've said time and again, I don't know how to control it one hundred percent of the time." He rested his hands on the window and closed his eyes. "But I'll try."

I bit my lip and gripped my pants into my fists.

When I had found Igborg a few years ago, I had told myself that I would nurse him back to health and send him on his way back into the wild, where he belonged. Of course, I didn't feel bad that he never actually left me. But the thought that someone could *take* him from me and do who knew what with him made my stomach churn. He was all I had of home, besides Taraji and Mihrage. When they left, Igborg would be the only family I had left.

Mihrage's brows suddenly pinched and he tilted his head. "Igborg was here, eating the moths, and someone lured him out of the room with meat. That's all I see." He opened his eyes and turned them to me. "I am sorry. I cannot see beyond that. I cannot see their face or anything."

My stomach rolled again and I looked down at my hands. "I was supposed to keep him safe." I gripped my pants tighter. "And that . . . *pirate* had to take him from me!"

"Caspara," Taraji said, placing her hand over mine and leaning close in an attempt to comfort me.

I pulled away and stood. "I'm not about to stand by and let Sinbad get away with this!" I snatched the dagger I'd stolen with my father and marched from the room.

"Caspara, you don't know that it was him," Taraji said, rushing after me.

"You could get in more trouble," Mihrage added. He reached for my arm, but I pulled away before he could get a grip.

"I don't care. He'll know who did take Igborg." I didn't slow. I didn't stop. I burst into the dining room, which held two sleepy-looking men and a woman. "Where is Sinbad?"

All three looked at me, the most awake they'd probably been in a few hours.

One man had glossy, drunken eyes and slurred out, "The pira'? The crazy kid es lookin' for treasure . . . some kind."

The woman sighed. "He doesn't know. None of us have seen him."

"Which room is he staying in?" I stabbed the dagger into the table in front of them.

Mihrage finally made it into the room and grabbed my arm. This time, when I went to pull away, he grabbed the other too. "Stop this, Caspara. You don't want to get us in trouble."

"Yes, I do. If it gets me Igborg back, I'll cause whatever trouble I can!" I stomped my heel on his foot, making him grunt and flinch.

"Caspara, you're causing a scene." Taraji pulled the dagger out of the table. "We're going to help you find him, but you aren't any good if you get arrested for violence."

I scowled at Taraji. She was right. I couldn't find Igborg if I was locked in a prison cell. I'd proven that once before when I got arrested trying to save my father. I sucked in a breath and slowly let it out through my nose, then turned to the strangers.

"I apologize for my outburst." After snatching the dagger back from Taraji, I stormed over to the door, pulled it open by the handle, and stepped out into the still-cool morning.

The morning sunlight painted the clouds orange while

the sky itself was still dark purple.

"If I were a pirate that just stole a dragon and was supposedly also seeking some sort of treasure, I would flee to my ship and leave as soon as possible." I looked over my shoulder at my two friends. "I'm going down to the docks to see if I spot Sinbad. Pack our things and meet me down there."

"Caspara!" Taraji shouted after me.

But I was already running.

I could only assume they went back to the room as I sprinted down the dirt road toward the docks. My stomach was tied in knots—I could get lost in the darkness or get attacked by a wild animal, even a robber (though I felt I had a better chance fighting against a human), or worse, I Sinbad could be gone by the time I reached the docks and I would never find Igborg again.

I skidded to a stop, nearly missing a gap in the trees that opened right up to the beach as the rising sun lit up the docks.

One ship in particular bustled with activity as the crew made their ship ready to sail. I couldn't discern what they said, but I didn't need to. My heart told me *that* was where Igborg was hidden.

No matter how familiar I was with living in the sand, there was no secret way to run through it. But I tried my best.

"Sinbad!" I shouted as soon as I got close enough I knew the crew could hear me. "I demand to speak with Sinbad!"

Sinbad's hair caught in the wind as he stood on the edge of his ship, holding on to the ropes. "Ah, Lady Caspara! You seem particularly upset this morning," he called. "Did you lose something?"

I made it to the docks but realized the ship was already moving. I tried to measure the distance between myself and the ship while I ran as fast I could. Even though I was a decent swimmer, I'd never swam in the ocean beyond the shore.

"Give me Igborg!" I shouted.

His smile froze and his eyes darted from the ship to the docks. "You'll never make it. Perhaps we will someday meet again." He flourished his hat.

I narrowed my eyes and planted both feet on the edge of the docks, launching myself forward. For a moment, I felt at home, bounding between the rooftops of buildings. But buildings didn't move. With fingers outstretched, I sorely missed and plunged into the icy waters. It stole my breath, but I had Igborg to think of and surfaced.

In those few seconds, the crew had dropped their sails and the ship was moving far faster than I could dream of swimming.

"No! Igborg!" I screamed, still moving my arms through the rough waves to try and catch up.

But it was futile.

I would never be able to swim fast enough to catch Sinbad's ship, and now I was yards away from the shore.

I stopped trying to swim and tears filled my eyes.

Igborg was gone. The one thing I had left that was my companion.

I had to hunt down Sinbad. What was the name of that island he said he was sailing to? What if he'd already sold Igborg to someone here?

I had no recollection of swimming back to shore, only that I dragged myself onto the beach and collapsed, exhausted and heartbroken.

"Caspara!" Taraji was kneeling in the waves in front of me, not caring she was getting her clothes and shoes wet. She pulled me into her lap and held me tightly.

That was when I started to cry.

"Did he have Igborg?" Mihrage asked, rubbing his hand over my back comfortingly.

I sniffled and looked up at him. "I-I think so. He-he didn't admit it, but . . . he acted like it. And now I've lost him too!"

Taraji leaned away from me and held up the golden lamp. "You could use your second wish and get him back."

My breath caught.

But I'd been so worried about Igborg, I hadn't even thought to look for the magic lamp. "Why didn't they steal this too?" I asked when Taraji placed the rusty metal oil lamp in my hands.

"They didn't know you had it. It was under your bedding, remember?" Mihrage said. "Look at us, we don't look like we have any riches. And if you hadn't let them know about Igborg . . ."

Taraji gave him an angry glare.

He flinched. "I'm sorry. It's not your fault, Caspara," he said.

"But it is." My throat caught. "The only way to get him back is to wish for it." I took the lamp and rubbed it immediately.

"Good . . . morning!" Taylin said in a chipper voice once he paused to look and see what time of day it was. His navy blue skin seemed a bit brighter than normal and the gold flecks sparkled in the full sunlight. However, he grimaced like a wet cat when the waves crashed over his feet. "You are always in messy circumstances."

With Mihrage and Taraji's assistance, I climbed to my feet and onto the dry sand.

Taylin raised a brow. "What happened now?"

"Some pirates stole Igborg," I said.

He grinned. "And you need my help to get him back!" He rubbed his hands together eagerly. "All it costs is a wish."

Only a wish? I *only* had three of them total, and I was already down to two. I'd promised Taylin I would use one to free him, which meant this was my only wish left. I'd used the first to give Sultana Shahira's magic back because that was Abudar's only wish, and after we escaped the caves, I knew he deserved that much in return for his kindness toward me.

The responsible wish to make would be to help Abudar. But Igborg was all I had left of a family.

"What's wrong?" Taylin asked.

"I just thought of Abudar. He's missing too. I just need to think of a way to make a wish in order to save them both."

Taylin scowled. "No trying to sneak in an extra wish." He wagged his finger, scolding me, and then used that same finger to dry all of us off. "One or the other, or both and use all of your wishes."

I swallowed and glanced at my friends. Abudar had his own magic and his own family to save him. I was all Igborg had. "I'm sorry, but I've got to go and save Igborg. You'll have to continue on your own, and we will catch up later."

Taraji blanched. "What are you saying?"

I turned to Taylin. "I wish for a boat that will sail on its own and take me to Igborg." I clutched the feather pendant on my neck for comfort.

"Not the wish I thought you were going to make, but . . ." Taylin winked and clapped his hands together. A plume of gold glitter fluttered through the air. "You know, you could have just wished for me to rescue Igborg."

In my overwhelmed state, I hadn't even considered that wish and looked at the jinni with wide eyes.

The gold glittered magic floated over to the ocean and took form into a ship far more solid-looking than the one Irilibus had chartered for us.

"Kids, we need to get on board the ship!" Irilibus said, having just walked down the path from the inn.

"You can't go after Igborg on your own!" Taraji objected, seizing my hands. "You'll have to face Sinbad and his pirates, and that's dangerous! Come with us, and we can all go after Igborg together."

"She already made the wish, and her ship is here," Mihrage said.

We all turned to see a ship at the end of a dock with Taylin standing in the captain's spot, wearing a preposterous gold-and-black costume.

"Why should *you* have to save your sister?" I asked Mihrage.

Mihrage looked past me, slowly taking in our surroundings. "When I was a boy, when I was learning about my magic, my mentor took me into the forest and told me to listen to everything around me. I'll never forget what he said. He told me, *Mihrage, the most important thing you can be is true to yourself.* As a child, I didn't understand, but I've grown to understand more and more the older I get."

I bit my lip and looked at the ship again.

"Caspara, being true to who you are doesn't mean

letting go of who you were. For me, being true to who I am means helping those I can. Because if I don't, who will?"

Mihrage didn't need to be specific. I knew he spoke of himself *and* my responsibilities as sentinel. I had turned away from them, vowed not to become one. But what if he was right? What if I could do both? Be true to who I was meant to be while also holding on to who my father raised me to be?

Mihrage nudged Taraji out of the way and hugged me. "Remember to think before you act. I know you're overwhelmed with the death of your father and that you feel a lot of responsibility sitting on your shoulders." He stepped back. "But you need to remember what your father taught you. Think before you act."

I nodded, grateful for him helping me recall rule number three. "I will. And you come home to us. Take care of Taraji."

He smiled. "You know I will. I have a promise to keep to her parents."

Taraji had her arms folded across her chest and she rolled her eyes at the mention of her parents. She jerked me into a hug. "Don't be stupid."

I didn't miss the glance Mihrage gave Taraji. They were worried about me. How unstable I must have looked to them. No, pitiful.

We separated and I walked to the ship Taylin had summoned. I paused right before stepping on to steal a glance at my friends. They had already boarded their ship and I could see Mihrage speaking with Irilibus, likely explaining what had happened.

What a fool I'd been to let Sinbad see Igborg.

How irresponsible I had been by not keeping my

dragonling safe.

Taylin gently set his hands on my shoulders. "This is a good opportunity to test out your skills as a sentinel."

I snorted and looked over my shoulder at the jinni. "You had to go there."

He grinned. "I did. Because you were trained in different skills than Abudar for a reason. Telama doesn't make mistakes. Come on and see the view of the ocean from the upper deck."

"If only Father could be here," I whispered. I hoped he would have been proud of me.

Six
Mithra

The stone warmed my fingertips as I rolled it from my index to my pinky and back. It was a familiar sensation now, even though I'd only had it a few days.

As I looked out over the city of Zunbar from my bedroom window, a thought creeped into the back of my mind: *Have you ever wondered how to gain more power? Not training, but real power?*

I stopped moving the stone and looked over my shoulder, as though I could see a person standing there. "What do you mean?" I asked out loud.

Go to The Veil. I will show you how to gain more power.

I removed my hand from my pocket and looked down at the ruby. There was a red light glowing inside Skeptically, I held it up to get a better look at the light inside. "How do you expect me to gain more power? Do you mean attending their lessons?"

I will show you. But you must get there first, and then I shall reveal my secrets to you. The light faded until the ruby was solid again.

I rubbed my thumb over the faceted surface, but the light didn't wake.

An eager flutter filled my stomach. Roshanak had taught me the only way to gain strength was through years of training, like what she had done. Hours of study, reading, and then applying those lessons into action. According to her, I needed to understand how magic worked, where it came from, and how to safely manipulate it. Sorceresses were "vessels" for the magic in the world surrounding them.

She also once told me there could be more sorceresses, if only they *saw* the magic. If they could look at the growing flower and see the tiny sparks from the sun warming the petals, the roots seeping up nutrients, and the little bees stopping to pollinate, they could see much more than just a pretty pink flower.

If they could look through the city and see the tiny birds roosting in the corners of the buildings, the way the wind danced with the fabric shades, the little lizards, scorpions, and bugs that hid under the market tables and wedged in the edges of the sand, they might be able to feel the wonders of the world around them. If others could see past the obvious things their eyes showed them, they could see the magic.

I threw a white scarf on my hair and one end over my shoulder and was poised to summon a portal when there was a knock.

"Who is it?" I called.

"Arash."

"Come in!" I smiled and turned to face my door.

The handsome man, my personal bodyguard, entered my bedroom. No other palace guard would dare do such a thing, but Arash was no other guard. The sword earring in his right ear glinted and he had a bit of stubble on his face.

"What brings you to my room so early in the day?" I asked, swaying my hips as I walked to him.

He slipped his arm around my waist. "I hadn't seen you yet today. I came to see if you would be practicing with Roshanak."

I couldn't hide my excitement and ginned. "I have a better idea. I'm going to go speak with The Veil. Come with me."

His dark brows pinched. "The Veil? What can they teach you that Roshanak can't?"

I shook my head. "I didn't say I was going to have them teach me anything. It's the ruby." I walked my fingers up his chest to the collar of his shirt so I could grab it and pull him closer. "I have a suspicion I need to confirm. Come with me?"

"I . . . I have responsibilities," he said softly, but hardly in a way that meant "no."

"Yes. And protecting me is your first," I said near his mouth, then pressed my lips to his.

Arash never could resist me.

He leaned into the kiss and then broke it and sighed. "All right. Only since you asked so nicely."

Remaining near him, I turned so I could create the portal. "*Iftah ya bowaba.*"

As usual, light swirled, creating a circle in the air with a mirror-like surface revealing a place beyond the main island.

"You're getting much better at that."

"Better than Abudar," I agreed.

Arash and I held hands as we stepped through, mainly because I wasn't sure how quickly the portal would close once I entered and I didn't want it to close on him or before he could join me.

Not knowing where the ruby wanted me to be, I opened the portal on the main floor of the new hideout.

"This is a bad idea," Arash whispered.

"Don't worry. I have everything under control." I smiled sweetly. "I was here just yesterday, remember?"

He shook his head. "Captain Nadeem will ask if I know the location. You know I can't lie to him."

"He won't ask for the location if you don't tell him you've been here," I said firmly. "And besides, you don't actually know what island they're on because you've only been there through the portal."

Arash looked at me sideways, but I ignored him and slowly headed up the stairs, my mind focused on any word from the ruby.

We did get several wide-eyed looks as we walked past young women in the land who were startled to see either myself as the princess, or Arash, since they hadn't seen a man since The Veil took them all to this island days ago.

Stop.

I halted so quickly Arash ran into my back. We had made it to the third floor of the main building and the rows of doors.

"What is it?" he asked, always on edge due to his training.

Go to the seventh door on your right.

The ruby hadn't shared any information with me about what to expect or what to do prior to coming, so I was putting all of my faith in a stone I only suspected belonged to my grandfather.

"We're almost to the end of the hallway," Arash pointed out.

"I am aware. I have eyes," I said dryly. I silently counted the doors until I reached the seventh, then paused for confirmation.

The ruby warmed in response.

I pulled my scarf down over my shoulders and knocked.

"Come in!" a voice sang.

I opened the door and found a lovely little room just big enough for a bed with a patchwork quilt, a bookshelf, and desk on a large colorful rug.

One lonely girl sat with a book open on her lap. She gave me a pleasant smile at first, and then her eyes widened in either horror or shock and she rose to her feet so quickly the book clattered to the floor. "Your Highness!" she blurted and curtseyed.

Yes, her.

"Hello. Forgive my interrupting you. Shorix wanted me to visit with a few of the girls here and offer my support. Did you participate in the Desert Trials?" On the inside, I was wondering what on earth the ruby wanted me to do *now*.

She met Arash's gaze and blushed. "Um. Sir." She curtseyed again and awkwardly tugged at her well-worn dress before she scooped up her book. "I did join the trials. I am ashamed I didn't even make it to the cave entrance. That is why I am actually excited to be here. I still get to train and will likely learn more than even those at the academy." She was all smiles.

Take the dagger from your lover, press me against the hilt, and drive the dagger into the girl's heart.

"Oh good." I quickly turned away from the girl to Arash. *I can't do that! Kill another person? Who do you think I am?*

You want more power, do you not?

Not by driving a dagger into their heart!

The ruby didn't respond right away.

Arash gave me a concerned look, and I busied myself by going to the girl's bookshelf, choosing a book at random and flipping through the pages. When the ruby still didn't respond, I placed it back on the shelf and selected another book.

Do you want to gain more power, yes or no? the ruby finally asked me.

Of course I do. But I stand firm that I will not take the life of another. If there is no other way, I shall drop you down the hole we climbed out of when we escaped the caves in the desert and no one will ever see you again. I felt a little bit ridiculous threatening a rock.

"Mithra?" Arash whispered. "Are you all right?"

I plastered a smile on my face. "Yes. Certainly. I thought I saw an important spell book, that's all." I placed the book back on the shelf.

The purpose of killing her is to take her power, Mithra. Of course, you could take her power another way, but it will be painful for you both, and she would live to be able to report what you have done to the head sorceress. You must decide if you are willing to risk that.

I glanced over my shoulder at the girl. *She's clearly from a low caste, and if she reports that the princess stole her power, there is a high probability they would either believe someone disguised as me did so, or that she never had magic in the first place. Either way, no one would suspect it was actually me.*

That's my girl. Send Arash out to guard the door and tell him not to enter. Take the weak sorceress by the hand

and say, "Qowetik melki."

"Arash, would you give us a few minutes? I have some questions." I looked up at him and gave him my sweetest smile. "Stand outside the door?"

He hesitated, glancing between us like he knew something was wrong, but he couldn't figure out what and didn't dare challenge me. Finally, he cleared his throat and bowed.

I couldn't decide whether or not it was a good idea to have him there. On one hand, he was guarding the door, but depending on what happened next, everything between us could potentially change. I was listening to a voice trapped inside of a ruby and about to steal the power from a fellow sorceress. What were the chances this spell would actually work? And how would Arash react?

"I didn't want men's ears listening, you know?" I said casually once he'd left. "We didn't properly meet. I am Mithra. You are?" I held out my hand.

"Nadine." She accepted my hand and closed her fingers around mine.

Say the words now. Do not hesitate. Qowetik melki.

"*Qowetik melki,*" I whispered, still doubting myself.

Electricity far more intense than anything I'd ever felt in my life ran from my toes, up my spine, through my shoulder, and down my arm into Nadine's hand.

She cried out in surprise and pain and tried to pull her hand away, but we were locked together. "What's going on?" she shrieked.

Purple magic glowed around her hand, pulled from her body, and bound together like the coils of a snake as it swirled around my arm into my chest.

When the last of the purple magic seeped into my body,

the force keeping our hands linked broke.

Nadine stumbled backward and collapsed to the ground while I sank into a chair, eyes wide and dazed.

She was yelling.

Tears streaked her face.

A set of hands cupped my face and pulled my attention to the matching face.

Arash.

He was concerned.

Why was he so worried?

He stroked my face, but I couldn't speak.

"What did you do to her?" he shouted to Nadine. He picked me up into his arms.

"It was her! She attacked me with some kind of magic!"

We were in the hallway now. What had Arash said to the girl? Had he told anyone on the way down the hallway what he suspected?

He suddenly stopped and set me on my feet. We were back where the portal had let us out. "Tell me what to do. Tell me how to help," he practically begged.

"I . . . need to . . . to get us back." My voice sounded so far away.

"How can I help?" he asked again.

I slowly shook my head. There was nothing he could do. My body felt . . . strange. My limbs felt heavy, like when we'd been in the cave and almost drowned. Pure exhaustion, and yet inside of my chest, my magic crackled like thunder before lightning.

I held up my hands and thought the words to the spell to create the portal: *Iftah ya bowaba.*

But I didn't speak the words aloud.

Only the strongest of magic wielders could use non-oral

magic, even if it was a basic spell.

Yet, as soon as I thought the words, the portal opened.

Arash opened his mouth to speak, but I stepped back into my bedroom and stumbled. His arms caught me and the portal behind us snapped shut.

"What in the . . . dry desert was that?" Arash demanded, trying his hardest not to curse. He grabbed my face again, concern lining his brow and anger burning in his eyes. "What happened in there?"

I smiled and slipped my hand into my pocket to hold the ruby. "I think it worked."

"Huh? What worked?"

"I took her magic." I let out a laugh and my exhaustion was suddenly overwhelmed with anxious energy and adrenaline. "I must go practice." I pulled away from Arash.

With his long strides, he easily got ahead of me and blocked the door. "What do you mean you took her magic? Mithra, I demand you tell me now."

I touched his cheek, still smiling. "Everything is going to change. For the first time in my life, my parents will see me. For the first time, they will see that I am just as important as Abudar. No. No, not just as important. That I am *more*. That I can be *more* powerful. They'll see me. They'll realize what they should have done my entire life. The ruby told me I could take the girl's magic, and I did."

"Mithra, this isn't you."

"This is the real me, Arash," I snapped, narrowing my eyes at him. "If you're not strong enough to be at the side of a powerful woman, then go away and I don't want to see you guarding me ever again. It's your choice." I pushed him out of the way.

With trembling hands, I walked to the palace practice

room. My hands tightened around the ruby.

For the first time in my life, the world would know my name, and not as the beautiful princess but as the most powerful sorceress in the land.

Seven

Taylin's magical ship sailed west along the coastline. I watched as the foliage faded away and cliffs rose along the edge of the land.

I'd always thought Sheblom was nothing more than rolling hills of red sand, but in the last two weeks, I had learned our landscape varied far more than I ever even dreamed. The Dragon's Lair caves lay buried beneath the sands west of Zunbar, their entrance in the bottom of a massive ravine. Layered orange and red towers of stone stood like guardians south of the city Balim. Zunbar was arid, while Halmu had been rather tropical.

My naivety toward my own land added one more reason to my list of why I felt I would fail as a sentinel. How could I represent the people of our country when I didn't even know what it looked like?

If only Father had lived longer. We could have explored the cities together.

I closed my eyes and let my tears fall. I missed his companionship. He would have climbed the riggings to the top of the mast and pointed out sea monsters that didn't exist or made faces out of the cliffside.

"We will reach Igborg soon," Taylin said in a comforting tone while he rubbed my back.

I dried my cheeks and opened my eyes. "I'm grateful you stayed with me. I know you didn't have to."

He rested his arms on the railing of the ship and nodded. "I couldn't leave you alone."

"But you could have. Everyone else has, why not you?" I sighed. "I didn't mean that." I leaned my back against the railing and looked down at my hands.

Taylin straightened and mimicked my position. "Two days ago, the only home you've ever known was destroyed. A week ago, you attended your father's funeral, and within that same week discovered the truth about your mother being Grand Sorceress Roshanak. You also learned that she did, in fact, abandon you. But she is the only one." He took my hand.

"When we get . . . home, Taraji will leave to study at the Zauberin Academy, and Mihrage will go with her."

Taylin shrugged and pulled me away from my moping position. "And you will go to the palace to be with the other sentinel, Prince Abudar."

I frowned. "You make it sound so easy."

He spun me around in a circle under his arm and smiled. "Caspara, I cannot fault you for being upset and sad, or hesitant toward your future. You're young for all of these events to fall upon your shoulders so suddenly. But they have. The way I look at things, you can choose to mope and be sad, or you can choose to act and maybe find some happiness along the way."

"Like you have?" I asked, unable to resist a grin when Taylin began dancing with me.

"Precisely." The jinni smiled.

"Do you believe things happen for a reason?" I asked.

"I believe fate does have a hand in our lives, whether or

not we want to acknowledge it." He stepped back and bowed.

I curtseyed. "Thank you. That was fun."

"And distracting." He winked and gestured a hand toward the left of the ship.

An island overwhelmed by a storm loomed on the horizon, and the ship turned toward it. A chill ran down my spine. Something about the island was wrong.

"Welcome to the island of Daryabar," Taylin said. "You may want to hold on to something as we get closer."

"Because of the storm?" I glanced at him.

He nodded.

"Do you feel that? The pit deep in your stomach?" Taylin's eyes shifted to me. "What you're sensing is the magic surrounding the island. The storm is ever-present."

As if the very ocean could hear Taylin's ominous tone, the waves began to crash against the sides of the ship. I instinctively ran to the mast to hold on.

Taylin cleared his throat. He opened the bag I had flung over my shoulder and looked inside, checking that his lamp was there. "All right. In order for me to stay safe, I am afraid I must hide."

"You can't leave me!" I almost shrieked.

He grimaced. "Yes, well, you see, I am afraid."

I raised my eyebrows.

"In case you haven't noticed, I'm not overly fond of water." His lip curled like a feline that had just sniffed bad milk.

I stared at him with wide eyes. "So you're going to leave me to *hopefully* make it to the island myself?"

Taylin grinned. "You do have one last wish."

"You're unbelievable! I don't know why I ever trusted

you!"

"I'll see you on the shore." He blew me a kiss and disappeared.

"You . . . worthless jinni!" I shouted.

The boat rocked to the right, and waves spilled over the side before it rocked left and the water that had made it onto the deck rolled toward me.

The next wave hit harder and added more water on deck.

And then the wind snatched the sails and dragged my little boat in toward a bay.

My heart pounded so hard I thought I might vomit.

I gasped when a wave slammed into me. "Sands! Someone help me!" I held on tightly to the mast with my arms and legs, clinging for dear life.

But there was no one to help me.

Another wave rose, this time cresting far taller than the ship, stretching up to the height of the mast. All I felt was the pit in my stomach drop. And then I was surrounded by blackness, and my fingers stung from being ripped away from the mast. Like a hand, the water gripped me and pulled me away from the safety of the ship. I tumbled through water, completely at the mercy of the ocean.

As I clawed through the water and fought for the surface, my lungs began to burn.

Which way was up?

Darkness surrounded me and my lungs ached for air.

A hand grabbed my wrist and dragged me through the water until I finally broke the surface and started coughing while gasping for breath.

Taylin looked at me with soaking hair sticking to his blue skin. "That . . . is the last time . . ."

"Shore," I coughed.

Another wave hit, forcing us below the waves. This time, we weren't nearly as deep and I managed to surface on my own.

Taylin looked at me. "You have to wish your way there."

"I can't! I only have one wish left!" I yelled, only to gasp when another wave headed for us. "Taylin!"

The wave slammed against my body, yet again dragging me below the surface as if there were something below the waves that wanted to devour me. My body twisted and rolled with the motion of the sea's current, and my arm slammed against something that could have been part of a ship or rock.

When my foot hit what I assumed was ground, I kicked off of it and urged myself toward the opposite direction.

"Wish for me to save you!" Taylin said from right beside me.

I met his pleading eyes.

I released the air in my lungs, no longer able to hold it, and gasped. But my lungs didn't fill with air. They sucked in water.

I was going to die.

This seemed to happen to me more than I wanted to admit—being put in situations where I was going to die. And I had a feeling this wouldn't be the last—if I survived.

Taylin grabbed my wrist.

And that was the last thing I was aware of before I was on the beach, vomiting water from my lungs and stomach and gasping for breath.

Taylin shook his head. "I don't know why I do it. Honestly. What is it about you that makes me feel like I have to keep rescuing you? I'm not supposed to want to do any of that without you using your wishes!" He shook his body like a cat would, and all of the water fell from him.

It was only then I realized that the beach was dry and the sky was clear. The storm was only over the water and not on the land. Looking past the jinni, the angry sea tossed with swells no one could survive. I couldn't see the ship.

I struggled to my feet and sucked in another breath. "How do we get to Sinbad?"

Taylin shook his head. "I don't know."

I snapped my attention on him. "What do you mean you don't know?"

"Your wish was only for the boat to take you to Igborg."

"After all we've been through, you're going to pull *that*? And it didn't!" I flung my arms out. "Do *you* see Igborg? Because I don't. And that ship should have made it through the ocean and onto land, if you were to make my wish fully come true."

Taylin opened his mouth, then paused and glanced at the sky then back at me. "Good argument."

I stared at the jinni. "Which means *you* have to make it so I can find Igborg."

"Then we find him." Taylin straightened his clothing.

As much as I wanted to strangle the jinni, I was still recovering from nearly dying.

Taylin folded his arms and tapped his toes, impatiently waiting for me to get up.

I finally got to my feet and stretched. "I'm going to climb that tree and see where we are," I said.

"Have you ever climbed a tree?" Taylin asked skeptically.

"No, but I've climbed buildings, and it can't be that

different." I wiped my hands on my wet pants and reached up to one of the branches and pulled myself up. My arm screamed in pain, but it didn't seem broken. In spite of my muscles protesting and the sharp pain in my elbow, I managed to get up onto the first branch and leaned my back against the trunk. "See?"

Taylin raised his eyebrows and folded his arms. "You do know you have an easier way of seeing things, yes?"

I climbed up to the next branch. "How is that?" I grunted and got up to the third branch. "I'm not using my last wish."

When I glanced down, I caught him rolling his eyes most dramatically.

Finally, I reached the top of the tree and gazed out over the island. It was nothing but trees as far as I could see, until spotted a stone tower far in the distance.

My heart jumped and I smiled. "It seems the rumors are right! There's a castle that's appeared here!"

"You're making the assumption this is the island that both has Igborg, some buried treasure Sinbad wants, *and* the very location where The Veil is hiding Abudar?"

"I . . . yes. No? Why not?" I looked down at Taylin but could barely see him through the branches.

"Oh, no particular reason. Other than this is Daryabar, an island that isn't supposed to exist, and the likelihood that The Veil would set up their hideout here seems rather . . . fortuitous."

I began climbing down. "I thought you believed fate had a hand in our lives."

"It seems more coincidental to me," Taylin corrected.

I landed on the ground. My adrenaline had long since worn off and my arm throbbed from whatever it had struck while I was drowning in the ocean.

I turned my arm and examined the bruise. "Sinbad didn't show us his map when he was telling his story. I have no idea where to even begin looking. So in order for *you* to fulfil my wish, *you* will lead the way to Sinbad."

I looked at the jinni.

Taylin ran his fingers through his dark hair. "Normally, I wouldn't be able to do such things, but since you asked so *nicely . . .*"

"It's Igborg, Taylin. A helpless little dragonling that was dragon-napped for who knows what reason." I looked up at him and gave him the best puppy expression I could. "You're not doing this for me. You're doing this for him."

"Don't give me that look." Taylin planted his hand on the side of my face and pushed me away. He grumbled something in a language I had never heard and waved his finger in the air to change his clothing from the gaudy pirate costume to the black-and-gold robes he normally wore.

"I *could* just stand here and start screaming." I shrugged.

Taylin sighed. "I don't think that's a good idea."

"Why?"

"Remember the magic you felt when we were out at sea?"

"Yes."

He looked around. "I still feel it in these woods. I don't think we should be drawing attention to ourselves."

"Then how am I supposed to find Igborg?"

Taylin held up both hands in the air, surrendering. "I'll fulfil your wish." He lifted his right hand to his mouth, kissed his fist, and then opened it and blew across his now-open palm. Gold glitter fluttered into the air and pointed like an arrow. "This direction."

"You'd better be right." I picked up my sopping bag and checked inside to see what, if any, of my supplies had survived. I had a waterskin, but all of my food was drenched with water. The dagger was still in there and, luckily, Taylin's lamp.

I dumped out the dripping packages of food that couldn't be saved.

Taylin looked me up and down and then somehow found it in his black heart to use some magic to dry me off. "There. All better. Now"—he wrinkled his nose and tip-toed around a bundle of seaweed— "let's go find Igborg."

Eight

I'd lived my entire life in a desert climate. I knew what it was like to walk in the sand in temperatures over one hundred degrees. But the water in the air added an entirely different sensation of suffocation to the heat of the jungle that I'd never felt before in my life.

Every part of me sweat—sweat slid down my spine, sweat dripped down my forehead, sweat, sweat, sweat. I stopped and leaned against a tree, breathing hard from the walk, and I finished off my water.

Taylin and I had kept our voices low while walking, just to be safe. The jungle was filled with sounds of birds and other creatures I wished I could identify because I'd never heard the clicking noises they made. We followed the magical golden arrow down the path through the jungle.

However, there was a point where we met with a path going left and one going right. The magic arrow pointed left, but something urged me to go right. Something deep down in the pit of my stomach.

I knew Taylin had summoned the arrow because of my wish, so it couldn't be leading us the wrong way.

Yet, I felt like I was *supposed* to go the opposite.

"You hesitate," Taylin pointed out.

I nodded. "I don't know why, but I feel like we should

go the other way."

"Your instinct is wrong. Magic is never wrong."

I turned to him. "Then why do I feel as if I should go that way?" I pointed.

He shrugged. "Who knows? But even if you feel that way, we must go this way or you'll never find Igborg."

I bit my lip and looked at the path to the right again. I knew the jinni was right, and I had to push away whatever it was I felt in my stomach.

We went left.

"How far away do you think we are?" I asked.

"I have no idea." Taylin tilted his head back to look up through the leaves of the trees. "The sun will be going down in a few hours, though."

I held up my empty waterskin. "I'm going to be needing more water before then."

Taylin looked at me. "You've got a final wish."

I frowned at him. "Nice try." I started walking again but heard a twig snap and the rustling of leaves ahead of me on the path.

"Summon me if you need me!" Taylin spun in a circle and disappeared.

"Don't leave me alone!" I shouted in a whisper, but it was too late.

The jinni was gone.

A gruff voice said, "If I have to cut one more tree . . ." It was followed by the sound of a sword hacking at tree limbs.

"Shut up, Nomil."

"Captain, this clearing will be a good place to set up a camp."

"That's why I'm having you cut the tree limbs, boys,"

Sinbad said as though he were bored. "I wouldn't have to deal with this if I were still in charge," he grumbled under his breath.

Using the skills I'd honed as a thief, I crept slowly through the foliage so the leaves wouldn't rustle and give me away. I slowly peered around the mossy trunk of a tree and saw the group of pirates cutting through the final bits of the tree branch. It dropped to the ground, revealing a nice-sized clearing beyond.

"Hey, there's a freshwater stream!" one of the pirates shouted and ran across the open space.

The other pirates soon joined, though Sinbad was a bit less enthusiastic.

My heart jumped. *Igborg!*

Igborg stood on Sinbad's shoulders, across the back of his neck. He had a little collar with a chain leading down to Sinbad's belt.

My blood started to boil and I clenched my hands into fists. I'd found Igborg. Now all I had to do was get him away from the pirate.

Unfortunately, that meant starting with a lot of waiting. Before we had parted, Mihrage had reminded me of one of the rules my father had taught me—rule number seven: always be ready.

Thinking of my father stole my breath and because I froze out in the open, I almost got caught by Sinbad when he glanced over his shoulder. Luckily, I managed to catch sight of his movement and darted behind the tree and slammed my back against the trunk so quickly I smacked my head against it and cringed as my head exploded with pain.

I held in a hiss and reached up to rub the now tender

spot on the back of my head.

After waiting several agonizing minutes, I leaned around the other side of the tree to see if Sinbad was still looking around. He was gone. I could just see the clearing and found Sinbad mingling with his men and helping them flatten the tall grasses.

Assess the situation. Make a plan. Okay. How many pirates are there? I counted seventeen men in addition to Sinbad. It was likely there were a couple more who had been left behind on their ship. Assuming their ship survived the magical storm.

I moved through the bushes, carefully pushing aside leaves as large as a person sometimes, and found a nice clear spot on a tree root beneath a plant holding a couple of adorable pudgy little tree frogs on it. I had a clear view of the pirates.

Igborg jumped from Sinbad's shoulders and glided down to the ground, immediately snatching up a large beetle and munching it down.

Sinbad looked down at him. "She should have taken better care of you. Caspara has no idea how incredible dragons truly are."

Igborg looked up at him, the wing of the beetle still sticking out from the corner of his mouth. He tilted his chin up and turned his head away.

"I know you can talk. You spoke with Caspara at the inn." The pirate crouched and held out a handful of nuts. "If you stay with me, I can teach you how to grow big and strong."

Igborg adored nuts, but he stubbornly kept his head turned away.

I couldn't help but admit that I felt an overwhelming

sense of love for that little dragon in that moment. He loved me. No matter what Sinbad did, Igborg would never choose to stay with him.

I set my father's bag on the ground beside my feet and licked my lips. It didn't matter if I was in the shade, the humidity in the air still made it unbearably hot. I would have to fill my waterskin at the same time I rescued Igborg.

So I made my plan—rest and keep an eye on the pirates, and at nightfall, when I had the shadows on my side, I would slip in and retrieve Igborg. I would need my lockpicks, which luckily hadn't fallen out in the waves, and all of the skills of silence my father had taught me and years of experience had improved.

I still wasn't an expert, though. Any of the older thieves could still sneak up on me, though I *had* managed to slip the coin pouch from Farhad the day before I went with my father to the merchant's house where he was captured.

I willed away memories of my father.

You can't keep breaking down into tears like this! Especially not with a band of pirates nearby. Get ahold of yourself!

The tears stopped, and I drew a big breath then lay down on the ground and used my bag as a pillow.

Once the pirates had munched on food and drank lots of water, they gathered together in front of Sinbad, all of them sitting in the shade.

Sinbad held Igborg in one arm. He looked so much bigger, the size of a cat or small dog. The pirate captain unfolded his map and examined the drawings I couldn't see.

"All right, we made it this far. I believe we are right here." He put his finger on the map and turned it to his men. "But the gods gave us the perfect opportunity to find it for certain. Dragons have an uncanny ability to sense treasure. Little Igborg here should be able to help get us started in the right direction."

I sat up.

Sinbad had stolen Igborg from me because of his dragon instincts to find treasure?

It would have been a good idea if Igborg had any idea what treasure was in the first place. Yes, I'd trained him to help me steal, but it wasn't as if he had a hidden hoard of trinkets or things he considered treasures. At least, not that I'd ever seen.

"How do you make him look for the treasure?" someone asked.

"Yeah, show us how dragons find treasure!"

The other pirates murmured their agreement.

Sinbad, however briefly, looked uncertain. But he expertly put on a scowl. "I am your captain, and you shouldn't challenge me."

"We want to see the dragon in action!"

Sinbad frowned and lifted the map for Igborg to see. "This is where we are going. Where the treasure is hidden. You know? Gold or diamonds?"

Igborg lifted his head to peer up at the pirate captain. "I know gold."

What Sinbad was too stupid to know was that Igborg's statement didn't mean he knew how to *find* gold, it meant Igborg knew what gold *was*. He'd stolen a lot of it and seen what Father and I or the other thieves had stolen.

But Sinbad foolishly grinned. "Wonderful! He can find gold. That treasure is bound to be hidden in a golden chest of some kind." He set my dragon down and, from my angle, Igborg disappeared in the tall grass. "If I hide this, you can find it. Close your eyes."

I watched with an amused grin as Sinbad took a gold coin from his pocket, turned around, and set it on the ground.

"Find it," Sindbad ordered.

The grass moved a little and I could see Igborg's spiked tail as he sniffed through the grass. He suddenly pounced and stood on his hind legs for the first time I'd ever seen with something in his front claws. "Treasure!"

Sinbad bent over and then scowled. "That isn't treasure. That's a bug of some kind. Find the gold."

Igborg blinked up at the man and slowly raised his hands to his mouth and shoved the bug into his mouth.

I had to clamp a hand over my own mouth to stifle the giggle building up. Poor Sinbad. He had no idea what he was getting into.

Igborg dropped back down to all fours and the grass moved a bit more.

"I don't think we're in any luck at all," one of the pirates grumbled under his breath.

"The dragon is useless," someone else said.

"No he isn't. He's young and inexperienced, clearly," Sinbad argued. "He just needs training." He bent over and picked up the gold and threw it to the ground. "Right there."

Igborg stood like he had before, on his hind legs, and held it up in his teeth. "Gowd!"

Sinbad rolled his eyes.

"Captain, all due respect, how long is it going to take the little dragon? Because this place is hot and sweaty and miserable, and we can just use the map."

Sinbad shook his head and placed his hands on his hips. "Give me the rest of the evening. If he doesn't help us find it tomorrow . . . well . . . we may have to abandon him here. All alone. With no way back to the main land."

Igborg somehow recognized the threat in Sinbad's voice and let out a growl.

"You'll never see Caspara again." Sinbad bent over and grabbed the gold coin and tried to pull it away. "Let go."

Igborg growled again.

"I said, let go." Sinbad jerked again.

But my stubborn little dragon pulled back, fighting the pirate for the treasure. Until Sinbad bopped him on top of the head with the knuckle of his middle finger.

Igborg let out a squeak and shook his head, dropping the gold immediately.

It took everything inside of me to not jump out right there and punch Sinbad across the face. I knew it would be foolish to react, because then the pirates would capture me too and I would be in no position to get Igborg out anyway.

I watched for the next couple of hours as Sinbad desperately tried to train Igborg how to find the gold. He started by hiding the gold just a little way away from Igborg and urging him to find it. However, Igborg refused to move. Sinbad had hit him, and he wasn't going to do anything for the pirate, whether or not he could.

Finally, Sinbad offered Igborg a couple of nuts, which he took with a bit of a scowl, but ate. Sinbad was a little smarter than I'd given him credit for because he realized Igborg would do anything for food. He should have realized that sooner, considering Igborg had literally left me behind so he could eat some meat from whoever took him from my room.

I had to give him credit, he knew how to train Igborg. Any hint in the right direction and Sinbad rewarded it.

Slowly, Igborg actually seemed to be catching on. He found the gold more frequently and further and further away. Was he sneaking a peek at Sinbad and watching him to know where to go? Or did he actually have that instinct inside of him?

The forest began to grow dark, and I looked up through the branches of the trees to gaze at the sky. The sun was setting.

Finally!

The pirates made fires and cooked a meal of some kind that actually smelled half decent. My stomach growled, rudely reminding me that I didn't have any food myself.

When Sinbad goes to sleep, I will sneak out, pick Igborg's lock, and take him away from here. I'll steal Sinbad's map so he can't find the treasure. Then, I'll fill my waterskin and maybe steal some food, if there is anything left to eat.

I repeated that over and over in my mind to try and keep it away from the thoughts of eating.

The pirates began to sing and eat, but instead of going to sleep right away, they began to drink and the singing carried on, and I wondered if they would ever go to sleep.

I must have dozed off, because when I woke, the pirates were passed out and the only sound I heard was the crackling of the two fires on the verge of burning out and a bird somewhere calling out in the night.

Wasting no time, I crawled out from under the tree and bush. My hands sank in the mud, and I grimaced but kept going.

I could practically hear my father's voice say, *Be as quiet as the shadows*. Rule number nine. He'd echoed that rule to me the night we'd broken into the merchant's mansion.

The pirates were lying haphazardly in the opening. I tip-toed around or over them, until I finally reached Sinbad. He had wrapped Igborg's chain around his hand, forcing Igborg to stay close to him and making it a bit more difficult for anyone to try and steal him.

A *bit* difficult.

I glanced down at the tattoo on my arm. *If I'm supposed to be a sentinel without magic, it must mean I have some sort of skillset that is important. Prove to me picking locks is one of those skills.*

It was a bit of a challenge aimed at Telama. I knew I could use a wish, but I might need that wish for something more important, like saving Abudar or trying to see if Taylin could bring my father back, or . . . keeping my promise to free Taylin.

I crouched beside Sinbad.

Igborg's nose twitched and his eyes flew open and his head lifted.

I grabbed his snout before he could make any sort of excited noise and pressed my finger to my lips, urging him to remain quiet. I glanced at Sinbad to see if Igborg's movement had woken him.

It hadn't.

The tip of Igborg's tail curled, and I knew he was resisting the urge to wag it.

I was just as excited to see him and made sure to wink and smile before I let go of his nose.

He licked my hand.

I removed the lockpick from the pocket I'd slipped it into and pushed the hook into the tiny lock. I thought working in a tiny lock would be more difficult, but there was only a single binding pin that had to be pressed and turned at just the right angle.

With silence and expertise even Farhad would have been impressed with, I opened the lock and Igborg was free.

He jumped into my arms and I gave him a little squeeze.

I glanced over Sinbad's body, trying to recall in which pocket he'd hidden the map.

Igborg must have realized what I was doing, because he jumped back down on the ground and walked to Sinbad's boot, then looked up at me.

I smiled and carefully lifted Sinbad's pantleg until I had access to the top of his boot. He let out a snore and I flinched, but used the moment to grab the map and pull it out, using Sinbad's noise to cover my theft.

Grinning proudly to myself, I picked up Igborg and placed him on my shoulder. It wouldn't be long before he was too big for that.

I used the same silence I'd used getting into the camp to make it to the water, fill up my pouch and get a drink, and then slip away.

Once I was out on the main path and running back toward the shoreline, I let out a relieved laugh. "I was so worried about you, Igborg!"

He set his claws on top of my head. "Igborg scared. And sorry."

"I'm not mad at you," I said. "You were hungry."

"Igborg no leave you again." He hugged my head and rested his chin on top of it too.

I giggled and reached my hand up to stroke him, then stopped walking. "Igborg . . . should we go steal the treasure?"

He made a silly chittering and squeaking sound that was

sort of a squeal mixed with clicking at the back of his throat. "Oh yes! Yes, yes!"

Nine

I opened the map and examined it in the dim light that barely filtered through the trees. I tilted it this way and that, trying to decipher the markings.

Igborg's stomach rumbled and I looked at him, entirely expecting to hear him belch. Instead, he let out a little fireball that made me jump, and it scorched the top of the map.

I gasped. "You can breathe fire?"

"I think so."

I looked around on the ground, picking up different sticks until I found one that was dry enough it could catch fire. "Do that again."

His belly rumbled and his throat gurgled and he belched out another fireball, this time a little bigger and just enough to make the tip of the stick smolder, but not ignite. He had to try twice more before the stick actually lit.

Using the bit of light, I held up the map and identified that the treasure was supposed to be located in a cave. I identified the clearing the pirates had camped in, only because of the creek that was labeled and the T in the road I'd taken with Taylin, the one where I felt I should have gone right.

Based on the map, and assuming I was in the location I thought I was, we needed to continue down the trail and then take a right.

I folded the map and tucked it into the pouch. "Were you truly able to sniff the gold like Sinbad was trying to teach you?" I asked Igborg as I began walking again.

He bobbed his head in almost a nod, but it was also side-to-side. "Sort of. Not with nose."

"If it wasn't your nose, what was it?"

Igborg shrugged and jumped down to the ground. "Like . . . hungry."

"You felt it inside of you?"

He nodded certainly this time. "You felt like that?"

For some reason, I looked over my shoulder. I hadn't heard anything, no pirates were following us, and there wasn't any person or any creature on the trail.

"I have felt like that before," I answered. "I saw a castle when I got here. I think it might be where Abudar is being kept, because I feel it probably the same way you mean."

"Are we saving Abu?"

I smiled. "Not yet. If he is here . . . then yes. But right now, I want to get back at Sinbad for taking you from me, so I'm going to steal his treasure. I know it's petty."

Igborg lifted his tail and pranced on ahead of me, clearly just as excited as I was.

Using the little torch on the end of a stick was barely enough light to keep me from stepping into holes and breaking my ankles, and Igborg warned me about a tree root or vines by hopping over them first.

More than once, I looked over my shoulders and I couldn't understand why.

"A cave!" Igborg shouted in the darkness, which did nothing to help my already-on-edge nerves.

"You could give a little bit of a warning," I said in a loud whisper.

Igborg gave me a sheepish grin, but it froze and then fell into a frown. "Caspara having new friends?"

I tilted my head. "New friends? What do you mean?" I followed his gaze and looked to my left, wondering what the dragon could be alluding to when I spotted the reflective green eyes of a cat.

A large cat.

I hadn't seen the panther because the pattern on its fur matched the shadows of the forest perfectly.

The predator wasn't moving, but the fading fire glistened off of its glowing green eyes. It crouched, tail flicking behind it.

I swallowed hard and moved as slowly as I could to remove my dagger from its sheath on my hip, just in case. "Igborg, start walking to the cave. Be very careful."

"Why?"

"That's a jaguar. It might want to eat you."

He gasped. "No eating dragons!"

The cat's eyes snapped to him. I essentially watched the panther realize the dragon was less than half its size and would be a much more suitable target.

"Igborg, fly."

"I can't see. Too dark. Not safe."

"It's going to attack you!" I grabbed a stick from the ground and threw it at the large wildcat.

The stick struck its side and it let out a hiss, baring its

enormous teeth.

And then it pounced from its hiding spot.

I acted on pure instinct when I ran toward Igborg and snatched him off the ground with one hand, rolling off the edge of the path right as the panther slid and missed its target.

With only a dagger to defend myself, I wasn't sure I could defeat the panther, but there was no way I wasn't going to try.

I let go of Igborg and jumped to my feet, then let out the biggest roar I could muster, letting all of the built-up frustrations about Sinbad stealing Igborg, my father's death, no one trying to find out who killed him, and facing I was mostly alone. I roared until I had no more breath and had to gasp for one.

It was enough to make the panther hesitate, likely wondering what sort of mutated creature I was.

But the panther was only momentarily distracted, and all of the muscles on its body rippled just before it ran at me again.

I sucked in my biggest breath and let out another roar, but this time Igborg stepped up to my side and let out a roar of his own.

The panther was barely deterred and landed on top of me with its claws grasping onto my shoulders. Its mouth went for my head, but I still had the dagger in my hand and drove it upward and into the panther's body, right between the ribs.

It let out a hiss and shriek that was horrifying.

I saw a flash of red and then another one as Igborg blew little fireballs at its side.

And then I heard footsteps running toward us.

"Oh no!" All I could imagine was that the pirates had heard and were coming, but at the same time I would rather have faced the pirates than the panther. I somehow managed to get my hands under the panther's jaw and push it away before it could sink its teeth into me, but I knew if it tried again, I wouldn't be able to hold it back.

The claws in my right shoulder tore down my chest and I screamed in agony.

"*Awqaf!*" a woman's voice yelled.

The panther flew off of me and into the nearby bushes as if someone had slammed into its side. It let out a frustrated roar, then took off into the wild.

I was lying on my back, gasping against the pain and desperately trying to keep myself composed as I looked over to see who my savior could be.

"In all the sands of time," I heard a man's voice whisper. It was somehow familiar.

And then the two of them knelt over me and my eyes widened. "Taraji? Mihrage? How did you get here?" I said in a high-pitched voice. I tried to sit up, but Mihrage pushed me down.

"You are very gravely injured," he stated.

"Obviously." I groaned and closed my eyes. "I must be so injured that I'm imagining you. I have to be unconscious."

"You're not unconscious," Taraji insisted and ran her hand down my arm. "It turns out that the only way to save Mihrage's sister is to get the same treasure Sinbad is after. That's how we got here."

"Mighty coincidental," I grumbled.

"She's in really bad shape. Do you know any healing spells?" Mihrage said, trying to keep his voice low as if I somehow wouldn't be able to hear him.

Taraji shook her head. "Those aren't spells I've been practicing. And I don't have any ointments on me either."

"I'll be fine. It only sounded bad," I insisted, even though I knew I had to be bleeding profusely. "Just help me get to my feet."

Igborg jumped on Taraji's side. "I have fire."

"That's nice." She smiled and patted his head.

"Fire help Caspara!" he tried again.

Mihrage shifted so he was at my head, then got his hands under my armpits and pulled me up to my feet.

I bit my lip and stifled a scream of pain, making it come out as more of a moan. "S-See? I'm fine," I lied as soon as I was righted.

Mihrage didn't let go right away. "Caspara, I'm worried about—"

"There's nothing we can do about it right now," I whispered. "Stop fretting."

"Mihrage, Igborg is right. Fire could cauterize her wounds," Taraji said.

"Please, let's get the treasure first," I insisted.

"I wish we had a way to heal you," Mihrage mumbled. "Your stubbornness is going to be your death."

"I have my father to thank for that."

He reluctantly smiled.

I looked at Taraji. "I will be okay. It's not that bad. Just a little scratch."

She looked me over, but I knew that she wouldn't be able to see anything in the darkness. "If you insist."

I did, because I hated people worrying over me.

But in honesty, pain shot through me with each breath I took, and it was far more than just a stitch in the side.

Mihrage crouched and retrieved my precious dagger, then wiped it off and handed it to me. I returned it to the sheath on my side.

Igborg stayed right at my leg, leaning against it as we both walked. He stole glances up at me now and again.

"Just ahead." Mihrage pointed to a gaping black hole ahead, and I knew it was the cave's entrance.

"I should have told you, when you cast that spell it was amazing to watch," I said to Taraji.

She smiled proudly. "I've been practicing in preparation for the academy. Getting a head start, you know?"

I didn't know, but I nodded.

If I'd thought the forest was dark, the cave was a black pit that made me flash back to a couple of weeks ago, when I had been part of the Desert Trials and vowed to myself never to enter another cave.

But the coolness was welcome.

"Igborg, can we have some light?" I asked. "Can you breathe your fire again?"

"He can breathe fire?" Taraji asked in amazement.

Igborg let out a fireball that shot down the corridor.

Mihrage smiled and patted the little dragon on the head proudly. "It seems to go straight, for the most part," Mihrage said. "We can keep a hand on the wall and have Igborg produce fireballs now and again to light the way."

"Do you have a stick that could act as a torch?" I asked. "It worked a little bit in the jungle. Come to think of it, the torch idea might work better if we wrap some fabric around the top first."

"I can find something," Taraji offered. She left to find a stick and pulled a bundle of fabric from her bag I assumed was a spare shirt or scarf. She tied it to the top of the stick and held it out to Igborg to ignite.

I placed my hand on my right breast while there was still darkness and flinched instantly. I was bleeding worse than I thought. I could feel it. My hand was soaking wet, as was my shirt.

I was in worse shape than I thought.

Ten

Taraji returned moments later, and a pathetic torch was soon in place, using Igborg's dragon fire. Fortunately, my idea made the fire much brighter than it had been in the jungle. That, or the tight space made it seem brighter. Either way, we knew where to go.

"Tell me how you got here and what happened while you were gone," I said. "How do you know the cure is this treasure?"

"I saw it. I . . . called on one of my visions," Mirhage answered.

"It was really fascinating to watch." Taraji reached out and took his hand.

"My boat crashed in the storm. Did yours?" I asked.

They both looked back at me, and Taraji nodded solemnly. "We don't even know if any of the crew survived."

I bit my bottom lip.

"But don't worry too much," she said with a bright smile. "We'll take this treasure back to Narshiz, you and Igborg will come with us, and we'll heal his sister, break the curse, and then go home."

I wasn't convinced it was going to be that easy, especially since we didn't have a way off the island.

We had to duck our heads to move through the cave. Luckily, there weren't any side corridors for us to wander down and get lost, and the cool air was a relief, even if the humidity still made it difficult to breathe. Somewhere, water dripped.

"I see it!" Mihrage suddenly announced.

I leaned to try and see past his shoulder or head only to flinch and recoil when pain pulled at the wounds on my chest. Something ahead glistened.

We all drew nearer and I finally managed to look under Mihrage's arm and see what he was so excited about. An opening had been carved into the wall with a pristine ledge. Upon that ledge sat a wooden chest that somehow seemed impervious to the elements that should have devoured it.

Mihrage looked over his shoulder at us with an eager grin. "Let's see what's inside."

Igborg suddenly scratched at my leg. "They're here!"

I looked down the cave's corridor but couldn't see anything beyond darkness. "Who is?"

"Pirates. I smell them." Igborg scampered up my leg and into my bag, in spite of his size.

A torch lit, revealing Sinbad's face and the pirates closest behind him.

Sinbad grinned. "Caspara! What a pleasant surprise. I must admit, I didn't expect you to show up, and I certainly didn't expect you to steal back what I rightfully stole."

I scowled.

"Had you not encountered that panther, which made enough noise to wake half of the jungle, I don't know that I ever would have found you."

I tightened my lips. "All we want is the treasure and to get off this island."

Sinbad tapped his chin. "See, that's the problem. That's the same thing I want."

We shouldn't have been there, not with Sinbad. And yet, there we were. In the middle of a humid jungle, inside a tiny cave dug into the side of a mountain, with swords between our shoulder blades.

Sinbad shouldered Mihrage out of the way to step past him, but Mihrage snatched the chest from where it had sat for years, in spite of the threat of the pirates. "We got here first," Mihrage insisted.

Sinbad's eyes lit up with greed. "Oh what a pity you were here first and we can't take the chest from you." He leaned into Mihrage's face. "You can hand it to me, or I will take it."

"I need the treasure to save my sister. We arrived first, I have the chest, and—oof!" Mihrage grunted when Sinbad slammed his fist into Mihrage's ribs and Mihrage doubled over.

Taraji gasped and the pirate nearest her had to hold her back.

Sinbad jerked the chest out of his arms. "Thank you." He held it up to the light from the torch Taraji held and tilted it left and right. "A treasure inside equivalent the gold of a sultan," he whispered.

A grumble echoed behind us, and I feared the panther was creeping up from behind. At least the pirates would be attacked first.

I gave Taraji and Mihrage an uncomfortable glance.

"But how does it open?" Sinbad wondered aloud.

"We need a key," one of his men commented.

All of the pirates looked at the cave floor as if the key would materialize from thin air. Sinbad desperately tried, but failed, not to roll his eyes at their intelligence, or rather, lack thereof.

"There's something written on the belly of the chest," another man said.

Sinbad tilted it again. "Ah, so there is." His eyes silently moved over the words as he read to himself. "It's a riddle. *With me in hand, you wield the fate of men. Pierce the lock and discover the strength of ten.*"

"Wield the fate of men?" someone mumbled.

"You wield power!"

All eyes shifted to Taraji and me.

I raised my hands in defense of myself. "I don't have any magical abilities."

"It's true," Mihrage confirmed.

Their gazes all turned to Taraji.

She let out a nervous laugh, then tried to swallow. "I do have magic, yes, but you must understand that I've only ever manipulated sand. I don't know any spells that would unlock that chest."

"A sultan wields power."

Sinbad turned to the man who'd spoken. "You want me to take this to the sultan and ask him for a key?" He snorted and shook his head. "This is why I am the one in charge. You wield a sword, imbeciles. You also pierce men with it." He set the chest on the ground, withdrew his sword, and pressed the tip of it against the lock.

It didn't work.

Each one of Sinbad's crew attempted to stab the lock, but no manner of stabbing from Sinbad made the lock even shift.

Sinbad grabbed the box and threw it against the cave wall with a shout of frustration. The wooden chest bounced off and clattered noisily to the floor, but not a scratch had appeared on the ancient wood.

"What do we try now?" one of the pirates grumbled.

"I say take it with us and get out of this dank cave," someone near the back demanded.

"Perhaps it's not a normally shaped sword," Mihrage suggested. "Or perhaps it is one that bears an enchantment of its own."

Sinbad ran his hand down his beard and glowered at his four prisoners.

The back of my neck prickled. Swords weren't the only things that were wielded, decided the fates of men, or pierced. Daggers did too. And I had a dagger on my hip that I had acquired the night my father was taken from me. I'd stolen it at the same time my father had been bitten by the snake statue and used it to defend myself against Abudar.

"May I see the chest?" I asked.

Sinbad narrowed his eyes at me. "Sure. See if a woman can figure it out."

I glared. "Don't underestimate women. We might just be smarter than you."

"How *did* you manage to get Igborg's chain off?" Sinbad handed me the chest.

"I wished it off," I lied.

He held tightly to the chest as I tried to take it. "Try with your lockpicks, thief."

I rolled my eyes and fished the lockpick set from my bag, but I already had a feeling that the lock was enchanted somehow and would be impossible or nearly impossible to pick. As I fiddled with the lock, I examined the words of the riddle circled a symbol burned into the bottom of the chest. A symbol I'd seen before, on the hilt of the dagger I'd stolen.

My dagger was the key to this chest.

"Well?" Sinbad demanded.

I somehow managed to keep a straight face and put my lockpick set away. "Tsk. I don't know. Looks like you're going to have a difficult time finding the right sword to open it." I rose back to my feet and dusted my knees. I looked at Sinbad. "I could use some fresh air."

He waved his hand. "Everyone, get out and back to camp. These three stay with us until we get back to the ship. We can't risk them sneaking off and leaving us stranded. And if one of you truly knows the answer, we may be able to come to an arrangement regarding splitting the treasure inside."

Eleven

Not only was I absolutely exhausted from being awake all night rescuing Igborg and finding the treasure, but the injury from the panther seemed to be getting worse and worse. I had fallen far behind the others, except Sinbad, who seemed keen on me not escaping from him.

Igborg's little nose poked my hand from where he hid inside of the bag and I rested my hand on top of his head to comfort us both.

"The panther attacked you," he said, stating the obvious.

I didn't even look at him.

"May I see?" He reached a hand out, but I slapped it away.

"Don't touch me."

He rolled his eyes. "I might be able to help."

"And how do you plan on doing that? Calling upon a goddess or dove to bring you healing potions? That would be a fun detail to add when you tell this story to your admirers back in Halmu."

Sinbad chuckled, which wasn't the reaction I was expecting. "If I could do such a thing to heal you, I would do so. Just for you." He winked at me.

I drew a slow breath in through my nose to calm my

anger.

"But you truly are more injured than your friends know, aren't you?" It wasn't actually a question. "You need help as soon as possible, or the infection could kill you."

"Yes, well, seeing how we're now your prisoners, I suppose I'm just going to die."

"So dramatic you are." He laughed.

I tried not to make it obvious as I held my hand over my wound, but I could feel Sinbad's dark eyes watching me. "You said something earlier, in the clearing, about how you used to be a leader. What did you mean?"

He raised his eyebrow, but his face was expressionless. "I have no idea to what you are referring." Sinbad refused to say another word.

We reached their camp and all I wanted to do was lie down and sleep.

"Get them some water and then bind them," Sinbad commanded. He sat down with his treasure and tipped it upside down to read the bottom again.

The sun was beginning to rise. I found a boulder that looked comfortable and sat down.

Taraji immediately knelt at my side. "I can see the blood now. Why do you always downplay things?"

I shook my head. "It's useless to worry over things you can't fix."

"You should remember that," she said with a stern look that reminded me of her mother.

I rested my head against the tree behind me. Two of the pirates were already working to bind Mihrage to the tree across from me.

"Captain Sinbad, I need to take care of Caspara's wounds," Taraji said once she stood. "I need to get water and boil it and wash her wounds so infection doesn't set in. And then I ask permission to look for some herbs that may help as well."

Sinbad tilted his head, his dark eyes landing on me. "We can strike a deal, Caspara. Tell me the answer to the riddle and your friend can help you."

"I don't know the answer," I lied.

He smiled. "See, the thing with being a great storyteller is that it also means I can tell when others are."

"You mean you can identify liars because you are one," I said flatly.

He shrugged. "This is your only choice."

"I don't know the answer," I repeated.

"Tsk. Bind her." He waved his hand dismissively.

Taraji, however, pulled away from the pirates and stormed over to one of the fires from the night before. She glared hard at Sinbad while she snatched a cooking pot and carried it to the creek to fill it with water. Her glare never left him, as though she were daring him to try and stop her.

"Where do you ladies come from where women have such defiance and fire?"

"Aye!" several other pirates agreed.

Taraji ignored them and set the pot of water on a fire one of the pirates had just constructed.

Igborg rubbed his head against my hand and I closed my eyes when I felt his bumpy scales rub my fingers. "Are you thirsty?" I whispered.

"Yes."

"You'll have to get the water from the spring. Be careful," I urged, stealing a glance down at him. "I don't want Sinbad to take you again."

Igborg wagged his tail. "No stealing. Igborg safe with

Caspara." He rubbed against me again.

I didn't believe that after Sinbad had already successfully taken him from me once, but all that mattered was that Igborg believed it.

"Caspara, your shirt is soaked with blood," Mihrage said.

I looked down.

In the morning light, I could finally see for the first time just how awful the wounds were. Four distinctive claw marks ran from my shoulder, down my breast, and to about my bellybutton. They were deep and open and my shirt was indeed soaked with my own blood.

I swallowed hard, suddenly feeling very nauseous. "Oh. I guess . . . I didn't know it was . . . so bad."

Mihrage leaned forward. "Caspara, look at me."

I tried to, but I was finding it hard to focus.

"Taraji, catch her!" he shouted.

I tried to remain upright, but it didn't seem to matter what I wanted. My body tipped and I closed my eyes against a second wave of nausea.

When I opened my eyes, Taraji was on her knees with my head in her lap and concern written all over her ebony face. I felt like I'd been unconscious for an eternity, but it must have only been seconds, because Sinbad was still in the process of getting to his feet.

The pirate captain walked over, unamused, but I noticed his eyes narrow a bit when he looked down at me.

"We need to leave the island now," Taraji insisted, looking up at Sinbad.

He shook his head. "Not until I know about the key. Ah, and I would like my map back." He crouched at my side and dug through my pouch until he found his map.

My heart stopped.

The lamp was in my bag.

All of my pain was replaced by fear and I tried to sit up. But Taraji pushed down on my good shoulder and shook her head.

Sinbad glanced in my direction and held his map out. "You don't want me to have this back? Is there a secret you know about this you're keeping hidden?" He unfolded it and looked at the drawing.

"I'm going to get the water now," Taraji said. She helped me lie down.

I grabbed her arm and mouthed, "The lamp."

Her eyes widened and she gave the slightest nod.

Sinbad shook his head and finally tore his gaze away from his map. "It's not the map. What is it, Caspara?"

Taraji reached out and grasped my bag. "You shouldn't be going through her private property. It's not for you to take."

Sinbad held firmly and pulled. "Aren't you a thief too? Then you know to seize an opportunity when it comes your way." He reached his hand back into my bag, in spite of Taraji trying to pull it away from him again. There was the sound of metal hitting metal—my dagger bumping up on the lamp—and his brows furrowed. "What is this?"

"Sinbad, will you read the riddle again?" I asked, trying to distract him.

"A lamp?" Sinbad looked at me quizzically. "Of all the things to carry around, you've got an old bronze lamp?" He held it up in the light.

"It belonged to my father," I blurted. "He was murdered over a week ago, and I don't have much left to remind me of him."

For some reason, Sinbad's expression changed ever so slightly, as if he were analyzing me, or perhaps he recognized my father's name. But that would be impossible. My father didn't fraternize with pirates.

Taraji snatched the lamp away and shoved it back inside of my bag. "All she has is that lamp and this bag. Keep your hands to yourself." She put my bag beside me and then retrieved the pot of steaming water. She set it down at my side and turned her attention to Sinbad. "You wouldn't happen to have a clean handkerchief, would you?"

Sinbad narrowed his eyes at me. "Who are you?"

"I'm . . . I'm no one important. I'm just a thief. Although, some know me as Almas." I glanced at Taraji, hoping that's what Sinbad meant. What if he found out I was the other sentinel? Would he want to sell me off?

"You traveled after me like you had an expert sailor as your captain, and yet there was no one with you on your ship." He leaned closer to my face. "You wear a griffin feather around your neck. And you have tattoos up and down your arm. Furthermore, you travel with magical friends and have a pet dragon. And you know the answer to my riddle. What makes you so special?"

"I don't know anything about your—"

"I saw the expression on your face change in the cave when you read it!" he shouted. "You realized something inside of that dank place, and you will tell me." He rested his hand on my shoulder and slowly pressed his index finger between two of the scratches.

I let out a cry and recoiled in an attempt to escape the pain.

"You're hurting her!" Taraji shoved him.

"I am not patient," Sinbad said firmly. He kicked over

the pot, allowing the water to spill onto the jungle floor.

Taraji snatched the pot and righted it in an attempt to save as much of the water as possible. She jumped to her feet and held her right hand out. "*Itrabati!*"

Thin vines exploded from the jungle floor and wrapped around Sinbad's ankles. The sudden stop in his stride caused him to fall forward face-first, and he had to catch himself with his hands.

"How dare you!" Taraji shouted.

She was usually so patient and exploded only when pushed too far. She'd clearly been pushed too far. She stormed over to him, even though the pirates sprang into action and raised their swords.

"You truly care so much for this treasure that you're willing to let Caspara die? A girl you don't even know? Did you know she's one of the sentinels?"

I groaned. "Taraji."

"Did you know her father was murdered, likely by the grand sorceress, and our village was destroyed by the palace soldiers?" she continued.

Sinbad held up his hand to stop his men. "Your village?"

She folded her arms. "We're from the band of forty thieves."

Sinbad's eyes locked on me again, but then drifted to the feather pendant dangling from my neck. "Let me up," he demanded.

"Not until you promise to let me take care of her wounds and promise you'll let us go so we can return home."

He narrowed his eyes at her. "I will agree to that as soon as Caspara tells me the answer to my riddle."

Taraji raised her eyebrow. "Then it looks like you might be sleeping there tonight." She stormed over to a pirate, who flinched when she reached out and snatched his dagger.

"You can't take—" he began to object.

Taraji pointed the dagger at him. "I'm going to help my friend. Try and stop me." Taraji used the dagger to cut the bottom of my shirt off and used that remnant as a rag. She dipped it into the water and began dabbing at my wound, starting at the bottom and being as careful as possible.

"When did you learn to cast that binding spell?" I asked, trying to keep myself distracted from the pain.

She gave me a sheepish smile and bit her bottom lip. "To be honest, I'd never cast that spell before. I just got so mad because you need help and it just sort of happened."

"I'm proud of you. You're going to be an amazing sorceress." I smiled up at her.

No matter how gentle Taraji was, all I could feel was burning and then electricity when she reached the deepest parts of the wounds.

I could no longer stifle my pain-filled whimpers or hide the tears.

"I'm sorry," Taraji said. "I'm trying to be gentle."

I nodded. "I-I know." I squeezed my eyes shut.

"I wish I could help you," Mihrage said.

"I wish you could help too," I whispered. I could tell I was on the verge of passing out, but fought against it. Saliva filled my mouth and I didn't want to open my eyes.

"Oooh, those are ugly."

I managed to open my eyes just long enough to confirm I had accidentally summoned Taylin before my eyes fell closed again.

"Stay out of sight. We have no medicine," Taraji said

softly to him.

"She wished Mihrage could help," Taylin replied in just as low of a voice. "Do you have some secret ability to find herbs or medicine?"

Mihrage sighed. "I don't think the wish was literal. Just hoping, as people do."

"Jinni, if we don't get her help or take care of her wounds, she could die," Taraji whispered.

Taylin paused before answering. "I see you've tied up the pirate captain that took Igborg. That is very good."

"Will you focus?" Taraji hissed.

I could practically see Taylin's scowl and his poise shift to arms folded and hip out. "I am. I was only thinking you could commandeer their ship to get off the island."

"Do you have a way to find it? Because I don't."

"The pirates know where it is."

"Which helps us how?" Mihrage interjected. "They want the chest unlocked, their captain has it in his mind that Caspara knows the answer, and the only way they'll do anything is if we give them that answer."

"Why is that a bad thing?" Taylin asked.

"Because I need it to save my people."

"Ah. So you're being just as selfish as he is."

"Jinni, if you can't do anything for us, at least save her!" Taraji squeezed my hand. "Caspara?"

I couldn't find the energy to squeeze back.

Twelve

My head pulsed with a dull headache as I opened my eyes. The sky overhead was gray, and a rumble of thunder ran across the belly of the clouds. I looked down at myself to find my wounds had been properly bandaged, and by the feeling of things, also somehow medicated. I wasn't in nearly as much pain as I had been.

Taraji lay with her head resting in Mihrage's lap, and he had his eyes closed with his head resting against the tree, which he was still tied to. I felt guilty for putting them in such a situation.

I moved my arm, inadvertently bumping Igborg, who was curled up at my side.

He lifted his head immediately and gasped before he jumped to his feet. "Caspara! You're awake! Taraji!" He ran over and pounced on Taraji's side, which made even me grimace.

"Oof! Igborg, that's rude," Taraji groaned. She sat up, picking him up in her arms as she did so. "What did you say?"

"Caspara is awake."

Her gaze snapped to me and she smiled. "Caspara."

"I'm so sorry," I instantly apologized.

She shook her head and crawled over to me. "I'm glad

you're alive. How are you feeling?"

I shook my head and gave a careful laugh. "I don't want to try moving."

She bit her lip. "Taylin helped. But then Sinbad somehow saw him and . . . I'm really sorry."

I stared at her, not wanting to think about what she might be suggesting. "What happened?"

"Sinbad took the lamp."

I closed my eyes.

"Do you actually know how to open that chest?" she whispered. "Because we could just give Sinbad what he wants.

I sighed and nodded. "I think I do." I finally opened my eyes.

"How?"

I shook my head. "I think it might be the dagger I stole with my father the night he was arrested. The symbol in the hilt matches the one on the bottom of the chest."

"There is the answer. Very good, Taraji," Sinbad said.

I turned my head and I sat up too quickly. I let out a cry of pain and clutched my chest, but turned to look at the pirates.

They all stood in their clearing with Sinbad at the front and Taylin next to him. It was only when I spotted Taylin that I realized Sinbad was holding the magic lamp and not the chest.

As if I didn't feel guilty enough, a wave of guilt so deep I nearly vomited washed over me.

"A lamp from your father, you said. This isn't an artifact your father gave you. If he had a jinni, he would have used it to get his own wishes met," Sinbad said. "And now that the jinni is in my power, I no longer need your help. I will now be unstoppable and rich thanks to you," he gloated. He laughed and walked to my bag and removed the jeweled dagger. "Men, bind the other girl."

"Wait," Taraji protested. She tried to cast another spell, but one of the pirates clamped his hand over her mouth and dragged her to the tree near Mihrage.

"Don't be so rough with her!" Mihrage shouted and pulled against his bindings. A pirate shoved a gag into his mouth and then gagged Taraji as well.

My heart raced. Where was Igborg? I glanced around quickly and couldn't see him anywhere. "Did you steal Igborg from me again?"

"No, he must have run off." Sinbad carried my dagger to his chest and turned it over.

My chin trembled, but I sucked in a breath to try and calm my fears. "Sinbad, when you unlock that, please take us off this island."

Sinbad placed the tip of my dagger through the opening of the lock and smirked. "It all depends on what's inside . . ." He turned the dagger, unlocking the chest, and slowly lifted the lid. The greed in his eyes turned to confusion. "How is this possibly worth anything? It's a blasted feather!" He lifted it into the air and turned to me as if I had been the one to deceive him.

It was a white feather, smaller than a peacock's feather but far larger than a dove's. In fact, it was just barely larger than the griffin pendant I wore on my neck.

My eyes widened. "It's a griffin feather."

"Is it enchanted?" Sinbad asked. He turned it over in his hand and looked at Taylin. "Tell me, is this worth anything?"

Taylin's expression remained stern, if not hostile. "I

cannot tell you without a wish."

Sinbad growled and jerked the dagger from the lock then jabbed it at Taylin. It would have gone up through his ribs had Taylin not disappeared. "You worthless creature!" He rubbed the lamp again. "I made a request!"

"I don't answer requests," Taylin said as he reappeared. "Only wishes."

Sinbad's lip twitched. "Answer me."

"That feather has no worth to you," Taylin replied.

Sinbad let out a frustrated shout, shoved the feather inside of the chest, and threw the chest on the ground, breaking off the lid from the bottom. "All of this for nothing!" He ran his fingers through his hair. "No. Not nothing. I have a jinni now. And you . . . you're the answer to all of my problems." He grasped Taylin by the jaw.

"You have everything you need. What could you possibly wish for?" I asked.

Sinbad lifted his eyebrow and looked over his shoulder at me as if he'd forgotten I was there. He slowly grinned. "You know me as Sinbad the pirate. What if I told you I was actually the leader of Bessoriah?"

I looked him up and down and scoffed. "How could you be the leader? You're barely older than I am."

He released Taylin. "Because I overthrew my father. I thought the kingdom would appreciate someone who wasn't a tyrant, but I was wrong. They overthrew me and exiled me." He turned to the jinni again. "We will go to Bessoriah, and along the journey I shall figure out how to perfectly word my only wish."

Taylin glanced my way when Sinbad turned away and ordered his men to pack the camp. "I'm sorry," he mouthed.

I rested my hand over the bandages—which was all I

had on my torso. "You helped again when you didn't have to."

His lip tugged in an attempted smile.

"I'm sorry I didn't keep you safe."

Taylin licked his lip and then bit it.

"You can't leave us, Sinbad," I said and started to struggle to my feet.

He looked over his shoulder. "Watch me."

I looked back at Taylin. "You can't let them leave us."

"I can't do anything to stop them. You aren't in possession of the lamp. Perhaps someday we shall see each other again on shores of blue sands." He lifted his brows.

Tears filled my eyes as the pirates began to leave the clearing, talking amongst themselves about how much of a waste the voyage had been.

"Get back in your lamp, jinni."

At the command from his new master, Taylin disappeared.

I held on to my chest, bit my bottom lip, and forced myself to my feet. I had to lean momentarily on a nearby tree to catch my breath. Although the wounds had been wrapped, the pain had reignited when I tried to move.

Taraji tried to say something around the gag, but I couldn't understand her.

Igborg scampered from under the grass, dragging my jeweled dagger, which was officially shorter than him. "Got it!"

I sighed in relief. "Igborg. I thought he took you again! And how did you find the dagger?"

Igborg dropped the dagger at my feet. "Igborg safe. Member?"

Bending over was more agonizing than trying to stand,

and I let out a muffled cry when I righted myself. After a couple of gasps for air, I limped to Taraji and cut through her ropes.

She instantly reached up and tore the gag off her face. "Caspara, I can help Mihrage. You just stay there."

"I can . . . help," I gasped.

She placed one hand on my wrist and the other on the hilt of my dagger. "I know you can. And you've helped enough right now. Let me take care of Mihrage."

I nodded and released the dagger.

Taraji turned to her lover and cut through his bindings.

Mihrage hurried to me and moved my hand out of the way. "You're starting to bleed through the bandages."

"Get the feather," I said. "You can't do anything else for me right now."

He looked over his shoulder before turning and slowly approaching the broken chest. He crouched low and righted it, revealing the perfectly white feather lying on the ground. He picked it up with utmost respect. "What Taylin didn't say to Sinbad is that griffin feathers are about as rare as they are. This feather is worth everything to the right person." He lifted his eyes to me.

"And the most to you," Taraji added. "Let's get to the bay."

"I agree." Mihrage wrapped the feather in fabric from the inside of the box and tucked it in his pocket.

"And then what?" I asked. "Stand there and shout over the perpetual storm for help?"

Taraji shrugged. "Or you could call for your rug."

I blinked in surprise. That thought hadn't crossed my mind until this moment. "Assuming I could call for it . . . that might actually work."

"Get calling," Mihrage said. He stepped up to my good side and put my arm around his waist so I could lean on him. "We need all the help we can get in order to get ourselves off of this island."

"If this doesn't work . . . I might have a plan B," I said, leaning heavily on Mihrage for support.

"What plan is that?" he asked.

I hesitated.

"Caspara, what's you plan?" Taraji urged.

"I spotted a castle. I climbed a tree when Taylin and I crashed on the island, and there was a castle in the distance."

"A castle on an island that's is supposed to be fictional?" Mihrage asked.

"I believe it might be where The Veil is hiding and they have Abudar."

Taraji and Mihrage exchanged a look.

"You think The Veil is hiding here?" Mihrage asked.

I nodded. "I know we might not have a way off the island, but we need to rescue Abudar. If I manage to summon the rug, we can all get off the island then."

Taraji chewed her lip and then nodded. "Which direction do we need to go?"

Mihrage raised his eyebrow, but didn't disagree outright.

I shook my head. "I couldn't tell you from down here."

"Igborg help!" he said with excitement, leaping up on the boulder I'd used as a seat. He spread his hidden wings. "Igborg look!"

I smiled. "Okay. Fly above the trees and look around. When you spot the castle, face that way."

Igborg didn't hesitate. He flew up into the air—already doing much better at flying than he had been just a few days ago, though he still tilted in the stormy wind that began to pick up in the trees.

A gust pulled him back, but he fought to remain nearby. "I see it! A rock palace!"

Mihrage pointed in the direction Igborg faced. "This way, then."

"Come back down, Igborg!" Taraji called.

Mihrage began walking in the direction of the castle, guiding me along the way.

I sucked in a breath and attempted to summon the carpet. *I have no idea how to do this, or if you can even hear me. I'm trying desperately, and we could use some help getting off of this island and home. If you could help . . . that would be greatly appreciated.*

The storm overhead rumbled with thunder, and now and then the forest path was lit by flashes of lightning. The rain began to pour without so much as a warning drop.

We hid under the branches of the biggest tree we could find and used the chance to take a break and get some water.

Mihrage lifted his shirt to wipe his forehead. "I forgot how hot the islands can get, even with the storms."

"Is your island like this?" I asked.

He nodded. "Yes. It has very similar foliage."

"And a sunken city," Taraji added with an eager grin. "If we break the curse, the city should rise up out of the lake and the fish and birds on the island will change back into people!"

I looked to Mihrage. "That's quite the curse."

He swallowed his mouthful of water. "I didn't realize the curse had spread so much. I understand why my father was so desperate."

"Do you think you can help your sister?"

He brushed his hand on the pocket where the griffin feather was hidden. "I certainly hope so. Although I don't know exactly what magical properties it has or why I would be requested to find it, there has to be a reason."

As quickly as the rain poured, it let up.

I looked up at the sky.

Taraji peered up at it beside me. "I think we should continue on our way while we have a break."

"I agree," I said. My bandages were drenched and had begun to droop.

Taraji seemed to notice and rummaged through her bag and then took Mihrage's bag and finally found a shirt. She helped me put it on.

"This way," Mihrage said, beginning to head down a path.

"That's not the right way," I said without thinking.

He paused and gave me a confused look. "That's the direction we were headed."

I pointed what I believed to be north east. "*That* is the way we need to go."

"How do you know?" Taraji asked.

"I know this sounds pretty ridiculous, but I can feel it with my tattoo."

"Your tattoo is telling us how to get to the castle? That doesn't make sense," Taraji pointed out.

I rubbed my hand over my arm. "I think Abudar is on this island."

Both Taraji and Mihrage's expressions were exactly the same—astonishment and then disbelief.

"Why do you think that?" Mihrage asked.

"Well, remember when Dablin asked me where Abudar was? There was suspicion The Veil had taken him. And I keep feeling this . . . pull. Like . . ." I rubbed my hand on my heart and shook my head. "There's something inside of me begging with me to turn around and go to that castle."

"Like being hungry!" Igborg said with excitement.

I smiled softly. "Maybe like that."

"I don't know, Caspara," Mihrage said. "Won't The Veil suspect something if we show up unannounced?"

I frowned. "What else are we going to do? I've been begging for the magic rug to come and help us, and do you see it? There's no way they know who we are. Someone would have to recognize me from Balim."

Mihrage rested his hands on his hips. "I could try and call upon a vision to see if Abudar is indeed a prisoner there."

Taraji grinned. "You want to do that?"

Mihrage looked at me. "I want to try. If he's there . . . then we will continue on our way."

I reached out, took his hand, and squeezed it. "Thank you."

He looked around, then up at the sky. "I need to get into a little more open space . . ." He walked away from the trunk and root of the tree.

"You're going to be amazed," Taraji said, grinning in anticipation.

Mihrage knelt on the ground. He closed his eyes, stretched his neck left and then right, and then he leaned forward and began tracing his finger through the mud in seemingly absent designs. He rested both palms in the middle of the designs and shifted up on his knees, facing us.

Suddenly, Mihrage's eyes flew open. They glowed yellow, with no visible pupil. The symbols in the sand began to glow with the same yellow and then lifted from the ground and into the air around him.

"There are . . . people in the castle," he said with a deep voice that had an echo to it that didn't belong to him. "The women are . . . but I must see through the eyes of another. Yes, the rat."

Taraji's lip curled in disgust. "He's using a rat to see? Gross."

"I think it's brilliant," I whispered back.

"There *is* a dungeon. The cells are empty, but I see torches. They wouldn't have a reason for torches if they didn't have a prisoner somewhere. The last room. I can smell something. You can fit through that gap . . ." Mihrage paused. For a moment, the magic rippled, but then the glowing light intensified. "I'm not losing this. Go in."

I glanced at Taraji.

She wouldn't look away from Mihrage.

He grinned. "Abudar is chained in the dungeon of the castle. I see him."

"Is he okay?"

"He's been in there for, what, three days now? I can't tell if he's been fed, but they've definitely been attempting to get information out of him. He has some bruising, but mostly appears to be lonely." Mihrage closed his eyes.

The yellow symbols surrounding him lowered and came to a rest in his drawings in the dirt. When he opened his eyes again, they were back to normal.

Taraji nudged me, making me hiss. "Oops! Sorry, I forgot. Wasn't that amazing, though?"

I nodded. "It really was. Mihrage, I think you should keep practicing. That magic is different from anything I've ever seen. I can't even imagine what you could do with it." I smiled.

He chuckled and got to his feet slowly. "It takes a lot of energy, since I haven't practiced in many years."

"With all the problems we're having, now is the perfect time to become an expert."

He looked up toward the sky. "Did you say you summoned the rug?"

I followed his gaze. "I've been trying. Maybe I need to ask aloud?"

Mihrage shrugged.

I cleared my throat. "Look, if you don't want to come all the way out here, that's fine, but maybe you just got stuck without a way through the storm. Perhaps you could try flying over it? The sky is clear over the island."

To my absolute astonishment, I heard a flutter I'd only heard once before, the night the magic carpet appeared to return me home to my people with Abudar.

The rug swooped around me and landed on the ground. I couldn't possibly have smiled bigger.

"Do you still think you weren't destined to be a sentinel?" Mihrage suddenly asked.

I frowned. "What do you mean?"

He rested his hands on his hips. "What are the chances you would steal the very dagger that unlocks this chest? Weeks ago? And then somehow end up on this island where we could unlock it."

I flushed and poked him in the forehead, in his third eye. "It's not fair you can read my mind."

"Think about it, Caspara. Sinbad *happens* to come to the same island I have to go to, where we're looking for the same treasure? And not only that, it's coincidentally the *same* island where Abudar is being held captive? Do you truly believe you are not important?" Mihrage raised his white eyebrows.

I chewed on my bottom lip.

He took Taraji's hand and they both sat down on the rug, but she sat in his lap.

I walked over and sat in front of them, mulling the thoughts over in my mind.

Was I truly destined to be a sentinel?

Thirteen

I had been watching the sky drift into nighttime colors and the castle slowly draw nearer as we flew. The sunlight hit the windows just right and a yellowish glow reflected off the windows. My heart jumped and my tattoos tingled. I rubbed my hand over them.

"You can feel Abudar, can't you?" Mihrage said.

Without looking over my shoulder at him, I nodded. "I can. My whole arm is practically burning."

"It's a good thing we're going to save him, then," Taraji said.

I didn't know why I felt so nervous. Perhaps it was because I was injured and wouldn't be able to defend myself if we ran into trouble. But I knew deep down the churning of my stomach had a lot more to do with seeing Abudar than with any danger we might encounter. The last time I'd seen him, I had yelled at him and accused him of being the one who sent the soldiers to attack my village. I'd told him I wanted nothing to do with being a sentinel, or with him.

Igborg was snuggled up in my lap and snoring.

The carpet settled right outside the front of the castle. I looked over my shoulder at my friends. "How do you propose we get inside without looking conspicuous?"

"You need a shirt, for one thing," Taraji said.

Mihrage pushed Taraji to her feet and then removed his own shirt and handed it to me.

Taraji and I both noticed each other looking at him from the corner of our eyes, but I recovered much faster than she did and took the shirt and pulled it over my head.

Taraji cleared her throat and started fiddling with her hair to look busy. "We sneak in together. If anyone stops us, I will pretend to be a new sorceress."

I nodded slowly. "That could work. And if anyone sees me, I could say I'm new and lost."

Taraji shook her head. "I was talking to Mihrage. You can't come in."

I blanched. "Excuse me? And why not?"

She gestured her hand up and down toward my side. "You're in no shape, Caspara. I'm not going to argue with you. If we get stopped, what happens if they take you into a room thinking you're a new sorceress? How would you get out?"

"I'm not just going to sit out here and wait!" I argued back. "You know me better than that."

Mihrage put his hand on my shoulder. "I know you're normally a fighter, Caspara, but in this case I actually agree with Taraji. If someone so much as bumps you, they will want to help you."

"How is that bad?"

He sighed. "Then we have to get you out too."

I looked between the two of them, feeling betrayed. "You expect me to just . . . sit here?"

"Igborg will protect you." Mihrage smiled and picked Igborg up. "Won't you?"

"Yes! Igborg blow fire too." His chest rumbled and Mihrage quickly turned the little dragon around so Igborg exploded the fire away from his face.

Mihrage set Igborg down. "Get some rest, Caspara." He rubbed his hand on top of my head in a gesture he used to do when we were kids.

I scowled at them both and turned away. How could my body betray me this way? How could my friends?

"We'll be back soon," Taraji said.

I was supposed to sit out in the forest, just outside of the castle, and not help them? There had to be *something* I could do. *Especially* as a sentinel!

Instead, I begrudgingly sat down on a rock and held my chest while I pouted.

Igborg crawled up in an attempt to lie at my side, but he'd grown so much over the past two weeks, the small space he attempted to lie on wouldn't fit his current size. He made a grumbling noise in his belly and slid off the side of the rock, then looked up at me for help.

I scooted over. "Here you go. Now there's more space." I patted the larger spot.

Igborg hopped up and this time smiled and lay down.

Waiting with nothing to do was worse than being stuck in a cave or walking through a jungle. At least I had been *doing* something.

Feeling exposed, I got up from the rock and walked a little bit into the trees to make sure I was well hidden, just in case.

The sun set and billions of stars appeared over the castle. Torches and candles began to light in the windows and I found myself wondering what it would be like to have magic, to just . . . say what I wanted to happen and have it actually happen. Essentially, every sorceress was her own jinni.

Don't be jealous, Caspara, I said to myself.

"What are you doing out here in the forest?"

I practically jumped out of my skin. I hadn't even heard the two girls approach, let alone seen them.

Even Igborg was caught off guard. He jumped to his feet and let out a roar.

One of the girls had her hair up in two buns and she gasped. "Is that a dragon? You have a dragon?"

I glanced at Igborg, then back at them. "Yes."

"May I pet him?"

I looked at Igborg. "Don't say anything," I whispered before looking back at the girls. "Yes, you can pet him. He likes to be scratched under his chin, like a cat."

She hurried forward and started scratching under Igborg's chin.

He began to purr.

"I haven't seen you before," she commented. "You must be new. I'm Jamila. This is Nadine."

"My name is Caspara. Um. What is your special type of magic? I mean, I know we're learning different . . . spells, but what is the one you were born with?"

Igborg crawled into my lap.

"I play with fire," Jamila said with a grin.

Igborg's tail began to wag and he jumped off my lap. "Me too!"

Jamila gasped.

I rolled my eyes at Igborg.

He sheepishly tucked in his tail. "Sorry, Caspara."

Jamila giggled. "You must be a very brave dragon."

"What about you, Nadine?" I asked.

Jamila glanced at Nadine, whose face dropped before she turned away. "She lost her magic," Jamila whispered.

"She claims Princess Mithra used a spell to steal it, but it must have been a sorceress who took on her face. Princess Mithra would never do such a thing."

I swallowed hard. I didn't know Mithra all that well, and certainly not enough to say for certain whether or not she would do something like that, but I wouldn't completely dismiss the idea. It all depended on what Mithra wanted out of it.

"We're going inside for dinner. Want to join us?" Jamila asked.

Dinner sounded amazing. I was positively starving, but all I could think of were Mihrage and Taraji's warning of not being able to make it back out.

"Thank you for inviting me, but I want to look at the stars a bit longer," I said reluctantly. I tried to stand but groaned when my muscles shifted and pain radiated up my wounds.

"What happened?" Jamila asked.

"I got a bit of a scratch." I reached down to my ribs and held them.

"If I still had my magic, I could help," Nadine said. "I was rather skilled at healing wounds."

"I'm . . . terribly sorry," I replied.

She walked over to me. "May I see them?"

"I don't know . . ."

She ignored my response and lifted Mihrage's shirt. "How long have you had the cuts?"

"I got them last night."

"These bandages need to be replaced. Come with me, I'll help you. I might not have my magic, but I can still be helpful." Nadine's stoic face finally cracked with a little smile.

So much for staying outside and out of danger.

I followed the girls to the front doors with Igborg staying close to me. He suddenly reached up and tried to climb my pants to get into my bag. I didn't think I could bear his weight on my cuts, but I could tell he was nervous about being seen, so I helped him climb in.

"This way," Nadine said.

We walked through the packed dining room bustling with dozens of young women eating their dinner and talking in excited tones.

I tried to keep my head down and attempted to be unseen.

Nadine continued up the flight of stairs and to the second floor, where about a dozen doors were lined up. She stopped beside one of the doors, placed her hand on the doorknob and said, "Nadine."

There was a clicking sound and then she turned the doorknob and opened the door to reveal her room.

"Are all of these bedrooms?" I asked.

Jamila smiled like she'd been waiting for me to ask. "Each door is enchanted. When we speak our name while holding the doorknob, our bedroom appears. In reality, I suppose we could have an infinite number of rooms!"

Nadine pulled her chair away from her desk. "Sit down and I'll look at those wounds."

I was extremely uncomfortable all of a sudden. Whether or not we were all girls, I didn't know them and didn't exactly want to take off my shirt and bandages to expose myself. But it was necessary if I wanted help with my injuries.

My thoughts immediately shifted to Taraji. Had she and Mihrage already made it to the dungeon? What would they do if they got outside and I wasn't there? Would they realize I'd been taken? No, they would think I intentionally slipped inside. And then they would be annoyed they had to get back in to save me.

"Where are you from, Caspara?" Jamila asked, jolting me out of my thoughts.

"A little village outside of Zunbar," I answered. Our village had never had a name.

"I could tell," Jamila replied without missing a beat.

Nadine rolled her eyes and set a small bowl down she'd been putting ingredients into. "Jamila is from an upper-class family, in case you couldn't tell. She has no manners."

"I do too! Though I do suppose mentioning I could tell you weren't rich wasn't very kind, was it?"

"We're working on it," Nadine said. She unwrapped the wounds and grimaced. "Ooh, that looks like it hurts."

"Unbelievably." I gritted my teeth. "Especially now the bandages are off."

"These are going to require stitches," Nadine muttered. "You'd better get Shorix."

"No!" I exclaimed a bit too quickly. Shorix would recognize me from Balim and might recall that I had no magic and therefore was no sorceress and didn't belong there. I swallowed. "Please don't bother her with something so trivial. Is there no one else who can stitch the wounds?"

"Shorix could probably heal them," Nadine pointed out.

"So could Thanab," Jamila said.

Nadine scowled.

Jamila rolled her eyes. "She and Nadine were learning the healing magic at the same time when Nadine's magic was taken."

"Go and fetch her," Nadine said rather reluctantly. "I'll

help Caspara lie down on the bed."

"I don't want a large audience," I said, looking at Jamila. "Please don't tell anyone else."

Jamila smiled. "I won't. Promise. I'll return in a flash!" She rushed out of the room.

"How did this even happen?" Nadine asked as she took my arm and helped me get to my feet.

"Panther. It went after my dragon and I had to protect him." I hissed when I started to move and had to hold my hand over my wounds to keep them closed while we shuffled slowly to the bed.

Igborg hopped up on the bed and waited for me to sit and slowly lie down. He then curled up right at my side.

"I'm going to put some salve on your wounds. Just enough to help with the healing process and hopefully the pain until Thanab gets here. Are there any areas in particular that hurt?"

"All of it." I closed my eyes.

Not two seconds later, Jamila returned. "I've got Thanab and no one else!" she announced proudly.

Thanab was a short girl with a pudgy face and kind eyes. "Oh my sands! Jamila said you were severely injured, but I didn't believe her." She hurried over and looked over Nadine's shoulder.

Nadine leaned back. "Can you heal this?"

She shook her head. "Not fully, no. Not after a day of using energy on practicing. But I can get them closed enough they shouldn't bleed any more. Like scabs."

"I'll take anything at this point," I said.

Thanab poised her hands in the air and closed her eyes. "Ishfa el-jerouh." She moved her hands in a memorized motion.

"She forgot to mention, the healing process may tingle a little," Nadine said to me.

Tingle?

Not so much.

Pain pulsed through my wounds with the beating of my heart. It felt as though my flesh was being pulled together. It was sheer agony that stole my breath—until that pain ebbed and the tingling sensation Nadine mentioned began.

Thanab dropped her hands and opened her eyes. She staggered a little and gulped a breath. "That is as much as I can do."

I looked down at myself and was relieved to see thick scabs over the wounds. They looked a day or two old instead of nice and fresh. "Thank you," I said and sat up, wincing just a bit as my scabs tugged.

"You should get to your room and rest," Nadine said. "Thanab can check on them again tomorrow."

I nodded. "Of course." I retrieved Mihrage's shirt and pulled it over my head. "Thank you for your kindness."

"We will see you at breakfast!" Jamila grinned.

I nodded, knowing full well they wouldn't see me at breakfast. They wouldn't see me ever again.

Nadine had to nudge Igborg awake, and he scurried off the bed and floated down to the floor by my side as we left the room. I went back down the stairs and, without so much as a second glance from any remaining sorceresses, I walked out the front door.

Fourteen

I spotted a shadow sprinting from the side of the building toward the open space and boulder where Mihrage and Taraji had left me. When I looked that direction, I saw two figures.

I realized instantly that the shadowed figure was running toward them, and if it were a sorceress, Mihrage was in danger of being caught. Taraji could easily explain herself away as being out late, but not Mihrage.

Gritting my teeth against the pain I knew I would soon experience, I took off running after the shadowed figure. I couldn't risk them catching my friends off guard. I couldn't risk them causing harm or worse, turning us all in to the sorceresses.

They had almost reached the space when I jumped and wrapped my arms around their neck, expecting to tackle them to the ground. However, they gripped my wrists around and threw me over their head. I hit the ground on my back and gasped in agony, positive some of my scabs had cracked.

The person's face was shielded by a scarf, but their eyes looked confused.

I used that moment of hesitation to kick them in the groin.

The figure grunted deeply and doubled over.

I rolled to my feet, far more slowly than I normally could, and unsheathed my jeweled dagger from my hip and pointed it to their neck. "S-Stop what you're doing!"

"Wait!" They stepped back. The voice was deep, definitely a man's.

I gritted my teeth and shuffled my feet through the dirt, driving toward them again.

They held their hands up and stepped aside when I thrust my dagger forward, punching my wrist. Pain exploded up my arm, and I had no choice but to drop my weapon.

"I said *wait*!" the voice repeated.

"Caspara, stop!" Taraji shouted behind me.

I glared and dropped to my knees and swung. He hadn't moved fast enough, and I swiped both legs out from under him, dropping him to his back. I sat on top of him and held my blade to his throat. "Why are you going after Taraji and Mihrage?"

"Caspara. Look at me."

He knew my name?

I froze to process that he'd actually said my name before I pulled the scarf off of his face. "Abu . . . Abudar!" Excitement burst in my heart. I leaned down and crushed my lips to his.

Which shocked me as much as it seemed to shock him.

He held a hand on my cheek, but flinched. "Your blade is still to my throat."

"I'm so sorry. I didn't mean to." I sheathed it immediately and flushed. "The last time we saw each other, I was so rude to you."

"Yes, you were."

I scowled. "You could at least try not to agree with me." I punched him in the shoulder, but not hard.

Abudar smiled. His dimples shone. He reached up and wrapped a strand of my hair around his finger. "It's good to see you too."

My heart fluttered and the humid jungle melted away. Abudar was alive. Safe.

"How did you know I was here?" Abudar asked.

"I didn't. I mean, I sort of did, once I was on the island," I confessed and then realized Mihrage and Taraji stood just feet away, watching us, and I was still sitting on top of Abudar. I blushed and scrambled off, only to drop to one knee with a whine of pain.

Abudar instantly got up on his knees and placed his hands on my shoulders. "What is it?"

"Mm. I . . . I got attacked by a panther last night." I held my hand tightly over the wounds, as if clutching them could take away the pain.

He looked me up and down, glanced at the others, then lifted the bottom of my shirt enough to reveal the scabs on my stomach, which had indeed cracked and were again bleeding.

I swatted his hand away on instinct.

He grimaced a little. "Sorry, I just wanted to check your injury."

"Oh. Right. Of course." I flushed and looked down. I lifted the shirt this time.

"Caspara . . ." He sort of sighed my name in pity and reached out to rub his thumb near one of the scabs.

"Abu!" Igborg squealed and jumped on his leg.

Abudar patted his head. "It's good to see you too, Igborg. I need to take care of Caspara and then I can give you a snuggle."

Igborg flicked his tongue and looked at me. "Caspara hurted."

"I'll be okay. I promise," I insisted.

He raised his eyebrow. "I don't believe you."

I looked at him and then pushed his hands away so I could get to my feet, but Abudar steadied me. "A sorceress healed the worst of the wounds. The scabs just broke open."

Taraji folded her arms. "You went into the castle?"

I gave her a completely unapologetic smile. "It wasn't my fault. They found me."

She rolled her eyes. "Always so stubborn."

Abudar got to his feet. "How did you even get here?"

I looked at my friends, then him. "I heard The Veil took you. But Mihrage's father showed up to arrest him, so we were going to save his cursed people, but then—" I winced from pain, which also stole my breath.

Mihrage continued the story for me. "A pirate named Sinbad stole Igborg. Caspara went after him while Taraji and I went to my home in Narshiz to see about the curse. We all ended up on this island because Sinbad was seeing the same treasure I needed."

"And here we are," Taraji added.

"Is there anything else I need to know?" Abudar asked.

I licked my lips. "Sinbad took the jinni. They left us on this island to die."

"It's a good thing we aren't doing that," Mihrage said as he approached. "And we have a way to get home," Mihrage said and gestured to the carpet leaning up against a nearby tree.

Abudar smiled. "The magic rug. It found you again."

"We can't go home yet," I said.

Mihrage shook his head. "I meant my home. Or . . . old home. I have to help my sister."

I looked at Abudar. "We can't all fit on the rug, so I'll wait here while it takes them to Mihrage's island. Do you want to go with them or with me to get the jinni back?"

He hesitated.

"Don't worry about me," I hurried to say. "You don't need my problems pushed on you. You've been imprisoned the past few days. You need to go home." I turned to the rug. "Take Abudar back to the palace and then come back for us."

The rug lay down on the ground.

Abudar gestured to Taraji. "Go ahead. You and Mihrage can get to Narshiz, and I'll stay with Caspara."

Taraji opened her mouth, but Mihrage took her by the shoulders and guided her to the rug. "We will see you at home," Mihrage said to me.

Taraji scowled. "I suppose we will. Be safe, Caspara."

"I will be." I smiled and waved to them.

As soon as they were out of earshot, Abudar stepped up to my side. "I don't know how to explain it, but I knew you were coming."

I looked at him, surprised by the revelation.

Were we more connected than I thought?

"Abudar, from the moment I arrived on this island, I felt like I *needed* to find you," I said. "I saw the castle yesterday when I crashed on the island, and some part of me *knew* you were there. I just felt like you were close." I looked down at my tattoo. "I felt it in my tattoo. I wanted to go there because I could sense *you*. I knew you would be there."

Abudar gave his crooked, dimpled grin, and his amber eyes glittered. "Can't stop thinking about me after all, huh?"

I scoffed and turned away so I wasn't looking to his eyes. I couldn't bear it. "Don't tease me." Being so close to him, smelling his familiar scent of cedar wood, cotton, and anise . . . it burned my heart.

"I'm not teasing you," he insisted and stepped around me so we were face to face. "Are we going to completely ignore the fact that you kissed me when you tackled me?"

I blushed madly and hoped it was dark enough outside that he couldn't see it.

"Caspara."

"What is there to talk about?" I finally met his eyes. "It was an accident. We both know we never should have kissed. You are engaged to Roseline, who I'm sure is out looking for you too."

"But if you feel for me the same way I feel for—"

I pressed my finger to his lips. "Don't. Don't say anything further. We cannot be together and you know it. You can't marry a street rat over a princess." I wished the rug flew faster, because I really wanted to get away from Abudar and didn't have a way to do so. My heart ached because I *did* want Abudar.

"You could use one of your wishes to become a princess," he pointed out.

I dropped my hand. "And change everything I am? Everything that makes me . . . me?" I shook my head. "There are better things I can do with that wish. I could use it to set Taylin free."

Abudar heaved a sigh. "Or you could use it to bring peace between the royal family and the sorceresses."

"See all of the things I could wish for?" I sat down on a thick log. "Why would I wish for something for myself when I could help everyone else with a wish?"

"Maybe because you actually deserve to have good things happen in your life?"

I laughed.

He didn't.

"Abudar, we need to take care of one thing at a time. Our . . . feelings or relationship aren't a priority. After you get back to the castle, I'll . . . go back to the thieves. And things will go back to how they are supposed to be."

"Supposed to be?"

"Yes. You in the palace, me with the thieves."

He heaved a sigh. "You're still not going to be a sentinel at my side, hm?"

I hesitated and then shook my head. "No." But I began to wonder to myself what was really holding me back.

It wasn't a question I could answer in one night, especially this kind of night. The longer we lingered, the higher chance we had of a sorceress spotting us.

"I'm going with you," Abudar suddenly said, breaking my concentration on the dark sky.

I looked at him. "You really don't have to. I've done plenty of things by—"

"What am I going to do when I get home?" he asked. "Eat a big meal and sleep and then . . . what?"

I shrugged. "Tell me why The Veil wanted you in the first place?"

Abudar rubbed the back of his neck. "They only wanted me on their side."

"You've been here for days and that's all that happened? They just asked you nicely to join their cause?" I asked skeptically.

"They kept me locked in a dungeon," he said flatly.

"Well, did they hurt you?" I demanded.

That cocky grin of his appeared and I felt my ears grow hot, but he didn't bother pointing out my humiliation. "They were very kind," he reassured. "They fed me and made sure I had blankets at night. They honestly only wanted to know if I would support their cause that all sorceresses should be allowed to learn all forms of magic."

"Then why didn't they let you go when you said yes?"

He shook his head, eyes drifting to the forest. "I have a feeling there was another reason they were keeping me there, but I don't know what that reason is."

Something in the air shifted and drew my attention, and moments later, I realized it was the magic carpet returning for us. It settled on the ground and I walked over and gingerly started to lower myself down onto it.

Abudar held on to my elbow, offering me a bit of balance and help as I finally sat down all the way. "How do we find this pirate of yours?" he asked.

I looked up at him. "He said something about being a leader of . . . what was that country?" I rubbed my forehead. It was the first time I'd noticed the dull dehydration headache. And then, clear as if Taylin were standing beside me, I recalled what he'd said about where we would see each other again. I turned to Abudar. "Do you know a country with blue sand?"

"Yes. Bessoriah."

I nodded. "That's where we need to go."

Fifteen

"Caspara." My father stood on a grassy hill in an open space surrounded by light. He looked like he always did—a groomed beard, kind green eyes, and an expectant but patient smile.

I grinned so wide my cheeks hurt and reached out for his extended hand. "Baba!"

He pulled me into his warm embrace and kissed the top of my head. "Stop worrying about what you might get wrong. What if you don't get anything wrong?"

I could stand like this forever.

"Caspara, there's another thief rule I want you to remember." He stepped back and looked down into my eyes. "Make your own decisions. Don't always do what I did. And always remember, I'll be with you forever, dune bug."

When I opened my eyes, my heart sank.

It had been nothing more than a dream.

But I realized I was curled up on my side, trying to protect my cuts, and my head rested in Abudar's lap. I immediately looked up and saw Abudar supporting his head in his hand with his elbow resting on his knee.

He breathed deeply, sitting up. Sound asleep.

The gold ring in his left nostril glinted, and for some

reason, I wanted to reach up and touch him. And I might have if Igborg hadn't landed on my chest. I grunted in agony.

"Blue beach!" he said with excitement.

Abudar sniffled twice and his eyelids drifted open. "Hm?"

"Blue beach!" Igborg repeated.

I pushed Igborg off of my chest and gasped a breath. My cuts ached but felt surprisingly better compared to how they'd felt the day prior. I groaned as I sat up. I looked down from the rug, through the misty clouds, and spotted the land below us.

The beach was made of blue sand, as if turquoise stone had been ground up and sprinkled across it.

"It's beautiful," I whispered.

"I didn't think we'd get here so quickly." Abudar groaned as he stretched and rubbed his eyes.

"Have you been to Bessoriah before?" I looked over my shoulder at him.

He nodded. "Only once, though. A few years ago, when I'd just turned twelve, my father needed to create some sort of trade or treaty, and he took me with him."

"Was that before the king was overthrown?"

Abudar's brows dipped. "I don't recall the king being overthrown. Father shares all of that information with me because I need to know what is happening in nearby kingdoms. Everything that happens has a potential of impacting our land." The last sentence sounded like a clearly memorized phrase.

I looked back down over the land. "Sinbad said his father was overthrown and he was exiled. He wants to be the leader of Bessoriah again, or maybe wants to have what is rightfully his by birth?"

"King Soran didn't have any sons. Only daughters. Perhaps Sinbad's father managed to overtake the throne for a short period of time?" Abudar rubbed his chin.

I looked at Abudar, who shrugged in response, but I wasn't comforted. Because perhaps Sinbad was worse than I thought. Perhaps his father had been the one to overthrow the king and failed, and Sinbad thought the kingdom should have been his *because* they were exiled.

The rug followed a river upstream until the trees broke, revealing a lake with buildings built right on top of it, with walkways in organized patterns above the water. Not a single walkway, however, reached the distant shore. Boats rested near the walkways in little harbors.

"Ah, I remember this city now," Abudar said. "They built the capital city on this lake to stop them from being invaded by attacking armies. Ages ago, they were continuously invaded. One of their kings, as I recall, had the people construct this city. Any kingdom or outside people who wanted to attack would have to do so by crossing the water, which would expose them to the watchtowers." Abudar pointed to a nearby watchtower and I realized there were six towers at the tips of each path, and that the walkways—and the buildings lining them—created a star shape.

"It's brilliant," I said.

He smiled. "It really is."

"I assume that is the palace in the center?" I pointed to the largest building of them all.

Abudar shook his head. "That is actually their temple. The palace is there." He reached his arm over my shoulder so I could better follow where he pointed, and perhaps so he could be just a bit closer to me.

The palace was much smaller than I imagined. In fact, it didn't look any bigger than the nearby houses. The only differences were the golden domed roofs, each with an inlaid stripe of turquoise.

"Any ideas on what to do once we get there?" Abudar asked.

I shook my head. "I'm hoping that by some miracle we beat Sinbad and can warn the people. But if he made it here before us and we knock on the front door . . ." I sighed.

"Igborg help?" He nudged my hand with his head.

I was reluctant, but Igborg was far less noticeable than we would be walking through the palace of a foreign country. Who knew what would happen if Abudar, the Prince of Sheblom, got caught sneaking about the palace of Bessoriah's royal family?

Abudar mistook my moment of silence for fear and nudged me. "He's growing up quite a bit. He might be very helpful."

I nodded. "I agree. Igborg, if you spot any pirates you recognize, you hide. Understand?"

He nodded and lifted up into the air.

I caught him by the tail. "Hold on just a minute. We are going to be by that big fountain there." I pointed to a nearby fountain near what I assumed were the merchant's quarters. "Come there before lunchtime. That will give us time to find something to eat."

Igborg nodded and I let go of him.

Maybe I could relate to my father just a little bit, how nervous he must have felt letting me spread my wings and gain a little more freedom.

"How are we supposed to pay for our food?" Abudar

asked.

I grinned. "Do you forget who you're with?"

Abudar rolled his eyes. "Just don't get caught, okay?"

I should have heeded his warning a little more. Unlike Zunbar, where the streets were tight and people were pressed together, the streets in Bessoriah were wide, and there weren't many people out this time of day. When I swiped a loaf of bread from one of the baker's tables, he spotted me immediately and shouted, "Thief!" and demanded I pay him.

I would have been able to escape if we'd been in Zunbar. *And* if I didn't have a goody-two-shoes prince with me.

Abudar grabbed me by the wrist and dragged me back to the baker. "Pay the man," he demanded.

I stared at him, dumbfounded. "Pay him? I can't pay him, I have no money." I gestured to *all* of me—Mihrage's too-big shirt with blood stains on it, my dirty pants, and my father's frayed satchel.

The baker scowled. "I can't sell it now that your filthy hands have been on my loaf, so you can't return it. Hand over whatever you've got." He stuck out his hand.

I stared at him, then turned to Abudar. "Perhaps *you* have something to give the man."

"And why should I pay for what you stole?"

I had no idea where to go with this. I was confused and didn't understand what he was doing.

Abudar finally gave me the slightest wink and I relaxed just a bit. "*Inhar*," he whispered.

The corner of the table suddenly collapsed and the baskets of freshly baked bread and rolls began to tumble down.

Abudar released me and scrambled to help the baker catch everything before it hit the ground.

I turned and sprinted away. I ducked around a corner and pressed my back into a doorway. I couldn't get the smile off of my face. *This* was familiar. *This* was what I was good at, what I'd been born to do.

At least, what I'd been born to do in Zunbar.

After a few minutes, I stepped out from my hiding spot. "Abudar?" I called hesitantly. I approached the end of the alley and peered around the corner, immediately grimacing when I did so.

Abudar stood with four guards with feathered helmets standing around him. If they were going to arrest him for helping out a thief, I couldn't allow that to happen. Abudar was shaking his head about something and then turned and began walking with the four strangers.

My stomach dropped.

How did he always get captured?

"Sands," I mumbled under my breath. I tore into the loaf of bread and ate a bite. I continued to nibble on it while following Abudar at what I felt was a safe distance.

Until two pairs of hands grabbed my elbows and jerked me to a stop. I paused mid-chew and looked up at the man on my right.

"Why are you grabbing on to me?" I demanded.

They were soldiers.

I gulped down the lump of bread. "I have somewhere to be."

"Indeed, you do. The baker identified you as the thief who stole"—he plucked the half-loaf from my hands—"a loaf of bread from him."

I smiled sheepishly. "I didn't notice you following me."

The man on my left chuckled. "We aren't supposed to be noticed. That's why we're called the shadow guard."

Shadow guard? That didn't sound good.

"The king will want to meet with you."

Sixteen

I looked away from the scar on the guard's face and focused on walking straight as they dragged me forward. I was suddenly grateful Igborg wasn't with me, but felt instant panic because he wouldn't know how to find me. Trying to be as discreet as possible, I glanced periodically at the sky to try and catch a glimpse of him but was unsuccessful.

From the sky the palace had looked small, so I wasn't expecting its grandeur at all. The homes we'd passed all had white plaster walls and short bronze domed roofs. The palace's white plaster walls were made of stone and hand carved with painted gold accents. The pillars at the front were pure white with a gold band painted around the top and a thin one at the bottom.

Two heavily armed soldiers stood in front of the gold doors with inlaid triangle turquoise stone. They stepped to the side, opening the doors as they did so.

We entered a wide-open space with a staircase to the right and to the left. A long gold-and-turquoise rug led to a throne on a pedestal, and a man with long black hair sat on the throne speaking with Abudar.

At least we'd be together.

Abudar laughed at something, and I was given the very distinct impression he wasn't under arrest.

"Forgive the interruption again, Sire, but we've captured a thief who stole bread from the baker," the scar-faced man announced when we got halfway down the rug.

The man on the throne lifted his eyes and bile rose in my throat. Sinbad grinned. "Caspara! I wondered if I'd ever see you again. I was just getting familiar with Prince Abudar here."

Abudar raised his eyebrow at me, looking like an unimpressed prince, but his amber eyes locked on me with question—how on earth had I managed to get caught after escaping?

The advantage we had was that Sinbad had no idea we knew each other. It was my turn to hopefully catch Abudar off guard.

"Did you say *Prince* Abudar? As in the prince of Sheblom?" I asked. I made sure to drop my jaw open and stare at him like I'd never before seen him.

Sinbad laughed out loud. "Caspara is one of the forty thieves," he explained to Abudar.

"Ah. We just recently destroyed their hideout. We've been trying to get rid of them for quite some time. I'm sure you can relate to the difficulties of having . . . roaches in every corner."

"I can indeed." Sinbad nodded.

I scowled. "I only stole a loaf of bread because I haven't eaten since *you* abandoned me on Daryabar!" I said, scowling at Sinbad.

"Daryabar? The mythical island?" Abudar asked.

Sinbad rolled his eyes. "We met in Halmu, and apparently she'd had too much to drink," he joked and then let out a boisterous laugh.

I wanted to punch him in the throat. He must have used

his wish, so where was Taylin?

Abudar heaved a sigh. "It was kind of you to welcome me into your new castle, Sire. I look forward to getting to know you as a ruler."

Sinbad nodded. "It will take my men the rest of the day to stock your ship. I recommend you stay the night, eat a proper meal, and get some rest. I'll have a servant run you a bath." He snapped his fingers and Taylin appeared out of thin air.

At first, the jinni's face was stoic. Taylin wore a black vest and golden pants, which made his gold-speckled navy-blue skin stand out more than ever. His golden eyes widened slightly when he spotted Abudar and grew wider when he saw me.

"Jinni, take Prince Abudar to one of our guest rooms and run him a bath. Then fetch him some clothes and a warm meal," Sinbad commanded.

With expert grace, Taylin stepped forward and bowed. "Follow me, Your Highness."

"What of the girl?" Abudar asked, casually wiping a bit of dried mud from the back of his hand.

"I haven't yet decided. She's a thief. She should lose a hand. Isn't that what you do in your kingdom?"

Abudar rolled his eyes. "Not for many centuries."

"Still . . . a thief without a hand has less chance of being able to steal successfully. And it would teach her a lesson." Sinbad stood and stepped down from his throne.

"You look ridiculous in the robes of a king," I commented snidely.

Sinbad smirked. "You should watch your tongue or I could remove that too."

"With all due respect, King Sinbad, I don't think taking

her hand will teach her any sort of lesson," Abudar commented. His eyes darted nervously, but I just couldn't believe Sinbad would ever take my hand.

Sinbad leaned down until our noses nearly touched. "Tell me, Caspara, which hand took the loaf from the baker's table?" He spoke calmly, but I could see the burning in his eyes.

I met the intensity of his gaze but held my tongue.

A slow, annoyed smile slid onto his face. "It would be wise of you to answer me."

"I don't remember," I admitted. "Probably my left. It's easier to slip items into my pouch on that side."

Sinbad's smile grew. He straightened and looked to his men. "Let's take her to the courtyard."

Abudar stepped forward, but Taylin held out an arm to stop him.

I couldn't help but look to him for help. Maybe I'd misjudged Sinbad. He was a pirate, yes, but we weren't on such bad terms he would honestly cut off my hand . . . were we?

"Your Highness," Abudar said.

"Go with the jinni, Prince Abudar," Sinbad ordered calmly without looking at him. "I'll eat lunch with you when you're ready." He headed for the front doors.

The soldiers, still holding on to me, pulled me after him. It didn't matter how hard I dug my heels into the rug, my feet slid. Helpless, I looked over my shoulder.

Abudar had been disgusted at the idea of cutting my hand off weeks ago when we'd first met in the prison. How was it now I was in the exact same predicament and yet would receive no mercy this time?

Abudar looked to Taylin. "Can't you do anything?"

He shook his head. "She doesn't possess the lamp. I am bound to the owner of the lamp."

"Even if he already used his wish?" Abudar whispered. "Why do you obey him?"

I couldn't hear what Taylin answered, but I had a gut feeling there was honestly nothing Taylin could do. And if Abudar used his magic to help me, his power would suddenly be revealed to the world, and who knew what sort of issues that could start between the two kingdoms?

I was dragged to a pristine white stone in the center of the courtyard in front of the palace, and my heart raced faster than it ever had.

"Sinbad, please. I have no way to pay for any food. I am starving. I had to eat something!" I pleaded.

"My question to you is, how did you even get here?" He looked down at me, his hands casually hidden behind his back. "Lay her hand out on the altar."

I struggled against the two men, gritting my teeth and even growling. The one with the scar managed to kick the back of my knees and drop me while the one to my left forced my arm out.

"I followed you!" I shouted.

"No, you didn't." Sinbad walked to the front of the alter and peered down at me. "Daughter of Kasim," he mumbled, then shook his head. "You're an embarrassment to his name."

The man on my left pinned my arm down.

I glared up at the pirate king. "How dare you. You know *nothing* of my father! You didn't know him. You have no idea what he taught me, what he meant to me."

"And you have no idea what he fought for," he countered.

"If you're referring to the griffin pendant, you could just tell me whatever you're hinting at."

Sinbad shook his head. "No. I don't think I will. Because you clearly couldn't ever live up to the order. You're far more pitiful than I ever imagined Kasim's child would be." Sinbad moved his arms quickly, pulling them forward and lifting them into the air. He had a sword gripped in both fists.

"Stop!" I shouted.

White light ignited the swirling tattoo symbols on my right arm, and when I yanked that arm backward and slammed my elbow into the scar-faced man, he flew backwards.

I stared at him with wide eyes.

The feeling of strength pulsed through me.

Sinbad drove his sword down toward my wrist. I jerked my left arm, but I'd hesitated too long. Sinbad's sword sliced through the air and down on my wrist.

A white light flashed, but instead of being terrified, I felt nothing but energy.

The sword's edge was bent and my wrist was fine.

Using my free arm, I turned just enough to punch the guard under the chin. His teeth slammed shut, his head snapped back, and he hit the ground in an unconscious heap.

I jumped to my feet and turned to Sinbad.

He took two steps back, the sword tip now dangling to the ground. "It cannot be. The sentinels haven't existed for centuries."

"And yet, here I am," I said. "I'm going with Prince Abudar, and you're not going to stop me."

"Caspara—"

"And I'm taking my jinni back too." I held out my hand.

"I know you hold the lamp in your possession. You wouldn't leave it out of your sight."

Sinbad's eyes narrowed. "You don't want to make an enemy out of me."

"I believe we've been enemies since you stole my Igborg."

Sinbad clenched his left hand into a fist, then grumbled under his breath how I was a "worthless woman" and reached into one of his robe pockets. And then another. "Where is it? I had the lamp in here . . ."

"Casparaaaa!" Igborg's voice sang from overhead.

I looked up to see my precious dragon diving toward me with Taylin's lamp held tightly in all four claws. I held out both arms and Igborg landed right in them.

"I got the lamp!" he announced proudly, oblivious that Sinbad stood just a few feet away.

I held him close to my chest. "I see that." I lifted my gaze to Sinbad. "I'm very proud of you."

Sinbad stood with his lips tight and his eyes narrowed in defeat. "It seems you've finally outsmarted me."

I rubbed the lamp and Taylin appeared before me. He grinned and wrapped me up in a warm embrace. "You did it!"

"Of course I did. Get Abudar. We're going home."

"How do you plan on doing that? I'm not providing you a ship now," Sinbad growled. He dropped his sword to the ground.

I grinned. "Magic carpet!"

The rug fluttered down to the ground at my side and I sat down on it.

I wished I could have captured Sinbad's stunned expression in a painting.

Abudar ran out of the palace, right over to me. He didn't sit, however, but grabbed my left arm and pulled it away from beneath Igborg to make sure my hand was still attached.

"I'm fine," I said. "Where were you?"

He held up the rusted lamp that belonged to Taylin. "I had to get this. I tried to run down here when I heard you shouting, but couldn't move fast enough." He breathed a sigh in relief and looked at me. "Could you be a little more careful next time?"

I laughed awkwardly. "I'll try."

Abudar sat behind me. "How did you knock those two out?"

"Uh. With my sentinel powers."

Sinbad remained standing at a distance while the carpet lifted into the air. Taylin disappeared from the ground below and Igborg snuggled into my lap, still holding on to the lamp.

"Caspara," Sinbad suddenly called.

"What?" I frowned down at him.

"Captain Nadeem can tell you about your father's pendant. There is much you don't know regarding the Griffin Syndicate. Speak with him when you return to the palace and you'll find out the truth."

"Griffin Syndicate?" Abudar muttered behind me.

"Thank you," I called down to Sinbad and the rug began floating away.

"You truly used your sentinel powers to fight the soldiers?" Abudar asked.

I nodded.

"How? Even when we sparred and tried to practice with Roshanak, your powers never engaged."

I looked over my shoulder and held out my arm to look at the now plain-black tattoos. "He insulted my father and my abilities. I wanted nothing more than to *prove* to him I was worth something more than just being a thief. Because . . . I think I might be."

Abudar reached out and entwined our fingers. "I know you are. I've been saying it all along."

I gnawed on my bottom lip and slowly pulled my hand away from his. "Thank you for putting up with me, even when I cause problems."

He chuckled. "You keep life interesting. When we get home, all I want to do is have a big meal."

"I couldn't agree more."

We both laughed.

"Oh! I managed to steal a few rolls from the baker. It's something to tide us over." He selflessly removed four rolls from his pocket and held two out to me.

"You don't have to share it with me," I said.

He lifted his gaze and almost scowled. "Why would you ever say something like that?"

"Because you're—"

"Stop it," he said firmly. "This isn't you. You don't talk like this. I don't care if I'm the prince. You are my other half, the other sentinel, and more importantly, you're my friend." He shoved the rolls into my hand.

"We haven't been friends *that* long." I gave him a bit of a smile so he knew I was teasing.

He grinned, his dimples showing.

I rolled my eyes.

He chuckled and reached out and tickled my knee.

"Stop it!" I laughed and pulled away.

Abudar's smile fell a bit and he leaned forward and

rested his elbows on his knees. He peeled a piece of the roll he was eating and held it out to Igborg. "I've had a lot of time to think, you know. About you."

"Abudar—"

"Let me finish. I should have been honest with you from the start about my engagement with Roseline, yes. But there was just something about you . . ." He shook his head. "It was wrong of me to build that desire in both of us when I knew we couldn't be together." He lifted his gaze to me. "But I want to talk with my parents when I get back. Because I should have the right to choose who I want to be with."

My eyes widened.

He actually *wanted* to be with me? A girl who could offer him no allegiance with a powerful country? Not even a dowry?

I shook my head. "Abudar, please. Don't ruin relationships between countries because of me," I said, tucking my hair behind my ear. "Your parents are trying to do what's best for you and our people. If that means allying us with another kingdom, how is that wrong? Besides . . . I like her. She's sweet."

Abudar looked away from me and down at the dragon begging for handouts like a puppy.

I leaned back against Abudar. "Maybe I'm considering being a sentinel."

His eyes lit up with excitement.

"And perhaps the two of us should ask the fates for some guidance?" I added.

He wrapped his arm around my waist. "If that's the only way I get to keep you by my side, I'll be more than happy to have you as my dearest friend."

I peered up at Prince Abudar's handsome face. I would have loved to try a relationship with him. But if he *did* speak to his parents, would they even give me a chance?

The thought of being a sentinel still overwhelmed me, even though I'd just tasted its power. Because how could I stand at his side and be his "other half" while if he married someone else?

Seventeen
Mithra

My blissful afternoon was absolutely shattered when the door of my balcony flung open and Arash came clattering loudly across the tile floor. From his pounding footsteps to the metal of his sword banging against whatever metal armor he had on, my peace was gone.

"Abudar has returned!"

My eyes flew open and I sat upright. I had been *trying* to enjoy some sun and have some peace from my studies while contemplating what I wanted the next steps in my life to be. I didn't anticipate Arash's announcement. Surely I'd heard him incorrectly.

"I beg your pardon?" I said, retrieving my robe to cover myself. I wore nothing but my undergarments.

Arash stood with his eyes down and his fist to his chest in respect for my privacy. "Forgive me for interrupting you. I was asked to fetch you immediately."

I rushed past him into my bedroom, taking only a moment to throw on something I could wear in public. I didn't even put on jewelry.

I pulled my hair out from my shirt collar and let it fall

down my back. "How did he get home? How did he escape in the first place? Why didn't a sorceress notify me *before* he made it back?" I slipped on my shoes and flung open my bedroom door.

"Caspara is with him," Arash answered.

A zing of anger shot through my chest. "Of course she is involved," I said through gritted teeth. "You would think she would have learned to keep her nose in her own business."

Arash rushed forward and pinned my hand between his and the door. "Mithra, you need to think about what to do with Caspara before you react. You knew there was a chance Abudar would be returned home, we just didn't know how soon."

"I haven't even had a chance to show Roshanak my newest skills since taking the magic from that student."

Arash pulled my hand away from the door and to his chest, standing so we touched. "Then we come up with a different plan. Getting Abudar out of the way didn't work. What is the next step?"

My eyes darted between his while I pondered. "I tried to get rid of Abudar and he is back. I did get the magic from that girl, whatever her name was, and it did help me."

"Then maybe you focus on the magic within that stone." Arash tucked my hair behind my ears, putting it back in order.

I nodded slowly. "And gain more power using its influence. It clearly has a lot it can teach me."

"Start there, then." Arash brought my hand to his lips.

I heaved a sigh. "I still want Caspara and Abudar separated. Did you see either of them long enough to get an idea if they're cozy again?"

He chuckled. "I think they're both fond of each other. They keep looking at each other and trying to be close without touching, but I think they both know there is a line with Roseline."

I rubbed my chin. "I could encourage Mother to move up the wedding. Once Abudar is married, he and Caspara cannot fall in love."

"But she's still his other half."

"Sands of time," I whispered under my breath. "Then you must get her out of the way until I grow more powerful."

"Me?" He blanched, his spine stiffened, and his arms dropped to his sides. "Why do I have to do that?"

"Because she trusts you! You're her brother. She would love to spend more time with you and get to know you."

Arash frowned, not sure at all.

"Do you love me or not?" I demanded.

"Of course I love you!"

"Then it does not matter how sweet she is or how much you might like her. I cannot get what I want if she keeps getting in the way!" I drew a breath to calm down and placed my hand on his chest. "Remember, you can be powerful too, Arash. Once I am the grand sorceress, you can be captain of the guard." I traced my fingers down his jaw. "Don't you want that?"

Arash licked his lips and finally nodded. "Yes. I want to be at your side."

"Good. Then I trust you can get rid of Caspara however you see fit. Make sure she doesn't get in the way again. By whatever means necessary, Arash." I raised my eyebrows at him, telling him I truly meant *any* means. "Then I will know you're on my side."

He nodded with uncertainty. "I . . . I will figure something out."

I felt as if I'd swallowed a stone. I felt guilty asking so much of Arash. They were siblings, after all. Caspara had even saved my life in the Desert Trials when she saved us from the octopus, and it was she who'd gotten us out of the caves, though I'd never openly admit it. To be honest, I did have a fondness for Caspara. It was rather unfortunate Telama had chosen *her* to be the sentinel, and now Caspara bringing Abudar back was about to unwind everything I'd been working for.

I entwined our fingers, and we walked down the hallway until we reached the stairs. Then he released my hand and fell into step behind me so no one would know of our relationship.

Excited voices from the library filled the hallways before we entered. Mother was hugging Abudar and stroking his hair, going on about how worried they had been. Father stood behind Abudar with his hand on his back, silently supporting him as well. Meanwhile, Caspara stood to the side, watching everything.

Their clothes stunk as if they hadn't bathed in days, their hair was greasy, and Caspara wore a shirt too long for her. Abudar looked positively impoverished. It was embarrassing, really.

"Abudar. You're back safe!" I made a show with the best amount of fake joy I could muster and threw my arms around him, making sure to hold my breath so I didn't breathe him in. "We were all so worried. Did they say why they took you?" I let go quickly, praying to the gods his smell didn't get on me.

Abudar sighed. "They wanted me to join their cause, to

convince Mother and Father that all sorceresses have the right to learn magic, and not just basic magic. They believe everyone deserves the chance to attend an academy, not only those who completed the Desert Trials."

"And do you agree?" Father asked.

Abudar turned. "They made a good case for it, claiming it would aid in the advancement of our people as a whole. Their main argument was agriculture. With more sorceresses, the small desert tribes have the ability to grow their own foods and sustain themselves through droughts." He shrugged. "I can't see why we shouldn't help if it's something within our abilities."

"These are heavily debated topics," Father replied. "There is a natural order to the world, and what happens when that order is disrupted?"

My jaw tightened. "One could argue that women naturally having magic *is* the natural order to our world."

Mother rested her hand on my arm. "We don't know what could happen, which is why we shouldn't rush into any decision. But Roshanak and Shorix seem to be on speaking terms now, so there is a chance we can move forward."

"Thank goodness Caspara was there to bring you home," I interrupted.

All eyes shifted to me.

I grasped both of Caspara's dirty hands. "How ever did you find him?"

"It's sort of a silly story." She let out a nervous laugh. "We ran into each other," she said. "I was with my friend Mihrage, trying to find a magical griffin feather to heal his sister and recover his land from a curse, and it happened to be on the same island Abudar was stuck on. It was a lucky coincidence, that's all."

"Yes. Lucky." I tried not to look at her like I was going to eat her.

Luck?

That she should end up on the *exact* same island where Abudar was being held?

That wasn't luck.

Mother approached Caspara's side and placed her hand on the girl's shoulder. "You're being guided." She used her free hand to touch the sentinel markings on Caspara's arm.

Caspara blushed. "I don't know about that . . ."

"I know you're nervous about being a sentinel, but too many things keep putting you back together with Abudar. I've never believed in coincidence."

Caspara looked to Abudar for help. "I still don't know. It's a bit . . . um . . . uncertain."

"Don't put her on the spot," Abudar interrupted.

Roseline ran into the room and paused only long enough to identify which of us was Abudar before she rushed to him. Concern lined her brow, and her blue eyes were filled with sleepless nights and worry. "You are quite all right?" she asked timidly.

"I am. Thank you," he replied.

She hesitantly reached for his hand and he graciously took it like the good little prince he was. "How are you feeling?"

"Much better now that you're back." She flashed a bright smile.

I didn't miss the pained expression on Caspara's face before she recovered and managed to hide it. I had suspected she had feelings for my brother, but I hadn't realized just how deep those feelings ran. It was sad, really.

But she could never marry Abudar.

"Will you be staying the night with us?" I asked Caspara.

She tore her gaze away from Abudar. "If that is all right with you. Unfortunately, my village was destroyed and I'm too far away to make it to our new location without supplies."

"Goodness, that's horrible!" I exclaimed and placed my hand on my chest. "Did your people survive?"

She nodded. "Yes, but only because Abudar warned them first. If he hadn't . . ." Her breath caught and she crouched to pick up her growing lizard that had been pawing at her leg. "I don't want to think of it," she whispered.

I smiled, hoping it didn't look as stiff as it felt. "How lucky for your people." I thought I would have been happier that no one died, but every time I took a step forward, Caspara was in the way.

The ruby tingled through my hip, and my new power seemed to react by sending that same tingling through my limbs.

Caspara cleared her throat when the silence became uncomfortable. "I do wonder if I might be able to have a word with Captain Nadeem?"

"I'll take you to your room so you can clean up," I offered. "And then Arash can help locate Captain Nadeem so you can have your conversation." I was about to loop my arm through hers but cringed at the cat-sized reptile's face and took her elbow instead.

"I'm afraid I don't have any other clothing with me," Caspara said.

I heaved a sigh and playfully rolled my eyes at her. "It

appears I must lend you one of my many kaftans."

She smiled. "Or you can simply bring me dinner. I don't want to inconvenience anyone."

I laughed. "Don't be absurd. I am no servant. Follow me. You can stay in the room you were in a few days ago, and I'll bring you an appropriate outfit to change into." I turned around and began the walk up the flight of stairs. "I honestly don't know how you stand getting so filthy."

"Oh, sand is easy to clean off. I got a lovely bath from the sea spray."

I looked over my shoulder to see what Caspara's expression told me, because I couldn't tell whether she was being sarcastic or truthful.

She was smiling.

I returned it. "Well, you should have enough time to scrub properly now. And your lizard friend."

The lizard's golden eyes blinked. "Dragon." He lifted his wings to prove it.

Caspara chuckled and patted his head. "She's teasing."
He huffed.

"Thank you," Caspara said. She walked past me into her room, and I ran my tongue over my teeth.

Things are getting out of hand, Princess. For every step forward you take, Caspara pushes you two steps back. If only you had more power, you would be that much closer to taking control. To being noticed.

"Mithra?" Caspara said, jolting me from my thoughts.

I put on my smile. "Yes?"

"I know things with Abudar missing the last couple of days have been stressful for you. You're a good sister, though, and I bet an even better sorceress." She grinned and set Igborg on the ground. "It's going to be amazing to see what you become."

Unsure how to reply, I nodded, and Caspara closed the door behind her.

Arash stood outside of my door when I arrived. "I think I know how to lure her away." He followed me into my bedroom. "She wants to speak with Captain Nadeem. I'll get her to the dungeons by telling her he is waiting there for her, and then I'll push her into a cell and lock her in. Abudar will believe she left during the night, and she will be safely secured and hidden away."

"Perfect plan." I gave him a kiss.

But the ruby tingled in my pocket.

While Abudar had been gone, I had tried out the new powers I'd stolen. Most basic spells I could now use without uttering the phrases for them. And at night, I dreamed of what my life could be like if I didn't have to memorize phrases ever again.

I could dominate any challenge.

I could out-cast Roshanak in any spell.

I could be on the throne . . .

My heart jumped in excitement. Could I be the *sultana* of Sheblom? I had never imagined such things with Abudar being the eldest and next in line.

Our country had never had a woman on the throne.

But I could be her.

I could be the first.

All you have to do is become more powerful.

"I know that look in your eye. You have another idea."

I nodded.

He stepped up behind me and wrapped his arms around mine. I loved it when he held me in this manner. Arash brushed his lips against my neck. "Care to share?"

"I want to be on the throne."

He paused. "You can be. When you get married to a prince, you will be on the throne." I saw the tightness in the corners of his eyes. He hated talking about me ever leaving him, and I couldn't blame him.

"No." I turned in his arms. "I want to be Sultana. *The* leader. The one in charge, not Abudar."

Arash's brows lifted in shock. "What? How?"

"I have to figure all of that out, but right now I must bring Caspara a dress so she can carry on with the rest of the day with my parents first." I hurried to my closet. "I needed to go to the sorceresses again. Take more power from them."

Arash blinked. "Mithra, isn't that dangerous?"

"I'll be careful."

When I gave Caspara the dress, I wasn't even sure if I said anything to her that made sense. I couldn't even recall what I said. As soon as her door shut, I returned to my bedroom.

Arash waited by my window.

"You'll stay here this time," I said.

His eyes darted to my door then back to me. "Then I should leave your room. Will you find me when you return?"

"Yes. And you can tell me about Caspara."

He dragged me to him and kissed me, then winked. "Your ambition is inspiring."

I playfully pushed him away and created the portal, like I had before. When I looked over my shoulder, Arash had just left my room and closed the door behind him. I stepped into the familiar, cool castle.

I rubbed my thumb over the ruby in my pocket. *Guide*

me to the one I should choose.

First, you must perform the spell we were practicing.

I nodded silently and stepped into an empty space beside the stairs where no one would see me.

I concentrated on each word of the spell required to give me Roshanak's features—her high forehead, cold brown eyes, the curve of her nose that looked like Caspara's, her high cheekbones. I only wished I had a mirror to ensure I'd cast the spell correctly.

Are you ready now to have tangible power? Are you ready to absorb all of the girl's power enhanced by the sacrifice of her life?

I stopped beside a window overlooking a courtyard where several sorceresses were finishing up their practice for the day.

Sacrifice? You mean . . . kill.

Murder is not the same thing as sacrifice. To sacrifice means to give up for the sake of something better. Is this not better for you?

To become more powerful than Roshanak, to grow in strength beyond Abudar even as a sentinel, and to eventually take the throne . . . could I take the life of another?

"Yes," I whispered aloud. Hearing my voice say it, accept what I was about to do, made my hands tremble and my stomach roll.

The girl in the green-and-gold kaftan. She is the one you want.

I spotted the girl the ruby had chosen.

It would be easy to distract her from the group. Each step felt heavy as I continued through the hallway until I reached one of the entrances into the courtyard.

"I'm learning how to manipulate water for the first time, can you believe it?" a girl in common beige clothing said.

"I know, it's incredible! I'm learning how to shift the shapes of rocks," her friend replied.

"I never imagined being able to learn different spells."

They were so engrossed in their conversation they didn't even notice me standing there.

A group of five girls giggled as they made their way into the hallway.

"Grand Sorceress Roshanak!" a girl gasped.

I turned to face her and she bowed respectfully.

"Can I help you find something?"

"That young woman in the green-and-gold kaftan. What is her name?" I asked.

She looked in the same direction I was. "That's Parisa. She's one of Sorceress Shorix's favorites."

"Why is that?" I asked.

The girl sighed. "She's a quick learner. She's already picked up three different elements of spells.

I smiled. "Thank you. Go on, I'm fine from here."

Luck seemed to be on my side finally. Parisa had lingered behind to speak with one of the sorceresses, and we would soon be alone. Even though that one student had seen me, I debated whether or not to allow the sorceress see me. I'd pushed my luck by taking the magic from another as myself, but even with Roshanak's face, I had to be cautious.

Only once all of the students left the courtyard did I approach its doorway. Parisa and her mentor were finishing up their conversation and I heard her say, "Good luck, Parisa," before she exited.

I stepped back against the pillar so she couldn't see me as she turned the opposite direction.

Parisa stepped into the hallway and turned. When she saw me, she gave a little squeak of surprise. "Grand Sorceress. To what do I owe the pleasure?" She bowed.

"I heard you are a rather talented."

Parisa smiled proudly and lifted her chin. "I am, indeed. I am the first to have mastered spells beyond what we have been told our entire lives would be our only spells."

"That is wonderful news." I smiled. "May we go on a walk?" I gestured to the door at the end of the hallway.

"Certainly." She positively radiated in excitement, and who could blame her? A young sorceress having a private meeting with the sorceress in charge of teaching the prince and princess was unheard of.

We exited the main tower and followed a path down to a stream and to a little waterfall. There were a few benches around and I took a deep breath of the humid air.

I tried to swallow as fear gripped me.

This was a terrible idea. Everyone would know I had been here. Someone would uncover that Roshanak was in two places at once, and they would blame me. If they did, I would be arrested and . . . would my own father execute me? Or would I be exiled?

Do you accept that I can help you? I hadn't anticipated the stone's words.

No, I admitted. *I am terrified. What if something goes wrong?*

I am here by your side to help. Take a deep breath. This is to make you more powerful. You will be the envy of all. Everyone in the land will see you.

I knelt at the stream and dipped my fingers into its clear surface. Within the ripples of the water, I could have sworn I saw a man's face looming over my shoulder. I slowly looked over my shoulder, only to see Parisa taking a seat on a nearby bench. When I returned my gaze to the water, the strange face shifted with the waves. I couldn't see the details.

Do you find yourself capable of taking her life to better your own?

"I can't imagine why you would visit me," Parisa stated, clearly trying to prod information out of Roshanak.

I slowly drew a breath in through my nose, calming my nerves.

Could I take her life?

To become the greatest sorceress of all time, to become the sultana of Sheblom . . . yes, you can.

I got to my feet and looked at my own reflection. Yes. I could.

A surge exploded in my chest, like electricity, and tingled all the way down into my fingers and hands. Black smoke materialized in my left hand. It took form into a black staff with etchings of magical symbols down to where I held it in my hand. At my grip, the etching changed to look like snake scales and had leather straps wrapped around it, with black and orange strips of silk dangling down.

Ah, you've done it. By accepting your destiny, you have strengthened your power.

I didn't need the ruby to tell me. I could feel it. I gripped the staff's handle with my other hand and twisted, and just below my hand grip, the staff separated and I held a dagger in my hand.

"Forgive me for not responding," I said softly, then turned my head to look at the girl. "I have been a bit preoccupied with my thoughts as of late."

Parisa looked up at the clear blue sky. "I heard about

Prince Abudar being missing. I hope you find him. But I must be bold and admit meeting you has been a dream of mine since I was a child. Do you think I could learn more about magic directly from you?" Her eyes were alight with hope.

"I am afraid . . . that won't be possible," I replied softly. I stood, mere inches from her, the dagger in hand.

Her brows furrowed. "Is something wrong?"

"*Qowetik . . . melki.*" I thrust the dagger forward.

Red light burst from the wound, seeped into my staff, and into my hand. My head fell back and I looked up at the sky as a silent cry left my throat. I thought the energy from the first girl had been incredible. It was nothing compared to the power causing my entire frame to tremble.

This . . . energy, this strength filled me like I had never before felt.

My entire body quaked.

I collapsed to my knees, withdrawing my dagger from Parisa's chest in the same movement. She slumped to the side on the bench, looking as though she'd fallen asleep.

You must rise and return home, young sorceress. No one can see you here.

I slid the dagger back into my staff and used it to get to my feet. I barely had time to think of the portal, let alone try and summon it, before it stood before me.

I stepped through it and into my room, then looked at my hands, still tingling.

A black viper with prickled scales down the sides of its face and at its nose slithered across the floor toward me.

Without a flicker of fear, I crouched and reached out my hand. "You are my familiar."

"Yesss. I am Sssamira. Together, the two of usss shall

do wonderful thingsss."

Eighteen

Mithra had been kind enough to give me one of her many nightgowns with the dress I'd worn to dinner, and it fit me perfectly. Though, I didn't feel beautiful. All I wanted to do was to fall down on a bed and sleep. The wounds down my torso had healed, for the most part, but still pinched now and then.

As I sat on the chair in front of the mirror, combing my long black hair, I couldn't help but think on how vastly different my life had been compared to the princess. We were the same size, had the same length of hair, the same determination to get what we want. But I had been raised in the streets by only my father since my mother had abandoned me because I didn't have a speck of magic to my name. Mithra had been raised in a grand palace with servants, far too many clothes, and a family who seemed to love and adore her.

But she hadn't shown up for dinner, and I had seen through her excited façade when she walked into the room and saw Abudar.

It made me suspicious.

I stood after hearing a knock on my door and opened it. I hoped it would be Abudar but was startled when I opened the door to see my mother, Roshanak. I still didn't know what to call her and stood awkwardly with my mouth trying to form something beyond "Hello."

My mother put on a smile. "I was told you'd returned. Sultana Shahira invited me to join you all at dinner, but I didn't want to make you uncomfortable since we didn't part on the best of terms the last time you were here."

I stepped back. "Would you like to come in?"

"I should probably . . . yes. Actually, I would." She smiled and entered.

Igborg lifted his head from the foot of my bed and then set it back down to follow her movements with his eyes.

She sat on the chair beside the window. "I am glad you've returned to the castle. And I'm proud of you for rescuing Abudar."

"At dinner, Sultana Shahira mentioned that you and she were speaking with Shorix for his return. You would have brought him home if I hadn't." I shrugged.

My mother frowned in thought. "Perhaps. Are you . . . staying long?"

I shifted my weight uncomfortably. "I haven't fully decided yet. Though . . ." I hesitated. Did I dare confront her? Would she be furious with me? And what would happen if she was?

"Speak your mind," Roshanak said.

"You lied to me. About everything."

Her brows lifted. "Pardon me?"

"You abandoned me in a crate by the docks when you realized I had no magic. My father took me away from you because you didn't want to raise me. You were ashamed to be the grand sorceress with a magicless daughter."

Roshanak's entire expression softened and she glanced at her hands resting in her lap. "You're correct," she replied softly.

"And you lied to me about my father being murdered," I added feeling a bitter sting in my heart. "The first few days I was with you and knew you were my mother, you lied to me over and over when you should have told me the truth from the beginning."

"I still don't know how your father died," she said, looking directly at me. "None of us do. Even Sultana Shahira looked into it. You can ask her."

"You promised to take me to his funeral." Tears filled my eyes. I wiped at them. "Did you send the soldiers to destroy my village? And don't lie to me this time."

Roshanak's eyes widened. "To destroy your village? Why on earth would I want that, Caspara? You live there. I wouldn't have risked the soldiers killing you. I want you to be a sentinel, I've taught you about their history and tried to get you and Abudar to work together."

"Do you truly want me to be a sentinel?"

"Yes." She answered without hesitation, and the expression on her face didn't change when she spoke. She was being honest. She did want me to be a sentinel, and she hadn't sent the soldiers after my people, even though that's what Abudar had told me.

I sat down on the foot of my bed beside Igborg and placed my hand on his back. He rolled to his side so I could rub his belly.

"If you didn't send them . . . who did?" I muttered out loud.

"I don't know."

I shook my head and looked at her. "Why did you send me to get the lamp from the caves?"

Roshanak watched me. "I wanted a wish."

"And what would you have wished for?" I asked.

She heaved a sigh. "I would have wished for the sorceresses to have equal opportunity in the land, that we wouldn't continue to be suppressed."

I shook my head. "But you can have that by working with Sultan Zayne. And surely Sultana Shahira can write a story now that she has her magic back."

Roshanak nodded softly. "Both are valid options. And in fact, Shorix will be arriving soon to go over options with us so the sorceresses can return to Sheblom."

I smiled a bit. "See? You didn't need a wish after all."

"I suppose I didn't." She smiled back. "Because of that . . . my wish would change if I had one."

"And what would it be now?"

"A second chance at getting to know and raise my daughter." Tears glistened in her eyes and swelled to the point a tear trickled down her cheek.

I bit my bottom lip and my chest tightened. "Maybe second chances aren't for the weak."

"Hm?"

"Thief rule number fourteen. Second chances are for the weak. At least, that's what Father said."

"He raised you well." Roshanak rose to her feet. "I'll leave you alone so you can catch up on your sleep. Should you need anything . . . just let me know."

I nodded and stood to walk her to the door. It was a bit . . . strange. I wasn't angry with her like I thought I would be. I still wasn't positive I should trust her, but then again, maybe I'd been looking at her wrong all this time because I had an expectation she didn't meet.

After blowing out the candle on the vanity, I climbed into the bed and watched the candlelight from the nightstand dance across the ceiling like little sprites.

My mind was immediately taken away to the night of my father's funeral, when I'd danced with Abudar by the firelight. We were happy. We'd laughed. He'd held me while I cried.

I dug the palms of my hands into my eyes, trying to push the memories away. Because all I could focus on was his stupid handsome smile and bright eyes, and I'd been forced to see that smile and those eyes locked on Roseline at dinner.

Instead of dreaming about Abudar and what I wanted in my heart, I changed my thoughts back to my mother and second chances. I could have been raised in the palace. She could have been at my side my entire life. She could have helped take care of me when I was sick, when I scraped a knee, or when I needed someone to talk to.

Neither of us had that relationship.

But perhaps we could.

I closed my eyes and tried to relax.

I was teetering on the edge of sleep when there was a soft knock on my door. I looked toward the sound, wondering for a moment if I'd actually heard it, but then it came again.

I rolled off the bed and walked to the door and opened it, only to blink in surprise. "Arash."

"Oh, forgive me. You were clearly in bed, I can come back tomorrow," he said, fumbling uncharacteristically.

I shook my head. "I was only surprised to see you, but I am grateful for any distraction." I grabbed a robe and put it on. "Where are we going?"

He blinked. "Going?"

I tilted my head. "You wouldn't come to my room at

night for any reason other than to show me something. Am I correct?"

"What if I only wanted to talk?" he asked, raising his eyebrow with a playful smile.

"Then you can come in." I stepped back, opening the door all the way.

He chuckled, shaking his head. "All right, you were correct. I did want to show you something, and Captain Nadeem will meet us there."

"How did I know, I wonder?" I laughed and closed the door behind me.

Arash smiled, and for a moment I saw my father. My heart twisted. He must have seen the expression on my face, because his smile dropped. "I must look a lot like him."

I swallowed my tears. "It's not your fault."

He nodded slowly. "I wish I'd known him. Anything about him."

I looked sideways at Arash. "I . . . suppose I never thought about it. You not knowing him. I know nothing of Roshanak, other than our few meetings."

"Perhaps we should swap stories." His smile returned, though smaller.

I reached out and took his hand. "I thought I was all alone when I found my village burning. I forgot I had a brother and that you must be feeling sorrow to some degree too."

He squeezed my hand. "That's what I want to talk to you about," he said. His eyes looked brown in the dim light, though I knew they were green, and he glanced around for others. "I want to take you to the dungeon."

I raised a brow.

He rolled his eyes. "Not that way."

I nodded, dropped his hand, and gestured to the left and then the right. "Which direction?"

"This way." Arash turned to the left, guiding me to a set of side stairs. "You may know, I work directly under Captain Nadeem. He's training me to hopefully take over his position when I become old enough, or when Prince Abudar takes the throne."

I nodded, lifting the hem of my nightgown so I didn't trip on it on the way down the stairs. "And he will be down here?"

Arash continued speaking, ignoring my question. "I helped him with the investigation when we were told your father was executed. But there was something about his death that bothered both of us."

We reached the main level. Arash put his hand up, silently ordering me to stop, and leaned his head around the corner to see if anyone was coming. Silently, he motioned me to follow him across the hall to the next flight of stairs leading down.

"What has bothered you?" I whispered when I thought we were far enough away.

"There was no blood anywhere. The cell showed no sign of a break-in—no scratches on the lock or any of the walls or bars." He stopped at the bottom and turned to me. "But the most important thing is, we never found a body."

I stopped dead in my tracks and narrowed my eyes. "You want me to believe you didn't find a body?"

"Correct."

"We had a funeral. They buried his body in a grave in my village." I pointed toward a wall, completely unsure if that was southeast.

"I don't know who they buried, and I don't know how

they got a body. I'm telling you the truth, though, Caspara." He walked all the way through the empty dungeon to a cell at the very back.

I'd seen that cell in the vision of my father. He had been chained to the ceiling, covered in sweat, and Arash had slammed the hilt of his sword into my father's ribs.

Arash unlocked the door and opened it. "Go look around."

I entered the cell and began examining it myself. "Roshanak could have used magic to clean up after she killed him, if it was she."

He shook his head. "It wasn't her, but I thought the same thing about magic being used instead of a blade. I asked Abudar to come himself and see if he sensed any remnant of magic. Sultana Shahira and even Mithra came at separate times as well." He shrugged and lifted his hands helplessly. "There's no sign that magic killed him. There wasn't even evidence that magic was used to clean up any blood if he was killed another way."

I stopped in the center of the cell and turned in a circle. "But it makes no sense. If there was no body, then how do you know he was murdered?"

"We don't."

I turned and locked eyes with him. "Then what makes you believe he's dead?"

Arash hesitated, then answered, "I don't."

My breath caught. "You . . . you believe him to be alive?"

He nodded.

I turned again, looking at the smooth stone walls of the cell. My father—*our* father—had been locked up in this very place. I had seen Roshanak demand answers from him and Arash hit him, but . . . there had been a funeral.

And Arash didn't believe him to be dead?

But Father would have shown me some sort of sign he was still alive, even if it was a risk to his own life. Perhaps the griffin pendant?

I gripped it.

No, he would have sent a message with Omar. Was it he who sent the guards to find us in the desert? Had he actually slipped out of this cell, alive, and sent them to rescue us? Another thought panged in my mind that he could have written a message somewhere in our home and I missed it.

I heard hinges groaning and whipped around in time to see the door seal shut and hear the lock click.

My eyes widened when I saw Arash through the window on the opposite side.

"I'm sorry," he said before my words caught up with my brain.

"What is the meaning of this?" I asked.

Arash's eyes softened. "I didn't want to do this, but it's the only way to keep you alive."

"What do you mean keep me alive?" I stormed over to the door and grabbed the bars of the window. "Arash, let me out immediately!"

He stepped back. "I truly am sorry, Caspara. You were given so many opportunities to stay away from Prince Abudar. You can't seem to. Now you must stay in the dungeon or I'll be obligated to kill you. I don't want you dead by my hand or any other, so the only way to keep you alive is to lock you in here."

"Arash, release me!" I shouted and shook the door.

He shook his head. "I love her too much." He pushed

the door to the window until it pressed against my fingers.

"Is Roshanak behind this? No. No. Mithra? Arash, if you truly are my brother, answer me!"

He pressed harder until the metal piece that sealed the window pinched my fingers between it and the bars. "Let go, Caspara. I'll make sure food is delivered to you and you are kept safe."

"Arash, please. Please don't leave me in here."

"I have no choice!"

My chin trembled and I was finally forced to let go of the bars.

The metal snapped together and the window bolt squeaked shut.

I slammed my fists against the door. With no backpack, lockpick, or weapon, I had no way out. I didn't even have the lamp.

And this time, I couldn't rely on Igborg either.

I pressed my forehead against the door.

Even though I had been locked up in prison before, there was something different about being trapped in the very cell my father had not only been tortured in but killed. Or not, if I believed Arash. And this time I was locked up because I was "too close" to the prince.

In that moment, I didn't know what to believe, because Arash had locked me up and left me there.

I rested my head on the stone wall and looked into the ceiling, through the only opening in the room aside from the door. The opening was barely two feet wide, by the looks of it, and blocked off by bars.

The cool desert breeze floated into the stuffy cell now and then.

Unfortunately, being locked up allowed me a lot of time

to think.

I recalled the vision I'd had with Abudar where Telama told us we were sentinels, and tried to remember how I'd felt. I'd thought I could do it, be the person they wanted me to be, what everyone was claiming I needed to be. A sentinel. A powerful being meant to protect the land from dangerous . . . beings? Magic? Its own people? Whatever the case may be, I supposed. And yet, I was locked away in a cell.

I hadn't been able to save my father, keep the lamp and jinni hidden, or protect my dragon.

Some powerful sentinel I was.

I *had* wanted to learn what it meant to be a sentinel at one point, until my village was destroyed.

Now?

I massaged my temples.

I needed Taraji or Igborg to speak with. I'd even talk with Taylin, or Farhad. the leader of the thieves. I needed to speak with my father.

Being true to who you are doesn't mean letting go of who you were.

I looked down at the tattoos on my arm, the markings I'd spent so long trying to pretend weren't there, the foretelling of my fate controlled by others that had nothing to do with me. But what was the worst that could happen if I accepted this "fate" of mine?

When we had traveled through the Dragon's Lair cave, I thought I needed magic to help. But in some situations I had proven I had developed skills better than magic. I'd been the one to fight the octopus, with Arash's help, and I'd managed to leap to safety across a chasm without magic to help, not to mention actually climbing out of the cave and dragging Abudar, Arash, and Mithra out of it too.

Perhaps I'd been thinking of the idea of a sentinel completely incorrectly. I thought "sentinel" meant I would have to be a guard of the people. Maybe being a sentinel didn't mean saving everyone; maybe it just meant protecting them or looking out for their needs and concerns. A liaison between royalty and the people?

Not only had I rescued the prince *and* princess, who were both powerful magic wielders by their own statements, but I had also saved my brother, a trained palace guard.

What *was* the worst that could happen if I decided to be a sentinel with Abudar?

If I didn't marry him?

If I might die defending those I love?

Any of those things might happen to me anyway.

Who was to say I wouldn't die protecting my friends and family running into Sinbad again or getting swallowed by a Sand Cloran—a giant snake-like sand creature with five rows of teeth? I could die from heat stroke any day!

I smiled to myself and looked down at my swirled tattoos. The worst thing that could happen would be giving up before I tried.

The room filled with starlight, but when I lifted my head, I realized the starlight had floated in from the opening overhead, literal glittering dust that took form into a tall, thin woman with gray-and-white hair pulled up in a delicate bun.

My heart jumped and I scrambled to my feet. "You wouldn't happen to be a weaver, would you?"

She smiled and nodded.

I had met her sisters before her.

"Do you know what happened to my father?"

Again, she nodded.

"Tell me." I stepped forward and reached up to grip my father's feather pendant.

The third weaver, the weaver of the past, placed her finger to her lips and shook her head.

My brows furrowed.

She walked to my side and faced the room, then reached over and touched my hand holding the pendant, then pointed to the floor, silently telling me to place it there.

I followed her direction and rested the silver griffin feather on the floor in the center of the room.

The woman shook her head and motioned with both hands in a little scooting wave.

I tilted my head in confusion. "You want me to move it?"

She nodded and pointed.

"Oh! The moonlight!" I replaced the pendant on the floor, but this time under the rays of the light of the moon.

The weaver smiled and nodded.

To my astonishment, the silver absorbed the white light of the moon and began to glow. I stepped back, toward the wall. With silent hand motions, the weaver of the past extended her arms and moved them in circles, urging the light from the pendant to stretch into the room.

Like a ghost, my father's form appeared. His features were nothing but white outlines, but I knew every detail of my father, and although the white lines were simple, I knew those shapes made my father's face.

I ran to him, wanting nothing more than to embrace him. "Baba!" I reached out to touch him, but my fingers went through the image.

He paused his pacing and his fingers reached up to his

face as though ten days ago he felt my touch. His eyes scanned the room and I wanted to scream that I was right there, that I would save him. But the white form walked through me as he resumed pacing back and forth across the room.

Although tears stung my eyes, I didn't allow them to fall, because the weaver's presence gave me real hope that my brother was right and our father was still alive.

The door became framed in white, and the memory of the door opened.

Father paused.

A man entered the cell. It wasn't Arash, because this man had facial hair. Perhaps this was Captain Nadeem? I'd only met him once, out in the desert when he'd rescued the four of us after the trials, and I could only vaguely recall what he looked like. Yet he didn't wear the clothing of the royal guard.

Whoever it was, his lips moved, but no sound came from them. He shook his head and gestured with one hand, his other politely placed behind his back.

I looked at the weaver. "What is it they are saying?"

She shook her head.

I turned back to the scene, frustrated that I couldn't discern what the two men said to one another. Father was being adamant about what he said, pointing to the ground, his brows furrowed in frustration.

The second man shook his head and stepped forward to grasp my father's shoulder.

They stood with their heads lowered.

Father trusted this man enough to let him near, to let the stranger hold his shoulder. Who was he?

And then the stranger, the man my father trusted, drove

his blade forward without warning.

"Baba!" I shouted and ran forth, but the ghosts of the past only dissipated as I passed through. With my hand to my trembling lips, I turned to the weaver. "He really did die?"

I'd watched the blade drive through my father's chest. I knew he couldn't have survived. He couldn't have. A man had slain my father.

The weaver smiled, pointed to her eyes, and pointed to the images. They moved backward in time to the moment the blade entered my father's body. There, the two beings froze.

She approached them and motioned me nearer by curling her finger.

Tears streamed down my cheeks, but I walked to her side and she took my chin, turning my face to see the images closer. She reached over my shoulder and pointed to a wisp of white at the entrance of the hole where the sword sank into my father's flesh.

Then the beings moved in slow motion. The sword drove through, but the smoke stretched away and upward into the air.

I shook my head. "I don't understand. Is that my father's soul? Going to rest in the lands beyond ours?"

The weaver grinned and held up her hand with her index finger close to her thumb, indicating I was close. She waved her hand, dismissing all images save the smoke.

The smoke floated more like a living being than smoke from a fire. And then wrinkled fingers stretched up into the air toward it. The orb settled in her grip and she began stretching threads from it and weaving them through a loom.

My heart began to race and I grasped my chest. "Gavair." I turned to the weaver and looked at her with wide eyes. "Your sister Gavair weaved his spirit?"

She nodded.

My mind began to race. Could it be?

I recalled that night in the cave when the sentinel's mark on my arm allowed me to unlock a magic door in the wall of the cave, revealing Gavair's workshop of looms. I had watched her weaving one of the hundreds of rugs before my eyes, and when she snipped the final thread, the rug came to life.

But there was a tiny detail of that memory I hadn't seen the first time. Or rather, hadn't focused on. Just before Gavair snipped the final thread, she had lifted her fingers from a tiny lantern and placed the white light on the rug.

I had never felt my heart pound so quickly. "Are you saying . . . the magical rug that took me to my village, that saved us from the island . . . that rug she weaved is my father?"

No sooner had the thought come to me than that very rug dropped from the opening and flew around me in a circle.

I opened my arms to embrace it. The rug leaned into me, and I wished I could hold it even tighter. "Baba! It is you!" I turned my head to the weaver of the past. "Can I save him? Can I bring him back from this?"

The woman shrugged, held up her empty hands, and shook her head.

"Thank you. Thank you so much for showing me this." I held on to the corners of the rug and looked at it as though I could see my father's face. "If I have any power to return you to yourself, I will do that. I have a jinni who might be able to help."

The rug pulled out of my hand and wiped my damp cheek, then tapped my nose. I could almost hear him call me "dune bug," and I smiled.

I crouched and picked up the feather from the ground.

"Fate has guided me far too many times for me to ignore it. If I am to be a sentinel, then a sentinel I will be." I looked at the rug. "Can you help me get out of here?"

Nineteen

The rattle of keys in the lock startled me awake. I'd attempted to escape with the magical rug, who was also somehow my father, but even though Father could fit under the door, he hadn't been able to pick the lock. With the bundle of threads as tassels at the corners acting somewhat like hands, he still wasn't strong enough to grip the interior mechanisms of the door. So I had relented and fallen sleep curled up on the rug.

I wasn't expecting at all to hear keys. I climbed to my feet and planted my hands on my hips. "Realized this is a stupid idea, did you?" I said right as the door swung open.

But it wasn't Arash.

It was a man a bit older than my father with gray in his beard and wrinkles around his mouth and eyes.

He raised an eyebrow and studied me. "Well, here you are. I figured I would find you down here; I just didn't realize you were foolish enough to get yourself locked inside."

I frowned. "Why would I have come here on my own?"

"This is the cell your father died in. Prince Abudar told me you wanted to speak with me but said you didn't come down for breakfast so you must have set out on your own to find answers. I am Captain Nadeem."

I glanced at my father, then the captain. Although the guards wore bronze or steel scaled breastplates, Captain Nadeem's were gold and polished. Each scale had a symbol stamped into it I could only assume stood for accomplishments he had achieved in his years of service.

I ran my fingers through my hair, pulling it over one shoulder, and cleared my throat. "Arash led me down here and told me how you suspected my father wasn't really dead, but then he locked me in here and left."

The captain's caterpillar brows furrowed. "Why should Arash do such a thing?"

"He said something mad about keeping me away from Abudar and that he loves 'her' too much, which I can only assume to be Mithra."

The man nodded slowly. "I shall have to look into this matter. Why did you need to speak with me? I assume Arash told you what we know about that night, and I am afraid we still do not know how your father passed."

I shook my head. "I believe I have solved that mystery."

"Oh? How?"

I hesitated, knowing I would sound like a foolish, mourning *girl* if I told him the rug behind me was actually my father. Even in a world of magic, I couldn't expect the man to willingly accept my word when he didn't even know me, but maybe if he saw my father's necklace he might be more willing.

I held up my father's pendant. "Sinbad said you could answer some questions for me."

Captain Nadeem quickly looked over his shoulder, then stepped into the cell and closed the door nearly all of the way. "Caspara, there is much you don't know and I cannot tell you now."

I laughed. "My father thought he needed to keep secrets from me because I wasn't old enough." I held up my right arm, showing him my tattoos. "Like the fact I am a sentinel. And guess what? He died before he could tell me what it meant. Instead of raising me and training me to be what I was destined to be, he kept it a secret because he felt he couldn't *tell me now*. I deserve to know whatever other secrets my father held from me."

I knew my father lay on the ground just behind me and could hear everything I said, but I didn't know if the rug even had the ability to understand me. If he did, he deserved to know how upset I was for all of his lies.

His lips tightened, and again he looked over his shoulder.

"Tell me, Nadeem," I said firmly.

"I made a vow to him that you would never know. I am sorry, Caspara." He pulled the door open and gestured with one hand for me to exit.

Instead, I turned and looked down at the rug lying on the floor. "Are you going to tell him or am I?"

The rug didn't budge.

I gritted my teeth. "The rug is my father. His soul was woven into the rug by one of the three weavers." I folded my arms across my chest and scowled at Nadeem. "Since he's in here, you can tell me."

Nadeem, however, looked at me as though I had lost my mind, which was what I had expected. "Come with me. Let's get you some breakfast and—"

I stomped my foot. "Curse all of the sands! Tell me!"

He shook his head. "Caspara, all I can say is that you have no need to worry about it any longer. With your father's death, that necklace is nothing more than a piece of silver. Prince Abudar's wedding will bring peace to our land we haven't seen, and now that you and he will be working together to stop whatever evil may come our way, there is no need for us."

"Us? Who?"

"I've said too much already."

"Nadeem—"

"No, Caspara," he said firmly. "You do not need to know. Go upstairs. You've slept through breakfast, but if you get back upstairs and dress, you'll be ready in time for lunch."

I stepped in front of him, glaring hard into his eyes. "I met Sinbad. He told me to speak to you, and he said something about the Griffin Syndicate. Secrets always come to light. My father used to say that. Kasim. A man you seemed to know and perhaps even call friend."

Captain Nadeem's brows remained furrowed for several tense moments.

I stood my ground.

He finally shook his head. "I made a promise to a dear friend. Just because he is dead does not mean I will share his private deeds. Not even with his daughter. I am sorry, Caspara."

My lip twitched in anger. I spun on my heel and stormed out of the cell, not bothering to look over my shoulder at the rug still lying on the floor.

I wasn't sure if I should call it "father," because I didn't know how much of my father was really there. What if he only recognized me but didn't know I was his daughter? Could he understand and answer questions? Maybe it could and that's why it wasn't moving—because it was convenient to pretend to be just a rug when his daughter demanded answers.

Igborg was beside himself when I entered my bedroom. He ran over to me and started jumping up and down. "Where going? Igborg scared!"

"I know." I crouched and stroked his back. "Arash thought he needed to lock me away to keep me from Abudar."

"But why?" He cocked his little head.

I looked around the room as I slowly stood. "I don't know. There is something more going on here, Igborg. Father isn't dead. He's the magic rug."

On cue, Father as the rug flew up to my window.

I folded my arms across my chest. "Do you understand me at all?"

The rug floated mutely.

Igborg looked at the window, then up at me. "Baba is rug?"

I heaved a sigh and walked to the window to open it. "Supposedly. That's what the final weaver told me, more or less. But why would they make him a rug and not let him die like everyone else? Why did Arash lock me away last night in the dungeon? Who is trying to keep me away from Abudar?"

"Rosh . . . Ronanak? Mom," Igborg finally decided.

I shed the nightgown I wore and put on the same kaftan Mithra had allowed me to wear the night before. My cuts no longer needed to be bandaged, but they still ached as I dressed. "Roshanak doesn't make sense. She *wanted* me to train with Abudar." I paused at the mirror. "Unless she didn't." I looked down at my little dragon. "She could have been putting on an act that she wanted me to train with Abudar but had no intention of letting us become powerful.

After all, with the sentinels in place, she would have no role in the kingdom, would she?"

Igborg stared at me blankly. He was a great creature to talk to, but it was impossible getting good ideas from him. He was still too young and inexperienced.

Braiding my hair was impossible. I thought I would be able to, but reaching up stretched my cuts and bolts of pain shot up my arm. I ended up just pulling it back in a ponytail at the base of my head.

As I walked from my bedroom to the palace's dining room, I kept to the edge of the hall, ready to dart into any door should Arash appear.

There was a mystery in the palace I had only just discovered.

Igborg's nails clicked on the tile floor as he scurried by my side. Hopefully, if anyone heard him they would assume it was just a scorpion running around.

Finally, I reached the main floor and stepped into the dining room without being noticed—as far as I knew.

The only two in the dining room were Abudar and Roseline.

Abudar actually did a double-take, glancing away from Roseline, to me and then back. He stopped his conversation. "Why are you sneaking around the palace?"

"Who said I was sneaking?" I glanced over my shoulder and when I looked at Abudar, he had an eyebrow raised. I stepped right up to them. "I need a word in private. You can come too, I suppose," I added to Roseline. "But I need to talk to you before Arash sees me."

"Arash?" Abudar looked me up and down as if that would tell him what I was about to say. He unnecessarily took my elbow and guided me from the dining room and through a door to a small room.

Roseline followed, glancing over her shoulder as I had.

I didn't wait for Abudar to ask. "Something isn't right," I said. "I feel like something is starting."

"What do you mean starting?" he asked.

I pulled away and rested my hands on my hips. "First, I must know how much you trust Roseline. Because I'm going to make some accusations you may not like."

"I may already be aware," Roseline answered for him.

I looked at the blonde girl with bright blue eyes and nodded. "Arash locked me in the dungeon because I'm too close to you," I told Abudar. "Something is going on. Either with him and Roshanak or him and Mithra, but one or all of them clearly don't want the two of us to actually become sentinels."

Abudar rested his hands on my shoulders. "Not everyone is out to get you, Caspara. That's a big leap. If they didn't want us together, Roshanak wouldn't have started to train you or wanted you and I to be together in the first place. As far as Arash, he could just kill you."

I frowned. "Abudar. The Veil took you away and *someone* burned down my village. Arash locked me up, but he did say he didn't want to have to kill me to keep us apart." I lowered my voice. "I spoke with my mother last night and she seemed genuinely shocked when I accused her, and she brought up the same thing you did about training us. That leaves only one person. Mithra."

Abudar lowered his hands and looked at Roseline.

I continued, "And I found out that the magic rug that saved us is actually my father reincarnated. More or less."

His eyes widened. "The rug that's saved us is actually your father?"

I nodded. "The third weaver showed me last night when I was in the dungeon. She also showed me who killed my father, but I couldn't distinguish his face or why he did it."

"Why would the weavers reincarnate him as a rug?" Abudar mumbled.

I shrugged. "I don't know, but I find it strange. And that fate keeps throwing me and you back together and things keep happening like they're warnings that something bigger is coming and . . . I don't know what to do. Maybe you and I can connect again and speak with Telama?"

Abudar folded his arms and turned to Roseline. "Do you want to tell her what you were just telling me?"

"I was speaking with Abudar earlier today," she said. "I agree that Princess Mithra may be the one up to something. I don't know much about Roshanak, but while Abudar was gone, Mithra spent an awful lot of time in the practice room alone while Roshanak spoke with Sultana Shahira about getting him back from The Veil. Of course, Princess Mithra could have been keeping her mind occupied since she didn't know how to help, but . . ." She paused.

"But?" I prodded.

Roseline glanced between the two of us. "But she's started to be able to cast spells without verbally saying them."

I saw Abudar's expression shift to dread and faced him. "What does that mean?"

"Even Roshanak has to use her voice to cast most spells," he said softly and turned away from us. He ran his fingers through his wavy hair. "It means Mithra is somehow learning powerful skills beyond what she should be able to at her age." He shook his head and turned back around, clearly not sure how he should move.

I shrugged. "Is she learning from The Veil? Maybe they have methods Roshanak doesn't know how to use?"

Abudar shook his head again. "Magic has an order. Like a stalk of wheat grows from a seed, magic starts from somewhere. There are laws, like how the seed needs soil, water, and sun. Magic doesn't just . . . happen. A stalk of wheat doesn't just appear. Mithra *must* be doing something."

"But everything right now is speculation," Roseline added. "I wasn't able to get close enough to see beyond through the crack in the door she left open. We don't even know if she's doing something wrong."

When Abudar turned to me, my arm tingled.

And I knew he felt the same thing, because he rubbed his hand over the tattoos on his arm.

"You feel in your heart something isn't right," I said.

He chewed his bottom lip and finally nodded. "I believe I need to speak with my parents. We need to have a conversation with all of us to see what's going on and stop it before whatever it is gets out of control."

"If it's something bad," Roseline added.

But Abudar and I could feel it wasn't something good.

"We'll have to talk after their meeting with Shorix," Abudar concluded with a nod.

"I suggest you keep a low profile, Caspara," Roseline said. "If they discover you're not in the cell and Arash threatened to kill you, you're in too much danger to be seen walking about the palace. It may be best if you return to the thieves so you remain safe."

I hesitated. A flood of thoughts exploded in my mind, from not wanting to leave Abudar's side to wanting to hear the conversation the royal family would have with Shorix, but most importantly that being here was supposed to be my responsibility.

"What is it?" Abudar asked.

"If I am supposed to be a sentinel . . . I shouldn't be running. I should be here helping," I answered, ignoring Roseline and looking into Abudar's eyes. It took everything inside of me not to reach out and grasp his hand in front of her.

He stepped closer, and I knew as soon as he did so that he was resisting the same urge. "Is there a way for you to stay here and be safe?"

"I was raised a thief. Raised to be invisible. This palace has hundreds of rooms. I can keep myself hidden *and* I can use my skills to help."

He gave me a hopeful smile. "You're changing your mind?"

I nudged his arm with my elbow. "I can't let *you* have all of the glory in the next life."

Abudar laughed, releasing some of the tension sitting on his shoulders. He took my right hand in his and patted the back. "You used some of that power when you faced Sinbad. You're unlocking it. If you can find a way to overhear things today and be safe, then tonight you can meet me in the red tower. We can exchange information and try and reach Telama or figure out our bond or . . . something."

His hands lingered on mine.

"If worse comes to worse, I'll use my last wish to keep everyone safe."

"That's cheating." His lip tugged into a crooked smile.

From the corner of my eye I spotted Roseline shift, and I cleared my throat and pulled my hand out of Abudar's grasp. "Where is the red tower?"

"It's where my mother lived when she was young. Straight down the main hallway and to your left. Igborg can take you there. He likes the gardens in that corner." Abudar looked down at my dragon.

I'd almost forgotten Igborg was there. When I glanced down, he had his chest puffed out like he was proud of himself. "You wander around the palace at night?"

"Sometimes when Caspara snores."

I gasped. "I do *not* snore!"

He bobbed his head up and down. "Like a dragon. More than me!"

Abudar laughed, and even Roseline stifled a giggle behind her hand.

I hoisted Igborg into my arms. "I do not snore, you little lizard."

"Igborg not lizard." He pouted.

"And I do *not* snore."

"Sometimes you do."

I shook my head. "Ridiculous little dragon."

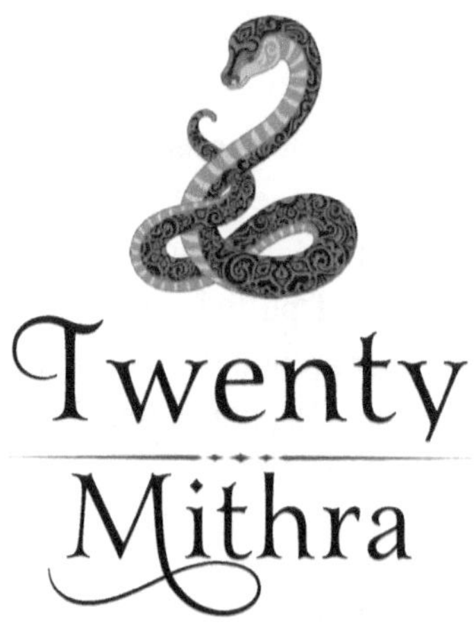

Twenty
Mithra

I rubbed the shimmering black-purple exterior of my skirts as I took a chair across from my father. He sat at his desk, looking over another letter. Judging by the exterior seal, it was from Kalekai, Roseline's home. Her sister had been ill, from what Father had explained.

He lifted his copper eyes to me. "Yes?"

I folded one leg over the other and looked down at the plum I was holding. "I was meditating this morning, as I do every morning, and a strand of thoughts came to me I never could have imagined." I rubbed my thumb over a spot that wasn't there.

"What sort of thoughts?" Father set the papers down and rested his wrists on the desk.

I lifted my eyes to him. "First, it was about Caspara's father, Kasim. He was a leader of the forty thieves, was he not?"

"Yes." Father's brows furrowed.

"But he was also mother's previous lover. Before she met you."

Father leaned back in his seat.

Even after nearly eighteen years, it was still a sore topic of conversation with him. Kasim and my mother had been childhood friends. True, she had also been childhood friends with my father until her father, Khorshid, the vizier to the sultan, made her forget when she left the palace with her mother to live in the city.

I smirked. His discomfort gave me a rush. I leaned forward. "The Griffin Syndicate."

Father's face became ashen and fear glistened in his eyes. He grabbed the pile of papers and nervously began tapping and stacking them into piles. "I don't know where you heard that, Mithra. I have work to do."

"I know you were faced with an incredibly difficult choice, Father," I continued. "Kasim wasn't threatening only your throne but your legacy. Most importantly, the future of your children. If you left him alive . . . if you had let him live, he would have ensured the throne was destroyed and commoners would rule Sheblom." I reached across the desk and took his hand. "You made the right choice."

Father's gaze snapped to me. His breath was heavy, caught between fear and anger.

Because this was a secret I never should have known.

I didn't learn any of that information from meditating.

That morning I had gone to the practice room all alone. Roshanak had been bothering me all week, trying to get me to practice with her, but I had grown bored of our little matches now that I was obtaining *real* power, and I wanted to see it in action.

I'd set the ruby on the floor in the center of the room and then looked over at the doors. The locks clicked into place, preventing me from being interrupted.

I rubbed my hands together eagerly and took a deep breath. There was magic I had never tried, never dared to access before now.

Dark magic.

Roshanak's first time using magic, she had used shadow magic. It was after that she learned how to manipulate other forms of magic. At least, that was what she'd told me. She had attended the Zauberin Academy herself as a youth, had trained under the best teachers. But all of them were adamant that dark magic was dangerous. She was encouraged to use her shadow magic no longer.

I was excited to try something dangerous. My body longed for it. I'd already killed a girl to obtain her magic and power.

One unfortunate but necessary step to reach my goals.

In that moment, I closed my eyes and felt the world around me as I had done so many times before. This time, I felt the shadows under the chairs, in the corner of the room, and between the tiny cracks between the planks of wood.

I felt my new companion, Samira, slide from across my shoulders, down my leg, and to the floor. Her energy only encouraged me.

I gripped the shadows and felt a rush of warmth and then cold. When I opened my eyes, the darkness had gathered around me and pulsed like a curious, living thing.

Careful now, Mithra, my ruby guide warned.

I grinned and reached my fingers out toward it. "Show me something I don't know. Show me who killed Caspara's father."

The darkness solidified enough to reach out and touch my fingers, but the instant we touched, my head flung back and I was dragged through dark hallways and surrounded by whispering.

"*. . . never be able to get revenge for . . .*"

"*Justice needs to be served.*"

"*. . . risking lives beyond ours . . .*"

"*I have no choice.*"

That final voice had been my father's. The other voices I hadn't recognized. I locked in on my father's voice and was taken to his office.

He sheathed his sword and grasped the handle of the door. "This is the only way to keep my children safe. The Griffin Syndicate cannot succeed."

He focused forward and yanked the door open, his decision made and Kasim's fate sealed.

I followed my father along the edge of the wall, through crevices of darkness in the memory. We went down the stairs and to the dungeon, then I watched my father, the sultan of our land, unlock Kasim's cell and enter.

"To what do I owe the pleasure of a private visit by the sultan himself?" Kasim asked in a bored tone.

My father stood before him. "I know why you wanted the dagger and serpent statue. You were hoping to gift the statue to Mithra, knowing of its magical properties. You were hoping that taking her hostage would help your cause and give you a way to manipulate me into forfeiting my throne."

Kasim's eyes narrowed. "Where did you hear such nonsense?"

"I am not a fool, Kasim! I know you have hated me since I took Shahira for my wife," Father shouted, his hand hiding a sword behind his back.

Kasim's expression didn't change. "You also murdered

my parents."

"The soldiers did. But still, I accepted you into the palace at my side as a trusted friend when you married Roshanak." Father gave a frustrated sigh. "I cannot allow you to ruin everything I have built or the legacy I will leave for my children."

"Then what will you do, Sultan Zayne?" Kasim challenged foolishly.

"May the gods someday forgive me, old friend." Father ran his blade through Kasim's chest so quickly, the poor old man didn't even stand a chance of reacting.

Or perhaps he accepted it because he knew his execution was necessary. Either way, Kasim's body crumpled to the floor and the darkness had given me my answer.

My father had killed Kasim.

As I sat in his office and watched the expression on my father's face when he realized I knew, I felt the darkness surrounding me, hissing eagerly like Samira in my ear.

Father stood and ran his hands through his hair, then clasped them behind his head. "Mithra . . . you can never utter a word of this to your mother." He looked at me with sorrow in his eyes. "It would kill her."

I stood, smiling, and walked around his desk to wrap my arms around him. "Of course I wouldn't say anything to her. You did what had to be done, Baba. Kasim would have killed you if you hadn't killed him." I stepped back. "And now, I believe it may be wise to get rid of Roshanak."

"What?" His arms dropped to his sides.

"You don't need her. You have me."

"She is the palace sorceress."

"I can fill that role!" I insisted. "I may be young, but

she's taught me everything she knows anyway. Besides, I've learned magic beyond what Roshanak knows."

He shook his head. "I don't know, Mithra. You are young. Perhaps when Shorix comes today, you can show her your skills and see if you're ready to take on more responsibility."

I stiffened. Shorix had mentioned no such thing to me. I gripped my hands into fists until my nails bit my palms. "I want her removed from her position, Father. I want to be the grand sorceress." I stepped forward and narrowed my eyes, using the ammunition I'd been building up. "What would happen if Caspara learned the truth?"

Father hesitated. "What's gotten into you?"

"Fire her." I turned on my heel and stormed out of the room. "Or I will."

Unfortunately, when I arrived at the practice arena to continue trying my new magic, Roshanak was there. I didn't intend to, but I visibly bristled.

Roshanak saw my body stiffen and placed her hands behind her lower back. "You're growing in power, Mithra. I wanted a word with you regarding that."

I folded my arms across my chest. "What do you want to know?"

"Your power radiates." She approached me but walked past and circled me. "Have you found an enchanted artifact?"

I laughed. "You don't think I could become stronger on my own?"

She stopped in front of me. "No. Not this quickly. It should have taken you years to get to this point."

"How can you even tell how strong I am?" I narrowed my gaze at her and moved my hands to my hips. "How do you possibly know I should have studied for so many years to be more powerful?"

"Because I attended the Zauberin Academy, I taught there, and I have been the palace's sorceress for the past eighteen years. I've seen both you and Abudar grow. He has the gift of a Sentinel and grew much faster than you. Yet all of a sudden, you have become more powerful than him in just the past week."

"Maybe you shouldn't underestimate a woman when she's invisible."

Roshanak's eyebrows dipped. "Invisible? Mithra, you're the most well-known woman in Sheblom. You're beautiful and—"

"I want to be more than beautiful!" I shouted and flung my hands into fists at my side, simultaneously stomping my foot. Behind me, a cool rush of air shifted my hair.

Roshanak took a step back and looked behind me. "Mithra. You've been practicing with darkness."

"Yes, I have," I said firmly. "And I don't intend to stop." The coldness behind me pushed forward until it stood at my sides and I realized I was pulling forth the darkness from wherever I could.

Roshanak shook her head. "You're strong, Mithra, but you aren't disciplined. You need to know how to control your power. You—"

"Don't need your help or training anymore," I interrupted with a proud grin. A grin because I knew what my next step needed to be.

Roshanak held her hands out before her face, her palms facing me. She touched the tips of her thumbs and index fingers together, creating a triangle shape, and then uttered the spell "*Ashriq,*" which sent an explosion of light in my direction.

I flung my arm up over my eyes silently summoning a magic shield to protect me from the brightness while also protecting most of the darkness surrounding me.

"You don't have to speak your spells?" Roshanak asked breathlessly, startled.

I took a step closer to her. "No. It's incredible what I can learn when you've ignored me. You've been so consumed by *Abudar* and bringing *Abudar* home, you completely ignored me. Which means I'm almost more powerful than you, in that regard." I held out my hand, silently summoning my staff, then pulled it apart to get to the dagger I'd used to kill the student sorceress. "*Qowetik melki*," I said and lunged at Roshanak.

Roshanak interpreted the words, and as I stabbed forward to end her life, she said, "*Ibtaqi*."

My movements instantly slowed, giving her time to avoid my death blow.

"Samira!" I shouted in frustration.

The viper slithered quickly into the room, heading for Roshanak. She didn't have a chance to tell me how shocked she was that I had managed to summon my familiar, or how disappointed she was that I hadn't told her.

Roshanak said, "*Iftah ya bowaba*!" A portal opened behind her.

"No!" I shouted in frustration and tried to run for her.

But Roshanak stepped backward, and the portal snapped shut before Samira or I could get to it.

The spell slowing me down disappeared as soon as she was gone, and I let out a shout of anger and frustration.

It's time you learn the truth of what you hold.

I looked at the glowing ruby, my chest rising and falling

in angered breaths. "And why would I want to talk about you right now? Roshanak just got away!"

Why do you think I chose you? Led you to me? I am more than a stone, young woman. What do you know of your grandfather, Khorshid?

Twenty-One

It turned out sneaking through the kitchen was easy. For me. However, with a starving and rapidly growing dragonling, it was almost impossible. He wanted me to take an entire lump of boar meat with us, and I had to compromise by slicing it in half and pointing out that if I had to carry the meat, I couldn't carry him.

He happily trotted alongside me the entire way up the stairs and to the floor we'd been staying on, grinning and eagerly licking his lips. Not wanting to be caught, I found a different room and sat down on the bed to eat while Igborg tore into his own lunch.

"Father?" I called, unsure what else to say.

The turquoise-and-gold rug squeezed under the door and rolled up to lean against the wall.

"Is that the best thing to call you?" I asked.

It seemed to nod its top half.

"You can actually understand me then?"

Again, it—or rather *he*—seemed to nod.

I sighed and licked some curried gravy off my bottom lip. It was the first time since learning the rug was my father that I'd actually had a chance to speak with him. "I have a billion questions I want to ask."

The rug didn't move.

"Why didn't you tell me about the feather? What is Nadeem hiding?" I asked.

But how could my father answer such questions? He had no mouth, no voice. I massaged my temple and took another bite of my lunch.

"Did Arash kill you?" I asked.

Father shook his rolled-up carpet head.

Okay, so he could answer yes/no questions.

"Did Captain Nadeem?"

Again, he shook his head.

I pursed my lips. "Is it someone I know?"

He nodded.

I heaved a sigh. "This is going to be a very long conversation." I set my food down on the vanity and looked at my own reflection. "Am I truly supposed to be a sentinel?" I looked sideways at the beautiful rug any royalty would be envious of.

The rug nodded and unrolled a bit, then rerolled. I could only imagine his frustration not being able to communicate.

"I wish you and I could have a conversation," I muttered.

On cue, Taylin appeared. He grinned bigger than he ever had. "I can grant that wish!"

"I know you can, Taylin." I straightened and faced him. "But if I do, you won't ever be free."

Taylin pursed his lips and tapped his chin. "What if I speak with him for you?"

"You can do that?" I looked him up and down, uncertain if I should trust anything the jinni said without a wish.

He rolled his eyes and raised an eyebrow. "Have I ever steered you wrong?"

"Fine. Then ask him why he lied to me all this time." I folded my arms.

Taylin hissed through his teeth, his pointed canines showing. "Yeah, he's really sorry about that. I mean, *really* sorry. He's apologizing profusely." He turned to the rug. "Slow down, I can't interpret everything you're saying if you're rushing through things. I know, but I can't tell her while you keep talking." He straightened his spine and then flopped down on the chaise chair beside the window.

I climbed onto the bed and sat cross-legged. "I'm ready."

"Kasim says that he's sorry he didn't tell you the truth about why he wanted to rob the house that night. When you told him about the dagger, he knew he needed it. The dagger is part of a story he uncovered when he stole . . . something from someone else. What did you call it?" Taylin looked at the rug.

Father unrolled and flung his top two corners out.

"Ah, he found a special book about mystical artifacts. He was hoping that the dagger would have magical components and could help him, but it was part of a set and he knew that meant he needed the other half."

"We found it on Daryabar," I replied. "I used the dagger to unlock a chest and inside was a griffin feather. Mihrage was supposed to use it to somehow save his sister from a curse, though I don't know whether or not it worked, because I haven't seen them since."

The rug seemed to slump.

"It seems that way," Taylin replied to him. He then looked at me. "Your father was hoping it would be something else."

"As was Sinbad. Perhaps the story was written that way

to hide the real treasure?" I shrugged. "But what does it matter now? What artifact were you looking for, and what were you hoping to do with it?"

"He was hoping to be able to . . ." Taylin paused and looked at the rug. "You don't want me to? And why not?" He rolled his eyes. "Things like that are what get you in trouble," he mumbled. "Fine, fine. Your father is refusing to let me tell you what he wanted with it, but I will tell you it has to do with what Sinbad wanted you to ask Captain Nadeem about." He raised his eyebrows.

I heaved a frustrated sigh. "Well, Captain Nadeem refused to tell me too." I climbed off of my bed. "I'm frustrated with you that you continue to hide things from me, even after everything I've gone through! Do you have any idea how much it hurt me when I was told you'd been killed? Or that I mourned at your grave? And Igborg did too! Or maybe you know and you just don't care."

The rug staggered toward me, trying to walk on two corners.

But I stormed away and to the door. "If you're going to keep secrets, then I will too." I held the door open just long enough for Igborg to decide to leave his munched-on meat behind, and I then slammed it shut behind us.

How in all of the sands of time could Father still want to keep secrets after everything?

How dare he!

Maybe I don't need him. I've been doing fine without him. I regretted thinking it the moment I thought it. I wanted nothing more than to have my father at my side. But what good was a rug I couldn't hold a conversation with?

I had more important things to worry about, like trying to figure out if Mithra was up to something or try and overhear the conversation with Shorix. I decided on snooping on Mithra, since Abudar would likely be in the meeting with Shorix, and then when we got together that night, I could fill him in on whatever Mithra had done.

The practice room was on the opposite side of the palace, and I glanced more than once up toward the ceiling. It was high enough off the ground I wouldn't be noticed easily by people directly under me, but I wasn't certain scooting along the edge of the moldings or leaping from the hanging lanterns was a better or less secretive way to travel to the practice room.

Instead, I opted for the highly more likely way of being caught—walking out in the open. I knew about the servant staircases, however, since Arash had led me down one to the dungeon. If the servants walked around the palace, they did so without being seen, which meant there were secret passages, which meant I actually *could* make my way around the palace without being seen.

I only had to find one of those entrances and then find my way to the practice room from there.

With my expertly trained thief eyes, I spotted a crack in the wall that didn't line up with the stones. Using that as my guide, I pushed my hand along the edge until I found the side that pushed open and entered the passageway behind it.

The dimly lit corridor followed the sharp angles of the walls. The first time I encountered a servant, I avoided eye contact at all costs but felt his eyes staring at me in silent confusion. By the fourth servant, I didn't care anymore if they saw me. I hadn't expected the corridor to be empty, but I certainly hadn't expected it to be so busy!

The secret doors on this side were labeled with the name of the room into which they entered, which made it significantly easier for me to find the practice room. There were no servants in this area.

I drew a deep breath and turned the handle as slowly as possible to avoid any sound. When I pushed the door open a crack and peered through it, I found Mithra up on a stool with a black staff in her left hand, waving her right through the air.

She suddenly stopped and thumped her staff on the ground. "No, no, no!" she shouted. "That wasn't right!" She jumped off the stool and kicked it over. "How am I supposed to become the most powerful sorceress in the world if I can't even summon a creature?"

What sort of creature would she try to summon? And why?

"You are close, Mithra," a man's voice said.

I looked around the room the best I could, trying to identify the man who spoke, but without being able to open the door fully, there was an entire half of the room I couldn't see.

"Use your familiar to support your spell. That's what a familiar is for. Feel Samira's energy and pull her power to you."

My brows furrowed. When had Mithra received her familiar? From what I knew, a sorceress earned their animal companion when they mastered their magic or found what they were supposed to be, or something along those lines. But I knew it was a big deal for a sorceress to earn her familiar. Did Abudar know?

"This is futile," Mithra grumbled. "Samira, come here." She looked over her shoulder and motioned with her hand.

It was only when the black coiled rope moved that I realized it wasn't rope at all, but a massive black snake. It slithered smoothly to Mithra and poised with its tail curled behind it and head held high. It was relaxed but still reached Mithra's shoulder.

Mithra stroked the snake's head. "This will be our first time connecting. I don't know how it will feel."

"I trussst you," the snake replied.

Mithra drew a deep breath and took her position. This time, however, she held her free hand with the palm extended toward Samira's head. *"Iftah ya bowaba. Akshifak."*

I recognized the spell to open a portal, but what I didn't expect to see was a portal lying on the ground. I expected even less to see that portal swirl with black light—if blackness can have a glow.

A sense of dread gripped my heart.

"Iqrab!" Mithra said and held up her staff.

A red ruby at the top of the staff glowed vibrantly, and purple magic swirled from her hand up and down the staff.

From the portal, a clawed hand reached up and gripped the edge of the floor, and then another. Its skin was gray. The creature dragged itself the rest of the way from the hole, revealing a ghoul with pointed ears, white glowing eyes, and a long tongue that reached out toward Mithra before it retreated behind yellowed pointed teeth.

Mithra smiled and I didn't recognize her.

I must have gasped or made some sort of noise, because Samira, the snake, whipped her head in my direction and flicked her tongue. With speed I never could have anticipated, she slithered in my direction and I had to quickly shut the door without slamming it.

I didn't wait to see what happened. I ran as fast as I could through the secret passages. I had to get to Abudar. I had to warn him about Mithra and the black magic.

Whatever Mithra was doing, it wasn't good, and she was placing everyone in the palace in danger.

Twenty-Two

I knew I was supposed to stay hidden, to wait until nightfall and meet Abudar in his room and give him the information I knew, but if the sultan and sultana were meeting with Shorix, they all deserved to know what Mithra had been doing while The Veil had Abudar.

Once I reached the main floor through the servant's tunnels, I didn't bother to remain hidden. I ran out in the open, across the hallway, and to the throne room—where I assumed the meeting would be held.

I burst into the room, interrupting the conversation.

Sultan Zayne sat on the throne with tight lips, his jaw tense, his eyes narrowed. I'd seen that look somewhere, I just couldn't place it.

Sultana Shahira sat at his side, and Abudar sat beside Princess Roseline across from Sorceress Shorix. My mother stood at the end of the circle, nearest the door, her back to me.

But all eyes shot to me when I interrupted.

Abudar stood. "What is it?"

I closed the door behind me and grabbed Igborg from the ground. "I went to spy on Mithra, like you asked, and she's definitely the one behind wanting to keep us separated and there's something even worse. She's definitely the one behind wanting to keep us separated. Not only that, but she's meddling in dark magic. I just saw her summon some sort of demon."

Abudar glanced at my mother. "Roshanak was actually just telling us the same thing."

My mother nodded. "This morning, I confronted Mithra. I received a letter from Shorix explaining how Mithra visited The Veil a few days ago and one of the young students claimed she no longer had the ability to use magic because Princess Mithra took it from her."

I gasped. "Nadine!"

Roshanak paused and glanced at Shorix.

The sorceress's eyebrows furrowed. "How do you know of her?"

I walked closer to them. "I met her when I rescued Abudar. It's a long story, but I was injured and she said she would have to get a different sorceress to heal my wounds because she couldn't anymore."

Shorix nodded.

Sultan Zayne extended his hand toward my mother. "Continue catching her up."

"I didn't believe Mithra had the power to do such a thing," my mother continued, now speaking to all of us. "To *know* such a spell is difficult on its own. But to have the strength to cast a spell so dark is another thing entirely."

"The biggest reason I came today was to speak with Roshanak," Shorix cut in. "Last night, my very best student, Parisa, was murdered. Her body was uncovered outside of our school. I spoke with all of the girls and a couple of them mentioned seeing Grand Sorceress Roshanak there after our lessons ended for the day."

"But it couldn't have been Roshanak, she was with us

last night," Sultana Shahira said.

Shorix shook her head. "That was why I had to come immediately."

"You think she took on Roshanak's features and . . . *murdered* someone?" Abudar asked in disbelief. "Mithra may be a lot of things, but a murderer?" He shook his head.

Roshanak folded her hands together. "I felt the same way as you, Prince Abudar. I feared she may have found an artifact, perhaps even one so dangerous it corrupted her mind. When I asked her about it, she uttered the very spell that would have ended my life and given my power to her. Luckily, I managed to escape."

"She tried to kill you?" Sultan Zayne asked, brows pinched.

My mother nodded.

The sultan's jaw flexed ever so slightly.

Where had I seen that expression?

Roseline spoke up. "I noticed she has been able to cast spells without using the words for them."

"I too witnessed that," Mother added.

"Why would she do all of this?" Sultana Shahira asked out loud. Though she was looking at Abudar, she seemed to speak to herself.

Abudar shook his head, answering her question mutely.

Sultan Zayne ran his hands down his face. "She asked me to fire you, Roshanak. She wants to be the grand sorceress. But I simply cannot believe she would kill a person so she could be a sorceress. She is one already!"

Roshanak shook her head and began to pace. "When I spoke with her earlier, she mentioned that she wanted to be seen, beyond people seeing her as beautiful."

"Did I mention she summoned a ghoul?" I interjected.

Again, all eyes settled on me.

I cleared my throat and held Igborg a bit tighter to my chest. "I *think* it was a ghoul. I could be entirely wrong."

"What do we do to stop her?" Roseline asked.

"I think we should talk with her," Abudar said. "We cannot be irrational. She's still the princess and a member of our family." He looked at his parents when he said that. "First thing tomorrow morning, one of the servants can tell Mithra that I want to practice with her or see her. We can all be in the practice arena, and when she arrives, we can talk with her."

"I can put a spell on the door to have it lock behind her," Roshanak offered.

"And I can ensure there is a ward on the floor to trap her, just in case she tries to use her dark magic against us," Shorix added.

"What do you think?" Abudar asked his parents.

"Did she tell you why she wants to the be the grand sorceress?" Sultana Shahira asked her husband.

The sultan slowly shook his head, as though searching his memories to recall her words. "No. But . . . she does have something to hold over my head and . . . I-I fear what your reactions will be if you were to learn it from her instead of me." He fiddled with the sleeves of his shirt.

Shahira's brows dipped. "What are you talking about?"

The sultan's eyes then settled on me.

With his attention, my stomach dropped and everyone else soon stared at me too.

He lifted his eyes to me. "I am sorry, Caspara. I am so sorry." He turned to his wife and took her hand in his. "You know all I have ever wanted is to protect our family and the people of our land. I made a decision on my own to do that, and I fear that decision has set wheels in motion I cannot stop."

"Zayne, what is it?" Shahira placed her hand on his cheek. "Tell me!" she begged.

"It was I who took Kasim's life."

And then I saw it.

That face, outlined in white the night the third weaver revealed to me the fate of my father. It was Sultan Zayne's face etched with anger and malice. Sultan Zayne's hand who drove forth the blade that slayed my father.

My breath caught.

Abudar snagged my hand and held on to me. "How could you do such a thing?" he almost shouted.

My body trembled in such fury, I couldn't get a word out. I had thought for the last two weeks about what I would do when I faced the person who had killed my father. Now, he stood in front of me.

The sultan.

My chest flared in anger and I had to turn away because I was afraid I might punch him square in the nose. Or worse. If I did that, I would get arrested.

Zayne shook his head. "He was part of an order, the Griffin Syndicate. I have been keeping a close eye on their movements for some time, but when he was brought to me, finally caught with the Serpent of the Duban, I had to stop him before he killed me and took everything from you."

"You killed him just so I would be king?" Abudar asked incredulously.

The sultan released his wife's hands and leaned forward.

I took a step back, instinctively grabbing the dagger on my hip.

Sultan Zayne didn't see my movement. "The syndicate wanted to do more than usurp the throne, Abudar. It wanted to destroy it completely, meaning they would kill anyone who remained in the bloodline. You *and* Mithra would have been killed. And then *they* would have taken the throne."

"But why would they want that?" I demanded. "My father was peaceful! All he wanted was what was best for our people and the poor in our land."

Zayne shook his head. "Kasim had this planned for years. He was going to use the Serpent of the Duban to . . ." His eyes finally settled on me and he heaved a sigh. "Caspara, I know you don't know any of this. But I can prove it to you." He dug into his pocket and withdrew a handkerchief. "The members of the order wear these." He held the handkerchief out to me.

I clenched my teeth and snatched the bundle from his hands and unwrapped it with shaking hands. My eyes widened when I revealed a silver griffin feather pendant just like the one I wore around my neck.

"That was worn by a thief who came to me just before the Desert Trials," Sultan Zayne went on to explain. "A woman warned me of their plans."

"A woman?" I whispered tightly.

He nodded. "Your aunt Jade."

I threw the pendant to the floor and got to my feet. "My father . . . you're saying he was a member of this *Griffin Syndicate* and that all they wanted to do was overthrow you? He was going to steal a serpent statue to help with that? And you killed him so he couldn't?"

Sultan Zayne licked his lips and rose to his feet as well. "It's a bit more complicated than that, but yes."

"Then why do you have members of this order sitting

by your side?" I snapped.

Sultan Zayne's brows pinched. "What?"

"Captain Sinbad told me your own captain of the guard is a member of this supposed order. But when I spoke with Captain Nadeem, he wouldn't tell me anything."

Zayne's shoulders slumped. "Nadeem was helping him?" he murmured.

Abudar looked up at me with pity. "I swear I didn't know."

"Caspara, I had to keep my family safe," Zayne said.

Without a care for my own life, I stormed up to the sultan and slammed my palm into his chest. "You *murdered* my father. A man who was once one of your friends! How could you think I would believe that you had no other motive and no other choice?"

Sultan Zayne looked down at me with sorrow in his eyes. "I *never* wanted to kill him."

"Then you could have come up with another way!"

"And how was I supposed to do that?"

"Talk to him!" I shouted. "Keep him locked in prison! You could have met with him and spoken with him about his demands and—"

"I did," the sultan interrupted. "On more than one occasion. He was always angry with me for how I took Shahira from him. When he lived in the palace with Roshanak, I would often catch him staring at her. More than once, I spoke with him about his actions and how they were inappropriate, but he was still madly in love with her."

Sultana Shahira appeared just as upset as I was. "I never saw this. Why didn't you come to me? Why didn't you tell me of any of this? I could have spoken with him."

Sultan Zayne reached out and took her hand. "I suppose

a part of me feared you still loved him too."

Her lip trembled and she pulled away.

"I don't believe you," I growled at Sultan Zayne and balled my hands into fists. "My father may have been a thief, but he never would have plotted *murder*."

Sultan Zayne shook his head. "You don't have to. But it's the truth. I am sorry you're learning things about your father that are difficult."

"They're lies!" I turned to Abudar. "They have to be! My father would *never* try and kill the sultan. He would never create a secret order to usurp the throne! And if you honestly felt guilty about killing him, *sultan*, you wouldn't have kept it a secret. You would have charged him with treason and had a formal trial and executed him in public with the entire city as witnesses."

Sultan Zayne's shoulders were slumped, his brows softened, and he looked at me with nothing but a helpless expression.

Abudar bit his lip. "Kasim hid from you that you are a sentinel. Perhaps that was also for a reason?"

I shook my head, my mind swirling. I backed up to a chair near the window and collapsed.

Everything I thought I knew about my father . . . couldn't be a lie.

Sultana Shahira made her way to me and knelt at my feet. She cupped my face in her hands and looked at me through tears in her eyes. "I am so very sorry, Caspara."

"Why would he do any of that?" I demanded, knowing she couldn't answer such a question if she hadn't even known about his death herself.

The queen of our land shook her head, just as lost as I was. "I don't know," she whispered.

My chin trembled and I felt hot tears sting my eyes. I rubbed at them. "You need to stop Mithra before she does something we're all going to regret." I stood and pushed past Sultana Shahira.

Abudar caught me and tried to pull me into his arms.

I pressed my hand on his chest and pushed him away, then shook my head. "I can't. Not right now."

Igborg ran after me as I left the room.

I had met with the sultan and sultana to warn them about their daughter, but instead found myself trapped in a nightmare I didn't even know was part of my life.

They could deal with the princess.

I needed to confirm whether or not Sultan Zayne was being honest with me.

Twenty-Three

I ran from the palace, across the gardens, and out of the gate. Igborg ran hard to keep up but eventually spread his wings and flew after me. I didn't stop until I reached Aunt Jade's shop, pounding on the door when I found it locked.

I heard the lock rattle and stepped back to wait impatiently for her to open the door.

Jade wore a pale blue kaftan and had her hair uncoiled from the two braids she typically kept it in. "Caspara! It has been some time since you stopped in for a visit." Her smile faltered. "What is wrong?"

I grabbed the pendant on my neck and jerked hard, snapping the chain, then held it out and dumped it in her hand. "You owe me an explanation," I demanded.

Her shoulders fell. "Let me get some tea," she replied softly.

Igborg scrambled his pudgy little body up onto a stool and rested his front claws on Jade's counter.

Jade returned a moment later with a bowl of water for him and a few cups and tea for the two of us. We sat at her table.

Jade stared at the pendant looking at her with accusation. She reached out and touched the edge carefully, as though it might cut her. "I had hoped not to see this again."

"You told Zayne my father was going to kill him?" I blurted, cutting right to the chase.

She shook her head. "Caspara . . ." She lifted her gaze to me. "I have seen so much bloodshed and heartache in my life. When Kasim lost Shahira . . ." She shook her head. "It was too much for him to bear. Even though he had me, our relationship was never quite the same. Everything changed once you and Arash were born, and I thought he would finally be happy." She smiled fondly.

"What changed?" I asked.

"Roshanak abandoned you." She closed her eyes and leaned back with a weary sigh. "He decided then that no one should be trusted. He still harbored a lot of anger toward Sultan Zayne, and I suppose he somehow blamed Zayne for what Roshanak did, though I could never convince him otherwise."

"Did you know Sultan Zayne killed him?"

Jade looked at me and new sorrow filled her dark eyes. "He did?" She hadn't known. She closed her eyes and leaned forward to place her head on her hand. "I knew he had been arrested and suspected it was for more than only theft, but . . . no. I didn't know Sultan Zayne killed him," she admitted in a whisper.

I looked down at my tea and watched the steam roll off of it. "Did Father . . . even love me?"

"Of course he did!" Jade didn't hesitate to grab my hand. "Don't you ever doubt that. He might not have been perfect and he may have done things I know he regretted, but there is no way Kasim never loved you. You were his world. He wanted everything for you."

"Then why hide all of this from me? Why lie?" I shook

my head, unable to comprehend.

Jade wiped a tear from my cheek. "I sometimes imagine it's because in his heart he knew he was wrong. But sometimes we're so stuck in our thoughts and views we cannot see the truth. Or what we might lose if we fail."

I shook my head. "I am . . ." I paused, searching for the right words to express how I felt. "My father . . . he was supposed to protect people. The fourth rule of the thieves is not to kill. The value of a life is more than that of gold. If the sultan was being honest, then . . . I am ashamed of my father."

"Do not be. You're an admirable young woman with a future of your own before you. What Kasim did will in no way reflect upon your own life. Your decisions are your own."

"Am I to forgive the sultan?"

Jade leaned back and sipped her tea. "I cannot answer that for you."

My gaze settled on the feather pendant. "What do other girls worry about when they're my age?" I asked, feeling defeated.

Jade laughed and I lifted my gaze to her, unable to hold back a little smile of my own at her warmth. She patted my hand. "They worry about boys, clothes, and their career." She stood and carried the tea cups back to the kitchen.

I looked around the small shop. In spite of how much I longed for a "normal" life, my life was anything but that.

Other girls my age *needed* to have the opportunity to worry about nothing more than their looks or husbands. They deserved to have a safe place to grow up. If I left Abudar behind to deal with his sister on his own, I would take that peace away.

I looked down at the black markings on my arm. I had been given them by someone who believed in me. Telama not only knew I could be a hero for my people, but she knew I needed the help of her and her sisters along the way. I'd never heard of a person who met all of the fates in their lifetime. I'd heard stories of Sultana Shahira saving our city, and I knew she was trying to save the sorceresses, but I'd never heard of a young woman who changed the world.

"What are you thinking?" Igborg asked.

I moved my gaze to him. "I think it's time I become a sentinel."

He trilled and wagged his tail. "Abu will be happy."

"I think he will be too." I went into the kitchen and hugged Jade.

"No matter what you learned about your father tonight, or what that may do to your opinion of him, just know that he loved you no matter what."

I let go of my aunt. "He's still around. I met one of the weavers, and she showed me that he was reincarnated as a flying rug."

Jade blinked at me and looked around. "A . . . flying rug?"

"I know it sounds silly when I say it that way, but it's true." I knew I could call for him and prove it, but I wasn't in the mood to see him or talk to him in that moment.

Jade reached out and placed her hand on my arm. "We'll have plenty of time to talk about him, and maybe one day I can see this rug you're talking about."

I placed my hand over hers. "Did you feel like you were betraying my father when you told the sultan what he was planning?"

Jade's eyes filled with sorrow and she nodded. "I loved

Kasim. He's all the family I had, besides you. Had I known Zayne was going to kill him . . ." Her voice caught and she touched her throat. Her chin trembled and she drew a steadying breath. "I have wept over it. But we cannot change the past. We can only learn from our mistakes and move forward. It doesn't mean we don't have regrets."

"I wish life wasn't so complicated."

"As do I. It appears we are some of the lucky few."

I rolled my eyes. "Lucky? Hardly." I released my hair from the ponytail I had it in, ran my fingers through it, and then adjusted the ponytail so it was on top of my head. "I'll speak with you soon."

"Good luck, Caspara. You're going to make an incredible sentinel." Jade gave me a proud smile.

It was strange to think that just three weeks ago, my life had been relatively normal for a thief. Taraji had been flirting with Mihrage, Father had been scoping out our next target, and I had been given the green light to lead that next mission. Now, I was a sentinel and the daughter of a man who wanted to overthrow the throne and of the grand sorceress, with a dragon as my companion, and who had a crush on the prince like every other girl in the land.

The palace didn't seem so grand as I approached it that night. I was exhausted from all of the thinking and worrying, and for some reason felt it was necessary to remind myself that I still didn't know if Mihrage had saved his sister from her curse and if he and Taraji had made it back to the thieves safely.

But I didn't go to my room. I found myself standing outside of Abudar's and was still trying to talk myself out of knocking while I raised my hand, but apparently I couldn't come up with a good enough excuse *not* to visit him and found myself knocking on his door.

He opened his door with his shirt off, revealing the muscles he'd clearly worked hard for. He smiled immediately. "Caspara. I didn't think you would come back tonight. To be honest, I didn't think you'd come back at all. And I wouldn't blame you, of course. Come in."

I hurried in and stood with my back against the tapestry in his room while focusing on the bed so I couldn't see him—no, the mirror! Oh, looking in the mirror I could still see him. The window. Yes, the window was a great option to stare at.

From the corner of my eyes, I saw Abudar fold his arms across his chest. "Caspara?"

"I'm ready to be who I was meant to be. I know I was able to defend myself against Sinbad because I am a sentinel, and I can't change what my father did, but that doesn't mean I forgive your father either. Still, you need my help dealing with your sister right now." I finally stole a glance at him.

Completely unashamed of being shirtless, Abudar lowered his hands to rest them on his hips and stood just a couple of feet from me. "Look, I know you're dealing with a lot on your own," he finally said. "But you don't have to *be* alone."

"That's why I'm standing in your bedroom instead of out in the desert," I replied. I fiddled with my fingers. How could I admit to him that I stood in his room because I *wanted* to be with him?

Abudar closed the gap between us with a single step and lowered his arms to his sides. "Standing in my bedroom instead of anywhere else?" he said softly.

"Where else would I go?" I asked. "You're the only

person . . ." I bit my lip, averted my gaze, and started to turn away.

Abudar grabbed my chin and redirected my gaze to his. "You have a whole family of people who love you. Your friends, the thieves, Igborg, even the jinni. But more importantly, I do."

I stared up into his amber eyes in disbelief. "You . . . what?"

"I love you, Caspara," he whispered. And, like he had the night in the courtyard, Abudar leaned down and pressed his lips to mine.

Even though I had fought against my desires and tried to talk myself into not wanting him because he was engaged to someone else, I melted into his touch. Because I did want him. I loved how he made me feel safe, how he respected me, and how he wanted the best for me. I wasn't ready to let him go.

I wrapped my arms around his neck and held him in for another kiss. And then another.

Abudar dug his fingers into my hair and our noses pressed against each other.

The only reason we broke was to breathe.

Abudar grinned down at me, his dimples showing.

And I smiled up at him the biggest smile I'd felt on my face since my father had been arrested weeks ago. But it slipped. "What about Roseline?" I asked.

He shook his head and set me back on my feet. I hadn't realized he'd pulled me up against his body. "We spoke about how we feel for each other and about the wedding. She admitted she's in love with someone back home, and I spoke to my mother about the wedding. She wants me to be happy and sort of likes you." He winked.

I moved my hand down to his cheek. "I like her too. She's been so warm to me."

"Do you want to give us a try, then?" Abudar's fingers played with my hair.

"Yes," I replied without hesitation. I kissed his lips. "Yes, I want to see if we can make this work. Because you're everything I didn't realize I needed in my life."

Abudar closed his eyes and pulled me close once more, and this time as I kissed his lips and tasted his tongue. He picked me up and I wrapped my legs around his waist.

He really was everything I didn't know I was missing. Abudar had always been honest with me, while my father—the only other man in my life—had lied about so much. Abudar believed in me, even when I didn't believe in myself. He was patient. He was kind. I didn't have a terrible life growing up, but I couldn't wait to see how my life would improve with him at my side.

Twenty-Four

I woke in my bed. Abudar had walked me to my room, holding my hand, both of us nothing but smiles. My cheeks had hurt from smiling so much. And even when I woke, I found myself smiling from ear to ear.

Igborg rested his heavy head on my belly. "I'm hungry."

"You're always hungry." I giggled and dragged him all the way up on my chest. "But I am too. We should eat before we confront Mithra." I held him close while I rolled off the bed.

I hummed as I set Igborg down on the window's ledge and opened the door of the closet. My jaw dropped. It was filled with all kinds of outfits to choose from. From full-length kaftans to long, comfortable shirts and pants. Either this was a room to store extra clothes by either the sultana or princess and simply forgotten, or it was specifically for guests.

"Caspara, you are happy," Igborg said.

I held up a yellow shirt and looked at myself in the full-length mirror. My gaze moved from the shirt to my face. I was smiling. "Yes. I am very happy." I looked over at the dragon.

"Why?"

"I think . . . because I'm going to be a sentinel, I'm in love with Abudar, and I think I have finally found where I belong." I walked over and kissed him on top of the head, then returned to the closet. "What color should I wear?" I called.

When I returned to the main room with a maroon-and-gold shirt in one hand and turquoise-and-gold dress in the other, I almost dropped them both when I walked out to find Abudar in my room.

"I wish you would have knocked!" I scolded and ducked back into the closet, but peeked my head out.

"I did," he said. "Igborg told me I could come in." Abudar smiled at me, his cheeks a bit rosy.

My heart fluttered. "What do you think I should wear?" I held both up.

"Definitely the maroon dress," Taylin said. From where he lounged on the bed.

I quickly looked over at the jinni and sucked in a breath. "I wish you would let me know when you were going to show up too!"

He laughed. "I had to come out and visit cute Prince Abu." Taylin jumped off the bed and threw one arm around Abudar's shoulders and patted his cheek. "I believe I should say congratulations?" He nudged his head toward me and wiggled his eyebrows.

Abudar's cheeks grew a bit more red. "We've only kissed. We aren't engaged."

"I'm so happy you two have finally confessed your feelings for one another!" Taylin squeezed Abudar's cheek like an aunt would and ran to me as I was about to close the closet door to change.

"You know, I may have to use my third wish on

something else," I said to him.

Taylin stopped in his tracks and frowned. "Why is that?"

"Abudar's sister is meddling with dark magic." I closed the door.

Beyond it, I heard Abudar heave a sigh and catch Taylin up on everything while I got dressed in the maroon kaftan. I left the closet while braiding my hair in a little more elaborate braid than normal. I took three thin strands and weaved them together from the front of my head, all the way across the top of my head, and down the back.

Taylin leaned against the wall beside the window, stroking Igborg's spine. "This is a difficult matter to solve."

"We're going right now to see if we can stop her. Oh, that reminds me." Abudar grabbed a basket I hadn't noticed from my bed. "I brought you and Igborg breakfast, since you're trying to stay hidden. And you look absolutely beautiful." His eyes drank me in.

I blushed and ran my hand over the expensive material. "Thank you. I think the room across the hall has a table."

"Yeah," he replied, but remained standing.

"Someone is a little lovestruck," Taylin said, leaning to my ear.

"Who?" Abudar asked, coming to. He then scowled a little and opened the bedroom door.

I couldn't help but smile as I followed him from the room and to the room across the hallway. Taylin followed, hands in his pockets, and I heard Igborg's little claws scurrying right behind.

Abudar set the breakfast out on the table and then pulled the chair out for me. He glanced at Taylin. "Maybe you should go away," he said in a low voice.

Taylin grabbed a handful of grapes and began eating them one by one. "I have been stuck in there for days. I want some sunlight. Pretend I'm not here." He faced the window and closed his eyes.

Abudar shook his head and sat down. He gave me an apologetic look. "I sort of wanted this a bit more romantic."

I reached across the table and took his hand. "I am happy to be here regardless of who our company might be. I don't think I'm getting rid of Igborg anytime soon, so he'll always be with us."

Abudar chuckled and looked down at the floor. "Where did he go?"

I looked around the room. "Igborg? Igborg!" I went to stand, but Abudar didn't let go of my hand.

"He will be fine," Abudar said. "Taylin would love to go get Igborg. Won't you?" He gave Taylin a stiff, demanding smile.

"Would you? He's probably headed to the kitchens. He's going to frighten your cooks."

The jinni rolled his eyes dramatically and dropped the three grapes left on the vine in front of Abudar. "Only because I love the little dragon." Taylin disappeared.

I giggled. "It's like having a child. Not that I would know what that's like."

Abudar chuckled, relaxing. He let go of my hand. "Mother, Shorix, and Roshanak have been creating a ward. It's like magic painted within a symbol that activates when touched."

"A magical trap. Sort of self-explanatory," I pointed out.

"Not all wards trap someone," he explained. "Some set off alarms, others release poison, you can even make one to explode. This one, however, *is* to trap Mithra. They're painting it on the floor in the practice room so when she enters she'll activate it."

I nodded. "That sounds good. And then what?"

"And then . . . they'll talk to her." He sighed. "I know we haven't always gotten along, but . . . she's my sister. I still love her. And if we're right about this, if she really is doing something dangerous . . . I want to help her. If she has a cursed artifact, it could have taken control over her without her even realizing it."

I stabbed two slices of the boiled eggs. "I can tell you love her. And you're right—if she needs help, we're the only ones who can help her."

Abudar nodded. "I only hope we're not too late."

"Don't think that way. You're always the positive one, remember?"

He chuckled. "Forgive my negativity." He scooped some lentils onto his naan and bit it.

Even though we both wanted to sit and eat slowly while enjoying each other's company, we didn't have much time before Mithra would be awake, eating breakfast, and then entering the practice arena to begin her daily routine.

After our rushed meal, we headed for the practice room.

However, we ran into Taylin, who stood at the top of the stairs. He pouted. "I can't find the little dragon. I thought he might be outside flying or lounging in the library, but I just cannot seem to find him."

I put my hand on Taylin's shoulder. "He's ravenous right now. I told you I believe he's in the kitchen. I'll go get him and you can keep him safe while we meet with Mithra."

"Caspara," Abudar began.

I was already headed down the stairs.

I found Igborg in the kitchen, as suspected. I spotted his tail up on a shelf behind a bundle of what appeared to be freshly acquired meat. I could hear the tearing of the fabric packaging and his happy little munching noises.

"Dragons," I whispered under my breath. "Igborg, you can't be in here," I said as I reached up to get him.

"I'm eating." He moved his tail away.

I grasped the meat and pulled it down, but he had gripped a chunk in his sharp little teeth and was pulling against me.

"You can still eat, but not in here," I said as softly as I could. "Abudar and I have to get to the practice room."

He growled. "I eat," he said through gritted teeth.

"Igborg," I scolded.

He shook his head, tearing off the piece he was trying to get. He gobbled it down, then spread his wings and floated to the ground at my side. "More, please."

"You're lucky you're so cute," I said.

He seemed to smile up at me.

I looked down at the meat in my hands. He'd already eaten half of whatever it used to be. I heaved a sigh and shook my head. "Taylin will take this with you and you can eat it in the room. But you have to stay there. Understand? You can eat all of this, but then you need to stay in there and soak in water or sleep. You can't let Princess Mithra know we're here, remember?"

"Oh. Right." He bobbed his little blue-and-green head up and down as though he'd completely forgotten, even though we'd been hiding.

I crouched and kissed the top of his head. "I love you so much."

He nuzzled me. "I love you too."

I returned to the top of the stairs, handed Taylin the lump of dragon-chomped meat, and turned to Abudar. "Are you ready?"

His lips spread into a big smile. "I'm sorry, I can't help it. I just . . . was trying to imagine if Mithra or Roseline would ever come up the stairs with a huge chunk of meat in their bare hands."

"I would say more than likely, no."

Abudar chuckled and held his elbow out to me.

I blushed and glanced over my shoulder at Taylin.

The jinni smiled softly, like a proud father. And that thought made my heart ache, because I hadn't seen the flying rug that was actually my father since before I'd snooped to find Mithra the day before. It was probably a good thing, because I might have held him over a fire last night in order to get answers out of him.

We entered the practice room and Abudar apologized. "Forgive us for being a little bit late. We couldn't find Igborg."

I looked down, trying to identify where the painted ward was.

Abudar guided me in a side step around the red rug and into the main area.

I immediately felt ashamed of my closeness with Abudar when I made eye contact with Roseline, then let go of Abudar. I rubbed my hands together and turned to Sultana Shahira. "He was devouring whatever meat your cooks were curing. He's so ravenous right now, he's eating everything," I said.

"Abudar used to do that," the sultana replied. "As he was growing, he would go through these times where he would eat three or four plates of food."

I smiled.

Abudar rolled his eyes. "I was growing. You can't blame me for wanting to eat. Igborg is no different."

"It just means you must be part dragon," I teased.

He gave me that special smile, the one with the dimple in his cheek, and my heart throbbed.

I blushed and hurried to get as far away from the main doors as possible. That inadvertently put me next to my mother, whom I had expertly avoided since we'd spoken about possibly mending our relationship and the meeting the night before.

"I don't know how Shahira and I didn't see it," she said softly, just to me.

"Mithra? How could you? You were worried about The Veil taking Abudar and half of the women in the land," I replied.

She shook her head and turned to me. "Kasim's death. Shahira and I spoke last night . . . she's heartbroken over the revelation that Zayne is the one who stole his life."

I looked at the sultana and noticed for the first time that she and Sultan Zayne stood several feet apart. "He believed the lives of his wife and children were at risk. Father would have killed him to keep me safe."

Roshanak nodded. "He would have. Are you saying you're forgiving him? How?"

"I didn't say that." I shook my head. "I'm definitely not there yet, but . . . I'm saying if he's speaking the truth, it might be an understandable reason. We'll figure that out after we solve the problem with Mithra."

My mother returned her attention to the room. "You've grown a lot over the past few weeks."

"I've had to."

Twenty-Five

The doors to the room suddenly flung inward and Mithra entered. She walked a few steps in, then paused. I noticed Roshanak's eyes dart and got the impression Mithra hadn't walked in quite far enough.

Sultana Shahira stepped forward. "Mithra, come in. We can all sit over here." She gestured toward the steps leading up to one of the platforms.

Mithra didn't budge. "I had the impression this was some sort of intervention, but I thought it would be between us as a family." Her eyes locked on me and Roshanak, then to Roseline, and finally to Shorix. "Disappointing."

"We only want to talk to you," Sultana Shahira said. "We're worried about you."

Mithra smiled too sweetly. "Worried about me? Aw. You see what extremes I had to go to for you to worry about me?"

Arash stood behind her in the doorway.

"I believe I know what this is all about. After all, we can't have anyone more powerful than the head sorceress of the palace." She turned to Roshanak. "It's unfortunate you had to tell everyone about my new skillset. But I've grown tired of this game and I'm ready now to show all of you who I truly am," Mithra said.

She held out her hand and a stunning black-and-purple staff appeared. At the top of the staff was a red ruby. The same red ruby I'd seen her pocket in the Desert Trials.

"I'm not a little girl anymore," Mithra continued.

Abudar stepped forward. "Mithra, we're worried about you. That is all. We know you're been growing in magic, and I want to make sure you're safe."

She laughed. "You want me to be safe? Do I look harmed to you?"

"No, but you could be performing spells that are dangerous," Roshanak cut in. "You've been manipulating darkness, and I don't know that you fully understand what you might accidentally—"

Mithra stomped her staff on the floor, and a black plume of smoke formed from the bottom of it until it solidified into a glorious black snake. "I would like you to meet Samira, my familiar. Tell me, Roshanak. If I am doing something I shouldn't be, then why has my familiar appeared? Didn't you always tell me we would receive our familiars when we finally reached the path we were supposed to take?"

Roshanak slowly shook her head. "No. A familiar appears when you've tapped into your true self."

"Then *this* is what I am meant to be."

I stepped forward. "Mithra, your family is worried about you. You should be grateful for that."

"Don't compare my life to yours," she snapped. "You have no idea what it's like to be ignored your entire life!"

"You haven't been ignored," Sultan Zayne interrupted. He began walking toward his daughter. "You have been nothing but spoiled your entire life. You've been given everything. The best lessons to further your knowledge of magic and the way our country works, celebrations for your birthdays that would be the envy of all, everything you ever wanted—"

"You think I wanted a birthday dance while *Abudar* was given parades?" she hissed. "Do you think I wanted to hear everyone in Zunbar talk about how beautiful I am instead of how wise or talented I am?" She laughed manically. "I gave you a chance to fire Roshanak and you didn't take it. I was going to wait to do this, but I believe now is the time. After all, I've been practicing all night. *Iqrab*."

"That's the spell with the ghoul!" I announced.

A portal opened in front of Mithra, and the ghoul I'd seen the day before crawled out of its hole. And then two more crawled out, dragging someone in between them.

All the air went out of the room.

The creatures held tightly to Taraji's arms. Her wide eyes searched the room, and when they landed on me, she cried out my name. "Caspara!"

"Taraji!" I ran for her, but Abudar caught me around the waist.

"Hold on. You can't go to her."

"I can't leave her with the ghouls!" I protested.

He grabbed my face and forced me to look at him. "You can't go alone." He raised his brows and held out the jeweled dagger I'd had in my possession.

I didn't know when he'd taken it out of my bag or how long he had it, but I didn't have time to ponder on those questions and accepted it from him.

He nodded and let go of me but stepped in front of me to face his sister. "Mithra, what are you doing with Taraji?"

She pulled her staff apart, revealing a dagger above the handle. "The final step. *Qowetik melki*."

"*Awqaf!*" Abudar shouted without hesitation. An

orange flash of magic struck Mithra's chest.

Mithra's hand froze in the air.

"I wish for you to save Taraji and Mihrage!" I shouted. I knew it was my final wish, that Taylin would likely disappear, but I couldn't let Mithra do whatever horrible thing she had planned. Of course, I also didn't know if she even had Mihrage, but just in case . . .

Taylin appeared from thin air, wrapped his arms around Taraji from behind, and disappeared all in the blink of an eye.

The ghouls looked around, confused.

Mithra, now unfrozen, let out a scream so loud and so full of fury it made the entire room tremble. The scream sounded like souls being ripped apart, and we all had to cover our ears.

Abudar suddenly collapsed and I looked over to see Samira coiling around him all the way up to his head, sealing his mouth shut.

The snake flicked her tongue at me. "Shall I bind you too?" I didn't understand how it happened, but it was as if Samira was shedding her skin—but that second skin was actually a second snake.

I ran, dagger in hand, toward the princess, a girl I'd once thought of as a friend.

Arash appeared from behind Mithra and intercepted me before I could even reach the ghouls. I'd sparred with Abudar, but not with my own brother, and our weapons struck with a metallic ring that filled the air.

"This isn't your place," Arash said, pressing his sword toward the hilt of my dagger.

"Mithra, please stop this," Sultana Shahira pleaded from somewhere behind me.

"I have set my course and chosen my path," Mithra snarled. "Ghouls, attack them all!"

I looked up at my brother. "Do you truly think Mithra's plan, whatever it is, is the right thing for our people? Our family?" I challenged.

He shook his head. "I would rather be on her side than against her. I love her." He stepped back, shifting his weight, and ducked under my arm to slam his elbow into my side.

The air exploded from my lungs and I doubled over but ducked a second blow that would have rendered me unconscious.

"Arash, she's murdered someone and planned to murder Taraji! My best friend!" I said, trying to appeal to the kinder side of him that I'd met in the caves.

A ghoul lurched at me at the same time Arash kicked out. I intentionally fell backward, which made Arash's kick strike the ghoul, which then turned on him.

I scrambled to my feet and saw the entire room had erupted into spells and chaos.

Roshanak and Shorix were trying to combine spells or attack simultaneously, but Sultana Shahira's wasn't able to finish her story. Sultan Zayne was pulling her toward the door to help her escape, and Abudar was still on the ground, groaning in pain as Samira tightened around him.

I had to take care of Abudar first.

I ran toward him, barely ducking a purple magical bolt of some spell.

Shorix disappeared. Had she summoned a portal and left us here on our own?

I jabbed my dagger into the snake's coils as soon as I got close enough, and the snake hissed in pain. "Let him go!" I demanded.

Samira's coils tightened.

I stabbed her again. "Release him!" My tattoos flashed white, just like the day I'd fought Sinbad's guards and engaged my power.

With new confidence, I straddled the snake and Abudar and moved faster than I ever had before to grab her by the head.

Her eyes widened in surprise. She should have been able to avoid my moves.

I pulled on her hard. "This is your last chance to free him."

Samira's coils released immediately.

I looked at Abudar. "Grab your parents and jump out of the window. The rug will catch you."

"How do you know? Did you tell it to meet us here?" he asked, getting up to his hands and knees while gulping in breaths.

I threw Samira across the room. "I haven't, but I know he'll show up. Just get them out and I'll get Roseline!"

The poor princess had huddled in the back corner of the practice arena. With no way to protect herself, I couldn't blame her.

Someone screamed, and I looked over my shoulder to see Shorix materialize just behind Mithra. She must have made herself invisible, but Samira had discovered her location and bitten her leg.

"Yes, Samira!" Mithra laughed.

The shadows in the room quivered, and I glanced over my shoulder at Abudar as fear gripped my chest. His gaze darted to me and I could see the whites in his eyes as fear overwhelmed him too.

"Hold her tight!" Mithra ordered as she turned. "*Qowetik melki*. And I shall use it well." Her face contorted into an evil grin, and she stabbed her dagger into Shorix's chest.

Shorix groaned in agony and fell to her knees.

"No!" Roshanak shouted.

I pulled Roseline to her feet and ran to Abudar.

"She's stealing Shorix's power," he said in bewilderment, eyes still locked on his sister. "She . . . she killed her . . ."

I grabbed his face. "Abu. Run, you idiot."

He blinked as he focused on me and nodded. "Run. Yes. Mother." He turned and took his mother's hand and ran for the nearest window.

"If you leave now, you'll miss the best part!" Mithra's voice sang.

A wall of moving shadows intersected our path and we skidded to a halt. We all turned to run to the opposite side of the room but were unable to.

Mithra walked to the center of the room, avoiding the ward Roshanak had created, absolutely radiating with power. She looked terrifyingly beautiful in a lavender gown with black beads and a slit all the way up to her right hip. Her long, black hair cascaded in beautiful waves, and her brown eyes almost glowed.

"Don't you want to know what all of this was for?" she asked.

I kept my shoulder to Abudar's as we slowly began stepping backward.

Mithra reached up and plucked the ruby from the top of her staff. "Don't you want to know where I got this ruby? *Why* I did? Mother, you should recognize it. You're the one who trapped your father in it."

Shahira's breath hitched behind me and I glanced at her.

Sultan Zayne's eyes were as wide as Abudar's had been. "No. Mithra, do not tell me that you found the ruby from his staff."

"Indeed I did. In the Dragon's Lair. While Caspara got herself a magical jinni, I got myself something better." She smirked.

"You don't understand!" Zayne said.

"But I do. And now Grandfather has enough power he can take on a physical form." Mithra slammed the ruby at the ground. "*Akshifak!*"

The ruby exploded, but the pieces froze mid-explosion. And then they reversed, pulling inward to implode into billions of tiny fragments as small as grains of sand. Those fragments came together, building on one another until a man stood at Mithra's side.

A man our country knew as Khorshid.

Twenty-Six

"If you ever needed a reason to bond as sentinels, now is that moment," Taylin muttered at my side.

I jumped at his sudden presence and tightened the grip on my dagger. "I thought you would disappear when I used my last wish!"

"Yes, well, about that . . ." He grinned sheepishly. "You technically get more than three. But that's beside the point. There's a sorcerer standing just a few feet away."

My gaze darted to Khorshid and then to Abudar.

"I think Taylin is right," Abudar whispered, trying not to draw attention toward us.

"But we don't know how!" I said, desperately trying to keep my voice low.

"As I've said before, I believe you're overthinking," Abudar said. He finally turned to me and held out his right hand, brows raised. "I don't think it's complicated."

I sucked in a breath. "Okay." I sheathed my dagger and reached my right hand out to take his.

Nothing happened.

Not like it had weeks ago in the desert when we'd climbed out of the Dragon's Lair Cave and our tattoos had glowed. Not even like when we'd had the vision with Telama and had touched then.

My breath caught and I looked down at our hands and then up at Abudar. "It's not working!"

"Because you need to believe in it. You need to believe in *you*. Remember what you were told in the caves? What the weaver said to you?"

Her voice came back to me, echoed all around me. *Your worth isn't dictated by gods or destiny, but by what you choose to do and who you decide to be.*

"It has been a long time since I've seen you, Shahira," I heard Khorshid saying.

I didn't look away from Abudar's warm brown eyes.

"To have one of the brightest sorceresses of all time, *and* one of the sentinels as children . . . the gods definitely blessed you, didn't they?" Khorshid continued.

I finally nodded. "I can be a sentinel. I want to," I said aloud. And I meant it. Because what else could I be? I hadn't been born to be a thief, nor a sorceress or princess. I'd been born to step up to this role, to take on whatever power came with being a sentinel, and to protect the people of Sheblom.

Abudar quirked his heart-skipping grin and warmth spread up my arm and into my shoulder. Our tattoos glowed and filled the room with a blue light.

"Grandfather," Mithra said. "Speaking of the sentinels?"

"Ah. Tsk. They think they can stop us now, Granddaughter." He laughed.

Abudar and I simultaneously turned our heads to acknowledge the dark sorcerer.

He stood with his arms folded across his chest, a cocky grin on his face, and his eyes had a red glow in the very center of his pupils. "I've only just woken. I can't allow you to confine me again." He snapped his fingers and the room filled with cobras.

"Samira," Mithra sang, summoning forth her snake familiar.

Samira's wounds had mostly healed from where I'd just stabbed her, but she didn't seem afraid of me or my dagger at all and came slithering toward us.

Abudar stepped back, but he summoned a ball of fire to his hands and drew an arch around him in a circle, sending a wave of flames from his feet out toward the small cobras and forcing them to slither away from him.

I grabbed the nearest object and threw it at the window behind me, shattering the glass.

"The window!" Arash shouted to Mithra.

Abudar came to and dragged his parents over to the window. He grabbed Roseline next, but she pulled away and jumped out on her own.

I grabbed Sultan Zayne by the arm. "You must jump out of the window."

"We will die!" he objected.

"No, you won't. I don't have time to explain right now, but my father is a flying rug and he will catch you, but you have to jump! Now!" I shoved him.

Sultan Zayne had to put all of his faith in a crazy girl he barely knew, peered out the window, then looked at his wife. "I'll jump first. If I survive, you follow."

"Take on the girl. I've got Abudar," Khorshid said behind us.

"There's no time!" Abudar said. He shoved both of his parents out to safety.

I began running toward Mithra and Arash, having no pre-planned idea at all on what I was going to do or how I would attack. All I knew was that I needed to be a distraction so the sultan, sultana, and Roseline could escape with their lives.

My mother created a shield of magic to protect the four of them, and that was the last thing I saw when I glanced over my shoulder.

Mithra moved her right hand upward, the palm extended toward the ceiling.

I let out a shout and jumped at her.

But bars suddenly sprang up around me, trapping me in a magical prison.

I might have been intimidated or frustrated before, but my tattoos warmed and the phrase echoed in my mind once more: *Your worth isn't dictated by gods or destiny, but by what you choose to do and who you decide to be.*

I put away my dagger and made eye contact with Mithra. "You and I are friends. Mithra, you know me. We helped each other in the caves."

She rolled her eyes. "You're honestly so pathetic. I mean, I like you. I really do, Caspara. But what use are you as a sentinel? You have no power."

I grabbed the bars. "You're wrong. I don't have magic, but that doesn't mean I don't have power." I gritted my teeth and pulled the bars with all of my strength. The power in my arm rippled and surged, and the metal groaned as I pulled a gap in the bars large enough I could fit through.

Mithra's eyes widened.

I lowered my hands and looked at them, then at her. I *didn't* have magic. But I'd told myself long ago that I wasn't weak. Now I had the power to prove it.

I let out a shout and jumped from where I stood, over the cobras trying to get to me and Abudar, and landed just a few feet from Mithra.

She scrambled to come up with a spell, but I crossed the short distance between us and punched her across the face. She cried out, flew through the air, and slammed into the nearest pillar. She crumpled to the floor, unconscious.

I turned to Abudar.

He stood facing off with Khorshid, his sword pushing against Khorshid's cobra staff.

One of the cobras Khorshid summoned struck at my boots, and I scrambled backward. Out of nowhere, Igborg swooped down, grabbed the cobra in his claws, and chucked him out the window.

I stared at my dragon with wide eyes. "What are you doing? You're supposed to be—"

"Helping!" he cut in.

I was about to argue, about to insist he was too young or not experienced enough, but all I could think of was how my own father had held me back by saying those very words to me, even if he meant it for my own good and protection.

"Watch out for the snakes," I said to him.

Igborg grinned. "I can help. I've practiced," he said proudly. He sucked in a breath so deep his belly bulged, and then his belly and throat glowed orange and he exhaled an enormous fireball at the cobras on the ground.

The fire exploded, burning them to crisps.

"Way to go!" I cheered.

Igborg cleared a path and I withdrew my dagger from its sheath.

"*Barq*," Khorshid commanded. A bolt of electricity moved from his staff into Abudar's sword, up his arms, and into his body.

Abudar's teeth grimaced together and he groaned in pain. When the bolt cleared through, he fell to his knees. I noticed the tattoos on his arm weren't glowing white like mine were.

I had to get him to believe in himself again. "Your sentinel power is tied to your magic!" I shouted. "Your magic will be strengthened through your abilities as a sentinel, but you have to believe in yourself."

This caused Khorshid to turn, and I drove my dagger forward, aiming for his chest.

He held his staff out. "*Ibtaqi.*"

My movements slowed as if I couldn't control my body. My arm raised so slowly, I knew I was in trouble.

"What did you do with Mithra?" He looked in the direction we had fought and spotted her, still unconscious. "She's still so . . . mortal." His lip twitched.

Surely my sentinel power would help me fight against the magic. I pushed against it with all of my strength, trying to break the spell forcing me to slow down.

Abudar climbed back to his feet, but a pair of ghouls still in the room grabbed him by the arms and ripped his sword from his hand.

"Jinni! We could use some help here!" I begged.

Taylin appeared to my right. His eyes went wide and he snapped his fingers, dissolving the spell.

Khorshid sneered. He stomped his staff in front of him and held out his hand.

But Igborg dove for him and let out a shriek I'd never heard from him ever. Covering my ears didn't hold back the sound.

The floor beneath our feet began to break apart from the soundwaves, and I stumbled to Abudar just as he used a spell to open a portal and kick one of the ghouls through. The ground broke from beneath the second ghoul. It held on to Abudar's arm for dear life.

I unsheathed my dagger and cut off its hand without hesitation, grabbed Abudar's arm, and said, "Open a portal and get us out of here!"

"*Iftah ya bowaba*," Abudar said.

The portal opened.

"Igborg! Here!" I called.

He stopped screaming and flew to my arms. The damage was done, the practice room was collapsing, and Khorshid was forced to leave us to save Mithra.

But something slammed between my shoulder blades just as Abudar pulled me through the portal and into the room I'd been staying in.

Abudar grabbed my bag, and thus the lamp, and turned to me, but his eyes widened. "Caspara, what's wrong?"

I was gasping. The pain in my back had stolen my breath, and I struggled to catch it. "A . . . spell. My back."

Abudar threw my bag over his shoulder and slipped behind me. He lifted my shirt.

"How bad?" I asked.

I felt his finger trace something. "It must be a curse of some kind." He placed his palm on the mark and said, "*Awqaf.* I don't know if that will stop it for good, but perhaps your mother would know. Do you feel any better?" He leaned around my side to look into my eyes, his own filled with worry.

The pain began to subside and I nodded. "Yes. It doesn't hurt so bad now."

"The mark is still there." He lowered my shirt and studied my face. "Do you feel any different?"

"No. Just hurts. It stole my breath a little." I set Igborg on the bed. "Though I can't carry you. We need to get to

Jade's, that's where the rug would have carried them."

"I've never been there."

"But I have. Maybe you could use my memories to find it."

Abudar drew a deep breath and placed his hands on either side of my face. "It shouldn't hurt much."

I looked into his eyes, worry gripping me.

"It was a joke. I was trying to ease the mood." He kissed my forehead then said, *"Iftah 'aqlak elai saouf ara zikratak."*

Flashes of memories flickered through my mind—fighting against Mithra, being on the island and getting attacked by the panther, seeing Igborg in the jungle, Mihrage's father showing up out of nowhere . . .

"Focus on your aunt's home," Abudar said.

But hearing his voice, my mind began jumping to Abudar. To the night I yelled at him and hit him because I believed he wasn't the one who burned my village. And then it flew to the night Abudar kissed me in the courtyard . . . the way he made me melt . . . the way his touch and his scent warmed me and made me want him. All of those emotions.

"C-Caspara," his voice said softly. The magic, and my memories faltered.

"Don't stop! I'll focus." I said, focusing my mind on the city and Jade's shop.

Abudar's magic took hold again. "I see it. Not too far away." He lowered his hands. "Is that really how you felt that night?"

I opened my eyes and met his soft gaze. "I did," I admitted.

He touched my jaw with his knuckle. "I felt the same

emotions. Mixed with confusion because of Roseline. I was afraid of losing you . . ." He entwined our fingers together.

I blushed, unsure of how to respond. I'd never been open with anyone like he was with me. I'd never been vulnerable. "I have never felt like this with anyone before," I admitted.

He chuckled. "I suppose we should stop wasting time and get out of the palace before my grandfather finds us." Abudar raised my hand to his lips and kissed it, then summoned a portal for us.

"*Itrabati*!" my mother said as soon as we entered my aunt's shop.

Ropes wrapped around me and Abudar, binding us both.

My mother sighed. "Forgive me. I wasn't sure who it was. *Inhal*."

The spell dissolved and we were freed.

Sultana Shahira ran forward and wrapped her arms around Abudar. "I was so worried. How did you get out?"

I looked down at Igborg. "My dragon helped us. Igborg used a powerful scream that made the room collapse."

"If he can scream like that as a dragonling, I can't imagine how much more powerful it will be when he's fully grown," Abudar said.

Igborg puffed out his chest, beaming proudly.

Jade stepped around the royal family and pulled me into a hug. "I'm so proud of you."

Roseline stepped back, ducking into a corner to get out of the way.

"Thank you." I smiled and hugged her back.

When she squeezed me, my back screamed in pain and I cried out.

Abudar caught me before I hit the floor. He looked at Roshanak. "Khorshid hit her with a spell. I don't know anything about dark magic or curses. Can you help?"

My mother knelt behind me and lifted my shirt. "Oh, Caspara."

"What is it?" I asked.

"This is the symbol of the *ein el hassad'*. The Evil Eye. It is a curse. One that will cause you weakness and bad luck. It's old magic, one that isn't used anymore."

"There has to be a way to counter it," I said.

She nodded. "I'll see if Jade can help me make the amulet." She looked at my aunt, who nodded. "It is easy to counteract. You don't need to worry too much." Roshanak offered me a smile, but there were lines at the corners of her eyes that were worry and not ease.

"That's a relief," Abudar said.

I wasn't so sure.

Twenty-Seven
Mithra

I walked through the front doors of the castle where The Veil had been hiding for several days. I'd chosen to wear a lavender kaftan with dark purple designs, even though I had wanted to wear something that broke tradition. Knowing I needed these sorceresses on my side, I had toned everything down.

Caspara had left a lovely bruise on the side of my face from our encounter earlier that day, and Khorshid had shown me the destruction to the practice room, which would take months to repair.

I knew I needed to get to The Veil before Roshanak or my mother could. I needed to have them as allies in order for me to successfully take the throne.

When I entered the hideout, girls left and right stopped and stared at me.

"I need everyone gathered together," I said. "Where is the largest place to meet?"

"The first floor of the tower," one of them said, pointing to the stairs in the dining room.

"Spread the word that this is urgent. I need every sorceress there, please," I commanded.

The girls glanced at each other, then split in different directions while I went up the stairs, past the bedrooms, and into the tower to the main floor.

Every girl I passed, I told them to fetch others.

Word spread like wildfire, and within thirty minutes, the room was packed with every sorceress The Veil had taken from our land.

I pulled a chair out and stood on it so more women could see me. "I know this is sudden, and I apologize for being so abrupt. Something awful has happened at the palace, and I knew I needed to come to you."

The sea of faces glanced at each other and whispered words of curiosity.

"Shorix came to the palace yesterday and informed my parents that Roshanak committed a murder here two nights ago. That she killed Parisa, a promising student."

Sorrow filled their eyes.

I took a deep breath, making sure to keep my expression soft. "But when Roshanak was confronted, she did something none of us expected. Shorix had come to the palace to sign the final treaty granting all of us the right to learn all magic. But Roshanak took that moment from us. She murdered Shorix and took the sultan and sultana to an unknown location."

Voices erupted with gasps or shouts of horror. Like the wind, the voices picked up, all of them in disbelief that Shorix was dead and Roshanak had killed her, that the sultan and sultana were missing, and that all they'd worked for was gone.

I raised my hand, silencing them. "Please. I know this

is devastating. I want to make things right and, until my parents are returned, I shall take the throne."

"What about Prince Abudar?" someone shouted from the middle.

I placed my hand on my heart and made a pained expression. "Abudar is deceived. A member of the forty thieves, Caspara, has somehow managed to corrupt him. Perhaps you know her better as Almas. Caspara is also the daughter of Roshanak and is on her side. She gave me this bruise when I tried to save my family." I turned my face and showed them all the bruise from Caspara's fist.

"Almas is a girl?"

"Roshanak has a daughter?"

"How did the girl bruise the princess?"

I gave them several moments to explore my lies. They weren't full lies, of course, but just enough I hoped they would join me. "I fear Caspara knows your location," I said, finally silencing their voices. "Because of this, I am opening the palace as a place of refuge. Furthermore, you will be allowed to visit with your families. To come and go freely."

Eager cheers rang out, mixed with some nervous clapping.

I looked to the women who had worked at Shorix's side. "I want you all to continue to teach the girls. They can come to the palace for lessons and stay there if they so wish, but I value you and what you've been teaching. I know I cannot replace Shorix, and I wouldn't want to. But please allow me to help as I can."

They all nodded.

A woman with graying hair stepped forth. "I am Khadija. I was Shorix's right hand."

I reached my hand out and took hers. "I cannot imagine

the pain you feel right now."

She wiped a tear from her wrinkled cheek. "We fought for so much, and I am pleased you have been on our side from the beginning. I am also grateful you are opening your home to us and feel this is the right thing to do."

I pulled her into a hug. "I want to do what is best for our people. This is a good place to start." I let go of her and smiled at the others. "I can open a portal to the palace and let everyone walk through who chooses. Retrieve your personal items."

The crowd hesitated to depart and looked to their leaders, those with whom they were familiar.

Khadija stepped up to my side, and I stepped down from my chair. "Ladies, it is time for us to move on to better things. Get your personal items and we will return to Zunbar. To our homes."

Finally, the girls departed.

I turned to the leaders again. "I do not know whether or not this should be public, but I wanted each of you to know I will greatly reward anyone who returns Caspara and Roshanak, dead or alive, to me."

They glanced at one another, then nodded.

Khadija sighed. "Such destruction. Such heartache."

I placed my hand on her shoulder. "And justice must be done. No matter how heartbreaking it is to realize the person you thought you knew is deceitful."

"Open the portal and we will begin the transition back to Zunbar," Khadija said.

I opened the portal and held it open while young women my age, a little older, and a little younger began walking through. Their leaders left with them.

Excitement began to make my fingers tingle because

everything I had worked toward for months was finally coming to pass. I hadn't known Khorshid would be able to be released from the ruby, but with his guidance I was going to excel in my powers far beyond anything Roshanak could have ever taught me.

I was the last to leave the old castle and step into my palace. "There are rooms available on the third floor for your choosing, and some on the second floor on the west side of the palace. The east side is for the royal family and is off limits. Otherwise you are welcome to explore as you wish. There is a practice room damaged on the second floor from our fight this morning that needs to be repaired, so avoid that area as well. Welcome to your new home."

The girls looked at each other, some clearly trying to hide their wonder and excitement, and others completely failing to do so. They began to walk, glancing back at me to make sure what they were doing was actually okay.

"I shall be in the library over here," I said, gesturing to the blue doors. "Please let me know if you need anything." I entered the library, and my grandfather looked up from the stack of papers he had spread out on the table he stood behind.

He grinned. "Did it work?"

I smiled widely. "Yes. All of the sorceresses are here now. I need to meet each of them, or perhaps Samira can find a way to search for someone with power or personality similar to my own. I need a set of hands willing to take Abudar's life so he can't take the throne from me."

Khorshid nodded and looked over at Samira, who had been curled up in the sunlight. "She should have the power to do such a thing."

I knelt beside my familiar and stroked her smooth

scales. "Bring me a girl who can aide us."

"Yesss, Mithra." She rubbed her head against my jaw before unraveling her coils and slithering off through the crack in the door.

"I didn't tell them about you, though," I said to Khorshid as I got back to my feet. "Some of the sorceresses are old enough they either remember what happened or have heard stories about you."

He looked back down at the papers. "That was wise of you. I shall do my best to stay out of the way and hidden. In any of my journals, did I write any spells?"

I glanced over the journals he had spread before him. "Hm. Not that I can recall. Mother cleared out the Red Tower when we were children. I don't know what she did with everything after that."

"Pity." He scowled. "There was a spell in there that would have helped me. I've been trapped in that stone for eighteen years and have forgotten it at this point."

I placed my hands on the desk across from him. "When you sacrificed those women and took their magic, was your only purpose to become a sorcerer?"

He lifted his gaze to me. "That was the first step. I wanted the throne and the power associated with it." His dark eyes were full of deep anger, and even I was intimidated by his look for a moment.

I tilted my head and straightened. "And yet you are fine with me taking the throne?"

"Yes." He turned and sat in one of the chairs.

"How do I know you won't stab me in the back when we get to the ideal position?" I challenged.

Khorshid smirked at me. "Mithra, if I wanted to kill you, I would have done it earlier today when you were unconscious and vulnerable. I could have taken the throne then, because there is no one around to stop me. But I like your tenacity and I feel like you would be a very powerful leader."

I studied him, then nodded. "And I am eager to continue learning from you. For now, I must make sure the sorceresses are getting comfortable in their new home." I walked to the door and looked over my shoulder at the grandfather I only knew from his journals.

He was still watching me with that same silent, cold expression.

I stepped out of the room and closed the door.

Yes, I'd grown in power, but he was powerful too. What would I do if he did turn on me?

Twenty-Eight

I sat on a floor pillow, a warm glass of tea in my hands that Madame Kiara had made. Sultana Shahira had sent me to invite Kiara over to look at the *ein el hassad'* mark on my back, and Kiara had made some tea while she poured through a book she'd brought with her. Shahira sister stood at her side, and the two sisters spoke in a hushed tone about what to do.

Roseline slowly wandered the room, looking at all of the different articles of clothing. Sultan Zayne sat by a window and Abudar sat at my side with his head against the wall behind him, dozing.

I reached into my pouch at my side and rubbed the lamp. "Taylin, where did you take Taraji?" I asked as soon as the jinni appeared.

"She's safe with the thieves. Mihrage was already there, so I didn't need to rescue him." Taylin sat on the floor beside me and looked at me. "What are those two worried about? Or rather, three." He nudged his head toward Shahira, Kiara, and Roshanak.

I heaved a sigh. "I have the *ein el hassad'* on my back."

Taylin lifted an eyebrow. "Evil Eye? How did you get that?"

"My grandfather is back," Abudar mumbled,

apparently more awake than I thought. When Taylin didn't reply, he opened one of his eyes. "The sorcerer? Khorshid?"

Taylin shrugged. "I can't say I've heard of his name. But I was trapped in that cave a *very* long time."

I scrunched my eyes in thought. "Can I just wish the Evil Eye gone?"

He shook his head. "Not that. It's not that simple. The *ein el hassad'* is a spell, and a spell must counteract it."

"Then I wish you to tell us the spell."

The jinni chuckled and shook his head a bit. "You're smart, Caspara." He rose to his feet. "Pardon my interruption, important people. I have a solution."

The three women all turned to him.

My mother's lips parted in surprise. "You found the jinni?"

I cringed. "Um yes, I did." I'd forgotten completely that I'd lied to her and had kept Taylin a secret until now.

The sultan lifted his head for the first time. He'd been sitting in the corner of the room, staring at his hands, brooding over something none of us could pull him out of. Not that I had personally tried, but Abudar and Shahira had, and even Roshanak had tried to give him breakfast.

Taylin pointed over his shoulder. "I know how to help with Caspara's curse, but it isn't going to be an easy solution."

"And what solution are you proposing?" Roshanak asked. "For ages, we have burned incense and spoken a phrase to protect against the *ein el hassad'*."

"True, but you can't protect against what has already been cast," he pointed out. "Yes, you must burn the incense. I believe the strongest and best would be to burn aloeswood."

Kiara pursed her lips and tapped her fingers on the counter top. "I may have some of that . . . I'm trying to recall . . . yes! I know precisely where it is!" Without hesitation, she ran out of the shop.

"That's all?" I asked.

He shook his head. "That is to essentially close the *ein el hassad'*, at least for the next day. Tomorrow, you will have to burn some more to keep it closed."

"And she has to continue to do this for the rest of her life?" Abudar interrupted.

Taylin heaved a sigh and threw his arms up in the air. "If you'll let me finish speaking, I'll tell you everything. No, it's not to keep the eye closed the rest of her life. In order to do that, you will need to acquire the scale of a dragon, which must then be engraved with the symbol of the *hamsa*."

The hamsa—a hand with an eye in the palm.

I looked at Igborg, who had jumped up and run over to Taylin.

Before Igborg could say anything, Taylin shook his head. "Not you, Igborg. Your scales are too small."

"And where are we supposed to acquire a dragon scale?" Sultana Shahira asked.

"The dragon we woke," I said aloud.

Abudar's eyes widened. "The desert dragon?"

I nodded. "It's taken up a home in the Ailorn Mountains. Since the thieves are there already, it would be convenient to take your parents there for protection, and then we can pursue the dragon's scale."

"You could be killed," Sultan Zayne said.

Abudar looked at his father. "And Mithra could have killed us too." He got to his feet. "We must prevent Khorshid from being able to see our plans, just in case he has some sort of ability to spy, or they will be prepared for whatever we do."

"I cannot lose you too." The sultan's voice cracked and he looked away. "How have I failed her so much?"

Abudar walked over and knelt in front of his father. "You did not fail Mithra. She chose her path. Maybe . . . there has to be a way back for her. We'll discover that path and bring her home."

"I've got it!" Kiara announced as she burst into the room. Without hesitation, she crossed to the small fire burning in the bronze bowl on the counter and tossed a handful of the aloeswood in. "There's just enough for tomorrow, but I'm afraid that is all I have." She held out her other hand, revealing the deep-brown pieces of wood.

A thick, resin-like scent filled the air, and I felt peace settle on my shoulders. I leaned back against the wall and my eyelids felt heavy.

Taylin crouched and took my hand. "It's already taking effect. Sit here for the next thirty minutes and take deep breaths. While you meditate, the rest of us will come up with the plan to stop Mithra once and for all."

"Mother, what was it Khorshid wanted when he was alive the first time?" Abudar asked.

Sultana Shahira glanced at her sister.

Kiara heaved a sigh and rolled her eyes. "World domination?"

"He wanted to have magic, to take the throne, and to get rid of all sorceresses. He felt women shouldn't be allowed to have magic, but men should."

Abudar frowned and climbed to his feet. "Then why would he ally himself with Mithra? She's a sorceress. That goes against everything he wanted."

She shook her head. "I don't think so. In fact, the more I think about this, the more it makes sense. Mithra was desperate for help, desperate to have the very same things he desired, and he knew he'd been willing to do whatever it took to achieve those dreams, so why shouldn't she?"

Abudar rubbed the back of his neck, a thoughtful scowl marring his usually bright face. "He's using her."

"That's my fear."

"If he's using her, at what point will he be done with her?" Roshanak asked.

The room went silent and everyone looked nervously at one another.

Sultana Shahira turned to Jade. "May I have some parchment?"

"You think you can write the story and have it fulfilled?" Kiara asked. "I thought you said the story you uttered this morning didn't work."

"I believe it didn't work because I didn't use the correct words." She withdrew paper from her pocket and handed it to her sister. "I allowed a gap somewhere within that story, and Mithra stepped right through it. I don't know how, but there must be something I missed." She looked from me to Abudar. "You already have a plan. I can help that plan by perhaps easing the fear of the dragon."

Abudar nodded. "That's a good idea. I don't want to harm the dragon, so perhaps we can trade the dragon for a scale."

As soon as the new paper was in front of her, Sultana Shahira began writing.

"How do we etch a dragon's scale with the hamsa?" Abudar asked, looking to Taylin, who remained at my side.

He grinned. "Just make a wish."

I was too relaxed to join in the conversation. In my drowsy mind, everything sounded like it was planned out, and that the execution of this journey would be successful. What did I have to add?

"I'll add in here that you will find a way to reach Mithra's heart," Sultana Shahira said aloud.

Abudar walked to his mother's side and leaned over her shoulder to see the paper. His beautiful eyes scanned the words and he nodded slowly, approvingly. "I think this sounds very clear."

"I see the hole," Kiara announced, having finished reading the story from that morning that Sultana Shahira had attempted to use. "You said that you would create the trap and Mithra would enter the room, but you didn't say she would step on the trap and be captured. That's the hole. Make sure in this story you're very specific about what the dragon will do."

Shahira chewed her bottom lip. "I feel like this is dangerous. I'm essentially controlling a living creature."

"You can't technically control someone," Taylin chimed in. "Your magic wouldn't allow you to make someone do what they wouldn't normally do."

"What dragon would *give* one of their scales to a human?" Abudar countered.

"Igborg," the small dragon said with a bit of a pout on his face.

I pulled him into my lap. "Your scales are too small."

Taylin smiled. "If this dragon chooses not to help that may be another hole in your story with Mithra. If she wasn't naturally cautious, she might have stepped on that trap and sprung it. But because of her caution, she was suspicious from the moment a meeting was requested."

"He has a point," Roshanak said.

Warm spread across my legs and I looked down, noticing for the first time my father's rug lying across my lap. I reached down and put my hand on it.

"I wish he could speak. That we could all understand him." I closed my eyes.

"I can still speak with him for you," Taylin offered. When I peeked an eye open, he added, "I'm a jinni, remember? I get to make your wishes come true. Even if you only meant them in jest." He winked.

I picked up the rug. And hugged it. "I wish you were a person again."

"I can't grant that wish," Taylin said gently. "Remember? I can't bring people back from the dead."

I wiped at my tears. "I know."

He paused and then said, "Your father is sorry for everything you've been through."

I felt my chest tighten. It wasn't out of sorrow. It was anger. "I have to know the truth. Was Sultan Zayne speaking the truth? Did he kill you because you were going to murder his family?"

"He doesn't want to respond." Taylin shook his head.

"So he *was* being truthful? My father was going to kill them?" My heart tore. If I didn't know that about my father, what did I know at all?

"He wants you to know he is here with you until you find your way. Once you can manage being a sentinel on your own—"

"You mean you're going to eventually leave me?" I looked down at the rug. "After everything I've learned and we've gone through, you're going to leave me?"

The rug wiped my cheeks with its corners.

"He said yes." Taylin gave an apologetic smile.

I lowered my head, fighting tears. I'd just gotten my father back and I would lose him *again*?

"It is the only way he will be at peace," Taylin said. He took my hand. "And the only way for your heart to find peace. He will shall carry you to the Ailorn Mountains."

"I'll open a portal," Roshanak said.

The rug turned to her.

She was watching it with an unreadable expression. And then she sighed and briefly closed her eyes. "You did a wonderful job raising our daughter. I seem to have failed in raising our son. Arash has taken Mithra's side."

"Only because he loves her," I said. "He told me so when we were fighting in the palace, and in the dungeon too."

"That's our way to her heart," Abudar said. He grinned like a child and clapped his hands together. "We get to Arash, and he can speak with Mithra. If we can get him on our side, he can help us save Mithra from whatever plan she has."

I got to my feet, already feeling significantly better. "Arash and I might have had a rocky start, but I think he's open to me. At least, I hope so."

Abudar held up a finger. "So the plan is . . . we get to the Ailorn Mountains. Mother, Father, Roseline, and Roshanak hide with the thieves. Assuming we can find them?" He looked at each of them as he spoke, then held up a second finger. "We get the dragon scale and you get rid of the *ein el hassad'*. Then you and I return to the palace and find a way to get Arash away from Mithra, which is by . . . doing what?"

I pursed my lips. "Showing up?"

They all stared at me like I'd lost my mind.

"I mean it. If I look through the window at Arash and wave to him to come talk to me—"

"What's to stop him from telling Mithra?" my mother asked.

"Then Abudar casts a spell to bind him." I shrugged. "But we must be careful about it."

"We're forgetting the biggest question of all," Sultan Zayne suddenly said. He stood and held his hands out in a helpless gesture. "How do we destroy Khorshid?"

Twenty-Nine

It was my turn for an idea. I cleared my throat and rubbed my arm. "You know, we do have some allies. Maybe the Griffin Syndicate wanted to remove Sultan Zayne from the throne, but what if they learned Khorshid was going to take it? Sinbad's back on the throne, perhaps his kingdom could help too? We also have the thieves, and if Roshanak can speak to The Veil, we can have all of them on our side as well. To be honest, it would be hard to lose with all of the help we have."

"Perhaps this can be my restitution for taking your father's life," Sultan Zyane said softly. "I can speak with the syndicate myself while you're doing your own tasks. I'll reach out to Captain Nadeem."

Abudar turned to his father. "Are you sure this is a good idea? You'll be at risk—"

Sultan Zayne reached out and placed his hand on Abudar's neck, his thumb on Abudar's jaw. "It is a risk I must take. If Captain Nadeem feels he must take me into custody . . . Perhaps I'm not to be on the throne."

Abudar shook his head. "You've made mistakes, we all have, but—"

"Not ones that cost another's life."

Abudar swallowed hard.

I saw Sultan Zayne's torn expression—his regret, pain, fear, sorrow. He went to look at Shahira but stopped himself, and I suddenly wondered if the two of them had spoken since Shahira learned he had been the one to kill my father and her friend.

"Mithra still would have recovered the ruby," I pointed out. "You had no control over that."

There was a knock on the door before it opened and Kiara's son, Lycus, entered. He grinned at me and waved before looking to the older women. "The guards are searching every building for Caspara, Roshanak, and Abudar."

"Me?" Abudar asked.

"The wanted posters say Caspara bewitched you and you need to be saved." He held up our wanted posters.

I took mine from Lycus, ruffling his hair a little with a small smile as I did so.

He grinned up at me.

My last wanted poster had a picture of Almas, a thief with most features hidden. This one was my actual face with every detail for anyone to see. It was quite a difference.

"Mithra has spread lies so quickly," Roshanak said.

Sultana Shahira said, "I don't think those are because of Mithra. My father was extremely cunning. He would be behind this."

"Is now a bad time to also tell you that The Veil returned the sorceresses and they're going to be training in the palace?" Lycus asked.

"*That* would be Mithra," Shahira said.

"She's already got the sorceresses." Abudar rubbed his neck.

"Remember how I complained about being a sentinel

because I don't have magic? You don't have to have magic to win," I pointed out. "Yes, it would help, but if we use our allies, maybe we can turn the tide and the sorceresses will switch sides." I nudged him with my arm.

Aubdar smiled a little and held up his poster. "I think I'll keep it. I've never been a wanted man."

I raised my eyebrow. "By the guards or by women?"

"Ouch."

We both laughed and he wrapped his arm around my shoulders.

Roshanak stepped to the middle of the room. "What I'm hearing is now is our time to leave the city. Jade, thank you for allowing us to find refuge with you."

"My walls will always be open to keeping you safe. All of you." She looked at the sultan.

He nodded his head to her and offered a slight smile of gratitude.

"*Iftah ya bowaba*," Roshanak said.

"You know, at this point I could probably cast that spell," I said to Abudar.

He snorted a laugh.

We walked through the portal to the Ailorn Mountains at the point where the Dumue River curved around it and into the ocean. It was the last place I'd left my people and carried on with Mihrage.

Now I was returning home.

"It's this way," I said, pointing to a path.

"How do you know?" Abudar asked.

I looked over at the magic carpet as it exited the portal. "My father showed me once. He took me here several years ago to show me where our people had once been forced to live to stay hidden, and how we'd come so far by actually having a village . . ." My voice died because we no longer had that village.

"Follow me," Father said. He began floating on ahead down the old path.

"Do you prefer the jungle heat or desert heat?" Abudar asked, running his fingers through his hair.

"Ask me in an hour after we've been walking," I replied.

As we walked, I slowed down to walk beside Roseline, who had been quiet this entire time. "You don't have to stay with us. In fact, you should probably return home so you don't get mixed up in all of this. My father could take you home," I offered.

"I thought about that, and while I do believe it would be good to return home, I also know you're going to need help. I can send for help from my own country, if someone will allow me to."

"Depending on how far it is, my father has a hawk that could send the message."

She smiled. "It's across the ocean. I don't know how far in miles, but I fear that's too far for a hawk to travel. I wouldn't want him to drown. But thank you for offering."

My gaze drifted to the tops of the mountains, where I had seen that desert dragon flying just days ago. And somehow we were supposed to negotiate with it in order to receive a scale.

An owl hooted to our right and I immediately smiled. That was the signal of whoever was on watch to notify the others so they wouldn't be caught off guard by strangers coming. The owl hoot meant we were a friend. Had we been a foe, the sound would have been a coyote howl.

The canyon grew a bit tighter and then curved to the

left. As soon as we rounded the corner, we were greeted by Farhad and other members of the thieves. He opened his arms to me and I embraced him.

"You made it back after all!" he gave me a warm squeeze and stepped back. "This must be the royal family. Ah. And Roshanak. I wasn't expecting to see you ever again."

I looked at my mother, who looked like she'd bitten a *gojeh sabz*, a sour green plum.

"I wasn't expecting to see you either," she replied simply. "But we aren't here for me."

Farhad looked over our slightly odd group. "I'm afraid staying with us will be much different than your lives in the palace. Over the next couple of days while you stay with us, you may be expected to help with hunting, fetching water, and preparing food. In our band of thieves, everyone must help one another or we cannot survive."

Igborg ran around me and jumped at Farhad's leg.

"My goodness, Igborg! You've grown a lot!" He picked up the dragon and laughed. "What has Caspara been feeding you?"

He was now the size of a large cat, or a small dog, depending on how one saw it. Igborg laughed, though it sounded more like a cough or upset stomach growl.

"He's been sneaking into the palace kitchen and eating entire animals," I said.

"Oh, Igborg would never do such a thing, would you?" Farhad laughed. He set Igborg back on the ground. "Will you be returning to us?"

I shook my head. "Not until this situation is taken care of. Abudar and I need to get to the top of the mountain and speak with the dragon."

Farhad's left brow rose high. "You *want* to go visit the dragon? It will devour you."

I heaved a sigh. "It is the only way I can get rid of the Evil Eye."

"Hm. I haven't heard of that curse being used in ages. Certainly not in my lifetime. Who cast it?"

"It's a long story." I glanced at the others. "If you want to share everything and update Farhad on what's happening, Abudar and I should fill our water skins and head up to the dragon before dark."

"Should we just go tomorrow?"

I looked up at Abudar. "We still have half of a day. Why sit around and do nothing just to do it tomorrow? Do you think Mithra is sitting around twiddling her thumbs?"

He frowned. "You could have just said no."

I placed my hand on his arm. "You know me better than that."

"At least stay long enough to eat some lunch," Farhad said. "I know two people who will be thrilled to know you're okay. Especially after Taraji was brought here by a jinni just a couple of hours ago after being missing for a couple of days."

The thought of seeing my best friends made my heart jump, and I hurried past him.

A couple of women were headed down a path to the river carrying baskets of things to wash, a couple of children were busy grinding herbs, stitching holes in clothing, and creating arrows or sharpening daggers.

I spotted Mihrage first. He stood out from the people of my village mostly because of his stark white hair. He had just dropped half a log on the ground and wiped his forehead with the back of his arm.

Taraji then walked over and began stripping the bark away with a tool—either she was carving a chair or preparing it to be used to make bedrolls.

"Caspara!" Mihrage shouted. His face lit up with a smile.

I sprinted toward them. "Mihrage! Taraji! You're both alive!"

Taraji jumped to her feet and met me halfway. Our bodies slammed together, a bit harder than we intended, but we both laughed with relief and squeezed each other harder than we should have too.

I closed my eyes. "Sands, Taraji. When I saw that Mithra had you, I thought I was going to lose you."

"You almost did. She wanted me to join her in usurping the throne, and I thought she was insane. *That* made her happy."

We let go of each other and she stepped back so Mihrage could give me an equally tight hug.

"I'm so grateful you used your final wish to free Taraji," he said softly. "I don't know what I would have done if I had lost her."

"Considering you will probably live two hundred years longer than me, you would have just found someone else to love," Taraji said.

Mihrage scowled and rolled his eyes. "First of all, we don't know Dalarians are even part dragon. Second of all, the longest any of us has lived was one hundred and fifty years old."

Taraji laughed. "That's still about seventy years longer than most humans live, *and* thieves tend to live less than that. Well, the lower castes at least."

"Did you lift your sister's curse?" I asked.

Mihrage nodded. "I can catch you up on that over lunch. And you can tell us all of the exciting things that happened with recovering the jinni and bringing Abudar back."

We swapped stories over the most delicious meal of lamb kebabs, seasoned basmati rice, and kofta pastries stuffed with minced lamb, garlic, onion, and pul biber for a bit of heat, seasoned with crushed nigella seeds.

Abudar had seconds, after asking, and even Sultana Shahira said, "I can't tell you how impressed I am by such delicious food."

That made Leila, Taraji's mother, extremely proud as she had been the one to cook the meal.

"How did you know you would need so much food?" I asked, licking my last bite of lamb from my lip.

"When your jinni returned Taraji, he said you would likely come here and to prepare for all of you," Leila replied.

I smiled. I needed to thank Taylin for that.

I leaned back a little and looked down at my bag. In all of the wishes I had made, had I even thanked Taylin once? I couldn't recall. Perhaps when we were in the caves and he saved me without a wish. He was probably able to do that because I wasn't actually limited in my number of wishes as he had made me believe. He could have helped me more, if I had known in so many more situations.

And yet . . . if I had relied on him for everything, how would I have learned anything? How would I have grown?

"I could sleep after that meal," Abudar said. He closed his eyes and rubbed his stomach for emphasis.

"To be honest, I could too," I said. But I got to my feet and dusted the sand from my bottom. "But evil doesn't take naps." I held my hand out to him.

Abudar accepted it and allowed me to pull him to his feet. "You're right." He groaned and stretched, then bowed to everyone gathered around the food. "Thank you for your hospitality. We shall return by this evening."

His mother stood and hugged him. "Be safe. Dragons are prideful."

"Nah uh!" Igborg whined. "Are not full of pride. Full of meat." He chomped down on a kebab Mihrage had on his plate.

"Igborg, that was mine," Mihrage scolded.

Igborg leaned back over his plate and spat it out, leaving a nice glob of saliva on top. "Sorry."

Mihrage rolled his eyes. "I don't want it now."

"Yay!" Igborg lapped it back up, followed by the rice.

Mihrage heaved a defeated sigh.

I chuckled at the amusing scene. It was fun to see Igborg's personality growing with his size. I walked a little way away, to where my father had rolled up under one of the few trees in the valley. "Are you ready to fly us up to a dragon?"

He unrolled on the ground.

Abudar hugged his father, again assuring his parents he would be safe.

Roshanak stood near me, awkwardly shifting or dusting sand from her clothes. "I suppose I should hug you as well. Though I know you will be successful. You're a fighter, and you won't give up even when you should." She smiled. "Some would view that as a fault, but for you it is a strength. Remember, if the two of you get in danger, you have to link together."

"We sort of did that earlier," I said. "That's how we fought off Mithra and Khorshid."

"Technically, we escaped because Igborg screamed and exploded the room," Abudar corrected when he made it to me.

I shrugged. "But we *did* connect. Even if it was only for a little while."

My mother's smile stiffened, and I could have sworn doubt was creeping in her mind.

But then I realized she must have felt genuine worry. I took her hand. She wasn't only worried for me. She had raised Arash, and he had sided with Mithra whom Roshanak had mentored. I couldn't imagine the guilt and shame she felt.

"We will be back by dinner time," I said and awkwardly patted her on the arm, then sat on the rug.

Abudar sat behind me and we took off. "You could have given her a hug at least," he said.

"I will. When we get back."

Thirty

"Big dragon!" Igborg screamed and slammed into my right shoulder, his eyes wide in panic, and he held on to me with his claws.

I looked around us in the sky and spotted the red shape drawing closer to us.

"That dragon is a lot bigger than I remember," Abudar said, worry in his voice.

"I remember it being exactly that big."

"Hold on!" Father shouted.

I gipped the edges of the carpet just as Father suddenly went directly upward just as the dragon exhaled a blast of fire toward us. Behind me, Abudar grunted, and when I looked over my shoulder, I realized I was pushing him back and off the end of the rug while he was desperately trying to hold on to the sides.

"Don't let go!" I called to him.

"You think?" he yelled back.

Father turned sharply, barely avoiding the dragon's heavily spiked tail.

Abudar let out a shout as he fell off the side of the rug, but somehow managed to cling on with his left hand.

"Abudar!" My arm warmed, and I knew my tattoos were glowing without having to see them. I reached my right arm down to Abudar. "Grab my hand."

Abudar gritted his teeth and pulled himself up just enough to catch my hand. Our grips locked and his eyes widened. "You can't pull me up on your own!"

My father spun upward, only to turn again and dive.

Igborg screamed.

I didn't let go of Abudar. With human strength, I wouldn't have been nearly strong enough to hold on. And Abudar recognized that.

"How are you doing this?" he asked.

I smiled, in spite of my stomach sliding into my throat with exhilaration. "Your magic is strengthened by your sentinel power. Because I don't have magic, it's my innate abilities that are enhanced. My strength, speed, and fighting sills. I think I'm figuring out how to be a sentinel!"

Abudar smiled up at me.

Father evened out and I was able to pull Abudar back onto the rug.

"The dragon's on your tail," I said.

Abudar looked over his shoulder. "Is there a way to talk to it?"

"I don't know if it can hear us, if we're too far away." I looked at Igborg, panting and holding his wings slightly out from his sides.

When he realized I was looking at him, he tucked his wings in close. "What?"

"Do you think you can talk to the big, scary dragon?" I asked.

"It tried to eat Igborg!"

I recalled the day we'd woken it in the Dragon's Lair cave and it had broken out and attacked us in the desert as we tried to make it back to the palace. Igborg had disappeared and shown up in the house Irilibus was staying in outside of Balim. Igborg had been exhausted and had a couple of small scratches, but he hadn't been gravely injured that day.

"Do you feel brave enough to try again?" I asked.

"Its chest is glowing. It's going to throw another fireball," Abudar announced.

Igborg whined.

I grinned. "You can show off your talents too, you know. I bet that dragon can't scream like you can."

Igborg finally smiled. "It can't! It did make big wind, though."

"Yes, but now it doesn't have sand on its side. And if you scream first, maybe you can knock it out of the air or surprise it."

Igborg spread his wings and allowed the wind to catch him and yank him off of the rug.

My heart jumped into my throat, and I reached back to grab Abudar's hand.

"I will never forgive myself if he gets gravely wounded," I said.

"I know you won't. But if he gets gravely wounded, he'd still be alive." Abudar kissed my cheek.

I frowned. "Wrong time for a kiss. We're watching Igborg fly toward a huge dragon!"

"Sorry! I didn't know what else to do!"

I rolled my eyes and looked back at Igborg. I didn't know if he was yelling at the dragon and trying to talk, but he blew a fireball toward the mountain.

The big dragon held itself still in the air by pumping its wings to stay afloat, but it didn't propel itself in any certain direction. It drew a big breath and struck the same spot on the mountain Igborg's fire had hit, but it engulfed a huge area of trees.

"Stay nearby," I said to my father as the two dragons grew smaller.

He turned and carefully began making his way back.

Igborg suddenly let out the same scream or roar he had in the palace. Out in the open, it wasn't nearly as ear-splitting, but it still made the rug beneath us tremble and I still tried to block the sound out by covering my ears.

The large dragon, however, faltered and almost fell from the sky.

Igborg stopped and looked over at us, then back at the dragon.

The red, spiked desert dragon floated down to sit on top of the mountain and tucked its wings in.

Igborg flew over to us. "He says to come sit. He wants to talk to us."

I caught Igborg and hugged him. "I'm so proud of you!"

He nuzzled my neck. "Thank you. You're so brave. I thought of you."

I kissed the top of his head. "I think you're the bravest creature I've ever met."

Igborg grinned proudly and puffed out his chest.

I kept my eyes locked on the dragon our entire descent. After all, I didn't know whether or not to trust the dragon.

Father finally landed several feet away, just in case we needed an escape.

"The little one said you brought me a gift," the dragon said. His voice was deep and crystal clear, and he showed his teeth to us in a smile I wasn't sure was friendly.

I got to my feet, still holding Igborg in my arms. "He wouldn't have said that, because we didn't bring you a gift.

However, we are willing to trade for one if you give us what we seek."

"And what would that be, little girl?"

I bristled.

Abudar must have seen me stiffen, because he set his hand on my shoulder and rushed his lips against my ear. "Don't react. This dragon will eat us both if we say the wrong thing."

I slowly drew in a breath through my nose. "I need one of your scales."

The dragon burst out in laughter.

"I was cursed by the *ein el hassad'* and was instructed to seek a scale from you in order to have it carved with a hamsa," I said over the dragon's roaring laughter.

His chuckle died down. "You have the *ein el hassad'*? Let me see."

I set Igborg by my feet, turned my back on the dragon, and lifted the back of my shirt.

Abudar instinctively lowered his hand to the hilt of his sword, flexed his fingers, and then dropped his hand back to his side, but his eyes didn't move away from the dragon behind me.

I felt the dragon's hot breath brush against my back, and then his tongue clicked.

"I have not seen the *ein el hassad'* in many years. Whoever gave you that mark has either been around as long as me, or has meddled in the dark arts."

I turned to face the dragon. "The second part. He is Khorshid, a sorcerer."

"A sorcerer in Sheblom?" The dragon cocked his head just like Igborg did, and for a moment I found myself thinking how cute it was because it was always cute when

Igborg did it.

"He is my grandfather," Abudar added.

The dragon's attention moved to Abudar for the first time since we landed. "I smelled wealth on you. You must be the prince. Interesting. A man with magic born from the same line as a sorcerer."

"He was supposed to be dead when I was born."

"Then why isn't he?"

I heaved a sigh and looked at Abudar.

"He was bound to a ruby, which freed him when it was shattered. I don't fully understand how, but it may have been tied to the magic he was doing in order to become a sorcerer in the first place. And then he conned my sister into thinking he would help her take the throne, so she aided in his release."

"Such an interesting world this has become."

"And things will only get worse," I added. "Can you imagine what a sorcerer could do to our land if he is able to take throne?"

"I imagine no worse than the other men who have already sat upon it." The dragon shrugged. "Though it would be interesting indeed to see a woman on the throne for the first time in history." A sly smile spread on his lips.

I swallowed hard and stepped forward. "What do you want for one of your beautiful scales?"

The dragon's orange eyes drifted to me and he lowered his massive head to make me look into one of his eyes. "I want the golden lamp sitting in your bag."

My heart stopped.

"Did you think I wouldn't feel the magic radiating from it? Or know it houses a jinni?"

"That . . . that isn't an option," I fumbled.

"Pity." The dragon straightened. "I can make no deal with you, human. Now, I can offer you a . . . oh, thirty-second head start to get back down the valley before I devour you whole."

I reached into my pouch and grabbed the lamp. "You're asking me to betray my friend."

"That isn't my problem, child."

I pulled the griffin pendant from my neck and held it out. "This is pure silver! It's worth more than this lamp."

The dragon laughed again. "Silver compared to a jinni who can give me all the treasure in the world I could possibly want? Why would I ever make such an arrangement? My patience is growing thin." His smile fell and he moved his tail up to his side, showing us the spikes, reminding us what would happen. "Shall I begin counting down from thirty?"

Taylin appeared and he cleared his throat. He stood directly in front of me, between me and the dragon. "I couldn't help but overhear. This . . . definitely wasn't anticipated. But you can always come back and find me," he whispered to me.

"Thirty . . . twenty nine," the dragon said.

"I am *not* betraying you," I said firmly.

"How else are we going to get you a scale?" Abudar asked softly. "We can't walk up to the dragon and pull one off of his body."

I turned to face Abudar. "You are forgetting that we are sentinels. Combined, our powers are enough to kill a dragon."

"You're not going to—"

"Of course not," I said, cutting off Taylin. "I simply mean, if we are strong enough to kill him, we should be strong enough to steal a scale."

"Twenty-two . . ."

Abudar shook his head. "I don't know. I don't see this working and ending well for us."

"When did you and I switch roles?" I asked.

"What?"

"When did you become the one to second guess? It's no wonder your sentinel powers aren't working." I reached both hands up and held Abudar's face. "Is it because you've admitted your feelings for me and now you're worried something will happen and you'll lose me?"

"How . . . how did you know?"

"Because I feel the same way. But instead of worrying and holding myself back, I'm using it as the fuel to the fire in my belly. I hold on to the thoughts of you to activate the tattoos and the power. You need to do the same." I kissed him.

"Seventeen . . . you're running out of time, humans."

"I have an idea," I whispered. I turned to the dragon and held up the lamp. "I'm going to trade with you."

The dragon stopped counting and smiled. "I knew you would see it my way."

"On one condition."

The dragon scowled.

"You pluck off the scale now. I have to use my last wish so the jinni can engrave the hamsa onto it. Only then will I give you the lamp."

The dragon flicked his tongue and huffed. "Deal."

Thirty-One

The dragon reached one of his claws to the scales on his tail. The scales were the smallest there, but they were still far larger than any of Igborg's scales, and the one he picked at was about the size of a gold coin. Just large enough to be used for what I needed it.

The dragon held the stunning scale up in his claws, then held it out to me.

I accepted it and turned the stunning scale in my hand. "This truly is beautiful," I said softly. "I have never seen such a beautiful creature up close." I looked up at him.

The dragon grinned. "No. You haven't."

"Igborg is amazing because he is a dragon, but you . . . you're something far more splendid." I held the dragon scale to my chest. "If Igborg could become even half the dragon you are, I would be proud. Surely no one else even comes close to your stature and strength."

As I spoke, the dragon puffed himself up more and more.

One thing I had learned about dragons by having Igborg was that they adored being praised. And by praising Igborg, I could often distract him.

I placed the scale behind my back and waved it, hinting for Taylin to take it and do his spell. "Because I will never see another dragon like you, may I get closer and see your claws? I imagine the farmers in the valley are envious too, since you've likely managed to slaughter their flocks."

The dragon clicked his claws against the ground. "Of course you may look. I didn't know you had such manners."

Taylin plucked the scale from between my fingers and I slowly approached the dragon and looked at his claws. They were slightly curved, and their length went up to my hips.

I gasped. "No living creature would survive even a swipe from these glorious claws! Magnificent. Do you have a name so I can tell stories of your beauty?" I looked straight up. The dragon was far bigger this close, and it took everything inside of me not to run away from the predator.

"Ah, a name, yes. And you can tell them of my victories. My name is Anzu." He lowered his head to me.

My eyes widened. "Anzu? Often known as Zu in the legends?"

He grinned. "You have heard of me?"

"Who hasn't?" I meant it honestly for the first time. "Our stories tell of the incredible storm dragon with power over thunder clouds who stole the Tablet of Destinies!"

Zu laughed. "You really have heard of me. I am impressed."

"I love hearing stories, especially when they are about magnificent creatures such as yourself. May I see your tail spikes next?"

The dragon proudly moved his tail a little closer to me and looked down at me with nothing but pride in his eyes.

I intentionally positioned myself with my back toward the dragon's eyes and lifted my own to my father, who rested nearby. I wished with all of my heart that he would realize I was giving him a cue to fly and pull me away from the dragon and then save Abudar and Taylin before the dragon could strike.

No sooner had I made the wish than my father burst forward, snatched me, and flew to Abudar. I reached my arm out, grabbed onto Abudar's forearm, and dragged him onto the rug behind me as it flew toward the trees.

Zu let out a roar of fury and I heard the crackle of a fire just before the rug shot upward like it had earlier.

Igborg flew as fast as he could to keep up, but Father had to maneuver unexpectedly and Igborg couldn't keep up.

"Taylin, please keep Igborg safe!" I wished.

"Done!" I heard him say, and Igborg disappeared from the air.

"Don't you dare wish me to safety," Abudar said, reading my mind. "I am with you."

Father flew straight down the side of the mountain, toward the valley.

"No! You can't lead the dragon toward the thieves," I said.

Father turned to the left just before hitting the valley floor.

"Now would be a good time to use some of my magic," he said, looking up at the sky. He sucked in a breath and held his hands up toward the dragon overhead. Abudar's arm sparked with white light.

I turned to face him and wrapped my arms around his chest. "I believe in you."

Abudar's chest expanded again, and this time the tattoos on his arms ignited just like mine. A bright-white shield formed from his hands just as a ball of fire hurtled toward us, but it hit the shield and exploded.

Zu shouted in anger yet again. He began beating his wings harder, and I realized it wasn't to catch up to us. A terrifying storm began to gather overhead with clouds so dark it felt like night, and flashes of lightning erupted like lightning bugs in summer.

"How do you counter a storm?" Abudar asked over the growing wind.

"I . . . I don't know! You can't?" I asked.

Abudar looked up at the sky. "When I used wind to try and counteract the wind he created out in the desert, we created a tornado. Hitting the spell with another of the same kind won't work."

Lightning struck a nearby tree, and the crack made me jump. Wind picked up and rain began to pour from the skies.

"Maybe you don't counteract it?" I said, not letting go of him.

He gasped. "You're a genius!" He laughed and pulled away from me to get up on his knees.

"Abudar!"

"*Iftah el samawat*!"

A ray of sunlight pierced the darkness right over us, splitting the storm and creating an area of safety away from the pelting rain and wind.

I wiped the rain from my face. "What did you do?"

"I made an eye to the storm," he announced proudly, looking back at me.

I saw a flash of light behind him.

"Watch out!" I screamed.

But the lightning struck Abudar square in the chest and sent him flying to the ground below.

"Turn around!" I ordered, falling to my belly so I could hold on.

Father whipped around, almost throwing me off.

We reached Abudar's unconscious form as Zu dove for him with claws extended.

I jumped off of my father to grab Abudar and throw him on, but I knew I didn't have enough time to do so before the dragon would get us both.

Letting out a yell of my own, I stood over Abudar and balled my hands into fists. I willed every part of my body to protect Abudar at all costs.

I punched my fist against the ground, but I certainly didn't expect to go sailing into the air, and I never could have anticipated slamming into the dragon's body with my own. If I couldn't anticipate either of those, there was no way I could have imagined that doing so would knock the dragon out of the sky.

I landed in a crouch and stared at the groaning dragon as he tried to catch his breath and get to his feet.

"Get on the rug," Taylin commanded, grabbing me by the arm.

I turned to him, my eyes frozen wide.

"I know. Yay, you flew. Now get on." He pulled on me. He had already managed to get Abudar on the rug.

I had to climb on top of Abudar, and then my father took off, leaving the injured Zu behind.

"What . . . just happened?" I asked Taylin.

He smiled. "You are a full-fledged sentinel."

Thirty-Two

We landed in front of the caves where the thieves had hidden themselves. As soon as the rug was on the ground, I ripped Abudar's shirt opened and gasped at the wound on his chest.

"Help!" I shouted.

His lips were purple and I pressed my lips to his and gave him my own breath.

Taylin showed up and placed his hand on my back. "Caspara, he will be okay." He placed his hand on Abudar's wound, and a golden glow radiated from his hand. "I know you well enough to not even have to wait for a wish. I'm getting to know your heart."

Abudar gasped a breath and opened his eyes.

I kissed him desperately, then threw my arms around Taylin and hugged him. "Thank you, Taylin," I whispered.

"Oh, it's not that big of a deal."

"It is to me. You've been so kind to me, even when you didn't need to be. You helped me even when I didn't make a wish, before I even knew your name. You've kept me safe and helped the ones I love." I looked at him with tears in my eyes.

He rubbed the back of his neck and shyly looked away. "It really wasn't a problem. I wanted to help you. You gave me a reason to want to."

I smiled. "You're a wonderful person, Taylin. And for that, I've got a wish for you."

"Caspara, you don't have to."

"I wish for you to have your love back. The one who wept for you so much she created the Dumue River when you were taken."

Taylin's golden eyes filled with tears. "Nahir. How can I ever . . ." His words caught in his throat. He touched my cheek and kissed my forehead.

"I know," I whispered.

Taylin picked up the lamp. He opened the lid of the lamp and reached in. With magic I didn't understand, as he pulled his hand out, Igborg returned to his normal size. He handed me the lamp and I returned it to my bag.

Taylin offered me another, grateful smile before disappearing.

"Abu is okay!" Igborg exclaimed and snuggled up against him.

I turned my attention to Abudar and smoothed his hair. "I'm glad you're okay."

"Me too," he whispered.

Sultana Shahira and Sultan Zayne were by our side a moment later. Shahira was checking on Abudar's new scar, and Zayne asked questions to make sure he was coherent.

I got to my feet and turned around.

My mother wrapped her arms around me and I hesitated.

"I heard the dragon and saw the storm. I must admit, I grew worried when I didn't see you." She let go.

"I outsmarted a dragon." I smiled.

Roshanak laughed. "I can't wait to hear about it."

"I really want to sleep," Abudar said with a heavy voice. "Help me get inside?"

Mihrage and Sultan Zayne picked Abudar up by his arms and helped drag him into one of the nearest caves. Farhad held the door for them and followed after.

"Why are you smiling? You almost died!" Taraji exclaimed. She grabbed me by the shoulders. "Do I need to shake you back into reality?"

I shook my head and let out a little laugh. "Taraji, it worked. Abudar and I . . . we linked." I looked at my mother. "As sentinels. We felt each other's power and . . . I was able to fly and hit the dragon and Abudar, he—he created an eye in the storm so it wouldn't affect us, though neither of us could have foreseen the lightning bolt, but still, it was absolutely incredible! You should have seen it!"

My mother smiled, seeming to be proud of me for the first time in my life.

"I think we might actually be able to fight Khorshid and Mithra and win," I admitted.

"It's incredible to me how much you've grown in such a short period of time," my mother said to me. She smiled. "I never imagined . . . I wish I had done things differently."

"I am the way I am because of how I was raised," I said. "Who knows what would have happened if I had been raised with you? We can't ever know that, and quite frankly, I don't think we should worry about it. We have each other now." I took her hand. "And we're going to kick Mithra to the moon."

My mother laughed.

As I ate dinner, we went over the plan again. We needed to be smart about our course of action, and it might take a few days to gather together those who would fight alongside us.

Sultan Zayne wrote a letter to Captain Nadeem requesting to meet him in the gulley where the entrance to the Dragon's Lair cave was. My father would deliver him there, they would speak, and if Captain Nadeem agreed to help, then he would be given our location.

I would go to Sinbad and personally invite him, since we had a little bit of a history at this point. Abudar would take Roseline to her home and see if they would help. Mihrage offered to invite his people as well. Taraji and Mihrage would help by spreading word to the nearest cities and their residents to give them a warning of Mithra's intentions.

Everything was perfectly planned.

The next morning, we had a hearty breakfast before we split to go our separate ways.

Abudar caught me as I was leaving the cave and dragged me back inside. He paused and looked at me with his beautiful, strange eyes.

"What is it?" I asked.

"I just wanted to tell you to be careful."

I smiled softly. "I know. I'll have my mother with me, so she'll stop me from being foolish and impulsive." I winked.

"I know, it's just that . . . so much rides on us and if we—"

I grabbed Abudar's face and kissed him. "I'll worry about you the entire time you're gone too. I love you too much."

He grinned. "Love me, huh?"

I flushed but didn't turn away. I didn't step away either. "Yes. I think I do. We're just kids, but I feel like I've known you my entire life."

He pressed the palm of his right hand to mine and guided our hands up in the air. Instantaneously, our tattoos glowed. "In a way, we have."

"Caspara!" my mother called.

I wrapped my arms around Abudar's neck and kissed him again. "I'll see you tonight, hopefully."

"Tomorrow at the latest. Hopefully." Abudar winked.

We left the cave hand in hand and then separated—my mother opened the portal for us to Bessoriah, and Abudar opened the portal to Kalekai for him and Roseline. Everyone else went their separate ways as well.

I did steal one last glance over my shoulder before stepping through the portal and into the city of Bessoriah just outside the doors of their palace.

"I've never been to this land," Mother commented, looking around.

"Well, their new king is adorable," I said dryly.

Mother walked by my side as I approached the main doors.

I recognized the guard on the left as one of the men I had knocked out, and he recognized me immediately too.

He straightened and glanced at his companion, me, and then up at the archers at the tops of the towers.

"I'm not here to hurt anyone. I need to meet with King Sinbad," I said. "Tell him I know about the Griffin Syndicate and my father."

"Don't move from that spot," the guard replied. He looked to his companion. "Don't let her in these walls before I return."

The second door guard was suddenly nervous, his eyes darting between me and my mother.

More soldiers appeared before the guard reappeared, luckily for us with Sinbad following behind.

"I didn't think I would see you again, Caspara." He looked me up and down. "You look radiant as always."

"Sweet of you to say so, Sinbad," I said. "I'm here because we need your help. Or rather, the help of Bessoriah's people."

He grinned. "I knew this day would come."

I took a few steps toward him, but he took a wary step back. I couldn't help but smile. "You're intimidated by me, Captain? You're frightened of a *woman*?"

"You're not any woman, Caspara." Sinbad raised his brows.

"Funny. Prince Abudar tells me the same thing." I batted my eyelashes, then shook my head. "We don't have time to waste on nonsense. Princess Mithra has released the sorcerer Khorshid and has taken the throne. Furthermore, she's put a bounty on my head as well as that of the grand sorceress and Prince Abudar himself." I held out our wanted posters.

Sinbad accepted them and looked them over. "You kidnapped the sultan and sultana? How is any of this my problem?"

"Because Mithra won't just stop at our kingdom," my mother said. "She will want to expand her power. If not her, Khorshid for certain. He will take Kalekai, Trembuley, and even Bessoriah. Then what will you rule?"

Sinbad looked down at the pages in his hands again, then at us. "You protect my kingdom from an attempted takeover in return for my help?"

I folded my arms. "Call it repayment for stealing Igborg *and* my jinni. You got what you wanted. The throne back.

The least you can do is help a country in need."

"Tsk. I'm not willing to put my people at risk." He held the papers back out to me.

I scowled at him and snatched them from his hand. "And you called yourself a friend of my father."

Sinbad's lips tightened.

"You're all talk, aren't you?" I said. "You claimed you wanted to make a change in Sheblom, so you joined the Griffin Syndicate, and all the while you only wanted what *you* wanted. Your throne back. Why won't you help others get their thrones back?" I straightened. "When Khorshid comes, I really hope he removes you from your throne and that you'll be stuck as a cabin boy on a ship." I turned on my heel.

"I didn't say you could leave," Sinbad sang.

"Funny. I didn't say we were staying." I ignited my markings. "Do you really want to upset a sentinel?"

Sinbad's jaw flexed.

"I didn't think so."

My mother opened the portal.

"If you change your mind, show up in Zunbar in two days. If you decide not to, we will remember that." I walked through the portal after my mother.

As soon as we reached the other side, I kicked a rock as far as I could and folded my arms over my chest.

"You can't expect everyone will help," Mother said.

"I would have hoped *some* of them would!"

"Caspara, the day is still young. The others have only just left."

"And now I have nothing to do to help!" I complained.

Mother raised her eyebrows. "There is always something you can do. Who else can be an ally?"

I licked my lips and looked over at Igborg, curled up on top of a rock and sunbathing, though his eyes were open and watching me silently.

"I have an idea . . . but you're not going to like it. I need you to take me to the top of the mountain."

"What? You're not thinking about—"

"That's exactly what I'm thinking." I walked to Igborg and hoisted him into my arms. "You can either portal me up there or I'll walk."

My mother frowned. "I don't like this idea in the least. Dragons are unpredictable and—"

"And his pride is wounded, but I can appeal to it. Trust me. Please?"

My mother heaved a sigh but raised her hands and cast the spell.

I walked out on top of the mountain and spotted the scorch marks from our battle with Zu the day before. I set Igborg on the ground. "Where would he sleep?"

"A cave," Igborg replied simply.

"Yes, but where is it?"

He looked around, trotted this way and that, raised his nose in the air and sniffed, then finally headed between rocks down a trail only he could see. "This way!"

I followed Igborg down a narrow path that gradually became rocky. The rocks slipped, but I managed to keep my balance.

Igborg stopped on an outcropping of rock and looked up at me.

I walked out on the outcropping and saw the narrow gap in the side of the mountain that was definitely the dragon's lair. There was a rotting pile of sheep bones just outside, and I had to plug my nose while trying not to gag.

"Anzu!" I called. "I've come to make peace with you."

I heard the rustle of scales and the familiar clicking sound of claws on stone as Zu rushed from the darkness to the entrance of the cave.

He pushed his face within an inch of mine and let out a loud snarl.

I took a step back and my foot slipped. I almost lost my balance, but quickly composed myself.

"You have some nerve showing up here to have a conversation when you deceived me!" he roared.

"I know. It was wrong of me," I said. "I made a promise to my jinni, though, and I needed that scale. But I have a better offering."

"Which is what?"

"Remember that hoard you left back in the desert?"

Zu leaned his head back and gave me a bored expression. "The one now buried in the sand from when I broke out?"

I hesitated but nodded. "I can recover it for you."

He threw his head back and laughed.

"I can use a wish to give it to you."

Zu's laughter stopped and he tilted his head. "I suppose that will be a proper payment for giving you one of my precious scales."

"I should also mention something else," I added.

"There's always something else with you humans." He sneered at me with distaste, like I was a rat stealing food from him and needed to be squashed. Essentially, that's exactly what I was.

I swallowed. "I need you to visit the city of Zunbar and distract the sorceresses so they come out of the palace."

He chuckled. "And burn it down?"

"No. burning anything down should be a very last resort, but try not to destroy too much. And you'll wait for my signal if I should need you to do such a thing."

He growled. "And remind me why I should trust a thief such as you?"

"Because if you don't, not only will you have lost your hoard, but you will lose your reputation. The mighty Anzu deserves far better things in life than being alone without a treasure, doesn't he? What would people say if they discovered your poor state?" I gestured to the sheep corpses for emphasis.

He looked at them, then back at me. "You're cunning, human. Cunning indeed."

"Do we have an agreement, then?" I pressed.

Zu leaned down again. "Should you need a dragon to destroy a city, I shall be there."

Thirty-Three
Mithra

I sat on my throne, stroking Samira's head while watching the corners of the room and pondering what to do next. I had the throne; now I needed to keep it. My grandfather had helped me reach my dreams, but I knew from reading his journals that he was the type of man who had no desire to share glory. He had scared off his own wife and children. They had moved into Zunbar and opened the apothecary Madame Kiara now ran, disguising their magic as herbal remedies so the sultan couldn't execute them.

If he did that to the people he was close with, those he loved, what would he do to me? I might have shared his blood because he was my mother's father, but other than that we had no relation. He knew nothing about me, and everything I knew about him was from words on a page.

"You're being very quiet," Arash said.

I shifted my gaze to him, having forgotten he was even in the room.

He stood at the side of the rug, watching me. "What is it?"

"Do you think Khorshid is able to hear what we speak of?" I asked.

He shrugged. "It is possible. In fact, it is highly likely he would know a spell to keep an eye on everything happening in the palace, if he is as strong as you say."

I looked over at Samira. She was curled up on my mother's throne with her head resting on the armrest between us, watching me with her emerald-green eyes. "Can you feel any magic in this room?"

She lifted her head and flicked her tongue. "I sssenssse it. But you are near."

"That's what I expected." I pursed my lips together in thought. "You cannot feel beyond me?"

"Your magic ssspreadsss across the room. It grasssps at the cornersss. I cannot tell what isss from you and what isss not."

I stood and stepped down from the throne, then took the few steps to Arash. "I want you to find Caspara and kill her."

Arash snorted and rolled his eyes. "That went over well last time."

I raised my eyebrow and grabbed him by his chin. "It would have if you had listened to me last time. What were you thinking locking her in the dungeon? You had to know she would find a way to escape! She's a thief and has a pet dragon!"

He frowned. "You agreed with me it was a good idea."

"I told you to keep her out of my way." I narrowed my eyes. "You failed."

Arash grabbed my wrist and pulled my hand away. "She is my sister."

"Only by blood! It is no different than Khorshid and I."

"I cannot kill her," he insisted.

Anger exploded in my chest and the dark shadows in the corners of the room elongated. "I have put my trust in you, Arash. I want you at my side, yet you won't do what I ask. How can I have a lover and guard who refuses to listen?"

He kept his eyes locked on mine. "Are you going to kill me too?"

For the first time in a long time, I hesitated. The question caught me off guard. I loved Arash. He was the only one who had paid any attention to me beyond what was required. He had always made me feel wanted and that I could do anything I worked hard for. I had worked hard for *this*. And he had always been at my side.

Would I kill him if he betrayed me?

"How could you ask me that?" I whispered, pain eating at my anger. My anger engulfed the pain, tore through it, and replaced it. I gritted my teeth and slammed my staff on the mosaic tiles.

The ground rippled and Arash fell to his knees.

I placed a fingertip under his chin. A fingertip which had black spreading across it like ink. "Do you still love me?" I demanded.

Arash's throat bobbed when he swallowed.

I was making him nervous. And he was taking too long to answer.

"I'll always love you, Mithra. But I must admit, I do not love what you are becoming."

I burst into laughter, which echoed in the room in a deeper, more sinister tone. "You don't love that I am becoming the queen Sheblom needs?"

"Look at your hands, Mithra," he said.

My gaze drifted from his handsome face to my hand under his chin. "What of them?"

"They're beginning to turn black. The darkness you're meddling with is taking over you. What happens when that blackness reaches your heart? Will you be capable of loving anyone but yourself?"

My gaze snapped to him, and I slapped him across the face with the back of my hand. "How dare you call me selfish!"

Arash kept his head turned away, and I saw a slowly growing red spot on his cheek.

I'd just hit him.

My heart skipped a beat and I took a step back.

I'd just slapped Arash.

A man I claimed to love.

"Arash," I whispered.

His jaw flexed. Slowly, he looked back at me and his green eyes were glossy, but he sucked in a breath and the look faded. "What would you have me do, Your Highness?"

"I . . ." Suddenly, I didn't know what I wanted. I turned away from him, confused, and forced myself to walk back to the throne. "If only Abudar were out of the way, I wouldn't have to be like this!" I shouted. "Kill him. Bring me his head," I commanded.

"As you wish."

I turned back to Arash and watched him get to his feet.

He bowed to me. Arash hadn't bowed to me in three years unless it was a formal setting with my parents or Captain Nadeem present.

Things between us had changed.

My heart ached.

Arash left the throne room.

I sank into my father's throne. "Samira, I have made a terrible mistake," I whispered. "Arash has never even been hunting. He's never killed a living thing, and yet I expect him to kill someone who has been a friend to him their entire lives."

"It isss to make you ssstronger. To ensssure your posssition on the throne, isss it not?" She rested her heavy head on my lap.

I closed my eyes and drew in a breath. The heaviness on my chest pressed in on me. "It is." I opened my eyes again. "With Abudar dead, not only can he not take the throne, but the sentinels will be extinct. Caspara will lose her own power and make herself vulnerable." I didn't speak to Samira but to myself, using my own words to try and comfort me.

But even as Samira closed her eyes, at peace with my decisions, doubt gnawed at me.

I stretched my neck and lifted and dropped my shoulders in an attempt to let go of the feelings inside. "I need to let some of this frustration out." I stood and left the throne room myself.

Samira followed. "Where will we go?"

"I want to practice with some sorceresses and test their strength."

"To protect you againssst Khorshid?"

I glanced down at my snake. "If it comes to that, yes."

Thirty-Four

Staying with the thieves with nothing to do but help make the next meal or brush fleece for yarn was *not* how I wanted to spend my time, especially not while everyone else got to be helping. At least Anzu was on our side. Sort of. I wasn't positive I *wanted* him on our side if he was willing to destroy all of Zunbar.

I sat in the shade and brushed one of the large bowls of fleece, picking out weeds that were stuck beyond all reason or other chunks that wouldn't separate. It was mindless work and gave me plenty of time to worry about everyone else.

My mother sat at my side, grabbed two brushes and a handful of wool, and said, "Show me how to do this."

I lifted my gaze to her. "You *want* to brush wool?"

"It will give me something to do. Didn't Farhad say I needed to help anyway?" She pressed the fleece against the brush and leaned a bit closer to me.

"Um. Okay. You just brush the two brushes together. Well, really you're only moving the top brush." I showed her how I held the fleece on the left and pulled the fleece down on the right. "It gets all the big stuff out and separates the wool so we can pull it into yarn."

Mother nodded and began brushing. "With enchanted

objects, this could go much faster."

"But imagine if everything was automated like that. What would people do for work?" I asked.

We actually exchanged pretty pleasant conversation as we sat and worked.

Sultan Zayne was the next to arrive back at our camp. "Where is Shahira?" he asked.

"Still with Taraji spreading information that the royal family wasn't kidnapped, I believe," Roshanak said.

"How did it go?" I asked.

He smiled softly. "Captain Nadeem will help us."

"That's wonderful! Sinbad and Bessoriah absolutely will *not* help." I sighed. "I have a feeling their people would have if not for the pirate who just took over."

"That is unfortunate, but I'll admit expected. I'll tell more about my conversation with Captain Nadeem when everyone returns," Sultan Zayne said.

As the day wore on, Sultana Shahira and Taraji returned, followed by Abudar.

"Roseline hasn't returned with you?" Taraji asked.

Abudar shook his head. "She wanted to stay home over the next couple of days but will rejoin us when we need them." He placed his arm around my waist and I leaned into him.

"Sinbad won't help. Surprise," I said.

"Come and sit to eat," Sultana Shahira said, guiding us to one of the many "tables" in front of the caves.

The tables were whatever might naturally be in place—a boulder or a tree stump—or what might have been able to be carried or made so far. Even chairs were being used as tables for some.

We all sat around the boulder that acted as our table and

Abudar looked at me. "Did you only cook while we were gone?"

"I helped, yes. But mostly I did yarn. And recruited a dragon," I finished with a laugh.

Sultan Zayne cleared his throat. "Captain Nadeem said that since we have left, the sorceresses from The Veil have indeed moved into the palace . . ." He continued to talk about everything we already knew, and I shifted from one foot to another and heaved a sigh.

The waiting was killing me.

That night, we left to meet Captain Nadeem at the edge of the Ailorn Mountains.

We all stood before Captain Nadeem under the last rays of the setting sun. My mother had her hands folded in front of her and my father lay on the ground with Igborg, myself, and Abudar sitting on him. Sultana Shahira sat on a stump Mihrage had retrieved for her, and Mihrage stood beside Taraji and Farhad toward the back. Sultan Zayne stood nearest to Captain Nadeem.

The captain looked at each one of us. "This is quite the impressive group, Your Highness."

"It is. Do we have the support of the palace guard?"

The captain turned to his sultan and nodded. "Every one of them. And I mean every." He stepped to the side and I gasped out loud.

Arash stood several feet behind him with his eyes downcast.

I scrambled to my feet and rushed to him. No one else moved, but there was something in his body language and the very fact that he was present that let me know he was in pain. I wrapped my arms around him, but said nothing.

He slowly patted my back.

I didn't let go. "Is it Mithra?" I whispered in his ear.

He nodded.

"Does she want you to do something you don't want to?"

Arash hesitated but nodded again.

Finally, I let go and leaned down so I could see his eyes. They were filled with such pain I wished I could take it from him. "Do you want to talk about it?"

He lifted his gaze from the sands and glanced at the familiar group of people he should have been able to trust. "I'd rather speak with you alone. Please," he answered softly.

I nodded. "I'm going to take Arash to get a drink at the river. You all can discuss a plan with Captain Nadeem about how we're going to get into the palace." I nudged my head toward the river, my eyes on my brother.

Arash followed me through the trees.

I sat down on the shore and patted the spot beside me.

Arash glanced behind us and then lowered himself to the spot I'd touched. "Mithra wants me to murder Abudar," he said softly.

My breath caught, but I held in the gasp. "Why?"

"It will keep him from taking the throne from her and weaken you as a sentinel." He grabbed a stick and stabbed it into the sand. He shook his head. "I wanted her to become stronger. I wanted her to discover herself and..." He sighed. "But she's become an entirely different person." Arash looked at me. "I don't know this Mithra."

"Maybe when we get rid of Khorshid, Mithra will return to the person you knew?" I offered.

"I hope so. Because if she stays like this, I cannot stay at her side. And that thought hurts more than anything I've ever known."

I handed him a water skin and sat in silence while he took a long drink. I looked down into the Dumue River. I hadn't seen Taylin since I'd sent him to recover his lover. Perhaps it was just taking him a very long time to convince her to leave the river behind?

"How do you do all of this?" Arash asked. "Deal with all of these emotions?"

I laughed. "I don't deal with them well. I blamed Abudar for burning my village when he had been the one to warn them. He'd told me as much, and I still didn't believe him. At Father's funeral, I cried myself to sleep. And now? I worry so much about Mithra and Khorshid, I can barely eat, let alone sleep. Don't tell anyone that. Abudar will tell someone and I'll be forced to drink a disgusting concoction." I made a face.

Arash smiled just enough to let me know I really was being a bit silly.

I pulled my knees to my chest. "I asked Aunt Jade what other girls my age worry about, because I don't feel I should have the weight of the world on me. But here I am, a sentinel. It's only by accident that Abudar and I have figured out how to connect and activate our powers, and we're still terrifyingly amateur at it. But this is who I am meant to be." My gaze drifted to the sunset. "I met all three of the fates, and you know what the fate of the present told me? She said, *Your worth isn't dictated by gods or destiny but by what you choose to do and who you decide to be.* For the last several weeks, I've been trying to figure out what that means. And then I realized I had a choice." I looked at my brother. "I could *choose* to be a thief like my father raised me to be, or I could *choose* to be the sentinel I was born to be."

"And you've chosen to be a sentinel," he finished.

I nodded. "But you have the same choice, Arash. Well, maybe not to be a sentinel."

He studied my face. "That's why I came here. As much as I love Mithra . . . I loved the woman I knew before she got her hands on the journals and before she acquired that ruby. I refuse to kill Abudar."

"Do you think there's even a chance you can convince Mithra to join our side and fight against Khorshid?" I asked.

Arash shook his head. "No. Before today, I had hoped. But no."

"And why not?"

"She struck me." His jaw tightened.

"I'm . . . I'm so sorry. That was wrong of her." I placed my hand on his shoulder. "There may be room in her heart, though. Even just a ray of light can pierce darkness."

"Look at you being optimistic." Arash gave me a tight smile.

I laughed. "Well, I'm learning." I stood and held my hand out to him. "You can help us. We'll figure out a way to get Mithra back on the right path."

Arash reached for me, then paused. "Give me a moment longer alone."

"Take as long as you need." I reached down and ruffled his hair.

He looked up at me quizzically.

I grinned.

His smile felt real for the first time since arriving. "Thank you, Caspara."

"Of course, Brother." I let Arash sit alone and returned to the planning. I resumed my spot beside Abudar. Captain

Nadeem was still talking about the different entrances to the palace. "I don't seem to have missed anything important," I said softly.

Abudar shook his head. "Not much. He's explaining that the guards have been positioned at each door and commanded to notify Mithra if any of us draw near."

I paused to make sure Sultan Zayne's question was being answered before I whispered to Abudar, "Arash was ordered to kill you."

Abudar raised his eyebrow and quickly looked to me. "Me. And?"

"Well, clearly he's not going to."

"That's good." He looked over his shoulder.

I rolled my eyes. "He really won't kill you. But Mithra doesn't know that." I raised my own eyebrows.

Abudar tilted his head. "Are you saying we should use that to get into the palace?"

Sultan Zayne cleared his throat.

Abudar and I looked at him.

"Do you have something you want to say?" the sultan asked. "Or can we continue?"

I cleared my throat. "I agree with what you've been saying about getting the soldiers and thieves to help." I stood back up and walked to the center of the half-circle. "Arash was commanded to murder Abudar to make me weak. If Arash takes me to Mithra, she will believe he's accomplished his task. That gets me in the palace."

"Wonderful. One of us," Sultan Zyne said flatly. "You can't face Khorshid on your own even if you are a sentinel."

I shook my head. "I don't plan on facing anyone alone. My father can carry Abudar to his room. Anzu is going to be waiting as well. He said he was happy to burn down

Zunbar, but I was specific that was not to be allowed. However, if he can draw out the sorceresses from the palace, that will give us a chance to face Khorshid."

"The sorceresses would need to feel pressured to respond to a dragon landing near the city," Sultana Shahira suggested.

"In other words, just landing nearby might not be enough," Roshanak added. "What if he demanded to speak with Mithra and The Veil?"

"I can tell him!" Igborg offered, excited to help.

"And the rest of us enter while they're distracted," Abudar said.

"This has the potential to work," Sultan Zayne admitted.

"We need a backup plan," Arash said, announcing his presence. "If Igborg could scream and break any of the walls, we can get in that way too."

Igborg sat up proudly. "Happy to help!"

I rubbed his head with a chuckle.

"We have another day before Kalekai can arrive and offer aid," Abudar said.

"And the Dalarian," Mihrage added. "With Roshanak's help, I was able to visit with my father."

Arash frowned. "Mithra could grow suspicious in that timeframe."

"She expects you to find Abudar and kill him within a day?" I asked.

He rubbed the back of his neck. "Hm. Good point. But no longer than that. I fear she might use a spell to see where I am."

"Can she do that?" Roshanak asked.

Arash shrugged. "I don't know what she can and can't

do anymore. Her magic is growing every day. I don't know if she'll be able to control it when you attack."

"Then we rest and build our strength for a day," Sultan Zayne said, making the final decision.

Arash and Abudar gave the same disappointed frown.

I sighed.

None of us wanted to wait around, but we had to make sure our allies could offer aid if we needed it.

Captain Nadeem left us behind, and Arash walked on my right side while Abudar walked on my left as we returned the thieves' new home. We would need to use them to warn the people in Zunbar to evacuate before Zu burned everything down.

I walked into the cave I'd chosen as mine, at least for now.

Abudar said, "*Ashriq*." The lonely fireplace sputtered to life. "You need some more wood," he pointed out.

"Then go get some." I smiled and sat down on one of the new bedrolls that had just been finished that day from the very yarn I'd cleaned. I pulled off my boots and lay down on my back with a groan.

"Igborg can!" he announced and scurried from the cave.

"This is where your people are living?" Arash asked, looking around our tiny cave.

"We have nowhere else to go," I replied.

Abudar sat on the nearest bedroll and also removed his shoes. "It's quite different from the palace, isn't it?"

Arash shook his head. "Nah, I wouldn't say that." He sat down against the far wall.

"Oh, careful with leaving your shoes out. Make sure you lay the opening down." Abudar demonstrated by turning his shoes upside down so the opening was pressed flat to the floor.

"Why?" Arash asked.

"Scorpions."

Arash raised his brows and looked at me to check if Abudar was being honest or teasing.

"There really are scorpions," I confirmed. "But Igborg likes to play with them, so I haven't seen any in our cave yet."

Abudar shrugged. "You never know."

Arash rolled his eyes and lay down on his back.

Igborg dragged some firewood in, trotting happily like a puppy who had retrieved a stick playing fetch. He tossed it onto the fire, then nuzzled up against my side and let out a happy rumble deep in his belly.

I closed my eyes and tried to focus on the comforting sound of the crackling fire. "Good night, boys. In a couple of days, all of this will be taken care of."

Thirty-Five

Abudar's breath became heavy and Igborg snored rather loudly. But like every night for several nights, I couldn't find any sleep.

I rolled to my side and opened my eyes to stare at the darkness. The fire was fading but still glowed with enough light I could see Arash's form across from me. I didn't know how I kept myself from gasping when I saw that Arash was sitting straight up, staring at Abudar.

I quickly lowered my eyelids until I had only a slit to look through.

Without warning, he stood and my instinctive reaction was that he had lied to me and was going to kill Abudar. I couldn't allow that to happen and sat upright myself.

Arash put his finger to his lips and then quickly looked away before he silently slipped out of the cave.

Confused, I followed him outside.

He leaned his hand against the mountainside and drew a deep breath. "Who is in my mind?" he demanded.

I kept myself hidden, even going so far as to crouch in case he turned, but stayed close enough I could hear him.

He pressed the base of his hand to his head. "I haven't found him. I'm in the desert . . . you can see through my eyes? Then certainly you see I am in the middle of nowhere with no sign of Abudar." He leaned his back against the mountain. "I don't want to talk about that . . . I need to sleep so I have energy tomorrow . . . I'll see you tomorrow night then . . . Please don't."

I wanted to check on him and ask what was going on, but I didn't dare. Whoever it was could see through him?

Finally, Arash closed his eyes and slumped to the ground. "I'm not made for this."

"For what?" I asked, deciding it was safe to talk.

He opened his eyes, but massaged his forehead. "Khorshid. Darkness. He was in my head and wanted to know what happened with Mithra and why I hadn't returned with Abudar's head and . . ."

I took his hand.

Arash looked down at our hands. "I'm grateful I'm not alone."

"Me too. I'm glad you're on our side. Do you think you can sleep?"

He shook his head. "I don't know. How do you try to get yourself to sleep on nights like this?"

I sat down beside him and looked up at the stars. "I try to dream. Imagine myself different places, going on adventures like meeting other princes or princesses, even swimming to the bottom of the ocean." I smiled. "And sometimes I wake up and it's dawn."

"You make it sound easy."

I looked at him. "I said *sometimes* I wake up and it's dawn. Not always. Sometimes I can go through an entire series of dreams and wake up and it's the middle of the night."

Arash looked out at the night. "Can we really get past this?"

"Of course we can," I said. "Especially since we have each other. That's something Khorshid won't ever have. If Mithra doesn't change her mind, she won't have anyone on her side either."

Arash nodded. "I hope you're right."

"I hope so too."

Eventually, Arash went back inside of the cave and lay back down. I joined him after I watched a star shoot across the sky and wished Taylin was happy with the woman he loved.

I'd just closed my eyes when I opened them again to Igborg tapping my head with his claws.

"Breakfast, Caspara! Come!"

I sat up and rubbed my eyes. Abudar and Arash were gone. I must have fallen asleep more easily than I expected.

I followed Igborg out to everyone already eating and looked up at the sky. "How on earth did I sleep so late?" I asked.

"You were exhausted," Abudar said and patted the sand beside him.

I sat and accepted the plate of food from my mother. "Where are the thieves?" I asked.

"Farhad sent them ahead early this morning to give time for the people in Zunbar to evacuate. They're hoping to get people out before the sorceresses wake and become suspicious."

I nodded. "I'll need to let Anzu know our plan."

"I did," Igborg said. He stood with his front claws on the edge of the stone and reached to the middle of it for a roll.

"How big will you grow, Igborg?" Abudar asked.

He looked at the prince with the roll stabbed onto his

claws. "I don't know. I don't know what kind I am." He shoved the roll into his mouth.

"Can you imagine if he gets as big as Zu?" Abudar asked. "There won't be a house big enough to fit him."

Igborg's eyes widened. "I can't live in a house? I don't want to get bigger!"

"It's okay," I tried to reassure him. "We'll figure things out later. If you get that big, then we'll make sure you have a beautiful garden with lots of trees. Maybe we can fly to one of the other countries and live in their mountains."

He pouted. "I like here."

"That's why I said we'll figure all of that out when you actually get bigger. Who knows? This might be as big as you get."

"I hope so," he grumbled miserably.

I scowled at Abudar.

"What?" he asked through a mouthful of food. "I didn't say anything."

"Yes you did. You made him all sad because he thinks he won't be able to live with me anymore." I pulled Igborg to my side. "I'll always love you, Igborg. I've loved you longer than I have Abudar," I added.

Igborg lifted his head. "You have?" He gasped. "You have! Long time before!" He stuck his tongue out at Abudar and grabbed another handful of food.

I chuckled and patted his rear. "You need some manners. I can get you a plate and you can eat off of that, but it's rude to steal food from other people's plates."

Igborg paused with the food halfway to his mouth and suddenly realized he'd stolen that food from Sultan Zayne's plate.

The sultan was scowling at him.

Igborg sheepishly lowered his hand. "I'm sorry."

"You *are* a dragon," Arash said. "You can't be expected to have the same manners as a human."

"Well, I don't know about you, but I'm ready." I stood.

Abudar looked at my plate, then his, then up at me. "Caspara, you ate probably five bites of food."

"I am ready to go. Come on, everyone." I slung my father's bag over my shoulder out of habit and for comfort. With Igborg now too big to carry my fancy dagger secured at my waist, all I had to carry was the lamp. I began to walk away.

My mother caught up. "We're using portals, remember? You don't need to walk off on your own. And we have plenty of time."

"I don't want to wait until tomorrow. There is nothing to prepare today," I argued.

"We can perfect the plan," Sultan Zayne said. "Military people do that all the time to ensure everything runs as smoothly as possible."

Thirty-Six

I felt more confident than I ever had in my entire life as I walked into the palace. This mess was going to be over in just a few hours. Abudar and his parents would return to the palace, the sorceresses would go home, Khorshid would be gone, and everything would go back to how it should be.

We rounded the corner into the throne room and all of my hope and excitement died.

Khorshid sat upon the throne with a smug look on his face. "Arash, I am pleased to see you have returned. And with one of our beloved sentinels. Where is the other?"

"Where is Mithra?" Arash demanded.

"Hm. Nearby. Now answer my question."

Arash remained holding me by the arm. "I mean no offense, but I report to Princess Mithra. She is the one in charge."

"Not anymore, I am afraid." Khorshid stood.

I felt Arash stiffen, and I went rigid myself. This was something none of us had considered. Well, I had known Khorshid was evil, but none of us thought he would have already taken the throne.

"What did you do with the princess?" Arash demanded.

"Do you wish to see her?" Khorshid waved his fingers in the air like he had plucked a hair from his sleeve and was trying to get rid of it.

A life-sized hourglass appeared in the corner of the room with Mithra trapped inside.

"Samira, my darling," Khorshid called.

"Mithra's snake?" I whispered to Arash.

The black snake slithered up to Khorshid and up his side to rest on his shoulders.

"Samira is not Mithra's familiar, but mine. She has been waiting for me to return and aided me in convincing Mithra to free me."

My heart jumped in both fear and excitement. If Samira wasn't Mithra's familiar, then Mithra wasn't hadn't discovered her true self. Her familiar hadn't appeared!

I turned to Arash and whispered, "She has a chance to be good!"

He was frozen in shock.

"Arash. We have to get Mithra out." I dropped my hands and ran for the hourglass.

"Not so fast, little sentinel," Khorshid sang.

I yelped when the tiles on the floor gathered together into a tentacle and grabbed on to my legs, dropping me to my stomach.

"This seems so familiar. Where has this happened before? Yes, with my daughter. Shahira tried to stop me but was too late. Your Aunt Jade was supposed to be the final sacrifice to push me to the pinnacle of power. But Shahira denied me for all of these years." As Khorshid spoke, the tiles covered me and pressed down on me. "I will finally get what I have always wanted."

"What do you want?" Arash demanded.

He snapped his fingers and the sand hanging over Mithra's head began to fall. "You have one hour to bring me the other sentinel."

Our plan had completely fallen apart, and we hadn't even had a chance to start to execute it!

Arash looked at me. "I need Caspara. She knows where—"

"Ah, ah. You know very well where he is. And if not, well, every second you waste is a pile of sand on your precious Mithra."

I looked over at the frightened princess.

Mithra had her hands pressed against the glass and her eyes pleaded for help. She tried to speak, but the thick glass blocked her voice.

I clenched my hand in a fist and slammed it against the floor, shattering the tile under me and creating a wave of energy that radiated outward, breaking tiles including those holding me.

"My goodness. You are feisty, aren't you?" Khorshid said in an almost-bored tone. "Samira, you'll take care of the girl, won't you?"

The snake somehow jumped from Khorshid's shoulders and headed straight for me.

I grabbed Arash. "Get the others, but warn Abudar," I said before shoving him forcefully toward the door. I turned around just in time to dodge a strike from Samira, though her tail coiled around my left ankle and tripped me.

Arash didn't hesitate, thankfully, and ran from the throne room.

"Your brother abandoned you, sentinel. Now you're on your own. Can you truly fight against a mighty sorcerer and his familiar?" Khorshid stood near the throne.

Samira might have had my leg, but I clung to the hope Abudar would soon be there and grabbed her tail. With strength that never should have belonged to a human, I managed to uncoil Samira's tail and free myself.

She let out an angry hiss and struck at me.

I dodged the first two times, but on the third I accidentally rolled into the hourglass holding Mithra. I looked at her.

Mithra was trying to stay on top of the rapidly-falling sand. She made eye contact with me and pointed quickly.

I turned as Samira's fangs sank into my left shoulder.

"I am strong with the power of forty sorceresses. How much stronger will I be with the power of the sentinels?" Khorshid's voice asked.

I had expected Samira's fangs to fill me with venom. What I felt was the opposite. Somehow, she was drawing from me. I felt the hair on the back of my neck tingle and goosebumps spring up from my scalp to my toes.

I let out a long gasp.

"Just a little more . . ."

"I'll have you know it's quite rude to steal magic from magical beings." I managed to turn my head just enough to see Taylin leaning against one of the windows with a gorgeous woman sitting on its ledge.

She had blue hair that cascaded to the floor like a waterfall and the most stunning blue eyes I'd ever seen. Her skin had a soft white glow to it.

Just his presence gave me the strength to grab Samira's jaw and start pulling her face away.

"You must be the jinni that has been traveling with little Caspara and granting all of her wishes," Khorshid said. He raised his staff, but the mighty roar of a dragon came through the open windows. "What in the sands of wonder is that?"

"Oh, that's Anzu," Taylin said with a smile. He winked at me and I felt a surge of energy.

Samira's tail coiled quickly around me, trying desperately to sink her fangs back into me. I pulled her head back further and further.

"I wonder if I could take the magic from a jinni instead," Khorshid pondered aloud.

I reached down with my other hand but couldn't get past Samira's coil for the dagger, so I reached down to the dagger in my boot.

"I don't believe that is a very wise thing to try," Taylin said. "Oh, I should have mentioned . . ." He paused.

An explosion of fire ignited behind him.

Khorshid's eyes widened. "You truly found Zu? The mythical dragon?"

"Not only him." Taylin lifted his hand and waved.

"Forgive me," I whispered to Samira. I drove the dagger upward through Samira's bottom jaw.

Khorshid whipped around and faced me. "No!" he shouted in pain and anger.

Samira's tail whipped around and slowly, from the tip of her tail, she turned into ash.

Khorshid fell to his knees beside her and let out a shout of pain.

All of the shadows in the room trembled.

He lifted his gaze to me, his eyes full of hatred I'd never before seen. The black in his pupils spread wider until his eyes were completely black. Khorshid stood and stomped his staff. "Did my dear daughter tell you where my strength lies?" he hissed.

Igborg dove through the window right as Khorshid opened a portal like the one I had seen Mithra open days ago, from which ghouls had climbed. Igborg opened his mouth to let out one of his sound-shattering roars, but a hand shot out of the portal as Igborg flew over it and snatched him out of the air.

"Igborg!" I screamed out and ran toward him.

But the ifrit climbed out of the black abyss, and I skidded to a stop. It was a demon from a world I knew only from stories and paintings, but no manner of artwork could truly show how horrifying the creature was.

It stood far taller than any man, with four goat-like horns protruding from its head. Purple-and-black snake scales adorned its arms and back, and along its back were porcupine quills. Its dragon-like claws held tightly to Igborg, and the third eye in the center of its forehead moved to me.

I took a startled step back.

Igborg clawed at the creature and still let out his roar, but the ifrit pinched Igborg's mouth shut between its index finger and thumb. Igborg whined and wiggled.

"Stop!" I begged. "You're hurting him!"

Taylin ran forward without hesitation and jumped for Igborg.

Khorshid held his hand out and spoke the spell to open a portal, which resulted in Taylin leaping through the portal and into the filling hourglass alongside Mithra.

I didn't know what was taking Abudar and the others so long, but also I didn't know how it was possible that Taylin had been captured. If I acted alone now, I risked failing. But how could I sit and wait any longer?

Especially since the ifrit had climbed the rest of the way out of the portal and another crawled out right behind it.

Somewhere through the windows, Zu let out another

roar that rattled the glass in the windows but didn't break them.

But no one was helping me.

I removed the dagger from the sheath on my hip and ran for the nearest ifrit, the one holding Igborg.

"Caspara, no!" Abudar shouted behind me.

But it was too late. My momentum was already carrying forward, and I had already planted my foot to leap.

The world slowed.

I saw the reflection of firelight glisten off of the demon's claws, the turquoise and green shades of Igborg's scales, the emptiness in the ifrit's eyes, and the movement of the ifrit's free hand. Its claws were extended outward, toward me. And I realized, too late, that the angle of my leap would cause me to land directly on those claws.

Somehow—by the gods, the blessing of being a sentinel, or training—my dagger hit its mark.

But so did the demon's claws.

Three sword-like claws pierced my abdomen as I drove my dagger into the ifrit's neck.

It made a gurgling sound, and black blood oozed from its mouth as it collapsed to its knees.

I gasped a breath, my own feet striking the stone floor when the demon collapsed. I looked down at the claws protruding from my body but was unable to make any sort of noise when the claws slowly retracted when the demon fell in a heap, dead.

I fell to my knees and weakly lifted my hand to touch the blood quickly soaking my shirt. Whose blood was pooling at my knees?

A pair of arms wrapped around me and I looked up to see Abudar holding me from behind. He picked me up into his arms and ran me out of the room while Igborg roared at Kasim louder than he ever had in his young life.

I didn't hear the sound.

All I could see were Abudar's brown eyes with amber stars around the pupils. Weeks ago, I'd hated those eyes. I'd thought Abudar was full of nothing but pride, a spoiled prince who worried only for himself.

But now I saw a different man. One willing to sacrifice his own life to save his people.

Abudar was saying something to me, something about "not listening" and "putting yourself at risk," or something near to that.

When I blinked, I was lying on the floor in the hallway and my aunt Jade loomed over me.

"You can't do this!" Sultana Shahira said. She pulled on my aunt's arm.

Jade turned to the sultana. "She will die if I don't."

"You healed from the wounds you saved me from, but if you do this . . . you can't heal from her wounds, Jade," the sultana pleaded.

My aunt hugged her. "We all have our destinies. This is mine."

"What do you mean?" Abudar asked.

Jade placed one hand on my stomach and the other on my forehead. She smiled softly. "You once asked me what my ability was as a sorceress. I have the ability to heal. But in order for me to do so, I must take their wounds as my own."

I tried to reach up and grab her hand or tell her "no" or anything to stop her from taking her own life.

"Shh. Let me do this for you." She kissed my forehead. "I love you, Caspara. I am proud of the young woman you've become, and I know you're going to make everyone in the world proud by what you do as a sentinel."

"But where will I run when I need someone to talk to?" I asked, feeling much stronger than I had seconds ago.

"Your mother and your brother." She squeezed her eyes shut and a wince formed on her mouth, though she tried to hide it.

That was the moment I realized she'd already begun the process of healing my wounds.

"Stop now!" I begged. "I can function like this, and then we can both live," I pleaded. I tried to pull away and looked up at Abudar for help.

He slowly shook his head. "We all know you can't face Khorshid with those wounds."

I looked back down at my abdomen. Jade had healed me so much already, and yet no scab had formed and the wounds hadn't even begun to close at the edges.

I rolled my head to the side to see Taylin dragging Mithra out of the room with the help of Nahir, and Mithra had Igborg cradled in her arms.

Jade collapsed and I sat up with minimal pain, more like a sharp breath to remind me where each claw had once been.

Pulling her into my arms, I broke down into sobs. "Thank you, Auntie."

"Anything for family," she whispered.

The magic carpet flew down the hall and scooped her up. My father wrapped around his sister.

I looked at Taylin. "I wish you could save her!" I said.

Taylin panted and lifted his gaze to me. He slowly shook his head. "I'm sorry, Caspara. She's too far gone."

I jumped to my feet and grabbed him by the front of his perfect vest. "You have to! I made a wish!" Tears burned my eyes.

He wrapped me in a hug and allowed me to break down into sobs.

Jade was the first casualty of our battle against Khorshid.

Thirty-Seven

Arash shielded Mithra with his body as pieces of the ceiling rained down on them—likely a residual effect of Igborg's roar.

Sultana Shahira rose to her feet and straightened her spine. She turned to face her father as he exited the throne room. "The sorcerer who had deceived the princess had a weakness the sentinels discovered."

"*Barq*," Khorshid said, and a bolt of lightning flew straight for Sultana Shahira.

Navid, her familiar, jumped in the way and took the blow.

"Without his serpent, he grew weaker and weaker until the sentinels were able to—"

"*Awqaf!*" Khorshid said, forcing her words to catch in her throat.

Abudar left my side and stepped up to his mother's side. "*Inhal.*"

His mother drew a breath and quickly said, "The sentinels were able to destroy Khorshid once and for all!"

Khorshid shouted in frustration and began a barrage of attacks.

My mother stepped up to the sultana's other side and she and Aubdar simultaneously cast a spell to create a shield, which most of the spells bounced off of.

"*Anadi al-ma'*," Nahir suddenly said.

"What are you doing?" Taylin asked, letting go of me to take the hand of his lover.

She smiled. "I am still one with the river." That was all she said before she physically faded into water.

The water stretched and built and flowed toward Khorshid and his remaining ifrit.

Abudar turned to me. "What is his weakness?" he asked quickly.

I looked down at my arm, at the tattoos I had grown up hating. "Light. He's meddled in darkness his entire life. Light would be his weakness. And light is what we are as sentinels."

Abudar smiled and grabbed my hand. "Yes, we are."

Although we hadn't needed to physically touch when we connected with the dragon, there was an added sensation of strength between us as our fingers interlocked. Perhaps it was Abudar filling me with his own strength after having lost mine from my injuries, or perhaps it was magic itself, but strength had returned to my body and made my fingers tingle.

Abudar spoke words I'd never heard him utter before. The ceiling Igborg had cracked fell, and direct sunlight poured into the palace.

The ifrit standing behind Khorshid let out an unearthly scream as purple-and-red blisters grew all over its body. It retreated backward, desperately trying to find somewhere to hide until it was too late and the sun had consumed it.

"Yield to us!" Abudar commanded, strength in his voice like I'd never heard before.

"I will die before I yield to you!" Khorshid snarled. "If

you want to play a game of light and dark, then I shall play. Take us to the Dragon's Lair!" He swooped his staff in a circle, and a red light swung around me and Abudar, but Arash grasped at the light with his hand and Mithra grabbed his pantleg with a warning shout.

In the blink of an eye, the five of us were in an enormous open space of a black cave. The only light was far overhead and barely a crack compared to the engulfing darkness.

But Abudar's and my tattoos glowed and warmed the space around us just enough I could make out silhouettes of stalagmites and stalactites surrounding us as though we were in the mouth of a dragon and they acted as the dragon's teeth.

"Now it is just us, as it should have been from the beginning," Khorshid said.

"You are foolish to think you can defeat us," Abudar said.

"We are sentinels, and we have connected in a way no one ever has before," I added.

"Almost. But not quite. And now, I am the one with the advantage," Khorshid gloated. Without uttering a spell, he lifted his arms and closed his eyes.

The shadows at the edges of our vision began shifting, moving, reaching toward us.

Mithra scrambled to her feet and leaned against Arash's chest.

Igborg, still in her arms, licked her cheek and looked at me. "How can I help?" he asked.

I studied the shadows. "If he can do that with shadow, can we do that with light?" I asked.

Abudar moved his attention away from one of the

shadows to his right to look at me. "Why not? Summon an army of light creatures to battle with the dark . . . I don't know how, but we can try."

I tightened my hold on his hand. "Give them my strength."

Khorshid laughed. "It took me months to perfect that spell, and it's the easiest of dark magic. If you haven't even tried to do such things between the two of you, how could you ever try to defeat me?"

"Go on, Abudar," I whispered.

Abudar drew a deep, slow breath and his gaze moved to the shadows edging near us, trying to squelch our meager light. I could see his mind working, searching for just the right kind of spell.

Without warning, hands grabbed our ankles and began dragging us apart. We both hit the ground hard, but neither of us let go of our hands.

"Don't think!" I said to Abudar.

Igborg suddenly scrambled over and exploded a fireball at my ankles, singing my toes, and then at Abudar, accidentally catching his pant leg on fire.

"Confounded dragon!" Khorshid said. A bursting sound filled the cave and the light overhead disappeared entirely. "You shall feel how strong darkness can be."

Igborg shimmied, his body rippling from the tip of his tail to the tip of his nose. I'd seen him do that when he was smaller and shedding his skin, but instead of shedding his skin—at least, from what I could tell—little flecks of light began filling the air. They looked like millions of tiny stars that began filling the cave.

Abudar grinned. "You're brilliant, Igborg." He got to his feet, dragging me with him, and said, "*Ashriq!*"

All of the tiny dusts of light began to grow.

I couldn't help but smile as the light filled the room and hope filled my chest.

"No!" Khorshid said and tried to pull the blackness down from the ceiling.

"*Ashriq*!" Abudar commanded again, making them glow even more.

And then Abudar and I linked. I saw through his eyes and I knew he saw through mine. We felt each other's mixed emotions and every tangible sensation in our bodies.

The light gathered together into one orb just as the blackness surrounded it.

Together, we gave the final command, "*Ashriq*!"

But at our final command, dull rays of light escaped and then suddenly exploded, filling the cave with nothing but light.

We turned to Khorshid. "Your weakness is light. You have forgotten what it feels like."

Khorshid stepped back, shielding his face with his arms. "Your light burns!" He desperately tried summoning darkness or demons or ghouls, but the spells hissed under the unwavering light.

Abudar reached his right hand out and placed it on Khorshid's chest. "Feel the light. Feel what you have long forgotten."

Khorshid dropped his arms and his eyes widened. They were no longer black, but a dark brown that softened in color until it was almost caramel.

Because we were connected, we saw every one of Khorshid's memories moving backwards—his deceit of Mithra, being stuck in the stone for eighteen years, being trapped in the stone by Sultana Shahira, the mighty battle against her and Sultan Zayne, him using Zayne to murder so many women, and even further back to before Shahira was born and he'd discovered the book of the damned.

"That started all of this," Khorshid said in a breathless voice. "I opened that book and bound myself to it."

We saw him slice the palm of his hand and drip his blood into the empty pages. The blood spread and revealed the secrets the pages hid.

And then guilt began to suffocate Khorshid as he relived every murder and evil deed he'd committed.

I dragged Abudar's hand away without physically touching him, and we watched Khorshid as he was overwhelmed by emotions he had buried for so long.

The sorcerer fell to his knees.

Abudar and I watched and began to separate into our own beings, satisfied that we had done what we were meant to do.

Khorshid had been defeated.

"I never knew I caused so much pain," he whispered with tears in his eyes. "I want to change. Please give me a chance!" He crawled to Abudar and grasped the hem of his shirt.

Abudar crouched. "Your blood runs through my veins. I want nothing more than for you to change and show the world you're more than the darkness you've hidden inside."

"My blood," Khorshid echoed. He lifted his head and cupped Abudar's face in his hands.

Mithra gasped and scrambled to her feet. "No, Abudar!"

I watched in horror as black lines seeped from Khorshid's hands into Abudar's face, seeping into the veins and spreading up toward his eyes.

Khorshid's lips twisted in an evil grin. "The ink from

the book linked to my blood. You have my blood within you. Which means I can take your sentinel power for my own!"

Righteous anger filled my chest and I ran toward Khorshid. I ignited my tattoos, summoned my strength, and dove for him.

But Abudar stuck his hand out and I hit an empty magical wall. His body trembled and I saw his eyes drift to me. He wasn't in control of his body.

"Abudar!" I screamed.

His tattoos began to change from white light to red and he groaned in pain as he fought Khorshid mentally.

Mithra grasped my hand. "I know how we can help him!"

"How?" I asked.

"We have to get into their minds and stop them," she said.

Arash shook his head. "I can't let you—"

"Please let me do this," Mithra begged. Her chin trembled. "This is how I right my wrong. It's my fault he's here in the first place. I don't need your permission, Arash, but I'm begging for it."

His shoulders dropped and he kissed her. "As long as you come back to me."

Mithra smiled and put her hands on my temples, like Abudar had once done when trying to open the portal to my aunt's home. "Good," she whispered.

"But it's not my mind you need to get into," I argued.

"You were just mentally linked with Abudar," she said. "Just do it again. *Iftah 'aqlak elai saouf ara zikratak.*"

Mithra was in my mind at that moment, a strange presence full of sadness. I mentally reached out for Abudar like I was reaching my hand through an empty room, trying to feel my way around it for just the right artifact to steal. Only, I was trying to find his mind.

I closed my eyes and remembered the way he smelled, like dry wood, fresh cotton, wet earth, and all with an undertone of anise. I looked into his eyes, the eyes that had confessed he loved me.

And then there were four of us sharing the small space of our minds. A ripple of pain and a groan seemed to come from each of us.

Undoubtedly, two minds in one was dangerous enough, but four . . .

"Abudar, I'm here," I called into the void.

A spot of flickering light caught my attention, and I recognized that Mithra and I stood in a tiny room. We exchanged glances and then both ran toward the light.

Abudar stood at the center and Khorshid stood across from him.

"You are mine now," Khorshid said, his lip twitching.

Abudar's light began to dim. "I will fight against you with everything I have!" He tightened his hands into fists and pulled them upward, physically willing his light to win this battle.

"Abudar! We're right here!" I shouted. But I couldn't step into his light. I couldn't reach him to touch him. "Now what?" I asked.

"He knows we're here," Mithra said. "We just have to find out how to find that spot. Do you two have a special moment or secret that could unlock his mind and let us in?"

I looked at Abudar, struggling to fight Khorshid, an older and much more experienced sorcerer. And then I smiled. "I know exactly how to make him see me." I focused on Abudar only, nothing else.

And then, Abudar stood before Khorshid in Mithra's gorgeous purple silk pants and purple-and-silver top that revealed his stomach—the outfit he'd worn during the Desert Trials when he had disguised himself as the sorceress Yasmin and deceived me until we reached the cave holding the magic lamp.

Abudar's concentration on the light broke when he noticed the change in his appearance, and his focus on Khorshid broke with it. Light surrounded him and reached out to where I stood with Mithra.

He smiled. "Caspara."

Khorshid snarled and took a struggled step forward.

I ran to Abudar and grabbed his hand. "I'm not letting you go. You can defeat him. But . . ."

His brows dipped. "What? Why are you saying *but*?"

"Abudar, you are an incredible sorcerer," I said. "You are strong, selfless, and kind. But you haven't allowed yourself to truly grow. You haven't found your familiar."

"You want me to try and find my familiar while Khorshid is crushing my mind?" he asked, a bit offended.

I looked into his eyes, reminding him that we were in his mind, but Khorshid was physically in front of him in the cave. "Yes," I finally said. "And you can call upon it with your own power *and* the power I share with you. We're one, Abudar. Sentinels. And Khorshid doesn't stand a chance against the two of us."

Abudar opened his mouth, I assumed to object, but I pressed my lips to his and silenced him.

Abudar's mind filled with light and with a strange sort of crackling noise, and I found myself on my back staring up at the sunlight still fighting with darkness overhead.

I rolled to my hands and knees and saw Mithra sitting up, breathing hard, and Abudar several feet away from Khorshid, who must have been thrown when Abudar took his mind back.

Abudar stood and he and I connected without touching. He looked at me. "I've always felt the crushing weight of responsibility, being the first born. Not only would I someday be responsible for running the entire kingdom, but because I am also a sentinel, I must also protect the entire kingdom. I envied Mithra because she didn't have those responsibilities and could have fun during lessons, learning how to grow flowers or change the weather. Those weren't practical spells for any sentinel."

I saw Mithra's entire expression change. For the first time in her life, she was realizing Abudar had feelings of inadequacy too.

Abudar looked over his shoulder at her. "You're my baby sister, and I'm going to protect you no matter the cost."

Like weeks ago in this very cave system, Abudar began summoning orbs of light. But they seemed to go to the sunlight, absorb little suns inside, and then spread until the entire cave was lit.

Khorshid had nowhere left to hide, though he desperately tried to call upon the darkness inside of himself or pull shadows from any crevasse he could.

Arash caught my attention. He had been walking the perimeter of the cave until he stood behind Khorshid with his sword in hand.

Mithra gasped.

I took her hand. "He's doing this for you," I whispered with Abudar.

"Someday, I shall return!" Khorshid said, and darkness

from his staff began to surround him, in spite of the light. "And when I do, you will regret having fought me!"

Arash hesitated.

Abudar reached a hand out and the sword glowed with light. He and Arash made eye contact and Abudar nodded. Arash stepped forward and drove his blade through Khorshid's body.

The light from the sword filled his body, exploding from each finger and from his mouth and eyes. A man who had once filled the world around him with darkness was consumed by the light he had so hated.

And then there was nothing.

Khorshid no longer existed.

Thirty-Eight

The light faded and Arash panted. "That was . . . intense," he whispered.

Mithra sprinted across the floor and wrapped her lover in her arms. "I am so sorry I put you in that situation. I am sorry for everything I did. I owe you such—"

"Shh," Arash interrupted. "There's plenty of time for all of that." He held her close and closed his eyes.

Abudar smiled at me and kissed the back of my hand. "I suppose I'll never know what my familiar might be."

I wrapped my arms around his waist. "Don't be disappointed. You must just need a little more time."

A high screech pulsed down toward us from the opening in the roof, and all four of us looked upward to see what it came from.

Large wings cast a shadow down at us, softening the light until we were able to recognize its shape. It wasn't a dragon. The wings were that of an eagle, as were the head and front legs, but the back legs and tail were those of a lion. It landed and looked directly at Abudar.

"A griffin?" I said stupidly.

Abudar stepped forward and bowed to it. "I am Abudar."

The griffin lowered its head and extended one leg as it

bowed too. "Finally, I have found you. I have been searching for a long time and caught glimpses of your location, but they would fade or disappear entirely and I could not find you."

The two of them straightened and Abudar smiled. "You have no idea how honored I am that you will be my companion."

"And why is that?" the griffin asked.

"The griffin is the symbol of the royal family," Abudar explained. "Our people haven't seen a griffin in many, many years. To have you return, and to be at my side . . . well, it is an honor, to say the least."

The griffin's golden eye shifted to me. "It is an honor to meet both of you, it appears."

"Both? Oh. This is—"

"Caspara," the griffin interrupted. He walked over to me and bowed. "I am Ophion."

"Oh. You don't need to bow. I'm just a . . . well, a thief. And a girl. And—"

"And a sentinel." Ophion lifted his head and made eye contact, and I felt ashamed for not being prouder of myself and what we had just accomplished. The griffin fluffed his wings and looked once again at Abudar. "I shall carry you and Caspara out of here and then the other two."

"I can make a portal and get us home," Mithra said, still holding Arash.

Ophion studied her a long moment.

She averted her gaze and seemed to hold a little tighter to Arash.

"Much conflict stirs your heart. But you have taken the first step toward righting your wrongs." Ophion turned his head to me. "You first. You shall place your legs in front of my wings. Abudar will sit behind them. This should prevent you from hindering my movements."

I followed Ophion's instructions for how to properly climb onto his back—one rule of which was to *not* pull on his neck feathers. I apologized ten times for that to appease him. Abudar got on behind me, seemingly perfectly.

Igborg trotted over and bowed to the griffin. Igborg was now the size of a large dog. "I am Igborg."

"I am pleased to meet you. When you get just a little bigger, Caspara will have to begin riding you. I will not carry these two around like I'm a horse," Ophion said.

Igborg laughed and looked at me. "You're making him a horse."

I shook my head at my silly dragon.

Ophion's wings pumped up and down until he lifted into the air. The beating of his wings was softer than Igborg's, who flew alongside us.

Abudar wrapped his arms around my stomach. "I can't believe that's finally over."

I leaned back against him. "It's a relief. I don't know what I'm going to do now."

"Spend time with me?" Abudar moved the hair from over my shoulder so he could kiss my ear.

"We've already been spending a lot of time together," I said with a laugh.

"I mean doing fun things, like swimming or painting or something," he said.

I looked at him and said, "Painting?"

We both burst out in laughter.

Ophion got us out of the cave and we headed back toward the palace, traveling over the familiar desert in a far more enjoyable form than walking.

"There is one thing we have to fix now," I pointed out.

"What's that?"

I cleared my throat and gestured to the smoke filling the air from Zunbar. "Zu?" I reminded Abudar.

"Oh. Yes, his destruction and reward."

We landed in front of the palace amongst a group of very confused sorceresses and entered through the broken doors.

Sultana Shahira ran to her son and hugged him. Sultan Zayne was right behind her and pulled both of them into his arms.

"Where is Mithra?" Zayne asked.

"She said she would use a portal to get back," Abudar said. "I received my familiar." He said with a broad grin while he stepped over some rubble and then gestured his open hand to Ophion.

The griffin nodded his head to the sultan and sultana.

"A griffin?" she said breathlessly.

My mother stepped over the rubble, and for the first time she didn't hesitate to pull me into her arms. "I knew you could do it," she said softly.

I smiled and hugged her back. "Thank you for all you've taught Abudar. He's very skilled. We definitely need to work on some things, like channeling the light, but I think we did pretty well. All things considered." I pointed to the destroyed roof of the palace.

Mother laughed and shrugged. "Minor sacrifice to keep those we love safe and alive."

Abudar looked up at the ceiling and the gaping hole in it while his mother and father met his new familiar. I looked around at the debris on the floor. With my new strength, I could help pick up all of it. We could easily repair the palace and any of the homes.

Taylin and Nahir walked over to me and Taylin pulled me into a warm hug. "You've become quite an amazing woman."

I laughed. "I'm still young. I still have a lot to learn."

Taylin handed me his lamp.

"Oh! I had made a promise to the dragon that I would give him the treasure from the caves. Can you magic that to his new lodging in the Ailorn Mountains?" I asked.

Taylin laughed. "You have such a silly way of wording your wishes." He winked. "I'll gladly do that."

"And one more thing. I sort of promised him that there might be a female dragon out there?" I gave Taylin a sheepish grin.

He put his fists on his hips. "And how am I supposed to go about convincing a female dragon to uproot herself for a dragon she's never met?"

I shrugged. "Maybe you uproot Anzu so he's not threatening our small kingdom?"

Taylin shook his head and sighed. "Only because I like you. I'll go speak with him." He kissed Nahir on the cheek before leaving.

I looked at the beautiful woman. "Thank you for helping earlier."

"You are most welcome, Sentinel. I have also helped put out the fires, and your guards are already at work relocating the families whose homes were affected." She bowed.

"Oh, you don't need to bow to me," I said quickly.

A soldier approached. "Your Highnesses, a boat from Kalekai and their soldiers have arrived."

"Ah. Welcome them here. We shall give them a place

to stay for the night, but I am afraid we no longer need their help," Sultan Zayne said. He looked proudly at his son. "We've gotten rid of the threat."

"The sorceresses may need to share rooms in the meantime," Sultana Shahira said.

"I know the spell to repair," Abudar said confidently. "Grand Sorceress Roshanak and I can work together to repair the palace before—"

"Help the people first," his mother insisted. "This is not an important part of the palace. Our people need their homes fixed."

Abudar nodded and turned to my mother.

"I am ready when you are," she said. She patted my cheek softly, and Abudar helped her climb over the rubble.

I smiled happily.

My entire life had changed. But I was going to be better for it.

I felt my father's presence before I turned to see the rug. I hugged it, which felt flat compared to hugging my father. I got the feeling he was ready to go, that he had fulfilled whatever reason the weavers had kept him around for.

"I don't want you to leave," I whispered.

A deep rumble pulsed through my chest and body, yet the ground didn't move. Bits of dust from the broken ceiling were disturbed and floated into the air.

I froze and my stomach tightened. The hair on the back of my neck stood. I looked over to the sultan and sultana and beyond and saw that every single person nearby had gone rigid with the same apprehensive tension I felt.

Again, the rumble pulsed, but this time it was much stronger, and then another pulse, and another, growing quicker and in rhythm like a heartbeat.

It stopped, and not a moment later, the earth beneath our feet fractured and split from the throne room, out the front doors, and arched through the courtyard.

"Rule fifteen," I said aloud, and all of my instincts took over. Of course Khorshid's death was too good to be true. It had happened too quickly.

I jumped from the pile of rubble, over the growing crack, and landed near the leaders of our land. "Ophion, take them somewhere safe!" I said.

"Although I respect your wanting to keep us safe, what kind of leader would I be hiding while my people are attacked?" Sultan Zayne countered, drawing the sword on his hip. "I will stand at your side and face whatever this is."

I shook my head. "Sire, it's your daughter."

On cue, Mithra rose from the seam in the earth and floated into the air several feet above it.

"But how?" Sultana Shahira breathed. "I spoke the story."

"That Khorshid would be destroyed," Zayne said.

"But not that his influence wouldn't linger," I added. "Tell another story, Sultana Shahira!"

Mithra crossed her hands in front of her, wrists touching, and then threw them apart. A silent wave of energy slammed into everyone nearby, making them fly or tumble through the air.

I hit the ground near one of the trees, and Sultan Zayne somehow grabbed on to Shahira and pulled her behind a pillar, which cracked after taking the brunt of the spell.

I sat up. "Khorshid tried to take over Abudar's mind before he . . . disappeared, or died, or whatever happened. He said they were linked through blood. He could have used that against Mithra too."

"You mean some part of him is still alive in her?" Shahira asked.

I didn't like the sound of it any better than they did, but I nodded.

Abudar ran up behind me, grabbed me under the arms, and dragged me behind one of the fountains. "How is Mithra here like that? Where is Arash? What happ—"

I pressed my finger to his lips. "She broke the earth and floated out of it. I think Khorshid buried a piece of himself inside of her like he tried to with you."

Sultana Shahira's voice echoed in the courtyard. "There was a sorcerer who took over his granddaughter's body. But he couldn't stand up against the sentinels."

The sorceresses still remaining in the courtyard began to scream in terror, and I was astonished when I turned to see all sorts of creatures climbing out from the crack in the earth.

"We got lucky the first time we fought Khorshid," Abudar admitted.

"Don't you dare doubt us now," I said firmly.

But unlike Khorshid's ifrits, these monsters didn't seem afraid of the sunlight, which was fading quickly.

"We blinded Khorshid with the light. We didn't destroy him with it," Abudar said, his eyes distant. "We need to give everyone here light."

"What do you mean? Physical?" I asked.

Abudar looked around. "Igborg!" he shouted.

The dragon dove down from the tree he'd been hiding in, and Ophion trotted over to us.

Abudar stood and faced his familiar. "Igborg has some kind of magical ability to make little orbs of light appear. We need everyone around here to have light, to *be* light to fight against Khorshid's darkness. How do we do that?"

"Shields of light," I said. "They can protect themselves if we give them shields, so start there. Igborg, can you do that special thing again?"

Igborg smiled and his skin began to glow beneath his scales. "I share my light."

I smiled and placed my hand on his head. A rush of energy shot through me and into him. The light inside of both of us connected, and this time the tiny flecks of light sparked with extra energy.

"Can you control them?" I asked him. "If you can, send them to each person here."

Igborg's body trembled and the orbs spread out, each one landing on a person's hand.

"These are particles of light!" I called out. "Will them into shields, and they will help protect you from the attacks of darkness!"

The command couldn't have come sooner, because black arrows began piercing the air, aimed at sorceresses, royalty, guards, and thieves alike.

"Kalekai's army is here!" Abudar announced.

The remaining particles of light from Igborg landed on those on the front line.

I wrapped my arms around Igborg's neck and kissed his head. "You are a remarkable being."

The soldiers took their positions without hesitation. The front line had shields land crouched, aiming their spears forward toward the monsters running toward them.

The sorceresses utilized their spells to try and ward off the attacks.

Igborg nuzzled me. "Did you ever consider maybe I am your familiar?"

I leaned back and looked down at him. "That's a cute idea, but I don't have magic. I'm not a sorceress, Igborg."

He licked the tattoos on my arm. "What do you think this is? What do you think being a sentinel means? It's more than being a protector, it's being a bearer of light. Light that is spread through sharing your magic, your heart, with others."

"When did you become so wise?" I asked. I looked at my arm and then at Abudar. "Bearers of light."

Abudar took my hand. "We don't need to use any fancy spells. They just need us."

Thirty-Nine

Ophion stepped up to Abudar's side. Igborg stood at my side. The four of us touched and light began to glow, not just from the tattoos on mine and Abudar's arms, not only from Igborg's skin or Ophion's feathers. No, the light spread across us until we radiated light.

Without fear for what could happen to us, we stepped forward and into the line of fire.

Black arrows hissed as they disintegrated near our flesh without piercing it.

No words needed to be said between Abudar and me, we could feel each other's thoughts. We both knew and agreed that there was still goodness inside of Mithra's mind and heart. We needed to reach it and get Khorshid's influence out of her once and for all.

We walked right by the creatures of darkness, the crack in the ground healing as we approached Mithra. Many monsters swiped at us with ragged swords, but all it took was the raise of a hand or claw to deflect the attack.

"Mithra, come down here and speak with us," we all said together.

"How are you doing this? How are you ruining everything I've fought for!" Her black hair floated in wind that we didn't feel.

"Because it is the wrong thing and you know it," we replied. "Samira was not your familiar. You are not on the path you were meant for."

"And yet I am winning!"

When I looked around, I saw the ghouls, ifrits, shaytan, and smaller imps running about and attacking anything they could get their hands on. Some of the sorceresses had been wounded and pulled back into the protection of the ranks. The Kalekai army was doing the same, but also pressing forward to hopefully gain an upper hand.

"You cannot win," we replied. "You have no chance. All you will do is cause harm to those around you. You cannot be the sultana of Sheblom."

She let out an angry scream and grabbed at the corners of the walls, physically dragging them forward to aid in the attack. They were nothing but shadowed hands.

Several grabbed on to soldiers or sorceresses. Several grabbed on to Zayne. And all of the people seized were dragged toward the darkness.

Ophion nodded his head, sending a ball of light that exploded, just like Igborg's fireballs had when he had first learned to use them. The balls of light extinguished the darkness and freed those trapped.

"Mithra, there is a part of your heart you have buried."

A flicker of a memory shot through my mind. It was brief, and for a moment I wondered if it was a memory at all. It was the moment, just a few days ago, when Mithra had released Khorshid from the ruby. The ruby had fractured, exploding into millions of particles.

And then, the memory slowed down and I saw one of those particles fly through the air and strike Mithra's heart. Khorshid's bond with her was from the ruby.

Abudar and I looked at one another, knowing we needed to get that ruby out.

But that also meant we needed to get close enough in order to do so.

Ophion charged to the right and Igborg to the left without Abudar or I commanding them to do so. They cleared the perfect path for Abudar and I to approach the princess.

Mithra touched her feet to the ground. They were completely black, as were her fingers. The darkness had begun to seep into her very flesh.

Abudar stepped forward to place his hand on Mithra's heart and pull out the ruby fragment, but six arms sprung from Mithra's back and grabbed the two of us, holding on to our shoulders and arms.

"I will *not* lose this time," she said firmly.

The darkness inside of Mithra and the light inside of us fought against each other. The black shadowed hands holding us crackled. Our light tried to seep into them, and Mithra's darkness tried to seep into us.

Something had to give.

Thief rule number thirteen—trust your instincts.

I knew this was a battle I wasn't meant to be part of. This was between Abudar and his sister.

I let go of Abudar's hand and stepped back.

Abudar didn't look at me, because he understood. For a split second, blackness surged onto Abudar's arm, then immediately disappeared.

"You're my sister," Abudar said alone. "I should have made you feel more wanted. We all could have done better. But the little girl I grew up with, the Mithra I know, the heart I am familiar with, was the little girl who found kittens in the streets and brought them home until they were better. You were the girl who challenged me to any magic battle and often won. You raised your hand during lessons and asked all of the questions and were never afraid to ask the uncomfortable ones."

He stepped closer to his sister and placed his hand on her heart. "Khorshid is not part of you. He never wanted to help you be a better person or make sure you succeeded in your life. Give me the ruby."

"People see me now! They notice me, how powerful I am, how much I can do! They see that I am a woman with power and stature! I can be a leader, I can do so many things."

"Yes, you can. But not like this."

Mithra gritted her teeth.

Abudar's hand glowed and his eyes narrowed in concentration. His fingertips began to press into her flesh through a slit of magic.

"No!" Mithra screamed, but Abudar's free hand held her close. "I want so much more!"

Abudar reached his fingers in and through that same sliver of light, produced the ruby fragment that had lodged itself in her. The final piece of Khorshid that remained.

Mithra collapsed to her knees as soon as she was rid of the ruby.

I ran over and dropped to my knees at her side to comfort her.

Abudar squeezed his fingers together and the ruby was absorbed by the light.

Khorshid was gone once and for all.

The earth slid closed and the beings of darkness scrambled to break out out into the world, but they couldn't escape the power of the sorceresses or the strength of the army.

"Where is Arash?" I asked gently.

Mithra pulled the necklace out from under her shirt, revealing a small hourglass with a tiny version of Arash trapped inside. She didn't meet Abudar's eyes as she lifted it up to him.

"You let him out," Abudar insisted.

"I . . . can't," she whispered. "I have no strength."

"Then let me give you some of mine." He took her hand and placed their palms together.

Mithra raised her eyes and met the gaze of her brother. Tears streamed down her face. She reversed the spell, and Arash appeared in front of her on his hands and knees. She lowered her gaze again and buried her face in her hands as she wept.

Arash crawled forward and pulled her into his arms.

"How could you want me?" she protested.

"You need someone to hold you. We'll deal with the fallout later."

Sultana Shahira and Sultan Zayne approached and held their little girl close.

I stepped away, giving them time together.

Arash walked with me and collapsed on the edge of the cracked fountain. "Is she going to be safe now?"

I sat beside him, and Igborg trotted over to lay his head in my lap. "I think so. Now that she has no influence from Khorshid, she should return to how she was. But I don't know if she can ever forgive herself for what she's done, and I don't know what her parents are going to do about the crimes she's committed."

Arash grimaced and ran his fingers through his dusty

hair. "I hadn't thought about that."

"Will you stay at her side?" I asked.

He looked over at the princess. "She needs friends. Even if we are no longer lovers, I cannot pretend I wasn't at her side all along." He looked at me. "I am as guilty as she is, because I knew and allowed it to happen."

I reached over and put my hand on his knee. "You and I are still family. We're here for each other. You aren't any more alone than she is, and we'll figure all this out."

Arresting Mithra and Arash were the least of our worries. We spent the next several days repairing the buildings of Zunbar and tended to the wounded. I needed to found out what happened with Taylin and if he'd gotten Anzu what he wanted.

Abudar and I found each other at some point during the night, and he plopped down in the street at my feet. "I can't do anything else."

I sat on the steps of the nearby home and yawned loudly. "I'm spent too. But I'm not sleeping on the streets."

Abudar leaned so he could rest his head on my lap. "Did you see your father?"

"No. He left," I said, looking into the distance. "I'm okay, though. He let me know he was ready to go. I'm lucky I got another chance with him."

"Did you get all of your questions answered?"

I started to play with Abudar's hair. "No, but I'm okay with that too. We can't know the answers to everything. I have a future and a purpose. What more could I ask for?"

"A bed?"

I laughed and sat up, forcing him to sit up, though he protested.

Ophion approached us and looked at Abudar. "The

homes are repaired. You need rest."

"Yes, we do." Abudar groaned as he got back to his feet.

Taylin appeared out of nowhere and I threw my arms around him. He laughed. "I am happy to see you too. I was thinking about your next wish and I should have been here to help with your battle, but I did get the treasure to Anzu and—"

"Stop." I stepped back and pulled out the lamp. "I have been looking for you everywhere. I wanted one last wish."

"Of course. Anything for you."

Nahir stood nearby and waited patiently.

"I wish for your freedom," I said.

Taylin stared at me, his grin falling. "What?"

"You heard me." I held up the lamp.

Taylin's gold sparkles lit up and he held out his hands. Golden chains, once invisible, glowed and shattered. He let out a laugh and enveloped me in a hug. "You're going to be just fine, Caspara."

I stepped back and watched Taylin embrace Nahir. She blew me a kiss and the two of them faded away.

Abudar hugged me from behind. "I guess this is your chance to start a new normal."

"Do I get to have you as part of my new normal life?" I looked over my shoulder.

"Absolutely." He smiled and kissed me. "Before we start our new normal life, I think we both need some rest," Abudar suggested.

"Caspara!" someone called from behind me.

I chuckled. "Why don't you go get some sleep? I'll take care of this. I love you, Abudar."

He entwined our fingers and smiled down at me. "I love you too."

Rules of Thieves

1. Always be aware of your surroundings.
2. Never get greedy.
3. Think before you act.
4. Do not to kill. The value of a life is more than that of gold.
5. Watch each other's backs.
6. Choose what is most valuable.
7. Always be ready.
8. Know your target.
9. Be as quiet as the shadows.
10. Trust other thieves.
11. Don't believe everything you hear.
12. Have a way out.
13. Trust your instincts.
14. Second chances are for the weak.
15. If it seems too good to be true, it probably is.

ALSO BY LICHELLE SLATER

THE FORGOTTEN KINGDOM SERIES
The Four Stones of Tern Tovan
(Exclusive to Newsletter subscribers)
The Dragon Princess
(Sleeping Beauty Reimagined)
The Siren Princess
(Little Mermaid Reimagined)
The Beast Princess
(Beauty and the Beast Reimagined)
The Phoenix Princess
(Snow White Reimagined)
The Crown Prince

Receive the prequel to *The Forgotten Kingdom Series* for FREE by signing up for my newsletter at:
www.LichelleSlater.com

CIRCUS OF THE STARS SERIES
Ringmaster
Marionette
Magician

Urban Fantasy
Curse of a Djinn

CHRISTMAS ROMANCE NOVELS
Secret Santa
Accidental Secret Santa

ABOUT THE AUTHOR

Personal dragon trainer, lover of glitter, writer of fantasy.

Reading has always been a huge passion, from The Hobbit to Goosebumps. Some of my fondest memories are at the library or being read to, and when I embarked on my journey of becoming an author, I did so with the dream of sharing the worlds in my mind with others.

I currently live in Salt Lake City, UT with my adorable King Charles, Perseus, and work full-time as a special education preschool teacher.

I am a USA Today Bestselling author and was nominated for "Unforgettable Book of the Year" for The Beast Princess and "Mind-Blowing Fantasy of the Year" for The Siren Princess at Penned Con 2020, and as "Best Debut Author" for Step Right Up (now Circus in the Stars: Ringmaster) at UtopiaCon in 2017.

Join my reader group on Facebook:
Lichelle's Book Wyrms

FOLLOW ME HERE

Instagram
@LichelleSlater_Author

TikTok
@LichelleSlaterAuthor

Amazon
www.amazon.com/Lichelle-Slater/e/B01MSU34EN/

Goodreads
www.goodreads.com/author/show/16150296.Lichelle_Slater